The Diehard
My Brother's Killer

Two Novels by
Jean Potts

Introduction by Curtis Evans

Stark House Press • Eureka California

THE DIEHARD / MY BROTHER'S KILLER

Published by Stark House Press
1315 H Street
Eureka, CA 95501, USA
griffinskye3@sbcglobal.net
www.starkhousepress.com

ISBN: 978-1-951473-74-7

Book design by Mark Shepard, shepgraphics.com
Proofreading by Bill Kelly
Cover Art by James Heimer

First Stark House Press Edition: May 2022

THE DIEHARD

Lew Morgan is a well-hated man. His friends and family would be happy if he just died. Grover, who runs the general store, is one of his oldest friends. But Lew, as owner of the local bank, doesn't intend to give Grover another loan. His son Whit is Lew's whipping boy, and Whit's wife, Dort, a controlling conniver who just wants Lew's money. And then there's Victoria, Lew's daughter, who is forced to compete for his affection with the other women in his life. They all hate Lew Morgan. You might say that Lew is in danger for his life. If only he had a clue that his brash arrogance rubbed some people the wrong way. If only Lew knew that at least one of these people plans to murder him…

MY BROTHER'S KILLER

Garth Sullivan lives in the same brownstone as his brother Howdy and his wife, Pamela. Garth once had a career as a woodworker, but that ended when Howdy accidentally caused the slicing of his two fingers. He once had Pamela, too. But now all he has is hate. A festering hate that only grows stronger with each dinner date. But Garth has a plan. It's a great plan, a wonderful plan. All he has to do to rid himself of Howdy is to fake his own death, and wait for the perfect moment to kill him. Unfortunately, he doesn't take Eunice into consideration. Eunice is their less-than-attractive neighbor, and she is in love with Garth. So when she sees him outside the building after everyone else thinks he's dead, she vows to keep his secret. But some secrets just can't be kept…

"Subtlety and sensitivity… and the quiet
authority of a first-rate craftsman."
—Anthony Boucher, *NY Times*

"A past mistress in the art of
dispensing psychological suspense."
—*Liverpool Post*

"Potts has a turn of phrase
that cuts like a knife."
—Paul Burke, *NB*

7

A Woman's Eye
By Curtis Evans

13

The Diehard
By Jean Potts

153

My Brother's Killer
By Jean Potts

256

Jean Potts
Bibliography

A Woman's Eye
By Curtis Evans

**Jean Potts' *The Diehard* (1956)
and *My Brother's Killer* (1975)**

All over the United States, apparently, women are sitting down and writing mystery novels that terrify mere men with their efficiency and their clear woman's-eye view of American society.
—R. M., "The Deadly Female" (review of novels by Jean Potts, Ursula Curtiss and Charlotte Armstrong), *Sydney Morning Herald*, 29 December 1956

If, as conventional wisdom has it, the period known as the Golden Age of Detective Fiction (1920s-1940s), was dominated by a quartet of British women mystery writers (Agatha Christie, Dorothy L. Sayers, Margery Allingham and Ngaio Marsh); the mid-century mystery writing which evolved out of the Golden Age over the course of the 1940s-1970s was hugely influenced by female authors of what was then usually termed "psychological suspense" (which in the last decade has become known as "domestic suspense"). With a few notable exceptions, like British authors Celia Fremlin and Shelley Smith, most of these mid-century women suspense writers, as the Australian reviewer quoted above observed in 1956, were either Americans by birth, such as Elisabeth Sanxay Holding, Charlotte Armstrong, Ursula Curtiss and Elizabeth Fenwick, or by adoption, as in the case of native Canadian Margaret Millar. Some of these women, like Armstrong, Fenwick and Millar, began their crime-writing careers during the years of the Second World War with relatively straight detective fiction, before moving intrepidly into the field of suspense. Noted regionalist American crime writer Jean Potts followed the path laid by these deadly duennas when she began publishing her own mysteries in the 1950s.

Potts' first two mystery novels, *Go, Lovely Rose* (1954) and *Death of a Stray Cat* (1955), were highly praised whodunits, the first book winning the Edgar Award from the Mystery Writers of America for the best first mystery novel of the year—Raymond Chandler's *The Long Goodbye* won the Edgar for best novel—and the second novel receiving acclaim from influential critic Anthony Boucher as being "even better" than its lauded predecessor. Boucher proclaimed *Death of a Stray Cat* "an unusually well-constructed detective story" with "virtues" that were "even more novelistic than deductive." Potts' third crime novel, *The Diehard* (1956), advanced this trend line even farther in the direction of straight literature and accordingly was roundly praised as her finest work yet.

In contrast with *Rose* and *Cat, The Diehard* is not even a whodunit but rather a *who'lldoit*. The central question in the novel is *not*, as per tradition, who killed Lew Morgan, the ruthless, recently widowed, self-made businessman who dominates the town of Turk Ridge, located somewhere in Chicago's hinterland. Rather it is who ultimately will be driven to kill him. Certainly there is no shortage of people who hate Lew, starting with the surviving members of his own family. There are:

> Whitt, Lew's weak, "mama's boy" son, utterly overshadowed by his masterful parent and cuckolded by his pretty, scheming wife, Dort, and her conniving male bestie, Tony, who see Lew as an obstacle to their plan to open a nightclub in the Windy City

> Victoria, Lew's socially awkward, unmarried, "daddy's girl" daughter, who has a sincere but gauche out-of-town travelling salesman boyfriend whom she knows her father will utterly abominate

> Grover Underwood, Lew's best friend from their schooldays and owner of Turk Ridge's longtime family grocery store, who stands badly in need of a loan from Lew's bank on account of competition from an encroaching chain store

> Sophie Barta, a Chicago beautician and romantic discard from Lew's past, when she was a gorgeous and accommodating waitress serving at Chili Joe's, who has a daughter named Arlene living in Turk Ridge (ostensibly a niece), in whom Lew has taken a beneficent interest

Contrastingly, there are two people who believe that to know Lew is to love him: his homespun, forthright Aunt Chat, who superstitiously has discerned portents of doom in her nephew's near future, and his longtime mistress, local schoolteacher Celia Colby, whom he has been freed finally to marry by the recent death of his wealthy, faded, wallflower wife, Olive. Both women to some extent are the better angels of Lew's nature, but will they be able to save him not only from himself but from the near and dear ones around him?

The Diehard is a superbly constructed suspense novel with interesting characters and a highly authentic small-town setting, something which was a specialty of the author, who hailed from little Saint Paul, Nebraska, a town of some 1600 souls when she was an adolescent and young adult residing there in the Twenties and Thirties. Perhaps the setting may seem a bit antiquated for 1956 to us in 2022, although it may well be that Midwestern burgs like Saint Paul and Turk Ridge were ten or twenty years behind New York, where Jean Potts, harboring cosmopolitan inclinations, had relocated in the late Thirties and lived for the rest of her life. The novel has all the small-town authenticity of Potts' debut 1943 mainstream novel, *Someone to Remember*, plus the stirring narrative drive of a classic of mid-century suspense (domestic or otherwise); and it was amply deserving of the hearty plaudits which it received from critics from around the globe.

In England, F. E. Pardoe, a future recipient of the Crime Writers Association's Red Herring Award, ringingly declared in the *Birmingham Post* that with her third mystery "Jean Potts establishes without any doubt what one had suspected from earlier two: that she is the most important crime writer to appear from America in many years…. [the] plot is original and developed with that loving care for detail which is the sign of the true craftsman." In the *London Observer* Maurice Richardson noted that Potts' "writing and characterisation were well above average" and that the book rang a most interesting variation on the melody of murder. Across the pond in Boston, Avis De Voto concurred with her British brethren, pronouncing in the *Globe* that "[a]tmosphere, interpretation of motive and sensitive writing make [*The Diehard*] an outstandingly interesting story."

When, two decades later in 1975, Jean Potts, now sixty-five years old, published her final crime novel, *My Brother's Killer*, the criminous landscape of mystery fiction had changed. That year the late Mary Higgins Clarks' debut suspense novel, *Where Are the Children?*, which initially had been turned down by a couple of publishers who considered its child endangerment theme too luridly depicted for sensitive female readers—made it onto the bestseller charts, reaping financial rewards undreamt of by most mystery writers and launching the nearly half-century crime fiction career of Clark, who was soon dubbed the "Queen of Suspense." Writers of mid-century domestic suspense like Jean Potts, many of whom like Potts would publish their final novels in the Seventies, came to be seen as a bit passé by comparison.

Certainly *My Brother's Killer* was by that time highly traditional, following the inverted mystery pattern set long ago by such writers as Francis Iles in *Malice Aforethought* (1931) and Richard Hull in *The Murder of My Aunt* (1935). In the novel, which is set primarily in a brownstone house and its environs in New York City, sullen, embittered Garth Sullivan hatches an evil plot to slay his brother "Howdy," an amiable fellow for whom he, Garth, holds nothing but hatred and contempt. (The reader may feel Howdy's cognomen alone is reason enough for murder.) Of course as we all know the best laid plans of murderous men have a way of going *agley*, whether in the novels of Jean Potts or Mary Higgins Clark (or Francis Iles or Richard Hull); and the entire criminal affray ends appropriately with classic irony.

My Brother's Killer earned far fewer notices in newspapers than *The Diehard* had two decades earlier, but the novel was championed in her "Gory Road" column by veteran Lenore Glen Offord, crime fiction reviewer for the *San Francisco Chronicle*, who, herself five years older than Jean Potts, had published some notably lauded mysteries, almost entirely during the 1940s. "The unfolding of the story is told with all of Miss Potts' great talent for realities in minds and physical backgrounds," Offord wrote enthusiastically of Potts' final crime novel, adding: "magnificent job."

In her Christmas Day roundup of the dozen best mysteries of 1975, the seventy-year-old Offord, decidedly feeling her years, confided wryly that a few months earlier she had "realized that I had been reviewing mysteries in chronicle columns for a quarter of a century—which somehow sounds longer than 25 years." She observed that "[d]uring all that time the mystery novel has been on the whole growing in skill and literacy; it's changed in attitude, sometimes—to my mind—for the worse, when its gone pornographic, and sometimes for the better, in social comment. Thank heaven, though, it's still with us—and in good health."

Unsurprisingly, one of the dozen novels which made it onto Offord's best-of list was Jean Potts' *My Brother's Killer*, one of only three mysteries on the list written by a woman. Who were the other two women crime writers? Bestselling Gothic novelist Dorothy Eden, a contemporary of both Potts and Offord, and … Mary Higgins Clark, still fervently wondering about the whereabouts of those children. Now, nearly fifty years later, the "Queen of Suspense" is dead and the mavens of mid-century mystery, long out-of-print, have come into their murderous own once again.

—February 2022
Germantown, TN

Curtis Evans received a PhD in American history in 1998. He is the author of *Masters of the "Humdrum" Mystery: Cecil John Charles Street, Freeman Wills Crofts, Alfred Walter Stewart and British Detective Fiction, 1920-1961* (2012) and most recently the editor of the Edgar nominated *Murder in the Closet: Essays on Queer Clues in Crime Fiction Before Stonewall* (2017) and, with Douglas G. Greene, the Richard Webb and Hugh Wheeler short crime fiction collection, *The Cases of Lieutenant Timothy Trant* (2019). He blogs on vintage crime fiction at The Passing Tramp.

The Diehard

By Jean Potts

To
The Professor

1

All through his wife's funeral, Lew Morgan wrestled with a nervous, unseemly urge to yawn. The struggle absorbed him: he was determined to act out his role of bereaved husband (though it was a strain, after all these years of doing as he pleased and the public be damned) without a hitch. He felt that he owed it to Olive. Not that she would know the difference, laid out there in the coffin. But all of Turk Ridge would know. A yawn would be, to Turk Ridge, the final, outrageous signal of disrespect.

As chief mourner, Lew sat in the front pew, with his son and daughter-in-law on his left, and on his right his daughter Victoria in her expensive black suit and her hat with its discreet little veil. There were also two stringy ladies, cousins of Olive's, who for some obscure reason had driven over to attend her funeral. And behind him row after row of curious eyes with himself as the target. He clenched his jaws against another secret crisis. Once more he drew out his handkerchief and patted his moustache, his trim line of a moustache that gave him a look of almost youthful jauntiness.

(It would have sustained him to know that this clenched-jaw, handkerchief-patting gesture of his was interpreted, by several of the funeral guests, as a commendable symptom of grief. "Poor man," one lady whispered approvingly to another, "he's taking it hard.")

The funeral was a big one. Turk Ridge, which had overlooked Olive for so long, suddenly remembered who she was. Or rather, remembered whose daughter she had been, and whose wife she was. The bank and most of the business places closed for two hours as a mark of deference. Not the Turk Ridge *Telegraph*, however; it was press day, and at this very moment the current issue was in the works, with a front-page column headed "Olive Whitt Morgan Passes On." There was precious little in the obituary about Olive herself; Whitt and Morgan were the significant names. In death as in life, poor Olive was eclipsed by her father, that "pioneering man of vision" who had run everything in town worth running, and her husband, who had picked up where Old Man Whitt left off. The *Telegraph* wound up with the customary tribute to Olive's virtues as wife and mother, a lyric description of the profusion of floral offerings at her funeral, and an extension of heartfelt sympathy to the bereaved family.

All very decorous. No mention was made of Celia Colby, who, as a casual friend of the family—nothing more—attended the funeral and then went back to teach the rest of her afternoon classes at Turk Ridge High School, with only a slight tendency toward absent-mindedness to show that today was a landmark in her life.

It would not have been decorous, either, to mention Olive's money, though all of Turk Ridge—except for Celia Colby, who had her mind on other things—was at least mildly interested in the subject. For instance, how much was there? And had Olive left it all in Lew's hands, or had she made her own distribution to her son and daughter? With most people it was only a matter of idle curiosity. But there were a few at Olive's funeral to whom it made all the difference in the world ...

To Lew the reading of Olive's will, which took place immediately after the funeral, was just a formality. He knew the provisions; he supposed that Victoria knew them, though he had never seen any particular reason to tell her and she had never asked; and as for his son Whitt— well, who cared what Whitt might be thinking or hoping or expecting? Not Lew.

Whitt's wife, Dort, was something else again. Lew knew very well what was going on in that pretty, bitchy little head of Dort's. He smiled a little to himself as he watched her settling down beside Whitt to listen. Very poised and proper she looked; every inch the politely interested, deferential daughter-in-law.

They had gathered in the big living room to hear old Mr. McVey read the will. He sat in one of the easy chairs, with his papers on a coffee table beside him, and his audience arranged in a loose semicircle in front of him. Lew and Victoria on one half of the sectional sofa; Whitt and Dort on the other. The lady cousins were there too, perched each on an occasional chair; they had driven back to the house from the cemetery, and nobody knew exactly what to do with them. So there they were.

Old Mr. McVey nodded piously at them all, like a Sunday school teacher greeting his flock. Then he picked up the will and began to read, pausing now and then to adjust his dentures.

It was a short will, and a very simple one. Olive made it fifteen years ago, when she first found out about her heart. All her property, real and otherwise—bank, lumber yard, farms, house, cash—went to Lew. Which, in view of the fact that he had been running everything ever since he married her, was neither surprising nor unreasonable. Victoria and Whitt had only to wait; their turn would come.

It was obviously what Victoria had expected. Whitt pulled at his ear nervously, but that meant nothing, he was always doing that. Dort? Well, Lew had to hand it to her: she hung on to her poise. If he hadn't been watching closely, he would have missed the glance she shot at Whitt; a glance loaded with secret rage. Whitt must have been watching for it too. He reddened. Then he went on pulling at his ear. Again Lew smiled a little to himself.

Mr. McVey, after shaking hands all around as a fitting close to the ceremony, departed. So did Dort; she had this Chicago company arriving tomorrow for the weekend, and the house was a shambles. A tender kiss for Whitt, sweet smiles for Lew and Victoria. Then she was gone. It was still only three thirty, and Lew began to speculate uneasily about what was expected of him for the rest of the afternoon. He knew his limitations when it came to this bereaved husband business, and he didn't quite trust himself with the lady cousins, who showed no signs of leaving, even now. Besides, they bored him. Let Whitt cope with them.

He couldn't very well turn up at the bank or the lumber yard, crassly concerned with business when Olive was barely underground. But what he could do was go see Aunt Chat. No one could possibly criticize him for paying a visit to his old aunt, who seldom got out anymore, even for funerals. And what a relief to Lew, what blessed deliverance from the bondage of his ill-fitting role! For with Aunt Chat, playing a role was not only unnecessary; it was impossible. The rest of Turk Ridge might forget that long-ago time when Lew had been a little boy from the wrong side of the tracks, before he got to be a big shot. But not Aunt Chat. He could no more fool her than he could fool himself.

When, fifteen minutes later, he pushed open the gate to her little yard, he had the feeling (as usual) that he was stepping back into his childhood. Nothing about Aunt Chat's place was changed at all. The flags along the brick walk were in bloom now, and the lilac bushes on either side of the porch; later in the summer there would be marigolds, bouncing Betty, four o'clocks, bleeding hearts.... The flavor of the old-fashioned names was extraordinarily satisfying to Lew. He paused in front of the small, square house, but he did not go up the porch steps. On a warm May afternoon like this Aunt Chat was almost sure to be sitting out in the backyard, in the lawn swing. As a child Lew had never understood why this wooden contraption, with its two seats facing each other, was called a swing. The most that could be coaxed out of it in the way of movement was a series of rusty, back-and-forth jerks, not unlike Aunt Chat's own rheumatic shufflings.

Yes, there she was, the great raw-boned old woman in her black-and-white percale (she made all her dresses from the same "pattren" with rick-rack trimming around the collar and long sleeves). Sunlight sifted through the delicate green leaves of the boxelder above her and fell in splashes on her bent head, with its little bun of thin hair on top and its molasses-colored side combs. She had a bowl of green peas in her lap; her gnarled hands went about the task of shelling them with the skill of long practice. Beyond the lawn swing and the boxelder stood the summer kitchen, with the pieplant patch beside it, and the pump house, all covered over with grape vines—the prettiest little place in the world, Lew had always thought. He had installed modern plumbing in Aunt Chat's house years ago, but she insisted (and secretly Lew agreed with her) that while city water was all right for washing, nothing could beat her old pump when it came to good cold drinking water. And in spite of the electric refrigerator in her kitchen—also installed by Lew— he suspected that she still kept her butter and milk cold in buckets which she let down into the well. She had always done it that way. Why should she change?

"Hi, Aunt Chat," he called, and the lawn swing creaked as she turned. Her mottled, weather-beaten face broke into a radiant smile at sight of him; she and Lew had always hit it off very well.

"Aren't you the one, sneaking up behind a person's back! I was just thinking to myself, be nice if Lew was to show up. How are you, boy?" She patted his sleeve—her version of a hug and kiss. "Set down. Tell me about the funeral."

Funerals were Aunt Chat's meat. She preferred them to weddings, or even to Decoration Day parades. But before Lew was fairly launched on his report, the delivery truck from Underwood's Store pulled up in front of the house and Grover Underwood himself came trotting through the gate with a little sack of groceries. The theory was that Underwood's made no deliveries after noon, but Grover was always making exceptions. He had gone to the funeral, of course—he and Lew were lifelong friends—and he still wore his good suit.

"I'll just set these inside," he said. "Hey there, Lew. Everything okay?"

"All okay. We had our session with McVey after the services, so that's over, too."

Grover paused with his hand on the screen door. "Oh?" he said. For a minute he seemed on the verge of asking something else. But he didn't, after all. He looked tired, thought Lew. Running himself ragged with that damn store.

"Much obliged, Grover," said Aunt Chat, when he came out of the kitchen again.

"Don't mention it. Well, I've got to be getting back. You haven't forgotten about tomorrow morning, Lew? Our conference ..."

"Sure. Come over to the bank about eleven thirty. I'll be there."

Aunt Chat waited till Grover was back in his truck. But not a minute longer. "Conference?" she said. "You and Grover got a conference tomorrow? He was telling me the other day things are bad at the store."

"Things are always bad with Grover," said Lew. "He's a good guy, but you know as well as I do that he hasn't got a grain of business sense. He's still back there in the horse and buggy days, trying to run the store the way his father and grandfather did. It won't work. I've been telling him for years it won't work, and it's no use, he either can't or won't see that he's got to change with the times if he wants to stay in business."

"You mean you ain't going to pull him out of the hole this time?" It was not so much a question as a thoughtful statement. Aunt Chat sighed. "Grover claims all he needs is a little time. It looks like the crops are going to be good this year, and if he can just get through the summer he'll be sitting pretty."

"I know," said Lew. "I've heard it all a good many times before. If it hadn't been for Olive I'd have refused him the last three loans. She always put in a word for him. But now— Because it's not really doing him a favor. It doesn't make any difference whether the crops are good or not, he'll still give credit to anybody that asks him for it—because Underwood's always has—and he'll be right back where he is now. He can't compete with the chain stores on that kind of a basis, I don't care how much of an institution Underwood's is. The name's worth something, I'll admit, and if Grover will listen to reason the chances are we can work something out. I hope so, for his own sake."

"Grover'd be lost, without the store. I don't know what I'd do myself, if I had to trade any place but Underwood's. He's real good about deliveries and all. I've always liked Grover."

"So have I," said Lew shortly. "He's one of my best friends." But you couldn't go on humoring a man forever, just because he'd gone all through school with you and was the best hunting and fishing companion you'd ever had. Not unless you were in business for your health. Aunt Chat just didn't understand.

"I was telling you about the funeral," he said to get her off the subject, and that did it. She listened with open relish.

"Sounds like they gave Olive a good send-off," she said, when he had finished with who all was there and who sent which flowers. "Poor girl. How did she look?"

"Why, about as usual. That is—I mean, she looked all right. Quite natural, everybody said." Though, now that Lew thought of it, "everybody" had no way of knowing whether Olive looked natural or not. For the past ten years she had been almost a recluse; only a handful of people had seen her, except at a distance, working with her flowers in the wide grounds back of the house where she had lived all her life. Lew himself found it hard to visualize her alive, she had grown so shadowy, so out of touch with the world. (He shifted fretfully on the lawn swing seat. Nobody could blame him. It wasn't his fault that his wife had chosen to fade farther and farther into the background.) The only picture he could summon up was of Olive at a distance, so slim that her figure looked tubular, like a limp strand of spaghetti balanced by some miracle on end. Or—with her halo of white, fluffy hair—like a dandelion gone to seed. Death had laid her out flat, but it had brought no change to her face, which remained pale, pointy-nosed, and above all withdrawn, closed up against life.

"Well," said Aunt Chat candidly, "she wouldn't have won any beauty contest, the best day she ever had. You didn't marry her for her looks, that's one thing sure." Her voice took on the stubborn note of one returning to an old bone of contention. "To my way of thinking, you hadn't any business marrying the poor thing. No sir. She wasn't no match for you, and you shouldn't ever have done it, Lew, I don't care how much it riles you to have me say it."

"It doesn't rile me. I did it, that's all. It's over and done with."

Aunt Chat tightened her mouth. "Uh huh. Over and done with. You've had your cake and et it too, all these years. And now that Olive's laid away, I suppose you're fixing to marry Celia Colby. When's the wedding to be? Tomorrow?"

"Day after tomorrow. We thought we'd wait a decent interval." It was an Aunt Chat kind of joke, and he gave her his sudden, genuine smile. The combination was too much for her. She cackled raffishly.

"I vow, Lew, you're the limit! Serve you right if Celia wouldn't have you, after all, the way you've kept her waiting."

"She'll have me, all right," said Lew. "It hasn't been all beer and skittles for me, either, you know. You had a happy marriage yourself, so you don't—"

"I had a happy marriage because I married the feller I wanted, not the one with the most money," snapped Aunt Chat, and in spite of himself Lew flushed. "There's some cold beer inside, in the ice box. Go fetch yourself a bottle, and don't give me any more of your sass."

Reduced thus to a naughty little boy—always, after smacking him, Aunt Chat had given him an apple or a "lickrish stick"—Lew rose obediently and went into the kitchen. The refrigerator and sink gave it a modern look, but time had left the rest of Aunt Chat's little home untouched. He peered into the front room, which had an airless, old woman's smell, and which was cluttered with knick-knacks—wishbones strung together, for some unfathomable reason, with pink and blue ribbon; crocheted pin cushions; locks of the hair of Aunt Chat's dead children framed on white satin; the enormous moustache cup that had belonged to her husband. Usually there was a quilt set up here in its frames; Aunt Chat was the best quilter in Turk Ridge. Lew used to kneel on a chair beside her, watching the pattern of tiny stitches, fascinated by the large, topless silver thimble and the deftness of her hands.

Here, even more than in the garden, he felt as if he had stepped back in time—not just to a place he remembered, but to a self he remembered, the core of his own true self preserved along with Aunt Chat's other treasures. He turned to the corner where his high school graduation photograph had hung for more years than he cared to count. It gave him an odd little jolt to find the space empty, only a darker rectangle on the faded wallpaper to show where it should have been. In a moment, though, he saw what had happened: the picture, mounted on heavy cardboard and strung on a bit of cord, had slipped off its hook and was lying face-down on the marble-topped table below. He went over and picked it up. The eyes of the boy he had been looked straight at him. Eyes at once bold and innocent, set in a thin, unsmiling face. The boy's hair was combed back in a startled-looking pompadour, and there was a defiant tilt to his head. He and Lew stared at each other—strangers trembling on the brink of recognition. All Lew could remember for sure about the boy was that he wanted to be a doctor and his graduation suit was too tight across the shoulders. The boy knew nothing at all about Lew. Would he have liked the man he had turned into? Would he have felt proud, ashamed, or merely surprised, at what life had done to him?

The prisms in the old-fashioned wind chime hanging in the doorway stirred, flashing violet and emerald splinters against the wall, and setting up a fragile clashing sound. Like a voice out of the past, so sad and ghostly that Lew stood quite still, listening, almost catching some faraway message ...

He gave his shoulders a little shake, replaced the picture on its hook, and went back outdoors with his bottle of beer.

"Took you long enough," said Aunt Chat. She was on her feet, tossing the pea pods over the fence to her little flock of hens. "I was beginning to think you'd got lost." She shook out the last pod and began the toilsome journey back to the lawn swing. Lew knew better than to try to help her; she had her own method of limbering up her stiff joints and did not welcome assistance.

"I was just taking a look around," he said. "I see you've still got that old picture of me. It had fallen off the wall, so I picked it up and—Hey! What's wrong?"

Aunt Chat had stopped in her tracks, and was staring at him with what he called her "spooky" expression. "What's that you say, boy?" Her voice was dramatically hushed. "It fell off the wall? Again?"

"What do you mean 'again'?"

"The second time in a week," whispered Aunt Chat. She put her hand up to her mouth, awe-struck. Behind her a couple of the hens paused too, brainless heads aloft, one foot dangling, in an attitude absurdly like her own. "Oh my soul and body, Lew, it's a warning. I never knew it to fail. It's a Sign."

"You bet it is." Lew grinned at her. "It's a sign you need a new cord on the picture. Or a new hook to hang it on."

"Don't scoff. It's a Sign. I've known it to happen time and again. When a person's picture falls off the wall, they're heading for trouble. Terrible bad trouble." The words hung, heavy with portent, between them in the sunny air. "It's come to me in a dream, too. I ain't been easy in my mind, Lew, there's something terrible going to happen. I can tell. I get this feeling. Like before Jesse died, it was like something had me by the throat. I just knew."

Everyone else had known too, if you wanted to get technical. Jesse, Aunt Chat's husband, had fallen at the age of eighty and broken his hip. It wouldn't have taken any special psychic powers to figure out what was going to happen to the poor old fellow. Lew thought this, but— exasperated as he was by Aunt Chat and her Signs—he didn't have the heart to say it. She looked too distressed, with her mouth working anxiously and her eyes—the same faded blue as his own—blinking at him. When he put his hand over hers, she clung to it; this touched him most of all. And she didn't resist when he started guiding her back to the lawn swing. Though her big frame was bent with rheumatism, and though Lew was of average height, she was still as tall as he. A great old girl, he thought; they don't make them like her anymore.

"Look, Aunt Chat," he said. "You know me well enough to know I've got no intention of dying just because my picture falls off the wall. I'm going to be around a good long while yet. I've lived hard and I expect I'll die hard too. It's going to take a lot more than Signs and bad dreams to kill me. Take my word for it, you'll have to think up some better way than that to get rid of me."

It took some doing, but he finally coaxed a smile out of her. "All right," she sighed as she settled down once more in the lawn swing, "have it your way. I'm just an old fool. You never did pay any mind to what anybody else said. No reason to start now, I guess." She folded her hands demurely, but Lew caught the wicked gleam in her eye as she shot her question at him. "What about the childern? I bet they're none too pleased, neither one of them, at having Celia for a stepmother."

"I don't figure it's any of their business," said Lew. "Do you?"

"They'll make it their business. Anyway, that wife of Whitt's will, or I miss my guess. She's got her eye on your money—why else did she marry Whitt?—and she's of no mind to split it with Celia or any other second wife of yours. You mark my word, Lew, that girl ain't to be trusted."

"Don't worry, I don't trust Dort." (Though, to tell the truth, he had a certain sneaking respect for his daughter-in-law; he suspected her of being as tough as he was. And she was good-looking, you had to give her that.) "Anyway, what can she do about it? Whitt wouldn't—"

Aunt Chat disposed of Whitt in short order: "Pshaw! She's got Whitt wrapped around her little finger. If she told him to walk on his hands he'd do it. She's a troublemaker, that Dort is. I saw it the minute I laid eyes on her. Her mouth turns down, and that's a sure sign, I never knew it to fail. You don't want to forget Victoria, either."

"Victoria!" Lew stared at her in genuine astonishment. His son Whitt—Lew would be the first to admit it—was nobody to count on, but his daughter Victoria ... To doubt Victoria would be to doubt his own right hand. She was that much a part of him, and always had been. "Why, Victoria knows she'll be provided for, no matter how many wives I marry. So will Whitt, as far as that goes. You're not trying to tell me Victoria's a money-grabber like Dort! Besides, she *likes* Celia! She always has."

Aunt Chat trained her bifocals on him and smiled pityingly. "Men," she said. "Well, if you don't see it yourself no use me trying to tell you. But you're mighty mistaken if you think Victoria's just another Olive. She's got a streak of you in her too, not that she shows it very often, but it's there."

"I know it. I know Victoria too well to think for a minute that she's going to start meddling in my affairs. Any more than I'd meddle in hers. I go my way and she goes hers. We always have. We always will." He became aware of the blustering note in his own voice and stopped. The silence didn't seem to bother Aunt Chat in the least. She was busy reanchoring her side combs, poker-faced, waiting for him to talk himself further into a corner. "I know you don't think I've been a very good father, but damn it all—"

"No, I don't. Victoria's level-headed, or you'd have had her spoiled rotten years ago, and as for Whitt, you never took any more notice of him than if he was a puppy that made a nuisance of himself once in a while. Land knows you haven't been a good husband to Olive, either, and it's always been my opinion Celia deserved better than she got from you." Suddenly she threw back her head and loosed her high-pitched cackle of laughter. "Blessed if I know why any of us put up with you, Lew Morgan!"

"Same reason I put up with you, I guess," said Lew. "Too old and lazy to change my ways." There, he thought with relief, she's forgotten all that spooky stuff, she's herself again.

But when he left, half an hour later, he wasn't so sure. Aunt Chat came around to the front with him to pick a pansy for his buttonhole and say goodbye.

"Lew." He was already through the gate, but at the urgency in her voice he turned. The late afternoon sun dazzled him. Were there really tears in Aunt Chat's eyes? Certainly her withered-apple face had an unfamiliar, tense look. "Lew. You take care of yourself. You hear me? I don't know, I've got this feeling...." She broke off and mustered up a smile and a wave for the girl who was hurrying past on the other side of the street. "Hey there, Arlene."

"Hi," the girl called back. "Afternoon, Mr. Morgan." She wore a red jacket, and she had long legs and a free-and-easy way of moving that reminded Lew of someone, another girl, years ago ... He couldn't place the kid herself for the moment.

"Who is she?" he asked Aunt Chat in an undertone, as he watched the girl whisk around the corner, out of sight.

"Arlene Barta. Works for her room and board at Miz Hall's and goes to high school. She's a nice obliging young one."

"Oh sure. Sophie Barta's daughter, you mean." Lew smiled a little, remembering Sophie, who had also been a nice obliging young one when, years ago, she had come to town fresh from the farm to wait tables at Chili Joe's. Very nice. Very obliging.

"Well," said Aunt Chat, "Arlene calls her Aunt Sophie. Sophie's brother and his wife raised her with their kids out on the farm. It ain't for me to say whether Sophie's her mother or her aunt." She folded her mouth up primly. Aunt Chat, like the rest of the female population of Turk Ridge, had disapproved of Sophie. A wild one, they all said; and they were right, Lew supposed. Wild and sweet. But her father had raised her too strictly. No wonder she cut loose when she got to town. She had wound up "in trouble," as they say, and it was anybody's guess who might be to blame. The list of candidates ranged all the way from one of the high school punks that hung around Chili Joe's on up to—well, on up.

Sophie herself never named any names. She went back to the farm— her brother's, not her father's; old man Barta would have beaten her within an inch of her life—and after a while word got around that she had gone to Chicago. After another while the gossip simmered down to an occasional rumor that Sophie was back for a weekend visit at her brother's farm. She never turned up at Chili Joe's, though. The place wasn't the same without her.

"Nice-looking kid," said Lew. Arlene Barta. Now that he thought of it, Arlene was one of Celia's pets (Lew's term; Celia herself was convinced that as a teacher she played no favorites). But she had been after him lately to manufacture a job for Arlene this summer, after school was out, so she wouldn't have to go back to the farm. "Of course you could find something for her to do, Lew, at the bank or the lumber yard. Typing things. She's so bright and quick, and she deserves a chance."

He turned back to Aunt Chat. Arlene Barta had provided only a temporary diversion; she had the pinched, anxious look again.

"You take care of yourself, boy," she repeated.

"Sure I will," he said, and patted her gaunt shoulder before he set off for home. No use trying to talk her out of it. But he would never understand how a woman as shrewd as Aunt Chat could be so riddled with superstitious notions. She had a gift for sizing people up (that was why Lew was so fond of her; she had always had his number and she liked him, anyway) but there wasn't anything mystical about it. It was a plain matter of using her eyes and ears, sharp to begin with, sharper now from long use. Why gum it up with all these trappings?

When he got to the corner he looked back. She was still at the gate, watching him. A shaft of slanting, religious-looking sunlight glorified her quaint figure and lent a quality of solemnity to her gesture—both arms raised stiffly in farewell.

Obscurely moved, Lew waved back. Of course Aunt Chat's signs and dreams were all of death. When you got to be that old, death must be your most familiar companion, constant as your own shadow.

He had a premonition of his own, a pang of how he was going to feel—lost, lost—when Aunt Chat died. There would be no one left to smack him when he needed it.

2

It didn't surprise Whitt in the least to find himself stuck with the lady cousins. This sort of thing was always happening to him. He was resigned to it.

Dad wasted neither time nor words. As soon as old McVey was out the door, he got Whitt aside in the hall. "I'm going to see Aunt Chat," he announced. "You look after the visiting vultures, Whitt."

Victoria was a little more diplomatic. She fabricated a nervous headache and—apologetically, piteously—went upstairs to her room. (A headache! She hadn't shed one tear over Mother. Not one tear.)

And it wasn't Dort's responsibility. They were his mother's cousins, not

Dort's. Besides, she had all this Chicago company arriving for the weekend. Somehow or other, "all this Chicago company" usually boiled down to one guest—Johnny—but Whitt wasn't going to let himself get started on that now. What was there to get started on, anyway? Dort and Johnny had known each other in Chicago for years, long before she ever married Whitt. Life was dull enough for her in Turk Ridge, without Whitt's pulling the heavy husband act on her, trying to make something out of a perfectly natural, perfectly innocent ...

So here he was, sipping iced tea with the lady cousins on the terrace. Not that they didn't take a cocktail now and then, they assured him— no old fossils they—but they had the drive home ahead of them. No sense taking chances. Alcohol and gasoline simply didn't mix. Whitt mustn't mind them, though, he must go right ahead and have a drink if he wanted one.

He wanted one the worst way. He had hesitated a moment—long enough for him to catch the aha-I-told-you-so look that passed between the cousins. That look had settled it. Dad would have gone ahead and done as he pleased. But not Whitt. Why was that? Why should he care whether these two old things approved of him or not? They were nothing to him, really ... He couldn't help it. He did care.

One of the cousins had a booming voice; the other one twittered.

"My, just look at those tulips," said Twitter, gazing rapturously at the garden. "The colors! Olive did love her flowers, didn't she?"

"A person's got to have something," Boom pointed out, and there was nothing to say to that. But Whitt felt himself bristling defensively. What was wrong, or odd, or pathetic, about loving flowers the way Mother had loved them? The way Whitt loved them too; the few happy memories of his childhood were of flowers and Mother's garden. Like one June morning when he had run out barefooted and all the roses were blooming, a swarm of red ones rollicking over the trellis, Mother had her arms full of pink ones, all dewy, and her face lit up ... Or like an afternoon in the fall when they raked leaves, with the bitter smell of asters and smoke in the air, and Mother picked the last of the splendid garnet-red dahlias and sighed as they started back to the house: "They're so nice and quiet. Flowers are so quiet, aren't they, Whitt?" Yes. Flowers were quiet and undemanding and beautiful. You could love them with no risk of their hurting you. They would never make fun of you, or brush you aside, or expect too much of you, the way people did.

"A lucky thing she married a man with such a good head for business," Twitter was running on. "Olive never could have handled it herself, if she hadn't had Lew to take hold when her father died. The bank, and the lumber yard, and the farms and all. Why, it makes my head spin to think of it! I may be old-fashioned, but I still think a man's so much better at these things than a woman, and I'll say this for Lew, he's carried on wonderfully."

"A lucky thing for him, too. He's done all right for himself." Again Boom stated the case bluntly, and this time she shot a glance of avid curiosity at Whitt. "I thought maybe Olive would split things up a little. But no. It all goes to Lew."

"It's simpler this way," said Whitt after a minute. Simpler, yes. But oh, Mother, Mother, why couldn't you have ...

The weight of the will lay like a cement block inside his chest. He should have known, he supposed. Victoria very likely did know, close as she was to Dad, and working with him at the bank as she did. But Whitt worked—or at least he put in his time—at the lumber yard. And had anybody bothered to tell him? Of course not.

He would have liked one of the farms, no denying it. But his first instinctive reaction had been something like relief. Here was a reprieve from having to cope with the intricacies of a fortune that he welcomed no more than Mother had. The minute he saw the look on Dort's face, though, his relief curdled. There she had sat beside him, poised as always, and nothing in her attitude had changed, though she must have been jolted down to her bones. But Whitt caught the lightning flash of fury in her eyes. The full withering force of it had not yet struck, but it would. And it would strike him, because he knew in his heart that he was to blame—not for the blighting of Dort's hopes, perhaps, but for the raising of them. Oh, he had never said in so many words that he would be rich and independent of Dad when Mother died. But he had done nothing to keep Dort from thinking so. He had let her go on with her soaring dreams ... What else could he have done? His abject dread of losing her might fade at times, but it never really died. She couldn't have stood it here in Turk Ridge for two years without something to sustain her. So she dreamed, and Whitt let her—indeed, he drifted into the habit of dreaming right along with her.

He felt the nervous sweat breaking out in the palms of his hands.

"Poor Olive, she hadn't been well for years," Twitter was going on, valiantly keeping the tea party conversation alive. "Still and all, it's a shock. It's always a shock. Of course we hadn't seen her in—mercy, I don't remember how long it's been! Long before you were married, Whitt, because we never met your wife until today. Such a lovely girl."

"Yes, isn't she?" said Whitt, with the surge of grateful pride that such comments always produced in him. The miracle of Dort's having married him! For a moment he forgot the weight in his chest, the strain of waiting for the storm to break.

"Victoria'll be the next one," Twitter predicted archly. "She's a quiet one—looks quite a bit like her mother, doesn't she?—but she'll surprise us all one of these days, just wait and see. I bet there's some young man she's keeping still about."

"Nobody special, as far as I know," said Whitt. There probably never would be, but let Twitter conjecture about Victoria's love life if it made her happy. Not that there was anything wrong with Victoria's looks. Or with her clothes: Dad had bought her a squirrel coat and hood when she was five years old, and he hadn't gotten any less extravagant, as time went by. The fact remained that, socially, she was a dud; as graceless and self-conscious as a high school kid on her first date. Maybe, if she had gone away to college— But she had chosen to stay here and work for Dad. "Victoria's quite the career gal, you know," he explained. "Dad calls her his right-hand man."

"Oh yes, she's always been her Daddy's girl."

"And always will be, if she doesn't watch out." Boom deposited her glass on the wrought-iron table and stood up. "It's time we got started back. We don't want to be too late."

"It was nice of you to come," said Whitt, and he wondered once more why they should have driven all this way for the funeral of a cousin they hadn't seen for years, a cousin who never answered their letters, except for a card at Christmas time. Was it curiosity? Family loyalty? A fondness for funerals in general? Surely it must be a stronger pull than any of these. Shaking hands with them in farewell, Whitt felt a throb of warmth toward the two old things who must still cherish an abiding affection for Mother herself. By way of thanks, he added, "Mother spoke of you often."

"We were just like this, as girls." Twitter crossed two of her scrawny fingers. She peered up at Whitt with a sly, wheedling smile. "As I told your father, we would so love to have something of Olive's to remember her by. Oh, nothing of value, you know, though I don't suppose Victoria would ever wear the garnets or the jade, much too old for anyone her age. Just something for a keepsake. You'll remind your father, won't you? There's a good boy ..."

After they had gone Whitt poured himself a straight shot and tossed it down. Abiding affection! Ha! Abiding affection for garnets and jade and anything else they could get their claws on. He stared out at Mother's garden, gilded by the sunset, and a wave of desolation rose in him. There was no one but himself to care about Mother, to feel even a twinge of sorrow for her lonely death, her lonely life. He alone knew what Dad had done to her. Which was to obliterate her. (And not even on purpose, not even noticing. All Dad had ever noticed about her was her money.) Whitt knew all too well the impact of a personality so much stronger, so much more ruthless than his own. It was like being out in a high wind; he had spent his childhood seeking shelter from it, cowering before the force of it. The bond of silent understanding between him and Mother was all that had kept him from being flattened. He had been a defenseless child. Now, of course, he was a man....

Suddenly he shivered. The wind was still here, he was still defenseless, and there was no one now to understand or care.

Dort had taken the car, so he walked home. Dad's house (even the old-timers were getting around now to calling it the Morgan place instead of the Whitt place) was on the edge of town. It was Turk Ridge's one estate, an imposing, old-fashioned house set in a vast lawn, with a driveway curving up to the front porch and an iron fence enclosing the whole business. Back of it stretched the open, rolling country; in front it looked down, with benign dignity, on substantial though more modest homes. Whitt and Dort lived in one of the new houses (their wedding present from Dad) on the other side of Main Street. There was a whole block of them, neat, rather pretty, each with brightly painted shutters and trim, each with a picture window. There wasn't any view except the shabby old grade school building with its playground worn to a nubbin by generations of children's feet, but the picture windows were there anyway. Whitt still felt shockingly public in his own living room, like a goldfish swimming around in full view. And he missed the spaciousness of the house where he had grown up. But this was one of the "stylish" parts of town; their neighbors were other smart young married couples like themselves.

Ordinarily Whitt would have enjoyed the walk home. It was such a soothing time of day, with robins skittering across the lawns along the way, and the late afternoon spring sounds—a lawn mower whirring, somebody hammering in a backyard, the clatter of kids on roller skates. But he could not shake off the desolation of that moment when he had stood on the terrace, looking out at Mother's garden, and seeing the sad landscape of her life and of his own. If only Dort ... The knot of apprehension inside him twisted even tighter.

And then as he was crossing Main Street a voice behind him called, "Hey there, Mr. Morgan!" and he turned to see one of the lumber yard men goggling at him: "I'll be damned, Whitt, if you aren't getting to be the spitting image of your dad! I'd of sworn it was him! I just wanted to ask about that order ..." No, it wasn't anything Whitt would know about (it never was); he'd see Mr. Morgan in the morning.

Whitt ought to be used to it. People so often took him for Dad, and whenever it happened it set off in him this queer reaction. In the first second he was always pleased—a quick, keen thrust of pleasure that turned at once into shame. Shame because he was not Dad, or anything like him except in the superficial things—the rather stocky build, the sandy hair and even teeth. Did he even want to be like Dad? Good God, no; and that was where the shame dug deepest: that he should be pleased, even for that quickly suppressed second. It was too much, the final ignominy.

He covered the last two blocks with his hands clenched tight in his pockets. It didn't surprise him to see the car with the Chicago license plates parked in front of his house. "All this Chicago company"—in a word, Johnny—had a way of turning up ahead of time for his weekend visits. As often as not he stretched them out at the other end, too, through Monday or even Tuesday. He was connected, in some way not very clear to Whitt, with the restaurant business; and though it didn't seem to be a full-time connection, Johnny was always rhapsodizing about the relaxing atmosphere in Turk Ridge and how terrific it was to get away from the grind for a few days. He pooh-poohed Dort's complaints about the dullness of small-town life: "You never had it so good, Baby," said Johnny with his infectious smile. And it was true that the familiar round of dinners, bridge and golf took on a festive touch when Johnny was here. All the jokes were amusing; all the girls—not just Dort—sparkled for him; all the cocktail parties were fun. In a way Whitt was grateful to him, as he was to anyone who could cheer Dort up. But whether even Johnny could dissipate the particular storm that was brewing right now was something else again. This was no ordinary crisis of discontent. It crossed Whitt's mind that it was also none of Johnny's business.

All the same, his heart lightened a little as he went up the walk. He could see them through the picture window. They were sitting on the sofa; Dort had her feet tucked under her, and she was listening intently to whatever it was Johnny was saying. Her ash-blond hair was held back with a black velvet band in an Alice-in-Wonderland effect. It made her face look, more than ever, all eyes and mouth. Wide, candid eyes. Lusciously drooping mouth.

She jumped up and ran to meet Whitt at the door. "You poor darling, I felt so guilty, leaving you to cope with those two old creatures! Was it too awful?"

Johnny stood up too, and shook hands with him warmly. "Awfully sorry to hear about your mother, Whitt. I can imagine what a tough day it's been for you. Would a drink help? How about if I mix up one of my All-Purpose Specials?"

It was extraordinarily pleasant, being fussed over like this (and Dort so unexpectedly sweet). Whitt's depression, now that it was evaporating, became the perfectly natural reaction to his mother's funeral. Nothing more. And because he was depressed about Mother, he had foolishly—even disloyally—let himself get into a sweat about Dort.

By the time he had worked his way through the second of Johnny's All-Purpose Specials, Whitt found life beautiful, Dort the loveliest wife a man ever had, and Johnny—yes, and good old Johnny the truest friend. He himself was a pretty fine fellow, when it came to that. You wouldn't find many Turk Ridge citizens big enough, broad-minded enough, to accept the Dort-Johnny situation for what it was, a perfectly natural, perfectly innocent ...

He was vague about how the subject came up. When he thought about it later, it seemed to him that Johnny's proposition was not news to Dort, the way it was to him. Maybe this was what they had been talking about so earnestly, when he saw them through the window. Most likely it was, because Johnny was full of it, bubbling over with enthusiasm. The sweetest little set-up anybody could wish for, a restaurant-bar right on Michigan Avenue—how was that for a choice location?—with a steady, solid clientele of long standing, Johnny had known the present owner for years, and the only reason he was willing to let it go at such a sacrifice was his wife's health, she couldn't take the Chicago climate anymore. It was a steal, take Johnny's word for it. The hitch was not so much raising the dough—Johnny knew half a dozen guys that would jump at the chance—as finding exactly the right partner. He didn't want to go into this with just anybody. This was a real good deal, too good to take any chances on.

"One end of the restaurant business I know from A to Z," he explained. "I know how to keep the customers happy, what the place ought to look like, how to keep the atmosphere quiet but not too quiet, all that." He grinned ruefully. "What I'm scared of is that I might louse the whole thing up on the other end—the everyday business details."

"That ought to be simple enough," said Whitt through the mellow haze that shimmered all around him. "Anybody with plain common business sense—"

"Not so common. To somebody like you, with your ability, it seems like child's play. But not to everybody. I'll be frank with you, Whitt, if you thought you'd be interested, I don't know of anybody I'd rather throw in with."

There was a moment of silence, before Dort whispered, "Oh Whitt, if we only had the money." She was sitting on the hassock at his feet, gazing up at him like a wistful child. "It would be a wonderful chance for you too. You know how your Dad is. Even if he'd let you take any responsibility down at the lumber yard, he'd never give you the credit you deserve. There's no future here for you, you've said it yourself. And what it would mean to me, to move back to Chicago!" She stretched her arms wide, a bird set free.

Whitt leaned forward and brushed his hand along her fair, silky hair. "I know, darling. There's nothing I'd like better." And it was true that, for the moment, his spirit soared with hers, off into a rosy world where he was magically successful, sure of himself, master of all he surveyed. Why not? After all, Johnny had picked him, and Johnny was no fool ... He thumped back to earth. "But a partner without any money isn't going to do Johnny any good, and all I can offer is expectations. I'll have it someday, but God knows when, the way things are tied up."

"It isn't fair," said Dort. "We shouldn't have to wait, just because your mother—" Suddenly she straightened up, her eyes wide with mounting excitement. "Whitt! It's your money. You've got it coming to you. What difference would it make to your Dad whether you get it now or fifteen years from now? He's got plenty, without your share. Why shouldn't he let you have yours now, when it means something to you?"

"Hey," said Johnny. "You've got something there. Just put it to him on a straight business basis, Whitt. You're not asking for any favors. You just want to clean up while you've got this chance. He'll listen to reason. I can give you all the figures, all you have to do is sell him on the deal. Hell, what have you got to lose?"

"Well, I—" Whitt's throat went dry. They made it sound so easy. They didn't know Dad. Or perhaps it was Whitt they didn't know—the craven Whitt who had so often before turned tail and fled at the first withering word from Dad. Their faces, blank with waiting, seemed to swim toward him in the dusk, blotting out the preposterous vision of himself undertaking to sell Dad on a deal. That vision belonged to the future, anyway. What counted here and now was Dort, whose eyes might light up in the next moment or droop with contempt—all depending on Whitt's next words.

He made what felt to him like a careless gesture. "Well, why not? It can't hurt to try."

From then on it was wonderful—all kisses and handshakes and jubilant plans and extra rounds of All-Purpose Specials. To Whitt, his ears ringing with the rare, sweet sounds of praise, his head whirling delightfully, the evening floated by like a dream. At some point they ate something delicious. At some point they switched to brandy; he remembered the feel of the snifter between his hands and the heady aroma. There was a lot of talk about figures, large, round, resounding figures. And at some point he must have gone to bed ...

He woke in the haggard dawn. His head was splitting. His heart pounded with dread. Of what? No matter of what. Just boundless, smothering dread. He jerked himself up on one elbow to see if Dort— of course she was there in the other twin bed; where else, where else? He lay back, weak with relief.

Fifty thousand dollars. You've got it coming to you. A straight business basis. Sell him on the deal. What have you got to lose? Fifty thousand dollars.

The voices buzzed in his ears like a swarm of gnats. And the faces swam toward him, larger than life, closing in on him: Dort's wide-eyed and ripe-mouthed, trembling between a smile and a curl of scorn; Johnny's swarthy, with the odd, light-colored eyes that seemed to glint like opals; and then that other face, so ironically like Whitt's own—even when he closed his eyes it was there, waiting for him. Straight mouth. Parrot nose. And pitiless, faded-blue eyes that stripped him right down to his abjectly quaking bones.

He began to sweat.

3

Halfway up the stairs Victoria realized that she was running again, the way she so often did nowadays. She couldn't explain it. She simply had this impulse to hurry, hurry, hurry. Just the other day somebody down at the bank had said to her: "What's your rush, Miss Morgan? Slow down a minute. There's nobody nipping at your heels." She knew that. It wasn't the feeling of running away. It was the feeling that, if she didn't hurry, she would miss out on something crucial—but what?—that was going on somewhere—but where? In her room upstairs? Ridiculous. And yet, as she opened the door, the sense of urgency surged up in her— *maybe it will be now, maybe it will be here*—and then dissolved, as it did time after time, all day long, into anti-climax.

Her room was a charming mixture of old-fashioned and modern comfort. It had a fireplace that worked, the great high ceilings typical of another, statelier generation, and a romantic little balcony that looked out over the garden. The furniture was of Victoria's own choice— uncluttered in line, light and cool in color. Shaggy, sage-green rug; wide bed with a built-in shelf behind it; lampshades like coolie hats; lemon-yellow drapes. A room as clean-cut and well-groomed as Victoria herself.

She tossed her hat and gloves onto the bed, unbuttoned the jacket of her black silk suit, and stepped out of her pumps. Even without their high heels, she was taller than average. Not as tall as Mother, though;

and her shoulders were broad, without the defeated droop that had been so marked in Mother. It was years, she thought triumphantly, since anybody had said she looked like Mother. The lady cousins might have, if she had given them a chance. Well, let them tell Whitt about it. Victoria wasn't interested.

She and Dad had both skipped out—and if not together, at least he wasn't off somewhere with Celia Colby. They were discreet, all right. Really, Victoria had to laugh at how discreet Dad was when it came to Celia Colby. It just showed how lukewarm he was on the whole subject. Dad wasn't the man to worry about a little thing like the proprieties— not if they kept him from getting what he wanted, and Celia ought to know it. She probably did know it, and couldn't bring herself to face it. A plain case of wishful thinking, if Victoria ever saw one.

She crossed over to her dressing table, fidgeted aimlessly with the bottles and jars on it, at last picked up her brush and swept it through her hair, hard, several times. Victoria's hair was perhaps her best point—dark brown, slightly curling at the ends, and shining with the good care she gave it. The girls envied her, they said, not having to worry about permanents. (Turk Ridge still called them girls, though they were all, like Victoria, past thirty. They were apt to refer to themselves as "the gals." There were half a dozen of them, all unattached, all with jobs of one sort or another. They played bridge and went to the movies together; sometimes they were invited to the young married set's parties. Not that there were ever enough men to go round, but it relieved the monotony.)

Yes, they envied Victoria. She didn't have to worry about permanents, and she had the only Cadillac convertible in town, and the only honest-to-God mink coat. She put down the brush and looked deep into her own eyes in the mirror. They would *really* envy her—wouldn't they?—if they knew about—

The phone rang. She leapt for it, and in the instant of leaping stopped short, a fumbling bundle of hope and dread. Surely, surely, he wouldn't call her. She had told him not to, she had made it so clear, and what if Dad hadn't left yet, or had come back for some reason? She sat down on the edge of the bed and picked up the phone.

"Miss Morgan? One moment, please. Chicago calling."

Her heart sank. It soared. It seemed to stop, while her mind darted back and forth between the operator who might be listening in and the click on the line that would mean someone was on the extension downstairs.

"Hello? Hello, Vicky? Are you all right? It's Fred."

"Yes, Fred. I told you not to—"

"I know, but you got me worried. No letter when I checked in at the hotel yesterday, so I figured you'd call me for sure last night—"

"I wrote you. You should have gotten it yesterday. Today at the latest. I can't understand why you haven't gotten it."

"Well, anyway. You all right? All set for Sunday? I hope I hope." The expression, one of Fred's favorites, reached out to her, warm and real as a handclasp. She could see him against the stereotyped hotel room background, sitting on the bed with his jacket off and his tie undone, his salesman's sample case beside him on the floor—a little bit paunchy, more than a little bit bald, his homely, lively face tilted to one side, while he hoped he hoped. For a minute she stopped worrying about who might be listening in.

"Oh Fred, I can't make it this Sunday. I just can't."

"Oh no." His voice sagged with disappointment. "I had it all planned, the whole day, I was going to drive you out to Buck's for dinner, and ... Why, honey? Why can't you come?"

The endearment set her off again; she cleared her throat nervously. "I just—"

"Is it your mother? Is she worse again?"

"She—she died." She hadn't meant to blurt it out. She hadn't meant to tell him at all. From the beginning she had used Mother's ill health (suitably embroidered, dramatized with well-timed crises) as her excuse. I can't ask you to my home, Fred, not as long as Mother's so sick. I'd love to have you meet my folks, but until Mother's better we're not having any company at all ... But Mother dead was no excuse, no shield against the day of disaster when Dad and Fred would meet. Her one defense, and she had thrown it away.

She listened, numb with apprehension, while Fred worked his way, inevitably, from shocked sympathy to offers of help. There must be something he could do. "Look, Vicky, just say the word and I'll jump in the car and be down there in three hours."

"No," she gasped. "No, no. You mustn't—I mean, thank you, but there honestly isn't anything you could do, Fred."

"Well, if you're sure ... I know how it is, a time like this. Of course you're upset, poor kid." She knew, from his groping reassurances, that he was wounded by her curtness, but she could not help it, she had never had a glib tongue. And especially not now, when all the circumstances were wrong, when he had caught her off balance, surprised her into telling the truth about Mother. She had *told* him not to call her. Tears of frustration sprang to her eyes.

"I'm sorry, Fred. I can't talk now." There. She was making it worse. He would never bother with her again. "Some other time. Only don't—I'll call you, Fred. I'll call you Saturday."

The rash promise was made. He seized upon it eagerly. "Saturday then. Day after tomorrow. I'll be waiting to hear from you. Take care, hon. Remember, anything I can do. Maybe we can figure out something for Sunday, after all. Maybe I can just take a run down there—"

"We'll see," she said faintly. "Goodbye for now."

She sank back on the bed, buried her face in the pillow, and wept. She had done everything wrong, all wrong, as usual. Why must she always get herself tied up in these cruel, self-conscious knots? The things she should have said to Fred, the things she wanted to say, sprang to her mind now with maddening ease. Now when it was too late, she felt her heart unclenching, opening out to him in a rush of warmth and gratitude. Gratitude that went back six months ago, to the day when he had sat down beside her on the train to Chicago and had struck up a conversation. (She could see the derisive glint in Dad's eye: "He picked you up on the train, you say? These traveling men! Real lady killers.")

How could she ever explain what that train trip, that pick-up, whatever you wanted to call it, meant to her? It may have been partly the pleasant strangeness of riding on a train, when she was so used to driving everywhere she went. But the Cadillac had been in the garage for repairs, and for one reason or another none of the girls went with her, on that particular Saturday shopping expedition. So there she was, alone, and in a rare, care-free mood. Even so, she shrank closer to the window, gazing out of it distantly, when Fred got on the train and sat down beside her, an hour or so out of Turk Ridge. Her automatic withdrawal was lost on him. "See that hardware store up the block? The big one. There," he said, reaching across her to point as the train pulled out. "I just sold that guy a five hundred dollar order. Quickest damn sale I ever made in my life. I had a couple of minutes to kill before train time, and bam! Just like that. Five hundred bucks worth. Care for a cigarette?"

Nobody on earth could have called it a lady-killer approach. In a way, it was not an approach at all, but the unaffected expansiveness of a man who had had a stroke of good luck and could no more keep it to himself than the sun could stop shining. He simply took it for granted that Victoria—or whoever else he might have chanced to sit beside—would be interested and pleased. And she was. Turning away from the window and the phenomenal hardware store, she looked into Fred's eyes and felt her face breaking irresistibly into a smile.

For one thing, he was so disarmingly homely. His hat was pushed to the back of his head, so she could see the sparse strands of no-color hair. His nose had a hump in it, and his mouth was too big. He was medium-sized, beginning to bulge around the middle, and his clothes were all right, except for his tie, which was terrible. But his eyes looked out at the world and all his fellow creatures with a kind of humorous, sociable curiosity. Something about him—Victoria had felt it instantly, like the touch of a magic wand—drew from her a spontaneous response that was brand-new to her, and wonderful. Here at last was a man who did not strike her dumb with self-consciousness. For that day, at least, he had set her free. And if, back in Turk Ridge again, the old bonds tightened about her as mercilessly as ever, she had that first Saturday—and other days with Fred, too—to be grateful for.

He took her, miracle of miracles, at her face value. He was not being nice to her because she was Lew Morgan's daughter, the richest girl in Turk Ridge. (Turk Ridge was out of Fred's territory. He did not know who Lew Morgan was.) He was being nice to her because, quite simply, he liked her. He thought she was good-looking. He thought she was smart. He thought she was fun.

No longer sobbing, Victoria lay back and stared at the ceiling, where shadows from the vines on the balcony shifted incessantly. The fault— and it was all hers, none of it was Fred's—went deeper than just saying the wrong things or leaving the right ones unsaid. It was a basic inadequacy. Her own. She was not capable of Fred's brand of honest, uncomplicated feeling. It must be so; otherwise why had she gone to such pains to keep Fred a secret from Dad and the girls and all of Turk Ridge? If she were true to her own feelings, she would be proud of him— as he was of her—eager to show him off. Instead, she had side-stepped, evaded, postponed, deceived him. (Yes she had. He didn't know about the Cadillac: she left it outside of Chicago and came in on the train to meet him. And the stories she made up about Mother being sick; and letting him think her coat was imitation mink; and pretending, when he gave her artificial pearls for Christmas, that she didn't have a string of real ones at home.) All because she was a coward and a weakling, afraid that she would not be able to preserve her picture of Fred—even though it was the real one, she knew it in her heart—if other people saw him differently.

The shadows on the ceiling flickered in their timorous, tremulous dance. "Other people." Another miserable evasion. She didn't give a snap of her fingers for anything the girls might say about Fred. He wasn't tall, dark, and handsome. But he was a man. An unattached man—his wife had died three years ago, and lonesome as he was, without home or children, he hadn't seemed to take much interest in anybody else, until that lucky day when he sat down beside Victoria on the train. (There was no holding back on Fred's part. Early in the game he had told her how much money he made, had taken her around to meet his friends, had made it thrillingly, alarmingly clear that his intentions were serious.) No matter what the girls might say, they would envy her.

There was only one person who could spoil Fred for her. Dad could; and she was terrified that he would. He had done it before, with the few boys, back in high school days, who had been brash enough to ask her for dates. And of course he had been right about them: one of them had turned out to be little better than a pool room hanger-on; one was a barber; one married well, and ran through every penny of his wife's money inside of a year.

But she was no longer a giddy high school kid with no judgment. She was thirty-three years old, and time passing, passing, and this haunting certainty that somewhere something important was going on without her ...

Exactly. There was nothing like loneliness to produce mirages. She closed her eyes, clinging desperately to her memory of Fred—the real, warm, living Fred who knew how to set her free. If he was a mirage, she could not bear to find it out. That was all. She was not brave enough to take the risk.

"Victoria! Hey! Anybody home?" It was Dad, calling from downstairs, and Victoria sprang up and rushed to answer him, as she had done ever since she was big enough to navigate.

"Right here. Be down in a minute." She gave her face a hasty inspection; Dad would notice if there were any traces of her crying fit. Well, after all, tearstains were in order, just after Mother's funeral. *Mother is dead,* she told herself solemnly. But inquisitively, too, probing to test the impact of *Mother is dead.* There was none. Just as there had been no impact, for Victoria, in *Mother is alive.* The same minus quantity. Or almost minus. She could remember a couple of times when Mother had aroused in her a mild, surprised curiosity—once when Dad slapped Whitt, Mother had suddenly gathered him up in her arms, big boy that he was (he always had been a crybaby); and then, when Victoria graduated from high school, Mother had gone to great, secret pains to make a corsage for her. Quite a pretty one, too, only of course Dad had ordered orchids from Chicago for the occasion. But what an unexpected gesture for Mother to make! Nobody had been able to think of anything to say.

Victoria put on her shoes and ran out into the hall. Dad was waiting at the foot of the stairs. Some trick of twilight, or perhaps just his attitude, with his face turned up toward her, made him look, for a moment, forlorn. But when he saw her he grinned and tossed his hat on to the old-fashioned hall piece.

"There you are," he said with satisfaction. "Everything under control?"

Meaning the lady cousins. "They're gone," Victoria told him. "At least I think they are. I let Whitt do the honors. It was a sacrifice, but he's so much better at that sort of thing than I am."

"You know, that's just the way I felt. One of life's little coincidences." They exchanged sidelong glances and laughed, in companionable guilt. Sobering, Dad made a fist and ran his knuckles along Victoria's forehead in one of his rare caresses. So he had seen the signs of tears. He looked slightly puzzled, but respectful. "I guess everything went off all right," he said at last. "Didn't it?"

"I thought so. If there have to be funerals at all—"

"Yeah. When I die I hope they skip the fuss and feathers. Just bury me and be done with it. Not that I'm planning on dying any time soon."

"I should think not," said Victoria curtly. "That's enough of that kind of talk. I don't know what we're going to do about dinner. Evvie got on my nerves so, crying and sniffling into the kitchen sink, that I gave her the rest of the day off. So we're on our own."

"Good for us." Dad rubbed his hands together in anticipation, and a pang of joyful relief shot through Victoria. He wasn't going off somewhere with Celia Colby tonight, after all. "I'll construct something. Be my guest."

What fun it was when Dad cooked! More fun than anything in all of Victoria's childhood. She remembered sitting on the high kitchen stool, her skinny little-girl legs wrapped around the rungs, hugging herself, rocking with giggles while she watched Dad cook. There were all sorts of variations to his act. Sometimes he was a voluble French chef, kissing his fingertips over the scrambled eggs, bursting into inconsolable fake sobs if the toast burned. Sometimes he was a mad scientist, chortling evilly as he concocted his brew. Sometimes he was a dancing cook, and pirouetted in a ruffled apron; or an opera-singing cook; or a juggling cook. Who cared if the food turned out peculiar? Not Victoria; she would have eaten sand and loved it.

A long time ago. But, following Dad out to the kitchen, she felt an echo of that childish delight ("Daddy's going to cook! Daddy's going to cook!") And he had the old twinkle in his eye as he made what he called a preliminary survey of the ice box.

"Let me see, let me see. No snails? No pomegranates? No nightingales' tongues? What kind of a household is this? My poor child, we shall have to rough it. We may be reduced to something so coarse as this steak."

"Oh the pain of it," said Victoria. "How about a drink?"

She mixed them each a Scotch, while Dad continued his rummaging.

Then she perched on the stool, sipping and watching. He had decided to make biscuits. There was no limit to his confidence in his own capabilities; he would tackle anything. Now and then Victoria slid off her stool to hand him things. She always knew what he wanted, without his having to ask. The magician's assistant, she thought, that's me. Dad's the star performer. But that was the way they both wanted it. Here was where she belonged, in her role of pert but admiring, dependable handmaiden. (The others down at the bank were sometimes shocked at the way she talked back to him. But he liked it.) Here was where she was happy. Happy ...

Her eyes strayed to the window above his head. The sky was still flushed with sunset, and against it the elm branches, freshly leafed out, shook in the restless, urgent wind of May. All the wide world outside, and here in this bright, cozy room no uncertainties, no effort required for her familiar role. Fred seemed unsubstantial now, hardly real. A mirage? Oh no, oh no. Her throat suddenly ached with the reality of the tears she had shed.

Dad, all unconscious of himself as a menace—but he was, a beloved, invincible menace—closed the oven door and dusted off his hands. "There we are," he said. He sat down at the table with his drink and smiled at her, drawing her back into the charmed circle. "This is nice, just the two of us. Maybe we should have asked Whitt to stay and eat with us, but what the hell, he's got Dort to keep him busy—and she's the one that can do it, if you ask me."

"Poor Whitt," said Victoria perfunctorily. "I understand Johnny's coming down again for the weekend. Supposed to get here tomorrow. But Dort was in a powerful hurry to get home. It wouldn't surprise me if he's here already."

"What goes on there? Do you know?"

Victoria shrugged. "I wouldn't need more than three guesses. They work awfully hard on the all-pals-together routine, and Whitt seems to go along with it. What else can he do?"

"I know what I'd do. I'd kick Johnny all the way back to Chicago, and then I'd take little Miss Dort across my knee and lick the daylights out of her. That's what she needs." Dad's face hardened, as it so often did when he thought about Whitt, into exasperated contempt. "But she'll never get it from Whitt. He'd let her get away with murder. Who *is* this Johnny, anyway?"

"An old, old friend of the family. Dort's known him for years," quoted Victoria glibly. "He's in the restaurant business. Or something. He looks like a gigolo to me. No, he doesn't either. He looks—well, he looks dangerous, somehow. As if he wouldn't stop at anything." But handsome, she thought. Too handsome. Too smooth. Too ready with the sweet talk. And under the silky surface a hint of something cold and cruel as a knife blade.

Dad snorted. "Dangerous nothing. He's as phony as a three-dollar bill. Strictly pasteboard. Not that I'd trust Dort any farther than I could throw her, either. She thinks she can pull any of her tricks on me, she's got another think coming. If it hadn't been for her, Whitt would have tended to business and finished his medical course—"

The old refrain, thought Victoria. Dad had never gotten over the disappointment of Whitt's failure as a medical student. Or perhaps it was a more personal disappointment that ate on him—his own youthful, unfulfilled ambition to be a doctor. He had imposed that ambition on Whitt, had crammed the square peg into the round hole willy-nilly, and he blamed everybody but himself for the inevitable fiasco.

"Biscuits are burning," said Victoria. "Of course that's the way I like them."

They ate at the kitchen table—with the exuberant relish that Dad's cooking always inspired in both of them—and then took their coffee into what was known variously as the back room, the library, the study, or the den. Whatever its name, it belonged indisputably to Dad, and though most of the furniture was rather shabby and helter-skelter, it was Victoria's favorite room, the heart of home to her. It had tall French windows—doors, really, opening out onto the yard stretching beyond the south side of the house—so that when the dark-green velvet drapes were pulled back the view of lawn and big old trees lent a feeling of tranquil space. When the drapes were drawn, the room took on a mellow, secluded atmosphere. Dad had a scarred desk in here, and a day bed where he sometimes slept. The carpet was an old-fashioned ingrain one, of a faded color that was like weather-beaten brick, and the book shelves on either side of the fireplace were jammed not only with books (all Victoria's childhood favorites were still here) but with almost anything else you could name—games, fishing tackle, golf balls, tobacco cans, boxes of shells and duck decoys, papers and letters—all jumbled together in the lavish confusion characteristic of Dad. In the middle of the room, under a bronze hanging lamp that could be lowered or raised on a chain, stood the old round table where they had spent so many evenings playing cards, its marble top hidden, between card sessions, by a green velvet cover that matched the drapes, one of its claw feet propped up with a chip of wood to keep it steady.

Several times, while they sat there with their coffee and cigarettes, Victoria came within an ace of telling Dad about Fred. It would have been so easy. Here she was, with the person who knew her best in all the world—yes, and who loved her best; he hadn't even called Celia Colby—enfolded in happy security and in the special dimension that Dad's presence produced for her. A projection of his own rich vitality? Maybe. Anyway, she had always felt more *alive* with Dad than with anyone else—until she met Fred—and in a way nothing that happened to her seemed real until she shared it with Dad. Fred was one of the very few secrets she had ever kept from him. He couldn't be kept a secret much longer. He had no idea that he was a secret. All the more reason why she should prepare Dad, instead of letting the whole thing burst on him without warning. And what better time than now, with Dad so relaxed and approachable, so obviously enjoying an evening alone with her? Surely, now if ever …

She leaned forward abruptly, poured herself another cup of coffee, and took several rapid sips. Quick, before her mouth went dry again—

"I'd kind of like to go fishing Saturday," Dad said lazily, oblivious to any crisis. "If I can talk Grover into taking a day off, I think I will. It would do him good to get away from the store. We might even stay overnight at the shack, make a weekend of it."

"Why not?" Victoria let out her breath in craven relief. "You haven't had a fishing spree in a long time."

"Of course Grover may not be speaking to me by Saturday. He's coming in tomorrow morning for a conference. That's what he calls it. You know as well as I do what he's after. Another loan."

"And you're not going to let him have it?"

"I am not." Dad straightened up; his brows drew together in an irritable frown. "Listen, I own more of the damn store than he does right now—and I have for some time—and I've got no intention of running a non-profitable deal any longer. I told him last year he was a fool not to sell out to that chain outfit, but he's got this pig-headed prejudice against chains … Why, hell, they offered to keep him on as manager. He'd have the same job he's got now. The only difference is, he'd be making money instead of losing it. Well, they're still interested, and this time I'm the one that's going to have the say. Grover can take it or leave it."

"Don't glare at me," said Victoria. "I'm not arguing with you. Only I think it would be a shame to fight with Grover. After all, you've been friends for years—"

"I know how many years we've been friends! But I'm still not in business for my health!" He got up and prowled over to the window, his hands in his hip pockets, his head thrust forward on his stocky shoulders.

"Okay, okay. I should think you could get around him, if you handled him right. You've done it plenty of times before." That was no lie; as far as Victoria could figure out, Dad had dominated Grover Underwood from the day they had started first grade together. It was an odd friendship, when you came to think of it—Grover was as mild and unspectacular as Dad was violent. Maybe that was why they liked each other.

Anyway, Grover and his troubles were responsible for Victoria's missing the boat the first time. (A reprieve? Or a wasted opportunity? She couldn't decide.)

The second time it was Arlene Barta. Again, Victoria had steeled herself to the talking point, and again Dad beat her to it.

"I've been meaning to ask you, do you think you could find some busywork for a high school kid at the bank this summer? Arlene Barta. She can type, Celia says, and she's bright and willing."

Celia and her lame ducks, Victoria thought bitterly; she's always got to be the lady bountiful. Especially when she can get somebody else to do the dog-work. But all she said out loud was, "Well, of course there's plenty of work. Do you think it would be worthwhile, breaking her in just for the summer?"

"Probably not. Though if she turns out to be any good we might keep her on part-time after school starts again in the fall. Celia says she deserves a break."

Oh sure. "She's Sophie Barta's daughter, isn't she?"

"Or her niece. There seem to be two schools of thought." He paused, thoughtfully. "You remember Sophie?"

"Everybody remembers Sophie. She was Bad Example Number 1, in all the better circles. I hope Arlene's not—"

"Oh no. Very well behaved, according to Celia. Even though she looks like Sophie." Again the thoughtful, rather cautious pause. Then Dad put down his cup with a pleased air of finality. "Well, so that's that. We'll give her a try and see what happens."

They had settled down to a game of gin rummy and for the third time Victoria was about to take her courage in both hands and broach the subject of Fred; she had actually gotten out the first nervous words: "Dad, there's something I—"

The phone rang.

She knew right away that it was Celia, from the way Dad's voice softened, after his first brusque "Hello." And then the automatic gesture of smoothing his hair (it was still thick and mostly sandy, only a sprinkling of gray on the sides), as if Celia could see as well as hear over the telephone, and he must spruce up for her benefit. "Hey there, how are you? Not a thing. Victoria and I were just starting a hand of gin rummy ... I don't know why not. Sure. Be right over."

So. No need any longer to be discreet or surreptitious. The twelve years of clandestine meetings, "chance" encounters, hush-hush weekends in Chicago were over. She's not wasting any time, thought Victoria, calling him up the very night of Mother's funeral.

Not that the affair—out in the open at last—was going to be news to anybody in Turk Ridge. Victoria herself had been aware of it for a good ten years, and she was one of the last to know. (That was what they always said about wives, wasn't it? Except that Mother hadn't counted as a wife.) It was common knowledge, gossip bandied about for so long that it had lost most of its snap. At one point there was talk that the school board might dismiss Celia. They didn't, though. After all, Dad was Lew Morgan. Celia went right on being the most popular teacher in Turk Ridge High School and getting invited to all the nicest homes, and she held her head up just as high as if she'd never heard of a back street affair, didn't know the meaning of the phrase....

Victoria unclenched her hands and forced a smile as Dad turned away from the phone. He looked eager as a boy.

"That was Celia," he explained. "You don't mind if I go out for a while, do you? I won't be late. Evvie'll be back before long, anyway. Or why don't you call up some of the girls, if you get lonesome?"

"Of course. I don't mind."

Halfway to the door he stopped. "What were you saying when the phone rang? Something about—"

"I don't remember myself. Nothing that won't keep, I guess. See you in the morning."

He was at the doorway now, impatient to be gone, but with one last, casually tossed off message. "Oh by the way, Victoria, Celia and I will be getting married, probably late this summer. No surprise to you, I guess?"

Her opinion, her feelings in the matter were of no more importance to him than that. Why, he had taken more pains to explain Grover Underwood and Arlene Barta, who made no real difference, one way or the other! While she—her face burned with humiliation—she was so abjectly dependent on Dad's approval or disapproval that she did not dare mention Fred. She had a furious impulse to say something cruel and savage, something that would destroy Celia for him ...

Ah, but she had no such power over him as he had over her. With a flick of his tongue, he could turn Fred into a cheap caricature, reduce him to a mirage, spoil him forever in Victoria's eyes. But nothing she could say would sway Dad one hair's breadth away from Celia. He knew how to be in love, and she had never learned. He had never let her learn.

"Not exactly a surprise," she heard herself saying carefully.

"Congratulations."

"That's my girl. I knew I could count on you." He gave her his big warm smile, waved jauntily. The door shut behind him.

You don't know anything about me, thought Victoria. Her hands began to tremble, and there was a strange, rushing sound in her ears. "That's your girl." You don't know. You don't know the first thing about me.

4

Every week day began, for Grover Underwood, with the ritual known as Opening the Store. He might complain about what a nuisance it was, but the idea of entrusting it to anyone else would have struck him as downright shocking. Pa had always Opened the Store himself; so had Grandpa before him. It was part of the Underwood tradition, like calendars at Christmas time and the bag of candy when a customer paid his bill.

So every morning on the dot of eight (you could have set your clock by him) Grover came trotting down the outside stairway that led from his apartment above to the store below. As long as his mother was alive, he had kept the big old Underwood house going—though how he did it, the way that furnace ate up coal, was a mystery—but when the old lady finally died he had sold the house and fixed up an apartment for himself above the store. He had grown very fond of his little home; he liked fussing around, doing his own cooking and housework. And then it was so convenient to the store—too convenient, sometimes; people knew that even on Sundays they could call Grover in case of an emergency. He knew they were imposing on him, but he never refused to go down and make up an order for somebody who had run out of sugar or needed an extra pound of butter on account of unexpected company. He took the store's motto: "Underwood's for Quality and Service" literally.

Down the stairway he came, a short man, rather stout, very neat in his gray suit, rimless glasses, and Panama hat (he would never have thought of leaving for the store without his hat). He had the sober, purposeful air of an aging dog bent on discharging his established responsibilities. At the bottom of the stairway he paused briefly, looking up and down Main Street to see that everything was in order, inspecting the sky to check the day's weather, and glancing with unfailing satisfaction at the curly gilt legend above the store: "Underwood & Son." Then he turned down the side street, into the alley, and let himself in the back door. The familiar smell of coffee, dry goods, and sweeping compound greeted him, and Muffin, the yellow cat, ambled toward him, yawning and stretching. He exchanged a few pleasantries with her while he poured fresh milk into her dish. It was going to be another nice warm day, he told her. Yes sir, the warm weather was starting in early this year.

The store itself was cool and dim, the way a store ought to be, in Grover's opinion. No gleaming enamel and glaring lights for him, thank you. Proper place for that sort of thing was a doctor's examining room. Or a lavatory. Though he was considering installing a refrigerated bin and putting in a line of frozen foods, when he got the new loan from Lew

...

He gave a little sigh and continued his progress toward the part of the store known as Mr. Underwood's office. This was in the middle of the great, high-ceilinged room, beside one of the pillars that marked the dividing line between groceries and dry goods. It consisted of an ancient rolltop desk (new in Grandpa's day, and every pigeonhole stuffed with bills and the memos. Indecipherable to anyone except Grover, which comprised his bookkeeping system), a swivel chair, and a hat tree. Here Grover deposited his Panama and changed into the alpaca jacket which was his uniform during working hours. It was molded to the stoop in his shoulders, and its breast pocket sagged with the weight of Grover's pen and pencil set and the case containing his "other glasses." Minus his hat, with his bald head exposed, he looked older, more than ever like a faithful old dog; the anxious lines in his forehead showed up, and his mild brown eyes seemed larger and rather wistful.

Eleven thirty, he thought; Lew said to come over to the bank about eleven thirty this morning. And without warning, as he stood there in the heart of the store, a gust of something that he could not name— panic? rage? desperation?—shook him from head to foot. Not only him, but the store too: before his eyes all the familiar things seemed to shimmer, as if caught in a long-drawn-out tottering collapse—the shoe-fitting bench, with its black leather seat; the bolts of percale and voile and cretonne behind the counter and in front of it the round stools where generations of Turk Ridge ladies had sat to pick out their dress goods; the ornate gold-framed mirror Pa had bought for the hat department ...

What if Lew said no?

Until this moment Grover had kept the question securely bottled up. It spurted out now, past all control, with a force that left him giddy. He had to lean against the desk to steady himself.

"I don't know what I'll do." He was actually saying the words out loud, in a strange, husky whisper. "I can't bear to lose the store. That's all. I won't bear it. I don't know what I'll do ..."

It passed as suddenly as it had come. Of course Lew was not going to say no. He knew that the store was Grover's whole life. Why, they were lifelong friends, ever since those first school days when Lew had bullied every other kid in their grade, only not Grover, for some mysterious reason he had singled out Grover, had trusted and defended and confided in him. Things had changed since then. Lew was no longer a tough little hoodlum from the wrong side of the tracks, just as Grover was no longer the plump, good-natured boy-who-had-everything. (That was how it had been, back then. The first bicycle in town, and all the candy he wanted from the store, and a real tent.) In a way, they had switched roles. But only in a surface way. Underneath was the same solid foundation of comradeship. Of course Lew was not going to say no.

With the appalling question once more safely bottled up, Grover got back to his routine of Opening the Store. Moving briskly toward the front, he whisked the dust covers from the stacks of overalls and work shirts on the center tables, folded them tidily and stowed them away in their place under the counter. He cast an admiring glance at Agnes' display of spring hats and graduation cards in the window. Then he rolled up the shades on the big double front doors, unlocked them, and propped them open with the pair of iron rabbits that had served as doorstops since time immemorial.

It was eight-fifteen on the dot. Underwood's was open for another day of business.

Already, in the self-service market across the street, a couple of early-bird housewives were moving down the aisles, picking out what they wanted. Self-service, thought Grover. What kind of service was that? Might as well run a damn cafeteria. But again he gave his little sigh. Somehow he couldn't get used to it, seeing people he still thought of as Underwood's regular customers doing their marketing across the street. They went there when they had the cash. They came back to Underwood's when they needed credit. Even some of the country people, the old-timers who had made Underwood's their Saturday headquarters since long before Grover's time—bringing in their eggs and butter and, after they had done their trading, lingering in the front of the store to visit. Even some of them.

One thing about it—and Grover had pointed this out to Lew last year—there wasn't room for two chain groceries in a town the size of Turk Ridge. And Lew had said he didn't know about that, and anyway the outfit that had offered to buy out Underwood's wasn't a grocery chain, it was more in the line of sundries ... "Turn Underwood's into a five and ten cent store?" Grover had cried out, and the idea still brought a flush of outrage to his forehead.

It was now time for the first cigar of the day. Grover unwrapped it, clipped it, and lit it with his usual fussy care. He particularly liked this ten or fifteen minutes at the beginning of the morning, when he stood in the doorway, contentedly smoking, and watching Main Street come to life. The mail truck rattled up to the post office from the depot; a clump of screeching kids sailed past on roller-skates; Doc Fletcher parked his car across the street, with the customary shriek of brakes, and hurried up to his office above the drugstore; Rudy Sorensen appeared in the doorway of his bakery and lifted a floury hand in greeting to Grover.

And Celia Colby came by on her way to school. She had a car, but unless the weather was really fierce she walked from Mrs. Walker's rooming house to the high school. She liked to walk, and you could tell it to watch her. There was something lunging yet graceful in the way she swung along. Celia wasn't the tidiest woman in town, Grover had to admit it. This morning her skirt—she was wearing a linen suit, the color of bachelor's buttons—didn't hang straight, and already wisps of her bright brown hair were beginning to work out of the knot at the back of her neck.

No, not the tidiest woman. But that careless touch only added to her charm. It was not in Celia's nature to bother with such non-essentials as straight seams; she could afford to leave that sort of thing to the mousy ones.

"Morning, Grover." Her big, sweet mouth broke into a smile; she paused, as she always did, to pass the time of day. They were old friends, such old friends that Grover could hardly remember now how differently he had felt about her when she first came to Turk Ridge. After all, it was thirteen years ago. Time enough for all the stormy, impossible hopes to die down, for all the sharp edges of sorrow to be smoothed away. He had fallen in love with Celia, but so had several other people, among them Lew Morgan ...

And somehow Grover had been maneuvered into the role of go-between and father-confessor. Maybe that was his nature; as it was Celia's to give and never count the cost; as it was Lew's to take, to get whatever he wanted, and on his own terms. No use blaming anybody. Celia knew what she was doing. Not at the beginning. But after the first few years she knew as well as anybody else that Lew had no intention of divorcing Olive to marry her. (Why should he? Celia was his, divorce or no divorce. And then there was Olive's money. A woman with any spirit would have divorced *him*, but Olive had never had any spirit. Only money.) As for Grover himself— Well, nobody on earth could have talked either Lew or Celia out of the affair. One was as heedless and willful as the other. At least Grover, relaying her messages to Lew, always there when she needed a shoulder to cry on, had not been shunted out of her life entirely. It was better than nothing. The irony of it? He had gotten used to that, too. You could get used to hanging, if it went on long enough.

She was chattering on now about the Junior-Senior banquet, and next week Commencement ... "The last Commencement, for me. I've got my letter of resignation all written, and we'll get married the end of the summer. Oh, Grover! Just think of it. After all these years!" She thrust her hands out impetuously and clasped his. Her gray eyes were shining. "I know it sounds awful, to be so glad, when somebody's dead ... I can't help it. I am glad. I've waited so long, and I'm so tired of all the sneaking and pretending. Last night when Lew came to call on me, right out in the open, I was so happy I could have bawled."

"Didn't waste any time, did he?" said Grover drily.

"We've wasted enough time, as it is."

Yes. The best years, for Celia, the years when she should have had a husband, a home, children—she had thrown them all away for Lew. There were still moments (now, for instance) when she looked like a girl. She had the compact kind of figure that was time-resistant, and the kind of fresh, thin skin that was apt to flush up like a peony when she was excited. But there were little lines around her eyes. The bright autumn-leaf brown of her hair was beginning to fade. She was no longer a girl. She was thirty-eight years old—a good fifteen years younger than Lew—but still no longer a girl.

"Well, there it is," said Grover vaguely, patting her square, freckly hand. Poor Celia, poor happy Celia ... Because it was dangerous to be this happy, Grover had a superstitious conviction that it was dangerous. No use warning her. She would have laughed at him. And maybe it was only a bit of jealousy on his part; she wouldn't be needing him, not even as a go-between, any more. Another moment, like the one when everything in the store had seemed to shudder before his eyes, threatened to pounce on him. He had a wistful impulse to tell Celia about his appointment with Lew at eleven thirty, to hear her impatient reassurances: "Why, of course Lew's not going to say no! What's the matter with you? He wouldn't think of saying no ..."

She was smiling up at him, absorbed, as always, in loving Lew. "I'll be an honest woman. Think of that, Grover. An honest woman at last!" she said before she set off up the street.

But she had always been honest, thought Grover, watching her sturdy, proud back. (There was sure-God something wrong with the way that skirt hung.) Too honest for her own good. With a little craftiness she might have finessed Lew into getting a divorce; in his own fashion he was as love-struck as she. But Celia had no tricks at all. Charm, but no tricks. And it was that same integrity that had made it possible for her to outface all the years of gossip, forcing Turk Ridge in spite of itself to accept and respect her. A weaker woman—and a luckier one—would have gotten herself fired. But Celia had missed out on that chance of escape, along with all the others.

She had turned the corner now. Out of sight. Grover teetered on his heels and took another puff of his cigar. And here came the staff of Underwood's—Agnes and her son Bud—right on the dot of eight thirty.

"Morning, Mr. Underwood."

It was one of the things about Agnes that Grover appreciated, her calling him Mr. Underwood. She was as old as he was; Pa had hired her to work in the store when she was still in her teens. Now she was gray-haired, getting rather deaf—a wiry, talkative little thing who had spent so much of her life at Underwood's that she didn't really feel at home anywhere else. There had been a break in her clerking career when she got married and had Bud. But then when her husband came down with pneumonia and died—just like that, as she always said, with a snap of her fingers—she came back to Underwood's, and here she had been ever since.

As for Bud, he had almost literally grown up in the store; Agnes had brought him to work with her when he was a baby because she had no one to leave him with, and he had started running errands and delivering orders while he was in grade school. Bud did the heavy work in the grocery department, besides such humble chores as sweeping out every evening and tending the furnace in the winter. He was a good-natured fellow, none too bright; Grover felt paternal toward him, and worried a good deal about how he and his wife managed to make out on his salary.

It was quite a busy morning. A good omen, thought Grover, it would have been demoralizing to have nothing to do but watch the hands of the clock creep around to eleven thirty. As it was, there was barely time to get things put away, after his session with Mrs. Johnson and her white summer shoes. ("No sir, Carrie, you'll be better off with the ties. I know your foot, and that cut-out's going to give you trouble, sure as you're born ...")

Agnes bustled over to help him. "Here, Mr. Underwood, let me do that. It's almost time." So she too was intent on his conference with Lew. He was aware of her, hovering at the edge of the office, while he changed from the alpaca to his suit jacket.

"There now," she said, when he was ready. She brushed a bit of lint from his sleeve. "All you have to do is show him the figures, Mr. Underwood. He'll realize, the minute he sees the figures." Their eyes met for a moment, in mute anxiety.

"Leave it to me, Agnes." He took his Panama from the hat tree, dropped it, and as he stooped to pick it up realized, with horror, that he was on the verge of tears. The only thing that saved him was Agnes standing there in her navy and white print, her face fixed in a stricken smile.

But once he was out on the street, he was all right again. He had always been a worry wart, he reminded himself as he climbed the short flight of marble steps that led to the bank. Last year he had gotten worked up in just the same way—and Lew had come round, there had been no catastrophe. He nodded to Victoria, in her place behind the cages. "Okay to go in? Lew's expecting me."

"Yes, Mr. Underwood." She looked peaked this morning. Heavy-eyed, as if she hadn't slept a wink, and her voice sounded faint and mechanical. Not that Victoria ever did give out with much warmth. An odd girl. Maybe Olive's death had hit her, after all. She hadn't seemed at all attached to her mother. Still, you never knew.

He straightened his shoulders and opened the door to Lew's office. It was a small room, looking out over the side street with its row of one-story, minor businesses—shoe repair shop, feed store, insurance office. Lew was standing at the window, idly, twirling his ring of keys. It was a nervous habit of his. Just about the only one; one of the things that made Lew so impressive was his air of immense—but controlled—vitality. Very few waste motions. A powerful natural poise that Grover had always envied. Even as kids—Grover in his expensive knickerbockers, Lew in his shrunken, faded overalls—he had managed to make Grover feel insignificant and undersized. And of course that was part of it—that Lew was simply, physically, bigger. So much younger looking, too; Lew still had his hair, and though his figure had thickened some, he didn't have an out-and-out paunch, like Grover's. You'd never dream we were the same age, Grover thought bleakly, I must look at least ten years older. And I don't only look it. I feel it.

"Morning, Lew." He took off his Panama and hesitated, just inside the door. (Hat in hand, he thought, as usual. The weight of all the other times when he had come here to solicit Lew's help pressed down on him, a shameful burden.)

"Come on in, Grover. Have a seat." He shoved a chair toward Grover and sat down at his desk, behind the crystal paperweight that had belonged to Old Man Whitt and the silver-framed photograph of

Victoria. He avoided meeting Grover's eyes. "Another nice warm day. Good fishing weather. I was telling Victoria last night, I've got a notion to take tomorrow off and go out to the shack. If I could talk you into coming along. How about it?"

"There's nothing I'd like better. Only—Saturday, you know. Hard for me to get away from the store."

"Hell with the store. Agnes can hold down the fort for a day. It'll do you good to get away. Me too. We're a couple of tired old men, Grover. We need a tonic."

Grover laughed, rather cautiously. Surely this was a good omen? Lew wouldn't be suggesting a fishing trip if he was planning to say no ... "Maybe you're right, at that. I guess I could—" He paused, then with a feeling of recklessness went on. "Sure I could. Why not? It's a deal."

"Good for you, my boy! Good for you!" Lew sounded a little surprised, very much pleased; Grover didn't usually make up his mind this quick. "Let's get an early start, and if we feel like it we can stay over and come back Sunday afternoon. Celia's got some shindig planned for the evening, so I ought to get back by six or so." At the mention of her name, his face took on a touching, boyish expression.

"I saw Celia this morning. Happy as a lark." The memory of Celia's happiness buoyed Grover up even more; he forgot that he had thought of it as dangerous. What with the excitement of tomorrow's fishing trip, and the growing certainty that it was a good omen, he felt on the verge of happiness himself. "Now to get down to business," he said, and he fumbled in his pocket for the figures; all he had to do was show Lew the figures. "Here's how things stand, Lew—"

He talked for several minutes, earnestly, with all the conviction he could muster. He had rehearsed it in his mind many times in the last couple of weeks; he had no illusions about his own persuasive powers and knew better than to depend on himself for any inspired ad-libbing. There was no indication, as he plodded on through his figures, of the violent shifts from hope to despair that were going on inside him. The sound of his own voice, so unflurried and deliberate, astonished him. But gradually, as he talked, he became aware of a profound uneasiness. Something was all wrong about the way Lew sat there, motionless, his eyes fixed on his hands, which were clasped on the desk in front of him. Not watching Grover, not interrupting him, not—well, not listening to him. That was it. Just letting him ramble on, with his own mind already irrevocably made up. Futility struck Grover like a paralysis. In the middle of a word, his tongue faltered, failed him entirely.

He waited helplessly, unable to look away from Lew's face, as if those features—straight, full mouth, trim moustache, parrot nose, arrogant forehead—were a map on which he might trace the geography of his own triumph or defeat. At last Lew looked up; in that instant Grover got a curious impression of anger (Why? What had he done or said to put Lew in a temper?) and he lifted one hand in an instinctively defensive gesture. He could not help it, he flinched before the fierce, faded-blue flash of Lew's eyes.

"All right, Grover. You've given me the picture. I've heard it all before, you know." Suddenly he struck the desk with the flat of his hand. The sound was violent and final, like a revolver shot. "Now you listen to me."

But it was not necessary for Grover to listen, any more than it had been necessary for Lew to listen to him. This is catastrophe, he thought, this is the way the end of the world feels, this deathly emptiness ... It did not occur to him to argue or protest. He wondered, a little fretfully, why Lew had to talk so loud, as if he must whip himself into a rage by saying it all in the harshest possible terms; "I'm not in business for my health ... You can take it or leave it, I own a damn sight more of Underwood's than you do, and from now on I'm going to have the say.... You and your old-fogey methods ..."

But at the end, after all the pacing between desk and window, after all the noise and the red streak that always showed up in Lew's forehead, between his brows, when he lost his temper—at the end he stopped in front of Grover and said, almost beseechingly, "Look, Grover, you'll still be managing the store, even though the chain owns it. That's part of the deal, to capitalize on the reputation Underwood's has built up all these years."

"No, thank you," said Grover primly. He was still holding the slip of paper with the figures ("All you have to do is show him the figures, Mr. Underwood.") and he folded it up and tucked it away in his pocket. "If you want to turn Underwood's into a five and ten cent store, that's your privilege, I guess. Nothing I can do to stop you. But if you do it, you can be the manager. I want no part of it."

Lew didn't take him seriously; he threw back his head and laughed. "Me manage a store? Why, Grover, I'd bitch it up inside of a week! I never could understand how you did it!"

Flattery, thought Grover; he thinks he can talk me into this, the way he's talked me into all the other things. He felt a cold, unfamiliar stirring deep inside him.

"We can thrash out the details later," Lew was saying. "These birds are coming in Monday to clinch the deal. You'll see, Grover. Once you get used to the idea you'll wonder why you didn't agree to it long ago."

Victoria stuck her head in the door. "Arlene Barta's out here, Dad. Do you have time to see her now?"

"I'm leaving," said Grover. "Got to get back to the store." When he stood up he could see, through the open door, Arlene sitting on the edge of her chair. A pretty kid. Looked enough like Sophie to be her. Grover's memory swooped back, years ago, to the evenings when he and Lew used to stop in at Chili Joe's, and there Sophie Barta would be, switching around with her loaded tray, and Lew watching her ... "Nice little dish, isn't she?" he had said once. It was before Celia ever came to town, yet somehow in Grover's mind that cruelly casual phrase contained the essence of Lew's attitude toward Celia, along with every other woman who caught his eye. He might as well have said it of Celia; it was implicit in the way he had treated her. A nice little dish. He had no inkling at all of what Celia really was, of what her life had been because of him, just as he had no inkling of what selling the store meant to Grover.

There it was again, the inner stirring, like something cold and smooth uncoiling. This time Grover knew what it was; he had not recognized it at first because he had never hated anyone before.

Behind him he heard Lew's voice, brimming with confident good humor (now that his show of anger had done the trick for him, now that—as he thought—he had Grover where he wanted him, in the bag): "Hello there, Arlene. Come on in. See you later, Grover. Don't forget, we're going fishing tomorrow."

"I won't forget," said Grover. He found, to his surprise, that he was smiling. "Sure we're going fishing. I wouldn't miss it for the world."

5

Sophie Barta often said—along about the fourth or fifth drink—that she wouldn't take Turk Ridge as a gift. No sir, not if they tied it up with blue ribbons and laid it out on a silver platter. Anybody that wanted any part of that God-forsaken, one-horse town was welcome to it. As for Sophie—thanks a lot, but she'd take Chicago. Luckiest day of her life, when she shook the hayseed out of her hair and headed for the big town.

Sometimes she got downright belligerent on the subject, as if somebody were arguing with her—which nobody ever was. "I mean it," she would keep on saying to the blurred, blank face of whoever was buying the drinks. "If it wasn't for Arlene, I'd never go near the place. It's the truth, so help me ..."

That was why it didn't make sense, the way she felt every time she reached this particular spot on the road to Turk Ridge, the last curve before the bridge. She never meant to slow down, but she always did, and as she looked out over the river glinting between the high bluffs on either side and the gentle roll of the fields, her heart seemed to lift like a bird taking wing. The same reasonless happiness she used to feel when she was a kid, dawdling along the country road to school, with her tin lunch pail and her books, under the wide, wide sky. She hadn't known any better then; life had been all anticipation, shimmering with mystery and the promise of wonderful, exciting things to come. Poor little wide-eyed fool of a kid. Almost nothing was left of her now; time had changed her, hardened her, faded her. Only this one spark remained undimmed, this secret lifting of her heart that nowadays never came except on the road to Turk Ridge. Of all places.

Sophie fussed with a cigarette, using it as an excuse for having slowed down almost to a crawl. Not that her second-hand coupe ever had broken any speed records. (It was the one thing she had managed to hang on to, when she and Charlie broke up for the first time, five years ago. House, furniture, even her clothes—let him blow it all in on his poker games. She didn't care, as long as she got the car. Got it, and kept it, through all the stormy, short-lived reconciliations with Charlie that had happened since.) Never mind that she couldn't really afford a car. That was what the other girls in the beauty shop kept telling her. It was beyond them, they said. No wonder she never got one cent ahead. But they didn't understand what it meant to her, to be able to drive out to Stan's farm under her own power instead of having to depend on him to meet her at the train. They didn't understand about Arlene, either. Why should they? All they knew was that Sophie claimed she hated the sight of her home town, and yet drove back there at least once a month.

She took a drag of her cigarette and let her eyes rest gratefully on the fields, cross-stitched now with young corn, and on the feathery willows at the river's edge. A meadowlark teetered on a fence post beside her and loosed the notes of his song; they rose and fell like a miniature fountain of pure joy. And the coarse green smell of freshly mowed weeds along the road drifted in through the window.

No, it didn't make sense. But, get right down to it, nothing else made much sense, either. You broke your back all day giving permanents and manicures and bleaches, and at night somebody—Charlie if he was around, some other joe if he wasn't—bought you enough drinks to keep you going, and after that it was just a question of were you going to peel their hands off of you or weren't you, and whether you did or didn't made very little difference, because next day was going to be the same, the mixture as before, anyway ... And that was your life. All of it—except for Arlene and the trips to Turk Ridge.

But how could you tell that to anybody else? How could you explain that you *had* to come back, because if you didn't have something to believe in you'd turn into a tramp?

That was the crazy part of it, thought Sophie. She flipped her cigarette out the window and stepped on the accelerator. As far as Turk Ridge was concerned, she *was* a tramp—because of Arlene. When all the time she herself knew that it was the other way around, Arlene was the only thing that kept her out of the gutter.

Arlene was all hers—her own, to believe in, to love, to possess. It didn't matter that Sophie had had to turn her over to Stan and his wife to raise, or that Arlene called her "Aunt Sophie." They belonged to each other, and they knew it. Why, ever since she was a baby, Arlene had lived for Sophie's visits; the first word she ever said was Sophie's name; the first steps she ever took were for Sophie. In her eyes, Sophie could do no wrong, just as—to Sophie—Arlene was the essence of all that was good and precious in this sorry world. And it would never change; Arlene was never going to get tired of her or fight with her, the way Charlie and the others had, she was never going to see the ugly seams in Sophie's life. Or anywhere else, if Sophie could help it. The wonderful, exciting things she dreamed of—as Sophie had, so long ago—were going to come true, for Arlene.

The difference was—Sophie smiled to herself, ruefully, proudly—that Arlene had brains, and brains had never been Sophie's long suit. Oh, she got by; she had managed to struggle through the eighth-grade exams, and, if Pop had let her, she would probably have gone on to high school. But Arlene won prizes, her report cards were an awesome procession of all A's, with "Excellent" and "Superior" vigorously checked all along the line. From first to last, her teachers had exclaimed over her. Especially this Miss Colby, this one that Arlene talked about so much lately. It was Miss Colby this, Miss Colby that, every other word. Sophie hadn't met her yet, but she was going to, tonight. Ordinarily she couldn't get away Friday night—Saturday was a big day at the beauty shop—but this was an occasion: Arlene was going to sing a solo between the acts of the Senior Class Play. She was only a Junior, but that was how good she was, they had asked her to sing between the acts of the Senior Class Play. Sophie wouldn't have missed it for the world. (But hadn't old Sourpuss at the beauty shop raised hell about her taking part of Friday afternoon and Saturday off! Yelled like a stuck pig.)

And before the play Miss Colby had invited them, Arlene and Sophie, to have tea with her. Get that. Not cocktails. Not afternoon coffee. Tea. Sophie couldn't help it, the thought of Miss Colby's tea party stirred up a whole flock of butterflies in her stomach. Was her new dress really all right? It had seemed stunning when she bought it, a black draped model with sequins—and she had found a little sequin skull cap to go with it—

but now she wasn't so sure. And maybe she had gotten her hair a little too dark this time? She glanced at herself anxiously in the mirror. *How do you do, Miss Colby. Arlene's told me so much about you, I'm very pleased to make your acquaintance.* She must remember not to laugh too loud—that ought to be easy enough, on tea—and she must watch her grammar. That old bugaboo that had haunted her all through school: was it I did or I done? Oh Lord, she couldn't for the life of her remember ...

The only thing she was sure of was that her new girdle was killing her.

Well, and Miss Colby's tea party wasn't all. It was many a long year since Sophie had appeared at a public shindig in Turk Ridge. Usually she stayed pretty close to Stan's farm. Oh, sometimes she and Arlene drove into town Sunday evening to the movies. But there was quite a difference between that and sailing into the school auditorium by herself (Stan and his wife wouldn't give up their Friday night pinochle club, not if Arlene was being elected president of the United States) in full view—not just of the country neighbors who were used to seeing her around, but of the townspeople, the ones that remembered her from Chili Joe's. She knew exactly the sly, speculating look that would come into their eyes, especially the women's, and the way they would buzz to each other, behind their hands.

She could see Turk Ridge now—the stand pipe, the cross on top of the Catholic church, the straggle of buildings, with Lew Morgan's big white house at the very edge. Lew Morgan.

Even now, it happened once in a while: she would be walking along the street in Chicago, when up ahead of her she would see a man with a certain set to his shoulders, a certain swing to his walk, and in spite of all she could do, her feet would hurry, hurry, her heart would set up a thick pounding ... It was never Lew, of course. One chance in a thousand. Even if it were, she wasn't sure she'd have the courage to speak to him. What was there to say? "Hi, Mr. Morgan. Where you been keeping yourself?" That was what she used to say, when he would come into Chili Joe's. The same as she did with all the others. Only not the same. Lew Morgan was the one she had been waiting for, all day long; the sight of him made her knees melt and her hands flutter like flags in a breeze.

The others (she didn't remember all their names anymore; she had been such a crazy kid, out of her head from too-sudden freedom) had been just for fun. She had liked them, every one, had felt a kind of rich tenderness for them. Ah, but Mr. Morgan, Lew...

She knew how it ought to seem to her, now that time had taught her what the score was. A man old enough to be her father, taking advantage of a reckless farm kid and then wriggling out of it cheap, at no more than the price of a beauty course in Chicago.

But it was not so clear-cut as that, either then or now. Because there were the others, and Lew knew it. (Trust Sophie not to play it smart.) And there was no getting around it, she could not feel wronged. She regretted the others, but never Lew, never for a minute, and she would have done it all over again like a shot.

She hoped, as the car bumped across the railroad tracks and headed up Main Street, that Lew Morgan wasn't planning to attend the Senior Class Play tonight. Things were going to be tough enough without that.

It was almost five o'clock when she parked in front of the high school, where Arlene was to meet her as soon as she got through practicing her song, the last rehearsal before tonight. "Trees." That was the name of her solo. Miss Colby was to join them here too, and then they would drive down to the Dew Drop Inn for this famous tea.

Tea. Sophie cast a meditative eye toward her big black handbag, into which she had tucked a good old pint, just in case of emergency. But no, she decided virtuously, it wasn't an emergency yet. No need to borrow trouble. She put in the few minutes' wait redoing her face (maybe her hair was all right, after all) and watching the group of kids who lounged on the front steps of the big square brick building. Now and then a little knot of them would drift off for home, calling back goodbyes and wisecracks to the others. A couple of the boys kept horsing around, trying to shove each other off the steps. Showing off for the benefit of the little blonde with the screechy laugh. The girls were none of them anywhere near as pretty as Arlene, Sophie noted with satisfaction. Though that was a cute skirt the blonde had on, striped, maybe Sophie could find one on that order for Arlene. She had always gotten more kick out of buying clothes for Arlene than for herself; no matter how broke she might be, she had never once turned up without some little present. This time it was a very special present, an ankle bracelet, sterling silver, with Arlene's name and the date engraved on it. Sophie could hardly wait to see her face when she opened it. For a minute, in the glow of anticipated present-giving, she forgot the butterflies in her stomach.

Then she saw them come out of the side door and down the long, curving walk to the car. Arlene and Miss Colby. It must be Miss Colby. A rather short, bareheaded woman in a wrinkled blue linen suit. She had her arm tucked under Arlene's (as if she owned her) and they were both laughing about some joke of their own. Arlene was a little the taller of the two, and there was something about the way she had her head bent toward Miss Colby that gave Sophie the queerest, emptiest feeling. She wished she had taken that drink.

She opened the car door and leaned out. "Hi, Arlene!" she called, and at last Arlene broke away from Miss Colby, ran the rest of the way and flung herself into Sophie's arms.

"Aunt Sophie! Aunt Sophie!" She dug her face into Sophie's shoulder in a fierce, brief caress. Her olive cheeks were flushed with excitement; between her long lashes her eyes sparkled like dew in the grass. Oh, she was the prettiest, freshest, brightest thing! Sophie's voice quavered when she asked, as she always did, "You been a good girl?"

Arlene's pony-tail bobbed up and down in emphatic assurance. The pony-tail had been Sophie's idea, the last time she was here, and it was just right for Arlene's pert, heart-shaped face, her hair had just enough curl for it.

She turned. "Miss Colby—" And Miss Colby stepped forward, smiling, her hand outstretched. "I want you to meet my Aunt Sophie."

Well, Sophie supposed, she was good looking enough, if you cared for the type. From the professional point of view, there was plenty wrong with her. Her hair could certainly stand touching up, and the way she wore it, pulled back and wadded up, didn't do anything in particular for her. Her make-up—assuming she had started out with any—had worn off during the course of the day, though she had apparently slapped on some lipstick not too long ago. And yet, in spite of all that was careless about her, she had the poise of a genuine beauty; the indefinable, luminous quality of glamour hovered over her like a halo. Sophie felt the pull of her personality—for it was more than just a matter of frank gray eyes and radiant smile—as they shook hands, and she knew, again with that queer, empty sensation, that she was no match for Miss Colby and never would be.

Why, the woman made a cup of tea at the Dew Drop Inn seem like an exciting little adventure. "Isn't this fun?" she said, as they settled down in one of the back booths, Sophie and Arlene side by side and Miss Colby across from them. The way she looked around at the streaked walls and the vases of paper flowers, you'd think it was the fanciest place in the world. "I mean, meeting you at last, after all Arlene's told me about you. I don't know if you know it or not, but you're one of Arlene's favorite people, Miss Barta—"

"Mrs. Hoffman," Sophie corrected her. "My husband and me are separated." Now why had she said that? Usually she was just as pleased to keep Charlie out of it. The less said about him the better. But for some reason she had to make it clear to Miss Colby that she was not an old maid, nor even anything so humdrum as a plain married woman, but that figure of sophistication, a divorcée. Or anyway, a near-divorcée.

"I'm sorry. Mrs. Hoffman. You know, it's amazing how much you two look alike. I suppose everybody tells you that, but it really is striking. You could pass for sisters anywhere."

"Mother and daughter, more like it," Sophie was astonished to hear herself saying. (Had Miss Colby heard the gossip? Sophie knew Turk Ridge; like as not the old hens were still clacking, to this very day.)

Whether Miss Colby had heard it or not, she didn't let on. "A mighty young-looking mother, Mrs. Hoffman," she said. "What'll we have? Cinnamon toast? Pecan roll? Apple turnover?"

"Nothing for me, thanks. Just tea," Sophie said with a sigh. Lord, could she use a shot, right about now! A double one.

Miss Colby and Arlene decided on cinnamon toast, and then, with a little jump of excitement, Arlene turned to Sophie. "Guess what, Aunt Sophie! You'll never guess, I've got a job this summer, thirty dollars a week, I'm going to stay in town and—"

"A job, Baby? You've got a job?" repeated Sophie, and out of the past she heard her own eager voice pleading with Pop: *Waiting tables at Chili Joe's, he'll pay fifteen a week and board, I can get a room for five, that's ten a week clear, please Pop, let me ...* He had let her, all right. She needn't have been scared, not with ten dollars a week as bait. And don't worry, he was right there every Saturday night to latch onto it, the mean old bastard, if she hadn't kept her mouth shut about getting a cheaper room she'd never have had a penny for herself.

"At the bank, Aunt Sophie. Mr. Morgan hired me this noon, and if I work out all right maybe they'll keep me on part-time this fall, after school starts. Saturdays off, and I start Monday after next ..."

"Isn't it wonderful?" Miss Colby chimed in. "A real opportunity. And what do you mean, if you work out all right? Of course you're going to work out all right. Why, by the time summer's over they're going to wonder how they ever got along without you."

"Just think, Aunt Sophie! Thirty dollars a week!" Arlene bounced beside her, eyes fastened on hers, waiting for the word from Sophie that would add the final drop to her cup of bliss.

"Why, I don't hardly know what to say," Sophie faltered. "Doesn't seem like you're old enough—what do the folks think?"

"I haven't told them yet." (That was how much times had changed, thought Sophie; she felt older than ever.) "Mr. Morgan was so nice to me, Aunt Sophie, he said he remembered you and asked how you were, and he introduced me to Miss Morgan, she's going to break me in on the job, and when I said did they want to give me a typing test or anything, he said 'What the hell, we'll take your word for it.' Just like that. He's such a wonderful man! Isn't it just too, too—" Words failed her. She stopped for breath.

"Sure it is, honey. It's wonderful. I'm—tickled to death."

"It was all Miss Colby's idea. She's the one that arranged the interview, and if it hadn't been for her I'd never have had the nerve. Oh, Miss Colby, I can't ever thank you enough!"

Miss Colby smiled at her fondly. "Nonsense. Nothing to it. I just happened to hear that Lew—Mr. Morgan—needed some help. That's all I had to do with it. You got the job for yourself."

So he was Lew to Miss Colby, thought Sophie. Very interesting. She knew very little of what went on in Turk Ridge anymore; Stan's wife wasn't the gossiping kind, and anyway, her social life did not often spread beyond her country neighbors to the town itself. But Sophie knew Lew well enough to be able to figure it out. He wasn't the type to let a little thing like a wife—sickly or something, as Sophie recalled it, anyway nobody ever saw her—cramp his style. And for all her ladylike airs, Miss Colby had plenty of the good old basic drawing power. It stuck out all over her.

Miss Colby had, in a word, everything. All that Sophie had ever had, plus all that she would never have. For instance, brains.

"Would you excuse me a minute," said Sophie, and back in the Ladies Room she wasted no time, she took a healthy swig out of the bottle in her purse. Thank God she'd had the foresight. More of a premonition of disaster, really. She wasn't sure, yet, what the disaster was. She just felt it piling up, like storm clouds gathering on the horizon.

And she was surer than ever when she stepped outside the Ladies Room and started back to the booth. Because Lew was standing there, his back to her, his hands planted on the table, bending down to turn on the charm for Miss Colby and Arlene. Sophie paused, fighting a wild impulse to hide somewhere, to run away ... But Arlene had already caught her eye. Not that there was any place to hide or run to, anyway. The whiskey seemed to tighten up inside her like a fist. She walked quickly over to the booth. "Why, hello, Mr. Morgan," she said, and it was just like the old days at Chili Joe's; she almost added "Where you been keeping yourself?" because her knees were melting, her hands fluttering, the same damn thing all over again.

It took him by surprise; for a minute he came very close to looking embarrassed. Then he held out both his hands. "Sophie! Sophie Barta! I'll be damned! Why, it's great to see you again, after all these years, Sophie. Just great. How are you? How's everything in Chicago?"

"Can't complain," said Sophie. She sank down in her place beside Arlene. Maybe she ought to say something else, something easy and casual ... "Everything okay with you? The family and all?"

They all got very solemn and quiet. "I guess you haven't heard about

Olive—Mrs. Morgan? She passed away this week. We buried her yesterday."

"Oh. I didn't know. I— That's too bad. I'm sorry to hear that."

"Yes." His eyes just flicked toward Miss Colby. "Well, it wasn't exactly unexpected, you know. She'd been in poor health for a long, long while. Her heart." With an effort—he made quite a business of the effort—he produced a smile. "Here, Celia, mind if I sit down a minute? Or maybe you don't want me horning in on your tea party—"

Sophie heard herself chirping, right along with the other two. Oh do sit down, Mr. Morgan. Of course you're not horning in, Lew. (Celia. Lew. Cozy as all get out.) We were just talking about you, anyway. Congratulating Arlene on her new job ...

That took care of the next few minutes. A lot of compliments back and forth, with Arlene looking starry-eyed, and Lew and Miss Colby beaming across at her as if they owned her. But she's *mine*, Sophie thought, staring into her teacup, while pride and resentment twisted in her. They're giving her a break and all that, things I couldn't do for her, but they don't need to think—comes to that, why shouldn't he give her a job? Why shouldn't he do a hell of a lot more than that for her? Thirty dollars a week, when by rights he ought to be sending her to some fancy school or college like Miss Colby must have gone to, music lessons, dancing lessons, all the rest of it. A lousy thirty bucks a week, and everybody acts like it was the crown jewels or something, and there he sits as close to his precious Celia as he can get in public, with his wife not even dead a week, bold as brass both of them.

Oh well. Skip it. Only how long was this tea party going to last? Not knowing she could not say, but they didn't need to prolong the festivities on Sophie's account. All she wanted to do was get out of here. Once that was accomplished, it would all get squared away, she'd have Arlene to herself, blow her to dinner at the hotel or wherever she wanted to go, get a grip on herself (maybe just one more small, very small, drink?) so she could do what she had come to Turk Ridge to do. Which was to make like a doting aunt while Arlene sang "Trees" between the acts of the Senior Class Play.

But it just wasn't Sophie's day. The tea party was only the beginning. The next number on the program, it seemed, was a stop at Miss Colby's place, where Arlene was to change from school to dress-up clothes. She had parked her good dress (the yellow eyelet Sophie had gotten her for Easter) at Miss Colby's at noon because the Halls, where she worked for her room and board during the week, were having a houseful of company and needed Arlene's room for the weekend. Arlene explained all this while she and Sophie drove down to Miss Colby's. At least they had these few minutes by themselves; Lew had volunteered to drive Miss Colby home in his car. And he didn't have to twist her arm, either, Sophie noticed.

"Don't you like her, Aunt Sophie?" bubbled Arlene. "Isn't she just super?"

"Very nice," said Sophie. "Seems like she and Mr. Morgan are real good friends."

"Oh yes. Have been for years." Arlene moved a little closer; her voice took on a hushed, impressive note. "Don't tell anybody, but I think they're going to get married, now that Mrs. Morgan's dead. That's what all the kids say. Isn't it romantic? I mean the way they've waited all these years."

Yeah, thought Sophie. I've got a picture of Lew Morgan waiting all these years. I've just got a picture.

"You tired, Aunt Sophie? You haven't been talking very much."

"Haven't had a chance." She forced a facsimile of her hearty laugh. "Not with a chatterbox like you around. Why no, honey, I'm not tired. I feel great. Don't you worry about me. You just keep your mind on that song you're going to sing tonight." She hesitated, halfway tempted to give Arlene her present now. No; better to wait till afterwards, make it sort of a climax. She'd been wanting an ankle bracelet for months. "If you do a good job on it, I might have a little surprise for you."

It was just one of the mistakes she was to make during the course of the evening. Just one of the minor ones. Lew's car was already parked in front of Mrs. Walker's rooming house; he and Miss Colby were waiting on the walk when Sophie pulled up. Smiling, both of them; Miss Colby radiantly, Lew rather uneasily.

"We've just had an idea," Miss Colby's voice had even more of the little uneven hum to it than Sophie had noticed before; it made everything she said seem exciting. "Why don't you two have dinner with Mr. Morgan and me at the hotel? We'll make it a little party. Arlene and I can get all horsed up now, and then we can go right up to the school house after dinner."

"We'd be delighted," said Lew. "Unless you have other plans." It wasn't his idea, that was for sure. Only there wasn't much of any way for him to get out of it.

Sophie let him simmer for a minute before she began, "Thanks a lot, but—" Then her glance fell on Arlene, sitting there with her hands clamped in her lap and her eyes fixed imploringly on Sophie's face. She was dying to go; it was written all over her. Dinner at the hotel with Mr. Morgan and Miss Colby! What possible reason could Sophie give for denying her a treat like that? None. She set her jaw and closed her eyes.

"Why, it's up to Arlene. Whatever she wants. It's her night to howl."

"Oh," breathed Arlene, "I'd love to!"

"Wonderful," said Miss Colby.

"Fine," said Lew. He looked just exactly the way Sophie felt, as if he couldn't make up his mind whether to groan or burst out laughing.

They trooped up the sidewalk together. One big happy family, you might say. Lew waited in Mrs. Walker's parlor, while Miss Colby led Sophie and Arlene upstairs, to her room. It was more living room than bedroom—a cheerful place, stamped with Miss Colby's own slapdash air. There was a studio couch instead of a regular bed, with a lot of bright-colored pillows and a cluttered end table beside it. The desk was cluttered too—magazines, letters, books, a pitcher full of lilacs. And a photograph of Lew, looking very stern and proper. Miss Colby had left her robe, a rose-colored chiffon affair, flung over the back of the easy chair, and a lone feathered mule lay on its side in front of the chest of drawers. The whole room smelled of the fresh, spicy scent she used.

"There we are," she said gaily, opening the closet door and taking out Arlene's dress. "Mmm, isn't it pretty. Your slippers are right here. Bathroom's next door. Go to it. Make yourself beautiful." She kept up a light-hearted line of chatter while Sophie helped Arlene dress, and while she herself skinned out of her blouse and skirt and into a black dress with a square neck. There was nothing wrong with the way Miss Colby was built, and the dress showed it. She pulled the pins out of her long hair, swept a brush through it a few times, and coiled it up again with no more than a glance or two in the mirror. Didn't take much more pains with her lipstick, either. All the same, when she was ready—with a pair of crystal earrings swinging almost to her shoulders as the finishing touch—she looked stunning. The way Sophie had wanted to look. And didn't. She was sure of it now; her dress was too fancy, and new girdle or not, it pulled across the hips.

But Arlene—ah, on that dress she had made no mistake. It was perfect, and when they walked into the parlor, with Arlene in front, and Lew gave an admiring whistle at sight of her, the tears welled up in Sophie's eyes. She had to bend down and pretend to straighten the hem of Arlene's dress in order to hide them.

Trust Lew to pour it on, for all three of them. Mock severity for Arlene: "Miss Barta, I warn you, you are not to wear that dress while performing your duties at the bank. Not under any circumstances. Why, we'd none of us get a lick of work done with anything as pretty as you around!" (Arlene blushed with pleasure.) The old-pals-together routine for Sophie: "How do you do it, Sophie? I vow, you don't look a day older than when you worked at Chili Joe's. The same good-looking kid." (The thing was that he could make you believe it. For all of a minute Sophie forgot her feeling that this whole evening was a perilous road along which she was sentenced to inch her way in a too-fancy, too-tight dress.)

And for Miss Colby he made what was apparently a special, secret joke: "Pardon me, Ma'am, but is this the train to Kalamazoo?" She held out her hand to him, laughing—an impetuous gesture, unguarded as a young girl's. In that instant Miss Colby's heart was in her eyes. Why, she's got it as bad as I ever had, thought Sophie (the melting knees, the fluttering hands), poor woman, poor Miss Colby ...

Then, when they were all set to go out the door, Miss Colby stopped short and started fumbling in her purse. "I was going to wait, but no, I can't wait another minute, Arlene. I'm going to give it to you now."

She was holding out a little white box tied with a bit of perky gilt ribbon. Everybody watched while Arlene opened it; everybody leaned forward to see ...

"Oh, Miss Colby," whispered Arlene. "Oh!"

It was an ankle bracelet, a replica—except that it was gold instead of silver—of the one tucked away in Sophie's bag, waiting for the moment of climax that was never going to come now. The same inscription: Arlene's name and the date. The letters gyrated slowly, gracefully, before Sophie's eyes.

"I had such a time," said Miss Colby, "deciding between the gold and the silver. I wasn't sure which you'd rather—"

"Oh, gold. Absolutely. I'd much rather have gold than silver," said Arlene. "It's exactly what I wanted. Perfect. Oh, Aunt Sophie, isn't it darling?"

"Lovely," said Sophie. Her voice sounded quite natural. She discovered that she was holding one hand behind her, busily balling up one of her gloves. "Oh oh. I seem to be missing a glove. I must have left it upstairs. Excuse me a minute, will you? I'll just run up and get it."

She felt light-headed; the stairs under her feet seemed extraordinarily far apart. But a little drink would fix that. Wouldn't it? Well, then, a not-so-little drink ...

She stood in the middle of Miss Colby's spicy-smelling room, with the good old bottle from her purse tilted up, pouring its raw, dangerous comfort into the emptiness inside her. Her eye fell on the photograph of Lew on the desk, and she felt her mouth curling up bitterly. "Getting pretty goddam respectable, aren't we?" she whispered to the picture of Lew. "With our wonderful Miss Colby that we're going to marry, and our jobs for Arlene, and our dinner at the hotel. Oh my yes, we're quite the solid citizen."

She gave a sudden sob. She could hear them talking and laughing downstairs, and Miss Colby called up had she found her glove, and she called back here it was, she'd be right down, and all the time disaster piling up, disaster pressing in on her.

Mustn't blow my top, she cautioned herself as she went down the stairs. (There had been some kind of a switcheroo while her back was turned; this time the stairs seemed extraordinarily close together.) Remember. Mustn't blow my top.

6

"So what goes?" asked Johnny, the minute she sat down beside him at the table in the hotel dining room. It was more diplomatic, they had decided, for him to be out of the way when Whitt came home from work. So the three of them had arranged to meet here for dinner, and Johnny must have known as soon as she showed up without Whitt. But he asked, anyway.

"So what do you think goes?" Dort slammed her bag down on the table and yanked off her gloves. "I knew it wouldn't work. I told you so from the beginning. Whitt's never stood up to his father in his life, and he never will."

"Still, it was worth trying," said Johnny mildly. "This way they've had their chance, both of them. I like to keep things on a sporting level, don't you know."

"But Johnny—" She stopped, but both of them knew what she had been about to say. That all they had accomplished by giving Whitt his chance was to point up how much he wanted his share of the money. It swung between them, a heavy pendulum of an idea that must not be put into words. Not yet. They had a good many moments like this nowadays, when Dort felt the presence of something perilous and silent as a tiger drawing close to them, closer. Did Johnny feel it too? It didn't show in his face. But then so few of the things he was really feeling showed in that dark, narrow face of Johnny's. Not that he was a deadpan. Not at all. His smile was easy and lively; most people never bothered to notice that it seldom went any further than his mouth, or that the glint in his eyes was of something far more subtle than laughter.

And this, of course, was fortunate for everybody concerned.

"Relax, sweetie." He flicked his lighter for her cigarette, and added casually, "They didn't quarrel, did they?"

"Of course they didn't quarrel. Whitt hasn't got the gimp to quarrel with anybody. Oh, I can hear him. 'Please, Papa, can't I have my pretty money?' And Papa gives him a pat on the head and says, 'Now, now, wait till you're older. Run along and play.' So Whitt runs along, like the good boy he is, straight home to cry on my shoulder, and I'm supposed to tell him it's not his fault, it's all that mean old Papa of his—"

Johnny laughed out loud. "Sure. I know. Now tell me what really happened. Where is he?"

"Home. Licking his wounds. Brooding over his traumatic experiences. Too upset to eat." She had gone through the motions of urging Whitt to come with her, but in a manner—she was expert at such things—that was guaranteed to keep him at home. This was an evening when she didn't trust herself with anybody but Johnny. Under the tablecloth she let her knee press briefly against his, an almost imperceptible token of all that was secret between them. She watched for the flicker in his eyes; permitted herself a small, triumphant smile when it came.

Then she went on briskly: "What really happened was that Lew turned him down. Flat. Just plain no soap. When Whitt gave him the song and dance about the restaurant Lew told him straight out that we're playing him for a sucker. We. Get that. Not just you. And if Whitt hasn't got sense enough to see it, then according to Lew it's time somebody told him. You're a rat, and I'm a tramp, and as long as Lew has anything to say about it we're never going to get our hands on one penny of Whitt's money, not one penny. Period."

"And what did Whitt make of all this?"

"Who knows? I had to pry the details out of him, if that means anything. You know how he clams up sometimes. He wasn't going to tell me anything except that Lew had said no. So maybe he halfway believed the business about you and me. He doesn't now, though." Again she permitted herself the small, triumphant smile. "Not after I went to work on him."

"Someday," said Johnny pleasantly, "I'm going to knock your pretty little teeth in for you."

"Well, what was I supposed to do? Let him go on believing we're making a fool of him? I don't like it any more than you do. But somebody's got to keep him happy—"

"Okay, okay. Keep him happy. Only just don't tell me how you do it."

"Whatever you say, sir." Her hands were trembling with elation. "As I was saying, I—persuaded him that what Lew said was all a pack of lies and that he ought to be ashamed of himself for even listening to it. So then he persuaded me to forgive him, and now all he has to do is forgive himself and we'll be right back where we started. Goody, goody."

The waitress, the heavy, conscientious one with the spaniel eyes, came up then, and they smiled gaily for her benefit. The smart young set dining out. If you weren't gay she worried, and when she worried she was inclined to hover. Johnny ordered drinks, and she plodded off contentedly. This was as it should be, the smart young set ordering drinks. All was right with her world.

"One other thing," said Dort. "Lew's going to marry Celia Colby. He told Whitt so. I just thought I'd mention it in passing."

There was a short silence, before Johnny asked what she had known he would. "How soon?"

"End of the summer. Another trauma for Whitt. They might at least wait a decent interval, he says. It hasn't even dawned on the poor dope that this is going to cut him out of a good chunk of what's rightfully his. He's fantastic, Johnny. Sometimes I wonder if he's all *there*."

"You didn't—"

"No, I didn't point it out to him," said Dort wearily. "But if we wait for him to figure it out it's going to be too late. Celia's going to be in solid. I wouldn't put it past Lew to palm off one of the farms on Whitt and split the rest of it between Celia and Victoria. I wouldn't put anything past him."

Here was the waitress with their drinks. Time for another round of gay smiles.

"End of the summer," Johnny said thoughtfully when she had left them to themselves. That gave them roughly three months. Again the pendulum swung between them, again Dort felt the tiger-presence edging a step closer.

"We can't even count on that," she said, very low. "They're just as apt to change their minds about waiting and dash off any day, any minute …"

As if on cue, the street door opened, and in they came. A regular little procession that—even at this distance, the length of the dining room— gave a curious impression of tension. Lew and Celia, smiling resolutely, with the kid between them. A good-looking kid; Dort remembered having seen her around town, but it took her a minute to come up with her name. Arlene Barta, that was it. Arlene Barta. And a couple of steps behind them a woman in a dress with a lot of sequins, a woman who moved with an air at once stately and cautious, as if she were carrying the Encyclopedia Britannica on her head.

"Who's the lady drunk?" asked Johnny.

"You've got me. Some relative of the kid's, I guess. Anyway, they look alike." So much alike, in fact, that it gave Dort a queer pang to see them. They were like the Before and After pictures in a macabre advertisement: See What Life Did To Me. You Too Can … Dort shivered slightly, and stole a glance at her own reflection in the mirror across the room. The pale gleam of her hair reassured her, and the provocative demureness of her dress with its full skirt and handspan waist. She remembered Whitt, so abjectly afraid of losing her, and here beside her was Johnny, unable, for all his suavity, to hide the fact that he was jealous ... No, she didn't have to worry. Yet.

Lew lifted a hand in greeting while the waitress was settling him and his little flock a couple of tables away. And Celia nodded politely. Not exactly unbridled enthusiasm. Well, Dort was used to it, or ought to be. But she had never forgiven Lew for— All right, she might as well face it, for not being the easy mark she had so confidently expected him to be. A woeful bit of misjudging on her part. But a perfectly natural one: Who would suspect Whitt of having a father like Lew? She had pictured another Whitt, only older and therefore even more malleable. Putty in the hands of his charming young daughter-in-law. Ha! It wasn't that Lew was blind to her charms. Not by a long shot. He observed them with considerable interest and admiration. And with complete detachment. She had not succeeded in denting that detachment, not once during the two years she had served time in Turk Ridge. Two years! She and Johnny had figured on five months at the most, before she would be back in Chicago—either with Whitt or without him, it didn't make a lot of difference—but with a nice fat bank account and plenty more where that came from.

Oh, it made her wild just to think of it. She couldn't afford to pull out now, after investing all this time, the most precious years of her life. The time to quit, if she was ever going to, was long past, way back when Whitt had brought her here as a bride. She might have, too, except for Johnny, with his take it easy, just be patient—simple enough for him, *he* wasn't stuck in this God-forsaken hole—and then she had assumed that it was only a question of waiting for Whitt's mother to die. Blame it on wishful thinking, on Whitt himself ... She would not waste her fury on Whitt. She knew who her enemy was, she knew who was responsible for her defeat. The way he looked at her sometimes, with those faded blue eyes of his—the fierce, knowing, ruthless eyes of a born adventurer. They made her feel transparent as a pane of window glass. Of course Lew saw through her. Why not, when he had been playing the same waiting game as she, for many a dusty year longer? They were birds of the same feather.

"Watch it, darling," Johnny murmured beside her, "your feelings are showing. You could be arrested for the look in your eye. Assault and battery."

"You think of everything, don't you? 'Watch it. Take it easy. Just be patient.' Everything except a way out of this mess. I'm fed up to here with waiting, waiting, waiting. I can molder here in Turk Ridge the rest of my life, and have nothing to show for it but a warped personality. Look at him. He's going to live forever."

"I wouldn't say that," said Johnny. "Not many people do." It seemed to Dort that there was something tentative in his tone, as if he were sounding her out, or giving her an opening ... Was it time, yet, to put it in words? They eyed each other warily, each waiting, perhaps hoping, for the other to take that enormous step between thinking and saying. Dort's tongue felt large and unwieldy in her mouth; she could not make it work. Another moment, and Johnny was going on smoothly, "Sure I think of everything. There's always another angle, that's my motto. And there is, you know. An angle that we've never so much as touched."

"All right, Mr. Bones. What angle you got reference to?"

"Victoria." He looked her straight in the eye. "Papa's pride and joy. He's never denied her anything she asked for. Why shouldn't she ask for the same thing Whitt did? She won't get the same answer he did, you can depend on that. And she knows as much about—well, shall we say life?—as Little Red Riding Hood. Any male over the age of fifteen who cared to take the trouble could have her eating out of his hand in no time—"

"Wait a minute," said Dort. Her voice was thin with rage, but at sight of the waitress pounding toward them on her conscientious rounds she produced a dazzling smile and lifted her glass to show that she didn't need a refill and that she was happy, happy, happy. The waitress changed her course. It was safe to go on. "Are you suggesting that you get cozy with Victoria? With me in a ringside seat? I'm a little slow about these things. I want to get it straight."

"Why not? It's an angle." He was watching her avidly, with the mean glint in his eye that meant he was getting even with her. Of course. For the business about keeping Whitt happy. She had forgotten that Johnny always paid you back. "It would take a little doing, to make sure Lew didn't catch on till it was too late. But not too much doing. A secret. A terribly romantic secret."

"You mean you would marry her?" asked Dort. "You would marry Victoria?" She knew she was playing right into his hands; there he sat, gloating, savoring every minute of it. Revenge, yes. But he would do it. Oh, never think he wouldn't. And the thought of it turned her inside out, like a wave of savage, physical pain—Johnny and Victoria, that well-groomed, frozen turnip; that miserable excuse for a woman who wouldn't know what to do with it if she had it ...

"If necessary," said Johnny coolly. "I think it's kind of a cute idea. You and Whitt, me and Victoria. We could have such nice family get-togethers."

"I won't have it," said Dort. Her voice seemed to be a long way off from her, a remote, mechanical click of a voice. "I will not have it. I mean it, Johnny. There's a limit to how much I can take—"

"You think there isn't a limit to how much I can take?"

No more caginess or gloating or cold-blooded baiting. He let the mask slip, he abandoned all pretense and showed her the honest desperation of his feeling for her. "Ah, Johnny," she whispered, as she always did. For it had happened before; not often, but often enough so that she ought to be prepared—the shortened tempers, the flare-up, and then, like a collision, as if there were a cord between them that would stretch just so far before it flung them back against each other, this instant of violent truth. And she never was prepared; it always hit her with the same brand-new impact. "Ah, Johnny, what are we going to do?"

It was going to be said now, and she felt a cowardly little wave of relief because Johnny, not she, was going to say it. His face had closed up again, but his hand resting on the table between them, made a nervous, clutching gesture. "There's only one thing left—"

Dort's glass, which she was in the act of lifting—her own version of the nervous clutch—was suddenly jogged nearly out of her hand; most of her rum and coke landed in her lap. She looked up to see the lady drunk of Lew's party swaying beside her, her eyes large with consternation.

"I *beg* your pardon! Oh, Miss, I'm terribly sorry. Barging into you like that! I don't see how I could have been so—"

Dort could have told her, but she didn't bother. "Never mind," she said shortly. She stood up and inspected the stain on her full, pale blue skirt. It was oddly shaped, rather like a heart. Or no, like a skull. A death's head. "I'll go in the ladies room and sponge it out," she said. "Before it has a chance to set. Back in a minute."

The lady drunk, still brimming with apologies, trailed along behind her, and once the door (coyly labelled "She") had closed behind them, she kept making fumbling efforts to help sponge. "Never mind," Dort said again. "It's cotton, it washes. No damage done." True enough—in more ways than one, maybe. It might even be that she and Johnny owed this poor fuddled creature a vote of thanks. What would they be saying, by now, if she hadn't jogged Dort's elbow just when she did? No damage done. Not yet. But sooner or later one of them must finish what Johnny had started to say. "There's only one thing left—"

"I guess we might as well introduce ourselves," the woman was saying, with that compulsive coziness that often prevails in ladies' rooms and beauty shops. "I'm Sophie Barta. Well, I'm Mrs. Hoffman, if you want to get technical, only Charlie and me aren't working at it right now. My home's in Chicago—" she paused briefly, impressively— "but I was raised right here on a farm outside of Turk Ridge. What a dump. Only reason I come back is Arlene. She's singing a solo tonight, at the Senior Class Play. She's only a Junior, but they got her to sing anyway. 'Trees.'"

"Oh, then you must be Arlene's aunt," said Dort, because some comment seemed to be expected.

Sophie Barta didn't answer for a minute. Her mouth trembled slightly, as if something hurt her. "Yeah. I must be Arlene's aunt." She had propped her bag, which was about the size of an ice bucket, up on the shelf below the mirror; now, after a moment's groping, she drew from it a pint bottle. It was a little more than half full. You could say the same for Sophie. "Join me in a little drink? Make up for the one I spilled. The thing is, it don't look right for me to have one outside. On account of Arlene. I have to set her a good example. Can't have her turning out like me." She unscrewed the top, and the raw whiskey smell rushed out to do battle with the other smells—disinfectant, liquid soap, stale powder. She waved the bottle hospitably toward Dort, who declined, with many thanks.

"No? Well, then. Cheers." The bottle tilted, gurgled, and the sequins on Sophie's bosom heaved in satisfaction. "I musn't blow my top," she explained solemnly to Dort. "That's what I got to remember, Miss— I didn't quite catch the name?"

"Dort Morgan," said Dort. "Mrs. Whitt Morgan."

Sophie stared at her. Then she gave an abrupt laugh, rather like a cough. "The hell you say. Small world, isn't it? I mean, us running into each other like this, and you turning out to be Lew's daughter-in-law ..."

The phrase caught Dort's attention. Lew's daughter-in-law. Not Mr. Morgan's daughter-in-law, the way you would expect. She felt a stir of curiosity, or perhaps it was more of a dim memory, some bit of gossip heard and half-forgotten. Sophie Barta, she thought. The name was certainly one she had heard before. It might be interesting to find out where.

She had been edging unobtrusively toward the door, but now she turned back to the mirror and took out her compact. "I think I've heard Lew mention you," she offered, patting powder on her nose.

"I doubt it," said Sophie, and again she gave the abrupt, disconcerting laugh. "But who knows? Maybe you have, at that. That's not Whitt out there at the table with you, is it?"

This wasn't according to the rules: Dort was supposed to ask the questions, not answer them. But she hung on to her smile. "Oh no. That's a friend of ours from Chicago. I'm from Chicago myself. And I'm like you, if I had my way we'd go back there tomorrow. Turk Ridge is pretty dead, if you've ever lived anywhere else."

"You can say that again," said Sophie with feeling.

"Here, honey, let me get my stuff out of the way, so you can see what you're doing." She made an unsteady move toward the ice bucket bag and her gloves.

"That's all right. There's plenty of room, if you want to do your face too—"

"Ah, what's the use?" Sophie made a face at herself in the mirror. "An old bag like me. Waste of time."

"Don't be silly," said Dort. "You're a very smart-looking woman. I noticed your dress when you came in. So smart. So—well, citified-looking."

"Yeah?" said Sophie hungrily. She smoothed her dress down over her hips, momentarily cheered. But then she sighed and slumped against the door jamb again. "I used to look a lot like Arlene, when I was a kid. Just as slim. Lord, this girdle is killing me."

"You still look like her. I knew right away you must be related." That at least was no lie. And oddly enough, Sophie looked better up close than at a distance, when all you got was the general effect of flashy clothes and blowsiness. Her skin was still clear, olive as a gipsy's, and not even cheap whiskey and too many men (somehow you knew at a glance that Sophie had been mixed up with too many men, all of them mistakes) could entirely spoil her great, sad eyes. Her hair was terrible; she ought to go on a diet; the mascara and lipstick had been laid on with a heavy hand; but there were still those eyes, and the sweet, vulnerable curve of her mouth. She must have been a wow when she was a kid, thought Dort. Again she felt the stir of curiosity. How did somebody like Sophie, who had left Turk Ridge years ago, happen to be on a first-name basis with Lew?

"You know something?" Sophie fixed her wavering gaze on Dort's face in the mirror; she leaned forward, like an orator about to press home some significant point. "I shoon't have come. No sir. Shoon't ever have come. All a mistake. You know how sometimes no matter what you do it gets all screwed up? You can't win, some days. That's me. And that's today. It's all screwed up, and all I hope is I don't blow my top ..."

"You can blow your top to me. That is, if you want to." In the mirror Dort watched her own face take on exactly the right expression—sympathetic but not too inquisitive, the understanding heart offered with no strings attached. "Look. I don't know you, and you don't know me, but sometimes that's the best way, to unload to somebody you're probably never going to see again." She turned and stretched out her hands in an impulsive, winning gesture. "It beats blowing your top out there, doesn't it?"

She had perhaps overdone it; Sophie's eyes filled with tears of maudlin gratitude, and her hands gripped Dort's convulsively, as if she were being rescued from drowning. "You know him. You're his daughter-in-law, for God's sake. You know how he is. Thirty dollars a week, and the poor kid thinks he's doing her a favor, she's walking on air, you'd think he'd handed her the crown jewels—" The dam had broken, all right, thought Dort. Flotsam and jetsam all over the place, and her only problem was going to be sorting out what was worth anything. The flood of broken, stormy words rushed on: "Gold. She wanted gold all the time, and I didn't know it, I've got it right there in my purse, all done up pretty, only it's silver, and *she* had to go and give hers first ... Poor woman, she's got it as bad as I ever had, and he's going to marry her. I feel sorry for her, I feel sorry for anybody that gets mixed up with him ... Thirty bucks a week. What the hell's so wonderful about that? He owes it to her, he owes her plenty more than that, if I'd only had the brains to play it smart ..." Sophie paused for a gulp of air. She ran the back of one hand across her eyes, smearing what was left of her mascara across her temple. But the next minute her fingers clamped tighter than ever around Dort's; she gave a terror-stricken sob. "You know what they want, don't you? They want to take her away from me. Oh, I can see it, they're not fooling me any."

"Now, Sophie, I don't really think—" began Dort. No doubt about it, it was going to take time to sort all this out. But just as certainly it was going to be worth it. Sophie might be on a first-name basis with Lew, but it wasn't out of any ordinary kind of friendship. There was a buried treasure of bitterness not too far beneath the surface. Dort probed cautiously. "You mean they want to take Arlene away from you? I can't believe—"

"Oh yes, they do." Sophie spoke quite calmly now. Her eyes stared past Dort, full of bleak knowledge. "And they can do it, too. Why not? They've got everything. Me, I'm just a slob. She don't know it yet, but some day she's going to be ashamed of me. Someday ... I can never remember whether it's 'I did' or 'I done.' Things like that." Sophie's grip slackened hopelessly. "Ah, what's the use? He'll get that, too, if he wants it. Haven't you ever noticed? He always gets what he wants, one way or another."

"I wouldn't be too sure about that," said Dort, and then (because you never knew, you couldn't be too careful) she added, "I mean, I'm not convinced they want to take Arlene away from you, as you put it. I think you're worked up and you're probably just imagining it." It was a little surprising, how relieved she felt when she could be honest with Sophie. There was something appealing about her. Not, of course, anything so appealing that Dort wouldn't be able to resist it, if the necessity arose. She had a hunch that the necessity was going to arise.

"Yeah?" Sophie was saying wistfully. She seemed to have reached one of those mysterious plateaus of sobriety. "Jeez, look at me. I'm a mess. Well, thanks anyway, honey. I guess I sure unloaded, didn't I? Think nothing of it, I do it all the time." She tried for an airy smile, and didn't quite make it.

"Don't worry," said Dort. "It's going to be all right. Everybody gets in a mood once in a while."

"Yeah. Well, thanks a million. Good luck." She ripped off a paper towel and bent over the sink, methodically setting about the repair job on her face. All that mascara, thought Dort, all that lipstick. No doubt there was room for everything, in the ice bucket bag. There it sat on the shelf, with Sophie's gloves wadded up beside it. They had their share of sequins, too.

"Goodbye," said Dort softly. "Good luck to you, too." She gathered up her own things from the shelf, and with them—so casually, almost as if by chance—one of the sequined gloves. Sophie was still bent over the sink when she slipped out the door and pulled it shut behind her.

"What happened to your lady friend?" asked Johnny, as she slid into her place beside him. "Her dinner companions are getting a little restive, I notice."

Dort glanced toward Lew's table, where the tension seemed to be mounting nicely. She couldn't quite suppress a smile. "I could be wrong, but I expect she's having a lady-like drink all by herself, while she replaces her face. We had the most interesting little chat."

"You're looking awfully damn pleased with yourself," said Johnny.

"Am I? Listen, Johnny—" She took a sip of the drink that was waiting for her and leaned a little closer to him. "I mean it was really an interesting chat. The lady's name is Sophie Barta ..."

As she said the name her memory clicked and came up with the bit of gossip that had eluded her before. Actually it amounted to no more than the standard small-town story of a "wild girl" (Sophie had apparently been pretty spectacular, in her way) who had got herself in a fix and left town. All very boring, when you didn't know the people. Dort had listened only because there was nothing else to do in Turk Ridge.

But now it was different. Now she knew the people. For several minutes she talked and Johnny listened. And it wasn't much of a problem, after all, to sort out Sophie's unburdenings. They weren't nearly as incoherent as they had sounded back there behind the door marked "She."

Sophie herself provided the only interruption to Dort's report. She emerged with regal step, face renovated, ice bucket bag hung over her arm, the imaginary Encyclopedia Britannica once more balanced precariously on her head. It was clear enough that she had killed the bottle. She paused, with a gracious smile, beside Dort's chair.

"Everything under control?" asked Dort.

"But definitely. Such a pleasure meeting you, dear. Maybe we can get together again some time."

"Yes, let's. You're here for the weekend?"

"That's right. See you around. Goodbye for now." She waggled her fingers, very genteel, and swept on to her own table, where an uneasy welcome awaited her.

Johnny's face, as he watched her progress, was thoughtful. And Dort could tell from his eyes that he was excited. They were like opals turned to the light.

He began to talk, casually, almost dreamily. "Did I ever tell you, Sweetie, the sad story of my cousin Albert? No. I don't think I ever did. Poor Albert. What happened to him shouldn't happen to a dog. He wasn't any mental giant, but then who is? Once in a while he drank too much, the way lots of people do. Sophie, for instance. That's what reminded me of Cousin Albert. Sophie. But aside from that there wasn't anything wrong with Albert. Except that he hated his boss's guts. The trouble was that so did a couple of other guys. One of life's little coincidences. They were brighter than Albert, these other guys, and it was the damnedest thing, the way they framed him."

"Yes?" said Dort. She felt her knees trembling slightly against each other. "Framed him—for what?"

"Why, for shooting the boss. What else? Incidentally, he was a real pill, this boss. He had it coming to him. And he got it, all right. It was a beautiful set-up. All the bright guys had to do was pick the right time and place. It wasn't hard to get Cousin Albert on the spot. A message that the boss wanted to see him took care of that. As I recall it, they used the boss's own gun. I'm a little foggy about the details. It—uh—it happened quite a while ago. Anyway, when the cops showed up, there was the boss laid out and poor Cousin Albert, with his mouth hanging open and a solid gold frame around him guaranteed to—"

"Drop dead! Why don't you drop dead!" The shout—a thick, choked sound that was like an explosion in the quiet of the half-empty dining room—came from Lew's table, and Dort knew that here it was, Sophie Barta was blowing her top again. She had surged up out of her chair, which clattered backward to the floor, and was leaning across the table, her hand waving in Lew's general direction, her eyes blazing. "There you sit, with Arlene between you and her, and you think you can take her away from me ... Don't you? Don't you? Well, you can't. She's mine, she's all I've ever had, and you nor nobody else ... Oh, we're so respectable nowadays, aren't we? So goddam respectable it hurts. Thirty lousy bucks a week. What's so wonderful about that, I'd like to know, when by rights you ought to—"

Lew stood up. "Now, Sophie," he kept saying, and for once in his life—Dort was happy to note—he looked completely at a loss. Not even angry; just nonplussed. There were perhaps a dozen other people in the dining room, every last one of them shamelessly gaping. The waitress came pounding over at an anxious gallop, but once on the scene she couldn't think of anything to do, either. Celia Colby sat with her face tilted upward, blank, frozen in a defenseless, listening attitude.

She had plenty to listen to, all right. Sophie plunged on, spilling out abuse, defiance, her own misery, in an incoherent flood. It seemed to go on and on; probably, though, only a couple of minutes passed before the kid stopped her.

All she said was, "Aunt Sophie. Please." In a low, trembling voice that made Dort remember Sophie's bleak prophecy in the ladies' room: "She don't know it yet, but some day she's going to be ashamed of me."

"Aunt Sophie. Please." She got out of her chair between Lew and Celia and went around the table and stood beside Sophie. She still had her napkin in her hand. She stood there with her head bent, and a slow, dark, painful flush spread up her neck, all the way to the roots of her hair.

Sophie stopped in the middle of a word. Her face took on a ludicrously startled expression, as if she had forgotten Arlene's presence. Then it simply crumpled up, and she broke into desolate sobs. "Damn you," she blurted at Lew. "Oh, damn you." She turned clumsily and, pitching like a ship in a heavy sea, floundered past the tables and out the door.

For a moment Arlene hesitated. Celia put out a hand, and Arlene half-turned toward her, longingly, pleadingly. Then she flung down her napkin, pulled her head up high, and walked quickly away and out the door to Sophie.

Lew took a step as if to follow her, and Celia jumped up. "No. You mustn't, you'll only make it worse. I'll go."

So that left Lew standing there alone. He rubbed his hand along his jaw and looked around the room, as if just now aware of all the avid eyes and all the straining ears. And suddenly he grinned. (You had to hand it to him, thought Dort; nothing could get him down for very long.) "All right, folks, the show's over," he said. "You can finish your dinners now."

There was a general exchange of sheepish glances, a clink of china and silver. But the glance Dort and Johnny exchanged, after they had watched Lew pay the check and leave, was far from sheepish.

"Let me see, where was I? Oh yes. Poor Cousin Albert," said Johnny in the same soft, casual voice. "I forgot to mention, I guess, that he'd had a fight with his boss a day or so before the shooting. A public fight. In a restaurant, if memory serves. Of course that didn't help him any. He swore up and down he wasn't guilty, he screamed he'd been framed, but he couldn't prove a thing. Not one damn thing. So who was going to believe him? Nobody." He smiled. "Nobody but me, that is."

"And me," whispered Dort. They leaned toward each other. But here came the waitress, conscientiously prompt with their coffee.

"Let's have a brandy," said Johnny. "I feel festive tonight." They turned on their gay, smart-young-set smiles. The waitress beamed at them. Under the table Dort felt the secret, exultant pressure of Johnny's knee against her own, and oh, she felt festive too, they were going to be happy, happy.

7

It was barely dawn when Grover heard Lew's car whirring up Main Street, and then the ritual beep-beep of his horn as he pulled up in front of the store. Two brief, muted beeps that never failed to send a tingle of excitement down Grover's backbone. Here we go, he thought, and a whole swarm of pleasant sensations crowded through his mind, released by that familiar signal—wood smoke, and the river smell, and the nip of frost in the air at pheasant-hunting time, the insect hum of deep summer and the lazy, easy dip of the john boat in the current. They had had their share of good times, he and Lew. Nothing could change that. But the good times were set apart now, preserved in the amber of a bygone age. Yesterday had sealed off forever one part of Grover's life. He smiled faintly. One part of Lew's life too, when it came to that.

His gear was already assembled and waiting beside the door—his rod and minnow net, the sack of provisions from the store, his blanket roll. He put on the battered duck hat dedicated through long custom to fishing trips, picked up his load, and let himself out the door.

The air still held the chill of night; Main Street looked ghostly in the pure, pearly light. But a delicate flush was spreading along the eastern rim of the world, and somewhere on the other side of town a rooster crowed with forlorn bravado. It looked like another fine day.

Lew opened the car door and leaned out as Grover made his way cautiously down the stairway. His eyes were still puffy from sleep, but bright and eager. "All set? Need any help?"

"Nope. Got everything," Grover answered in the same hushed voice. He swung the blanket roll off his shoulder and stowed it and his other stuff in the back seat, which was already cluttered with Lew's paraphernalia, crammed in every which way. "You are the messiest bastard," he muttered affably, while he rearranged and tidied. He always said this, just as Lew always complained about the length of time it took Grover to get started.

"Come on, come on," he said now, racing the motor. "We got something better to do than sit here all day while you rearrange the stock. Al claims the catfish are getting fatter and sassier by the minute. I called him yesterday and told him to get the boat ready for us. He said he'd leave it down below the bluff, where he always does."

Grover gave a little nod of satisfaction. That was what he had figured on. The boat below the bluff. They would stop at the shack first, leave the car there because that was as far as you could get with a car, and go the rest of the way on foot. There was a rough sort of trail, half-choked with underbrush, along the edge of the steep bluff, that would bring them eventually down to the river, to the place where Al always left the boat. In the secret watches of the night Grover had figured it out; he knew the right spot on that trail which he and Lew had taken so many times. He was counting on it—though of course, if for some reason Lew and Al had made a different arrangement, Grover too would have thought of another way. For his mind was made up. Nothing was going to stop him.

He felt a tranquil sort of gaiety as he got into the front seat beside Lew. It was queer, the way all the bitterness and turmoil of yesterday afternoon had boiled away during the night, crystallizing into this clear, pure resolution. The idea was no longer appalling to him. It was hardly even personal; he was finding it quite possible to enjoy the companionship of this trip with Lew just as if it were not the final one. Habit, perhaps. Or maybe the relief of knowing that at last, after a whole lifetime, everything was to be settled between them.

"I hope I brought enough beer," Lew said. "Nothing beats beer, when you're fishing. It's in the trunk, packed in ice. The way we did it last time. One thing we don't have to worry about is sandwiches. Victoria made us enough sandwiches to last all summer. And a dozen hard-boiled eggs—"

"Hell, Lew, I boiled up a dozen too."

They laughed comfortably. "Be so busy eating we won't have time to fish."

They were rattling over the bridge now; the river below them was dark and swirling. Along its bank the willows swayed in the early morning breeze, trailing their feathery fingers in the water. Girlish kind of trees, willows. Girlish time of morning too, all fresh, pale color that would flower, later, into the depth and shimmer of an early summer day.

"Nice day," said Lew. He glanced sideways at Grover. "You look tired, boy. What did you do, forget to go to bed last night?"

"No. I turned in earlier than usual. Too early, maybe. I couldn't seem to get to sleep." He had shuttled between his bed and the fat old leather rocker, staring into the darkness while his brain churned—aimlessly at first, producing only a welter of past, present, and future without meaning or pattern. But in the end, when the seething subsided, he had been left exhausted, purified, and most of all resolved, with his plan suddenly clear and hard as crystal. And the only traces of this memorable night were that he looked tired and that his hands shook, slightly but constantly. Astonishing.

"I had a rough night myself," Lew was saying. "Lord, the trouble women can kick up when they take a notion to!"

"Women?" Grover turned toward him sharply. "You don't mean Celia—"

"Of course not. Celia's a lady. She doesn't make scenes. Sophie Barta, that's who I mean. She got looped and created something fierce—as Aunt Chat would say—in the hotel dining room. A regular floor show. You should have been there." He laughed shortly and then went on to describe, not without a certain relish, last night's dinner party.

It shocked Grover. Not so much what Sophie had said; that was not exactly news to Grover, knowing Lew as he did ("Nice little dish, isn't she?"). But her violent, public way of saying it ... Violence always did shock him; he liked things to be smooth and mannerly. And yet here he was, with his plan ... A sense of unreality engulfed him. He looked down incredulously at his own neat, plumpish hands. Yes, they were really trembling slightly. Yes, they were really going to do what must be done.

Lew had paused, while he negotiated the turn on to the narrow, bumpy river road. Or he might be expecting some comment, or an answer to a question that Grover had missed. He could have missed quite a lot.

With an effort he collected his wits. "What did Celia make of all this?" he asked.

"I don't know for sure," said Lew. "But trust her to rise to the occasion. She got Sophie calmed down, don't ask me how, and she got Arlene up to the high school and on to the stage for her number— I'll say this for the kid, she rose to the occasion too. Celia was out in the car, holding

Sophie's hand, so they didn't hear her, but I did. A real little trooper. You know, Celia's right about her. A kid like that deserves a chance. I'm glad I decided to take her on at the bank. Damned if I don't think it might be a good idea to—well, to sort of adopt her. How does it sound to you?"

"I'm not sure. Sophie'd put up a howl, I suppose. Isn't that partly what was eating on her last night?"

"Partly. Mostly it was whiskey. She wouldn't stand in Arlene's way. She'd come round."

Grover hesitated, not quite daring to mention what bothered him most about the proposal. Victoria, he thought; that odd, frost-bitten girl who had never had a chance to be anything but Lew's daughter. Was that the kind of a chance Arlene deserved? And was Victoria expected to clap hands at the prospect of a younger, prettier adopted sister? With a queer pang he remembered what Victoria had been like as a little girl—shy, but lively and loving. But then she had changed, so gradually that he had hardly noticed. Now, when it was too late, he saw how great the change had been, and how sad.

"What's your idea? To stake Arlene to a college education?" he asked cautiously.

"College? Why yes, I guess so, if she wanted to go. Victoria didn't want to, you know. All she wanted was to stay home and work with me at the bank."

Grover's heart sank. The old, possessive pattern all over again. There was Celia, of course, who might see it too and save Arlene from turning into another Victoria. Not necessarily, though; there were a good many things about Lew that Celia didn't see.

And then Grover smiled to himself. What was he worrying about? After today Lew was not going to be a menace to Arlene or to anybody else. Of all things to forget!

"It might work out," he said comfortably. "You didn't finish about last night. What was the wind-up?"

"There wasn't any particular wind-up. Sophie passed out finally, and Celia drove her and Arlene out to the farm in Sophie's car, with me tagging along behind in mine to bring her back to town."

"Sounds complicated," said Grover.

"It was, brother, it was. She didn't say much of anything on the way home, and damned if *I* could think of anything to say. Not after the unloading job Sophie had done. Poor Celia. I'll make it up to her some way."

"How you aiming to do that?" asked Grover. He was genuinely curious; as always, Lew's adventures held a storybook kind of charm for him. He himself had never been faced with a delicate situation like this; and never would be, of course. There was nobody like Sophie in Grover's past. Nobody like Celia in his present, either. He thought, fleetingly, about the three or four girls he might have married, if he hadn't had Ma to look after. No, he didn't regret them. Nice enough girls. But not like Celia.

"Oh, I don't know," said Lew carelessly. "Some way. Celia's an understanding sort. And after all, why should she hold that business with Sophie against me? It was long before she came to Turk Ridge. I've never looked twice at another woman since I met her."

"Congratulations. Look out for that curve, will you? I'd just as soon not wind up in the ditch."

The dryness of his tone was lost on Lew, who was still absorbed in self-defense. "You know what Sophie was, anyway. Not that I'm trying to whitewash myself. I staked her to that beauty course because she didn't have anybody else to turn to. Not because I thought I was responsible for what happened to her. I doubt if she knows herself who it was. But she wasn't really a bad kid, she just went wild when she got away from that old man of hers. Turk Ridge was no place for a girl like Sophie, and nobody else was going to help her get out. So I did. That's all it amounted to."

"That's all," said Grover. "Tell it to Celia. She's an understanding sort." (Too understanding, when it came to Lew. She had put up with enough from him; it was time somebody stopped her from wasting the rest of her life.)

"More than I can say for you," grumbled Lew. "My pal. All I ever get from you is sarcasm. Insults. Not one kind word." Actually, he was in great good spirits. This was what he expected from Grover, this tart commentary that until today had hidden, beneath its disparaging crust, so much admiration and devotion. Only Grover knew that the devotion wasn't there anymore; it was dead; Lew's own heedless hands had killed it. And Lew couldn't tell the difference. He had no idea that now, in his role of sharp-tongued bystander, Grover was speaking the literal, complete truth.

"I can't see that you deserve a kind word," he said. He felt powerful and daring. "You got off cheap with Sophie, and you know it. It doesn't matter whether Arlene's your daughter or not. She could be, that's all that matters. You've gotten off cheap with her, too. Not to mention Celia. You knew damn well it was dynamite, letting the three of them get together, and still you went right ahead and—"

"Hey, wait a minute. It wasn't me, it was Celia—"

"You could have stopped her. All you had to do was tell her the truth about Sophie and Arlene. You should have done it long ago, when you first saw what an interest she was taking in Arlene. You had no business letting her find it out this way. You claim you had a rough night. What about the three of them? As a matter of fact—" He paused. Was he pushing his luck too far? No. Lew's brows were drawn together in a little frown, but he was taking it without resentment, as he had taken it on other occasions when Grover chewed him out. He still didn't see the difference. Grover's heart knocked with excitement. "As a matter of fact, I don't think you had a rough night at all. I think you got kind of a kick out of it. Didn't you? You like playing with dynamite. You always have. It's great sport, as long as it's the other fellow that gets hurt when the blow-up comes."

Lew blinked. "Good Lord, Grover. That makes me a prize bastard. You don't really think I did it on purpose, do you? I mean, without knowing it myself—"

"Wouldn't surprise me in the least," said Grover. But all at once his zest in his sly little game was gone. He felt withered inside, bereft. It was true: his devotion to Lew was dead, and with it most of the color and richness of his own life. The loss was his as much as Lew's. More his; much more his. Lew was not even aware of it, and nothing Grover could say would make him aware of it. Ah, but there was something he could do. Not yet. Later. In the final moment Lew would see the desolate truth, he too would know what the death of a friendship felt like. But for a little while longer Grover must go through the old familiar paces.

"Relax," he said. "That ends the sermon for today. We will now join in singing Hymn Number Seventy-four."

Lew's grin was relieved, a little shamefaced. "Had it coming to me, I suppose. Between you and Aunt Chat, I've been cut down to size, no two ways about it. She thinks I'm a bastard, too. Told me all about it the other day. What's more, the way she sees it, I'm going to get my come-uppance. Something terrible's going to happen to me."

They hit a bump just then. Luckily for Grover; it hid his guilty start. "Something— What? How does she know?" And for a crazy moment he believed that the old woman did know, had somehow divined his plan and warned Lew, and that Lew had come on this trip only to trap and outwit him ...

"She's been having dreams. You know Aunt Chat and her signs and portents. Don't ask me where she gets these spooky ideas. Though I used to take them for gospel, when I was a kid. Tell you the truth, that's why I made friends with you when we first started to school."

"How do you mean?"

"Well, that was the summer I fell off the barn roof and broke my leg. Had to stay in bed forever, it seemed to me. Aunt Chat took care of me, and to pass the time she used to tell my fortune. Tea leaves, cards, Ouija board—we worked them all to death. It always came out that I was going to be the greatest doctor in the world, I remember. And then there was this mysterious friend that kept turning up. Aunt Chat couldn't tell for sure from what the spirits said whether he was a grownup or a boy my age. But I was going to have a friend, and somehow or other he was going to exert a powerful influence on my life. How would I know him when I saw him? Why, naturally, there would be a sign—and I must say, you could always count on Aunt Chat to come up with a dilly of a sign."

"You bet. Trust her," said Grover. He laughed, to indicate mild interest. It was embarrassing, how curious he really felt about Aunt Chat's sign. Nonsense, of course. A superstitious old woman, half-believing herself what she invented for the amusement of a child. "What was it?" he asked.

"It didn't come through real clear, either. That made it more magical. But there was three in it somehow. Three times? Three weeks, or months, or years? There were all kinds of possibilities to watch out for. Three. And something round. No size indicated. It might be the moon, or it might be something no bigger than the head of a pin. And milk. Maybe something white like milk, maybe something wet like milk—it was anybody's guess. Three. And round. And milk."

"Very simple," said Grover. "A coconut with the shell off, at three o'clock in the afternoon." He breathed easier. Of course it was all nonsense.

"That's one that didn't occur to me. I favored pearls. Believe me, if your father had had three pearls in his stickpin instead of only one, they'd have had to pry me loose from him. But then I went to school that first day, and there you were at recess with those three milky-white marbles of yours, and that settled it. You were elected, boy."

"Yeah. You won them off me before the week was over."

"That's right. I kept the three of them for years. My good luck charm. Believe it or not, I've still got one of them." He fumbled in his pocket and drew it out. Grover would have recognized it anywhere, the smooth, frozen-milk globe with a clear, icy streak in it. It took him straight back to the dusty school playground, and the holes he had worn in the knees of his black ribbed stockings, and Lew, barefooted and swaggering— already established as the toughest kid in first grade—pushing his way into the marble game. Ma hadn't been any too pleased when Grover brought him home to play after school that first day, and practically every day afterwards. But Grover didn't pay any attention to her objections. From the beginning he had found Lew irresistible, a being from another, rougher, more exciting world who—marvel of marvels— had singled out Grover for his friend.

"Go ahead," the grown-up Lew was saying, with the same challenging air that had marked the boy. "Laugh at me."

"I'm not laughing," said Grover after a minute.

"Want it? It's yours by rights. I cheated when I won it off you."

"I know it," said Grover. "No, you keep it. You never know when you're going to need a little extra luck."

"Fifty years." Lew slipped the marble back in his pocket. "That's a hell of a long time, in case anybody asks you. Well. Aunt Chat was wrong on one score. I didn't get to be a doctor, but I found a friend, all right."

"A friend, yes. Though if I ever exerted any powerful influence on your life I don't know about it." He couldn't think of a single time when Lew had listened to his advice. Not that he had offered it very often. The last occasion was when Lew insisted on trying to make a doctor out of Whitt; Grover had spoken up, out of pity for the boy, and Lew had lost his temper and told him it was none of his business. And there was the time, shortly before Lew got married, when they had gone on a fishing trip— the very spot they were headed for now, only in those days the place belonged to Grover's father—and Grover had come right out and said what he thought about Lew's marrying Olive Whitt. You'll regret it, he had said; money or no money, you'll be making a mistake if you go through with it. Where had he exerted any influence that night? Where, for that matter, was the regret, where was the mistake? Somebody was going to marry Olive Whitt for her money. It might as well be Lew. Lew had said as much. You've always had everything you wanted, he had raged—in a bitter outburst that startled and bewildered Grover—you and your precious principles. You don't know what it's like to be poor.

He knew now, though. It was all the other way round. Including Aunt Chat's prediction. Not he, but Lew—with his verve and ruthlessness— had been the exerter of powerful influence. And now that influence had stretched all the way, and Grover was the complete have-not, bowing and scraping for a little of the money that had once seemed so insignificant to him.

"Why, of course you've influenced my life," said Lew. "Don't you remember? You lent me your bike, and I used to take Bessie Lally riding on the handlebars. My first romance, and I owe it all to you." He threw back his head and laughed.

The sky was lightening fast now; they could see the fiery edge of the sun pushing up beyond the trees. Half an hour later, when they reached the shack, it was full day, and the whole world seemed to sparkle and pulse with fresh color.

The shack had started out as just that—a dilapidated, deserted one-room hut that had been there when Grover's grandfather bought the land and that he never used except as an emergency shelter, in case he got caught in a storm. Pa had patched up the roof, repaired the chimney, and put in flooring so that the place was snug, though still rough and sketchily furnished. It had provided an ideal hang-out for Grover and his friends, when they were in their teens. But all that was changed, now that Lew owned the shack and the land. (Grover had signed it over to him, the first time he had to ask for help to keep the store from going under.) It wasn't a shack anymore; it had a gasoline stove and lamps, a separate bedroom with built-in bunks, easy chairs in front of the fire place, and a rug on the floor. Lew was figuring on putting in electricity and plumbing, maybe this summer. Grover knew what that meant. Television, and all the other gadgets that Lew doted on.

"Everything looks okay," Lew said as he unlocked the door and peered inside. "I don't even smell a dead mouse. Come on, let's get the stuff unloaded."

They made short work of it; after all these years they had it down to a system. Grover took charge of the groceries and ice, Lew of the bedding and fishing equipment. When they had finished they sat down on the door step, each with a can of beer. This too was part of the tradition. The cottonwoods above them fluttered in the soft, warm sun, and now and then a handful of blossoms drifted down from the gnarled old apple tree that produced the wormiest apples Grover had ever seen. And sour; just to think about them set his teeth on edge. Blossoms smelled good, though. There was a faint whiff of the river, too, a blend of mud and fish and wet, rotting wood. It tinged the air, even this high up. The shack was set back a bit from the path that straggled along the bluff's edge; even so, you could see a strip of water, brown and sleepy as a snake, from up here. That was the opposite bank. Under the bluffs, on this side, the river was deep, with a treacherously changeable current. As he lifted his can of beer, Grover noticed again how his hands were trembling.

Lew, who had been thoughtfully scratching his back against the door jamb, leaned toward him with an impetuous yet shy gesture. "Look, Grover, I don't want you worrying about the store. You know, the deal we were talking about yesterday. Maybe I said too much. It's just that I hate to see you knocking yourself out, year after year, and—"

Grover smiled briefly. "Never mind. It's not your fault I'm a failure."

"Who said anything about you being a failure? I didn't mean that at all," Lew explained, all haste and heartiness. "Of course you're not a failure."

"Oh yes, I am. All the way down the line."

"Shut up. There isn't a man in town that's better thought of than you, and you know it. You're the same kind of genuine, all-wool-and-a-yard-wide citizen your father was, and your grandfather before him."

But they didn't lose the store, thought Grover. I'm the one that's done that. No use arguing with Lew, though. He was off again, carried away by his own anxious, earnest pep talk.

"You'll see, Grover. It's going to be a new deal all around, and you're going to have the time of your life managing a live-wire store. We can't lose, not with your experience and reputation, and the chain back of us. Honest to God, you're going to wonder why you didn't agree to it long ago. Why, this time next year you'll be on Easy Street, with nothing to worry about for the rest of your life."

"Maybe," said Grover. He sighed. It would have been nice if, in this last conversation of all, Lew could have gotten his mind off money and deals. Nice, but too much to expect. He stood up, and as he looked down at Lew—still talking away, tirelessly enthusiastic, oblivious to what was so close to him, so very close—he felt a surge of obscure compassion. "I'm not worrying about it," he told Lew gently. "Why worry? It's all settled, and that's that. Don't get yourself steamed up. You aiming to sit here all day, or you coming fishing with me?"

Lew leaped up and clapped him on the back. "That's the stuff. I knew you'd see it my way, once you got used to the idea. You'll never be sorry, I guarantee it. Come on. Let's go."

They had quite a load, what with the beer and sandwiches and their fishing tackle. As usual, Lew carried a little more than his share. And— Grover had counted on this, too—he struck off in the lead, impatiently tearing his way through the underbrush, the wild grape vines and elderberries that choked the narrow path. Grover followed at a more sedate pace, though never losing sight of the vigorous figure in front of him. The bulging leather bag slung over Lew's shoulder swung jauntily as he forged ahead. What energy the man had! Even now, when he was no longer young, he still moved with the poised power that Grover envied so much. Occasionally he paused, to give Grover time to catch up, or to call out a warning about poison ivy, or simply to look around in frank enjoyment of himself and the bright spring day. He had always been happiest outdoors. When he first married Olive and took over the bank, he used to chafe himself into a rage of irritability, hardly able to wait for the weekend, when he could light out for the river or the hills and forget about the bleak bargain he was bound and determined to stick to. And usually Grover had gone along, like a faithful dog trotting at his heels ...

He pushed on, hurrying a little now, because the place he had in mind was not too far ahead. It wasn't really hot, but he was working up a sweat. From exertion. It couldn't be nerves; he felt detached and glassily calm, almost as if he were moving in one of those dreams where nothing touches or surprises you. Past the little clearing where they used to find bluebells when they were kids. And there, just beyond the bend, Grover had once come upon an orphaned baby coon that he took home with him for a pet. The familiar landmarks glided past; weeds, heavy with dew, slapped against his legs; a blue jay flashed across the path, jeering; inside his head a remote voice repeated mechanically, something terrible is going to happen, something terrible is going to happen.

"Wait up for me," he called, but Lew had stopped any way, just in the right place, where the path veered sharply, to the very brink of the bluff. When Grover came up to him he was peering over the edge.

"We ought to be able to see the boat from here," he said. "Yep. There she is." Grover's eyes followed his pointing finger to the boat, far, far below. It looked no bigger than a toy boat, fastened close to the fallen tree trunk where Al always left it. For a minute the glint of sun on river dazzled Grover. He felt his sweaty shirt sticking to his chest, which was all at once rising and falling, faster, faster.

He echoed Lew's words: "Yep. There she is." Then he dug his heels into the moist earth; half-bent, as if to pick up something or tie his shoe lace; and seemed to stumble, shoving heavily against Lew as he did so.

Everything was very distinct to him, and leisurely, like a dream. He heard Lew's startled grunt, saw him totter momentarily against the sky and in the next instant, with that instinctive poise of his, whirl and regain his balance. And then the dream splintered, it was all lightning-speed and ruin, and the something terrible was happening, he himself was plunging on past Lew, down, down ... Automatically his hands shot out and found something to clamp onto—a tough, knotty tangle of roots in the face of the bluff. He had stopped plunging. He clung there like a monkey on a trapeze, his legs dangling in bottomless air, his arm sockets ready to crack with the strain of his weight, his heart hammering. He looked down, and at once closed his eyes against the waiting, swirling river.

Above him he could hear Lew shouting. The words escaped Grover, and one of the lenses in his glasses must have been smashed when he fell, because Lew's face—much closer than the river—kept jumping in and out of focus. He had ripped off the shoulder bag and his stout leather jacket and was hitching them together into a makeshift tow-line. Now he flung himself flat on the ground and lowered his line. It was long enough; one sleeve of the jacket hung within Grover's reach.

"Hang on, Grover, just hang on and we're okay." Lew was speaking very calmly, very distinctly. "It'll hold. I can haul you up. All you have to do is grab ahold."

Grover's hand, his mindless, reflex-ruled hand, slackened its grip on the root, getting ready to stretch toward Lew's jacket and safety. Safety at any price ...

No. Not at this price. He spat out a mouthful of dirt and stared up at Lew's face, flickering crazily, one moment clear-cut and urgent, the next an anonymous blob. To be rescued by the hand he had planned to destroy, to be in debt to Lew for his very life, in addition to all the rest—

No. Failure that he was, dangling here in the extremity of defeat, he could still preserve one last shred of his own integrity. He could refuse to live at this price.

"*Grover!* Christ's sake! Grab ahold!"

Lew would never know. He thought they were still friends. Oh well. You couldn't have everything.

The line swung closer, almost brushing his hand, close enough so that he saw the milky-white marble roll out of the jacket pocket and bounce its way down the bluff. There goes Lew's luck, he thought. Mine too. There goes everything.

"No. I'd rather die." He wanted it to be a yell, but he hadn't the strength. It was only a whisper.

But it was the truth. He felt his mouth drawing back in an exultant, defiant smile. Then he let go of the root, and he was plunging again, this time for keeps.

8

"You shouldn't have done it, Miss Morgan," said Evvie, above the wail of the vacuum cleaner. "No earthly reason why you should go to work and make all them sandwiches for your Dad. Why, I'da been glad to do it if you'd only told me."

She would have been, too, even though she hadn't gotten in till three thirty in the morning, and she looked it. But the lacklustre gaze she turned on Victoria was full of reproach; whatever her shortcomings, Evvie put her heart into her job. She caught a glimpse of herself in the hall mirror and shuddered. "If I don't look like death warmed over. I don't know what hit Bill and I last night, seemed like we just lost all track of the time. It's a good thing his leave's up next week, or we'd neither one of us be worth shooting." She sighed, a bit complacently. "No kidding, Miss Morgan. You shoulda told me. I feel awful, you going to all that work."

"I didn't mind," said Victoria. "I made them last night." Why not? She had had nothing else to do. She wasn't like Evvie, with her string of beaus—she was waiting for Bill to get out of the Army, but she didn't let that cramp her style—her dates and dances and hangovers. As often before, Victoria studied, with a kind of wistful curiosity, Evvie's scrawny little body; her pert face, which still bore the traces of last night's make-up; her stringy bleached hair. She was no world-beater when it came to looks. Not even when she was done up in her dance-night best— spike heels, eye shadow, can-can petticoat, and all. And it certainly wasn't her brains that made her popular; the first year of high school had proved too much for Evvie. But she was born knowing a lot of things that Victoria still hadn't learned. She had never sat through a whole evening in tongue-tied, immobilized agony, as Victoria so often had. Or suffered the contortions of indecision—to call Fred, not to call him, to invite him here, not to invite him—that gripped Victoria at this moment. Or found herself wrenched between loving and hating the same person at the same time ...

"You can let the upstairs go till later," she said, as Evvie switched off the vacuum cleaner. "What I wish you'd do right now is run across to Mrs. Peterson's and see if she has any fresh cottage cheese this morning. There's a new recipe I want to try out. Cottage cheese souffle." She kept her eyes fixed sternly on Evvie, ready to stare her down if it was necessary. It wasn't. Evvie swallowed the story whole; the Morgans had a right to their whims. And Mrs. Talking Machine Peterson could be counted on to hold a willing listener like Evvie spellbound for at least twenty minutes. Which was exactly what Victoria wanted: twenty minutes to herself, so she could call Fred without having to worry about being overheard.

"And listen, Evvie, after you've finished the cleaning you can have the rest of the day off. Dad won't be back till late tomorrow afternoon, and I can fix something for myself tonight."

"Honest, Miss Morgan?" Evvie's bleary eyes lit up at the prospect of another big night, another hangover tomorrow. "Gee, that's swell. Bill's last weekend, and all. Gee, thanks, Miss Morgan."

Victoria smiled stiffly. The coast was clear now, in case she decided to invite Fred. Or, to put it another way, her bridges were burnt. No excuse, now, for not inviting him. When would she have another chance like this? If that was what she wanted, a chance— Oh, to be like Evvie, who knew, without having to think twice, what was swell and what wasn't!

"I better take some money, I guess," Evvie was saying. "It's twenty-five cents a pint."

"Oh, of course." Victoria picked up her purse from the hall piece, but even before she looked in her billfold, she remembered. Sixty-seven cents. She had meant to ask Dad yesterday, but she had kept putting it off—the way she always did—from minute to minute, and now here she was, with sixty-seven cents in her purse. She took out the half-dollar and gave it to Evvie. Seventeen cents. A gust of sudden rage shook her. She leaned against the newel post listening to Evvie's footsteps slap down the hall and to the tense, furious whisper inside her: Damn him, oh, damn him ...

All she ever had to do was ask. It sounded so simple. He wasn't going to put her on a salary, Dad said; why, he'd feel like a cheapskate, doling out so much to her on payday, as if she were just part of the staff instead of his daughter. Had he ever denied her anything she wanted? Of course not; everybody knew how generous he was, with his spectacular gifts and his unlimited charge accounts. All she had to do was ask. He would have been astounded to know how costly the asking was to Victoria's pride; how she hoarded and scrimped against the humiliating moment when it could be put off no longer. She couldn't possibly tell him how she felt about it; just admitting it to herself had always made her cringe with shame and disloyalty.

Until now. The sudden rage swept everything else aside. Seventeen cents, she thought; I have to ask him for every last penny, and oh, by the way, he and Celia would be getting married, probably late this summer ...

She hurled her purse to the floor, picked up the phone, and called Chicago. She made it short and sweet. At least Fred found it sweet, judging from the lift of delighted surprise in his voice. Even Victoria, absorbed in her anger, could not quite miss that. Sure he could make it tonight instead of tomorrow. Sure. Any time she said. Eight thirty? Earlier, if she wanted to— No? Okay, then. Eight thirty. He'd be there with bells on.

"It's a great big white house on the edge of town," she said, and the prosy, explicit directions she went on to give him convinced her, for the first time, that she was really inviting him here, Fred was actually going to see her in her natural habitat, as herself, Lew Morgan's daughter, the richest girl in Turk Ridge. With seventeen cents in her purse. All right. With seventeen cents in her purse. But Fred wouldn't see that side of it. Not with all the unmistakable signs of money, lots of money, staring him in the face.

She crossed the hall and looked in at the living room, trying to imagine how it would strike her if she had never seen it before. It was a room meant to be looked at, sleek and calculated; the interior decorator had been delighted with it. With a quaking sensation in her interior, Victoria turned away. No. She could not entertain Fred in this atmosphere of sterile luxury; it would blight even his buoyant spirit. Where then? There was the back room—but that was so steeped in Dad's personality that Victoria would not be able to forget him for an instant. The veranda, if the weather stayed pleasant ... Or the little sitting room where Mother used to sit with her seed catalogues or her embroidery. Victoria hurried down the hall and opened the door on that humble sanctuary with its rather touching mementoes—pictures of Whitt and of herself from babyhood on up, Mother's wicker flower box filled with potted begonias, wandering Jew and geraniums, and the bright embroidery flosses on the window sill, beside her little sewing chair. The interior decorator had left this room untouched. And the impact of poor Mother's personality was never going to overpower anybody. Yes. The sitting room would do. With pitchers of lilacs on the mantelpiece, and the photographs put out of sight, except for the one of Victoria on her Shetland pony, that was rather nice ...

She felt a surge of uncomplicated joy. Fred's coming, she thought, I'm going to see Fred tonight.

At that moment she heard the kitchen door slam, and then Evvie galloping down the hall, calling breathlessly, "Miss Morgan! Oh, Miss Morgan, isn't it terrible— Miz Peterson just heard it, not ten minutes ago, from the paper boy, she was so upset she could hardly— Just terrible. The worst thing I ever heard."

"What's the matter? What are you talking about?"

"It's Mr. Underwood. He's dead. Drowned. Him and your Dad—"

"*Dad? Dad's dead?*"

"Oh God's sake, Miss Morgan, no. Not your Dad. Don't look at me like that. Not your Dad. Mr. Underwood. Fell in the river some way and drowned while they was fishing. It took 'em all this time to find the body. Your Dad and Al. They're hauling the body back to town in Al's station wagon. Isn't it just terrible, Miss Morgan?"

"Oh, Evvie, are you sure?" She let go of Evvie's shoulders and leaned against the wall. Not Dad. She would stop shaking in a minute. Not Dad. Mr. Underwood. Drowned. That familiar, kind face streaked with river mud, the plumpish body (he wouldn't have been wearing his alpaca jacket of course, but somehow that was the way she saw him) bedraggled and limp. "I can't believe it," she said helplessly.

"That's just what Miz Peterson said, she couldn't believe it either, but it's all over town, the paper boy said. He heard it down at the store. Agnes just went all to pieces. He wasn't sure when it happened, but he thought real early, and it took them all this time to find the poor guy." Evvie sniffed. The time element seemed to have a morbid fascination for her. "There's the clock striking now. Half past twelve."

But Victoria had heard another sound. She rushed to the front door and flung it open. Dad was getting out of Doc Fletcher's car; he paused in the driveway a moment, nodding in answer to something Doc was saying. Then Doc drove off and Dad turned and started slowly up the steps. His face looked drained and dull.

"You've heard?" he said when he saw Victoria. He held out his hand in an uncertain, beseeching gesture that brought her flying across the porch to put her arms around him.

"All he had to do was grab ahold," he told her. "I can't understand it. No reason on earth why I couldn't have pulled him up. He knew it. He must have known it."

"Come on inside. Come on, Dad, we'll fix you a cup of coffee—" There stood Evvie with her mouth hanging open, goggle-eyed. "Evvie, go put the water on," she said sharply, and Evvie pulled herself together and scurried off.

They went into the back room. Dad sat down on the couch, sagging, his hands hanging down between his knees. "I've got to go back out there, later. Doc's going to pick me up. I have to show them where it happened, for the coroner's report. Besides, I left the car out there at the shack. My God, Victoria, I can't get over it. Grover—"

She got the brandy bottle from the book case and poured them each a shot. The warmth of it spread through her; she sat down close to Dad while he told her what had happened. Gradually the color came back to his face. His voice began to sound natural again. She had always known, by instinct, how to get him to relax. Just let him talk. Just sit close to him quietly, reassuringly, with now and then a murmur to show you understood. She was the one he had always turned to, even when she was a child ...

He put down his coffee cup and reached for the telephone. "I want to let Celia know," he said, and while she listened to him give the operator the familiar number her inner glow faded and gave way to a slow, creeping chill. She could not shake it off. Not even when it became clear—maybe someday he would learn who was dependable and who wasn't—that he was not going to get an answer. Celia had a phone of her own in her room at Mrs. Walker's; it was one of her little touches of luxury. She didn't have to connive for a few minutes' privacy—

Victoria was suddenly rigid. Fred. Fred was coming tonight. It hit her like a thunderbolt, the fix she was in, with Fred coming and Dad almost sure to be here (for of course Celia couldn't be depended upon to keep him out of the way; not Celia). She knew exactly how it would be. So exactly that she felt herself shrivelling already.

"Not there, I guess," said Dad. "Well, I'll get her later."

Any circumstances would have been bad, but these were the worst, the very worst. Dad's nerves were on edge to begin with; he was in no mood to be told that his daughter had taken up with a travelling salesman months ago and that the fellow was turning up tonight at eight thirty, honorable intentions and all. Supposing, that is, that Victoria could bring herself to tell him. Which she could not possibly do. He would see at once that she had invited Fred here behind his back, thinking he would be away, and he would know why. The shameful reason would leap out at him in banner headlines. There was no surer way of reducing Fred's visit to a shambles. But it would be just as fatal to let Fred show up out of the blue, without a word to Dad beforehand ...

"There's another thing," Dad was saying. "The funeral arrangements. There aren't any close relatives, but there's a whole raft of cousins. They ought to be notified, I suppose."

Fred must not come. That was the only way out. Fred must simply not come. Relief swamped her. All she had to do was get hold of Fred and tell him not to come. So simple, after all. Explain to him. Tell him some other time. Tell him anything. Just keep him away from here tonight.

"I can tend to that part of it," she said. Now that she saw the way out, she could hardly wait to take it. Her hands fairly itched to reach for the phone. "Agnes will know how to get in touch with the cousins, and anybody else that ought to be notified. I can run down right now and—"

Evvie charged in, balancing a tray of sandwiches and soup. As goggle-eyed as ever. More so; she had obviously been crying. "I fixed you a bite of something. Thought you might like a little broth, Mr. Morgan. It kind of hits the spot when you're upset. Oh, I just—" She gave a loud sniffle. "Oh, poor Mr. Underwood! He was always so nice and friendly. The nicest, friendliest man."

"Yes," said Dad. "They don't come any better than Grover." Again Victoria felt the shock of it, as if some good old fixture in her life had been whisked away without warning. Grover Underwood had always been there—slipping her and the other kids candy and gum when they stopped in at the store after school, patting her head, exclaiming over how tall she was getting, interrupting his Sunday afternoon card games with Dad here in the back room to help her with her arithmetic. Always there, and now all at once not there. Not anywhere. Dead. And she could spare him no more than a few minutes' regret, a few absent-minded tears before she rushed on, absorbed in her own problems. At this very moment the lump in her throat was as much for herself as for Grover. There was no time; she must get away from Dad somehow so she could call Fred. The potential calamity of his coming here tonight had a sharper impact, for her, than the accomplished calamity of Grover's death. No use pretending otherwise.

Still sniffling, Evvie fumbled in her pocket and came up with a half-dollar. "Here, Miss Morgan, here's the money back for the cottage cheese. Miz Peterson— Oh God's sake, I don't know if I even asked her! I'll go back if you want. I never give it another thought, after she told me about Mr. Underwood."

"Of course not, Evvie. It's all right. Let it go." (Sixty-seven cents. Enough for a call to Chicago, in case she used the pay phone in the drugstore? She wasn't sure. She would have to take a chance and call from the hall phone here at home. Whether she was alone in the house or not.)

Meanwhile, she must make herself sit still. She took a sandwich and smiled—a you're-dismissed kind of smile—at Evvie. "Thank you, Evvie. Thanks very much." When she and Dad were alone again, she repeated, "I can run down and see Agnes right now."

"Better wait a while," he said. "Till she's quieted down a little. She went all to pieces. Why don't you wait till Doc comes back for me? There's no rush. That'll be time enough."

In other words, he needed her. He wanted her to stay with him. In spite of all she could do—in spite of the sixty-seven cents, and Celia, and the urgency of calling Fred—she felt the glow returning. He looked so tired, not dull the way he had at first, but still mortally tired. Hollow-eyed, so that his beak of a nose jutting out seemed not so much arrogant as vulnerable, almost fragile. His plaid shirt was stained with sweat, his trousers with mud.

"Oh, Dad," she said huskily, "your feet. They must be wet. You ought to change—"

"No, I'm all right. No sense changing, as long as I have to go out there again and show them the place." He stared down at his big square hands. He kept stretching them out, clenching them, stretching them out again. She had a curious impression that he was on the verge of putting into words something he had shied away from until now, something important and secret.

But then Doc Fletcher rang the doorbell, and whatever it was was left unsaid, after all.

"Do you want me to go with you?" She said it against her will, standing in the hallway, aching to get hold of the phone and call Fred. She could not keep from saying it. And if he said yes, please do, she would not be able to keep from going.

But he said no, of course not. He gave her shoulder a quick, grateful pat. "I'm okay now. This shouldn't take long, it's just routine. See you later."

The minute he was gone she rushed to the phone. A little past two, according to the hall clock. Which was a creature of whims, sometimes fast, sometimes slow; a congenital liar. And it didn't matter in the least which lie the clock happened to be telling today. Because she was too late. Fred had checked out. "I see," she said, when the metallic voice of the hotel clerk stopped clicking. "Thank you." She hung up. Her hands fell, of their own weight, into her lap, and she left them there, crossed at the wrists, palms upward. She did not feel surprised, or panicky, or anything at all. Having checked out, where would Fred be likely to go? She had no idea. It was as if he had dissolved temporarily, to be re-materialized on her step at eight thirty tonight. She could no more prevent his appearance than she could conjure him up now, out of the nowhere that hung between.

After a while she stood up. It was shadowy in the hall; the day, which had started out so fine, must have clouded over. Yes, through the open door she could see the sky, no longer blue, sagging with gray clouds. Evvie was clattering dishes in the kitchen, the clock ticked away its lying life, a car turned in at the driveway, fast, with a sharp spatter of gravel.

It was Dort and Johnny. (Not Whitt. It was hardly ever Dort and Whitt.) She had on blue jeans and a bright red jacket, and her hair was tied up on top. Quite fetching, though she wasn't going to be able to work the child-bride angle too many more years. Beside her Johnny looked very tall and masculine and dark. Like a couple out of a movie. A couple registering concern, sympathy, willingness to be of help—just so much of each, according to some standard recipe.

"Victoria! We just heard, and we came right up. Is Lew here? Is there anything we can do?"

"God, what a business. Your Dad must be all cut up about it. You look pretty rocky yourself, poor kid." Johnny seemed about to reach for her hand, instantly suppressed the gesture when she shrank back against the wall. She didn't like Johnny to touch her; he was too much the expert, making a kind of production out of a simple handshake.

"Dad's not here," she said, but they went past her, anyway, heading down the hall toward the back room. Just as if they owned the place. It was Dad's room, Dad's and hers, but here they were, their eyes seeming to swarm over everything, their synthetic movie roles forgotten for one unguarded moment. Victoria felt a dim flicker of curiosity. What was Dort up to now? She hadn't come just to hand out loving kindness, you could bet on that. But she never did anything without a purpose, either.

"He'll be back, then," she said, after Victoria had explained, tersely, where Dad was. She perched herself on the corner of the desk and swung her blue-jeaned legs. "I mean, he'll probably be home this evening, won't he?"

"Probably." All too probably. Not a chance in the world that he would be anywhere but right here this evening, annihilating Fred once and for all. Suddenly desperate, she put her hands up to her cheeks.

Johnny was right there with the sympathy. "Poor Victoria. You look done in. Let me get you something—"

"Brandy," said Dort. She slid off the desk and picked up the bottle from the table. "She needs a shot of brandy. Poor Victoria. I could use one myself. Why don't we all have one?" Something in her face scared Victoria. Something genuine and violent that flashed out briefly from under the glaze of phony concern. Whether or not it had anything to do with Victoria—probably not, they were looking at each other, not at her—it made her want to get out of there.

"I'm afraid you'll have to excuse me," she said firmly. "I've got to go downtown and help Agnes with the funeral arrangements."

"Oh, really? You don't mind if we stay here and wait for Lew, do you? He may want a little moral support when he gets back." Dort was smiling slightly. That demure-wanton face of hers, with the oversized eyes and the pulpy, drooping mouth. What was she up to now?

"Why no, I don't mind," Victoria said at last. "I don't know what time he'll be back, but it's all right if you want to wait."

Oh, they did want to, they assured her. They did so want to be of some help.

All right, let them stay. What was the difference? When she got to the front door she saw that it was raining, gently but persistently. No wind, no fuss of any kind; just the rain falling like tears from the thick gray sky, sharpening the colors of grass and driveway, and setting up a faint tremor in the heavy plumes of the lilacs. There was a thump behind her; Evvie was grappling with the vacuum cleaner, getting ready to do the upstairs.

"Miss Morgan." Her voice was hushed, funereal. "You won't want me taking today off now, the way things are—" She paused hopefully.

"It doesn't matter, Evvie. You can go, just the same. I can manage. You go ahead."

There was a short, perfunctory argument before Evvie said, from the bottom of her simple heart, "Oh, Miss Morgan, you're so *good* to me. Honest you are. If there was just some way I could pay you back."

But there wasn't any way. Because Evvie would never in the world believe that Miss Morgan was not lucky and rich and sure of herself. Miss Morgan lost, destitute, helpless? Don't make Evvie laugh.

Help me, help me, Victoria wanted to cry. Somebody's got to help me. But Evvie, her skimpy body sagging under the weight of the vacuum cleaner, kept on climbing the stairs, and there wasn't any way.

That was when she heard it for the first time, the echo of her own voice gasping out, "*Dad?* Dad's dead?" Ghostly, incredulous, and yet fluttering with some other, indefinable quality that she could catch only out of the corner of her ear, so to speak. As soon as she listened for it consciously, it dissolved.

It was to haunt her for the rest of the day, unaccountably recurring, as tantalizing as a half-remembered tune. It kept bobbing up at odd moments while she helped Agnes make the arrangements—poor distraught Agnes who couldn't be persuaded to leave the store because Underwood's never closed on Saturday afternoon—while she talked to the undertaker, telegraphed the cousins, conferred with the Presbyterian minister. There it would be, her own voice, her own words to Evvie: "*Dad?* Dad's dead?" always with that mysterious overtone that slid away out of her reach, the instant she tried to identify it. She could neither catch it nor escape from it. In a way, she was grateful for it, just as she was grateful for the practical chores that filled up her afternoon.

"I can't thank you enough, Victoria," Agnes said when she left. "I don't know what I'd done without you to take hold and decide things. You're so capable."

Agnes, like Evvie, would never believe the truth, which was— Well, what? Victoria *was* capable. Everybody said so. Dad's right-hand man. But no one saw—she had not seen it herself until now—that her efficiency was only a mechanical device that she had hit upon, years ago, to keep her occupied. She had filled up her whole life with busywork of one kind or another; otherwise its emptiness would have appalled her. And the busywork had sufficed, after a fashion, until she met Fred. How could it ever suffice again, now that she knew what a makeshift it was?

She pulled the hood of her raincoat up against the quiet, steady rain and ran across the street to her car. The wet asphalt gleamed; lights shone, yellow and fuzzy, in some of the stores; the awning in front of the pool hall dripped forlornly.

I can't stand it, she thought. I can't stand to have him spoil Fred for me. He's got no right, but he'll do it, and I can't stop him. Because I'm only half a person, I don't quite dare love anybody else without him to say it's all right, and he never will, he never will ...

Whitt had just arrived and was going up the steps when she got home. He waited for her on the porch. "Dad's back," he told her, "and Celia's here."

As if she didn't know it. There stood the two cars—Dad's Buick and Celia's shabby coupe—in the driveway. But you could always count on Whitt to say what didn't need to be said. It's raining: that would no doubt be his next news bulletin.

For once he surprised her. "You all right, Victoria?" He put out his hand tentatively. "You look kind of—I don't know, kind of upset. You must have had a rugged day. Why, look here, you're shivering. You've caught a chill or something—"

In the failing light his face blurred into a dim version of Dad's face. Otherwise—such was the pitch of her despair —she might have given way and cried out help me, help me ... To Whitt, of all people! The only person in the world who was more of a weakling than she. Oh, they were a fine pair, she and Whitt. They could thank Dad, both of them—the loved one and the unloved one, it came to the same in the end—for what they were.

"I'm all right," she said shortly. "I'm tired, that's all."

He let his hand fall back to his side. After a moment he said, "I guess Dort and Johnny aren't here yet. I'm supposed to meet them here for a drink. They missed Dad when they were here this afternoon, so they were going to come back."

"They must have gotten tired of waiting for him," said Victoria. She had a sudden impulse to hurt Whitt—because she had almost appealed to him, because he was contemptible in Dad's eyes and therefore in hers. Just because. "How nice of them, to invite you too. It's going to be a regular family reunion, isn't it?"

His mouth quivered, just as she had known it would, and then his face went blank and remote. Mother used to look like that, most of the time. She brushed past him and opened the door. The sight of the hall clock threw her into a near panic. After six. She hadn't thought it was so late. Or was it the other way round? Had she been willing the hours to fly by, behind her back, so she would be spared the agony of counting them off? Two and a half hours, and Fred would be here. So little time. So much time. She felt as if she were smothering. And there it was again, her own voice haunting her: "*Dad? Dad's dead?*"

"You're sure you're all right?" Whitt had followed her in, and was watching her in a worried way. "You haven't caught a cold, have you? Better take a couple of—"

"Aspirins," she finished for him. She gave a harsh laugh. "Oh sure. A couple of aspirins will cure anything."

She hurried down the hall.

She could hear Dad's voice, a serious-sounding murmur, before she reached the door to the back room. Yes, they were in the back room; Celia had been allowed to invade Dad's inner sanctum, the heart of Victoria's home. The hall door stood open, and they were so absorbed in themselves that they did not notice her for a moment or two. And what a cozy little scene it was, to be sure. A fire crackled and flickered in the fireplace, and the light from the hanging lamp fell softly on the mellow colors of the rug and drapes. They were sitting on the couch, where Victoria and Dad had sat earlier, and—now, as then—he was staring down at his hands, stretching them out and then clenching them again, while he talked. Victoria did not need to catch any of the words. She knew, without that, that he was telling Celia what he had not quite told Victoria, confiding to this outsider what he had held back from his own daughter. Celia was making herself very much at home; she had one foot tucked under her, and she was picking absently at the fringe on the cushion beside her, frowning a little.

"You know that Grover wouldn't—" she was saying, in that distinctive, uneven voice of hers. Then she looked up and saw Victoria. Here it was, the famous Colby smile, switched on full force. "Hi, Victoria. Come on in by the fire."

That was big of her. Whose fire did she think it was? Whose home was this, anyway?

"Thanks. I don't want to intrude," said Victoria, and Dad had the grace to look startled. But only for a moment. He came over and took Victoria's hands in his, drawing her into the warm, bright room.

"You're all chilled and shivery, poor baby. Let me fix you a drink. Hello there," he added to Whitt, who was hesitating in the background.

She swallowed convulsively. "Dad, are you going to be here all evening? Because I—"

"Sure I am. I'm beat. All I want to do is have a couple of drinks and go to bed."

What was the use? She couldn't tell him about Fred. Not with Celia sitting there, all ears and smiles and condescension. Whitt, too, and Dort and Johnny due any minute. Two and a half hours. So little time. So much time. She stared up at him imploringly, and he was not even looking at her, he was smiling past her, at something Celia was saying. Something that Victoria did not hear; there was no sound in the world, for her, except the memory of her own voice. *"Dad?* Dad's dead?" At last she captured the elusive, haunting quality. At last she knew what had been in her heart when she gasped out those incredulous words to Evvie.

It was hope. She wished Dad dead. Nothing else could set her free.

9

"Committees are like that," said Celia philosophically. "They dwindle the minute there's any work to be done."

She was not at all surprised—nor even very annoyed—that the Junior-Senior banquet place card committee, which was scheduled to hand-paint the place cards this morning, had dwindled to one member. But she was a little embarrassed that that one member happened to be Arlene. It would have been easier, after last night, if their next meeting had turned out to be a group affair instead of a tête-à-tête. This way there was nothing to disguise the bald fact of their self-consciousness. And no excuse for not talking about the one subject that occupied both their minds. Better left untalked about? Maybe. If it were a matter of Celia's feelings only— But it wasn't; it was Arlene's feelings far more than hers. Or if Arlene were a full-grown woman, instead of a touchy, unpredictable adolescent— But she wasn't. The age gulf had never seemed so vast.

Celia gave her an opening (in case she wanted to use it) when she first appeared, breathless from running up the stairs to the Home Ec room, where Celia had laid out the paint pots and brushes on one of the long tables and hopefully set out chairs for the four committee members.

"Am I late?" Arlene had cried, her eyes skimming past Celia's to the empty, empty room. "I'm terribly sorry. Aunt Sophie drove me in, and we meant to get started earlier, only we had to wait for the neighbor boy, he wanted a ride to town—"

"How is she?" asked Celia, aware that her eyes were skimming too. So there was the opening.

"Just fine," said Arlene automatically, and for an instant their glances almost met. But for only an instant. Arlene whipped out of her jacket, tossed her pony-tail with a practiced hand, and rushed headlong into an explanation of how she had met Peg and Louise, they were terribly sorry, but they had this chance to go to Chicago and buy their dresses for the banquet, and when else were they going to do it, and Arlene was to tell Miss Colby they were terribly sorry about the place cards.

"That leaves you and me," said Celia. "Harlan just called and said he can't come either. He has to help his father at the creamery. Well. I suppose we might as well get started."

It was a picky, exasperating kind of job. The gilt paint had to be mixed with oil. Just the right amount of oil. Too much, and you got a hot butter effect; too little, and you got something like crumbs. The gilt was for the border. There was blue for the forget-me-nots. It took a steady hand and patience, neither of which was Celia's long suit. Especially not today.

She dipped her brush and sighed. No businesslike teaching, she thought: you jumped in all aglow with ideals, fired with the vision of yourself striking sparks from youthful minds right and left—Shakespeare, Shelley, Keats—and you wound up painting forget-me-nots on place cards.

But she would never have to do this again. Once more she felt the gush of her happiness, like a wonderful little fountain sparkling inside her. No more Class Day skits to write, no more Senior ring squabbles to settle, no more wienie roasts to chaperon, no more endless teachers' meetings to sit through.

Mrs. Lew Morgan. It was what she wanted, and it was all she wanted. Last night made no difference. None of the other humiliations had made any difference, either. The prying eyes and knowing little smiles. All Turk Ridge, speculating about her. And the time, years ago, when she was asked to resign from the Penelope Club, the Penelopes had never stooped to explaining why, they didn't need to, Celia knew that Doc Fletcher's wife had seen her and Lew coming out of that hotel in Chicago. The old guard of Turk Ridge, the Penelopes, so sure of themselves and their position that they were not afraid to be unfashionable or stuffy. Their snub had been, after all, such a triviality; it was funny that the sting of it still lingered. Maybe not so funny, either. The older Penelopes were cut from the same pattern, ladylike but durable, as Celia's mother. (And that had been no triviality, Mother's shock and sorrow when she found out about Lew. Mother was dead now; but she seemed still to hover uneasily over Celia, a loving, disapproving, anxious ghost.)

When it came to that, Celia herself was a lady, a Penelope born and bred. Ay, there was the rub. It was not in her nature to dissemble; until she met Lew life had never required her to dissemble. Well, she supposed she had learned. The hard way. Just as she had learned to grow some kind of a shell against the town gossips. A very flimsy shell, judging from the way she had felt last night, when she had had to sit there in the hotel dining room and listen to Sophie shriek out what all of Turk Ridge must have whispered (and snickered about, of course they had, behind Celia's back); what Lew himself should have told her, long ago ...

She felt Arlene watching her and looked up. But all she caught was the hurried dip of Arlene's head, bent again over her brush.

"The gilt's the hardest, isn't it? I think the gilt's simply gruesome."

"So do I. Oh, Arlene, yours look fine! Much better than mine. Mine wiggle all over the place."

Their voices ping-ponged back and forth, meaninglessly. It was ridiculous, and yet Celia could not quite bring herself to break up the pattern of chit-chat. Arlene might very well be too agonizingly embarrassed about last night for a single word. Whether or not she had gotten the full import of Sophie's outpourings, she must still be in a state of shock and confusion. And what she was feeling toward Celia herself was the biggest riddle of all. Had she any idea of what the whole business had meant to Celia? If so—teen-agers so often had a Puritan streak—Celia might be a broken idol, in her eyes. Or perhaps, striking out blindly, she had settled on Celia as a focus of resentment, instead of someone to be thanked for helping her deal with a drunk and disorderly aunt. (Mother, Celia corrected herself. A drunk and disorderly mother. Let's be accurate about these things. Not too accurate, though. Let's not delve too deeply into the matter of Arlene's parentage.) Of course it was possible: Arlene might never be able to forgive her for having been there, a witness to her shame. Anything was possible, with so many divided loyalties, so much bruised pride.

They went on chattering, helplessly, with now and then the glances that barely avoided meeting. They went on painting place cards.

And then all at once, in the middle of a discussion of the weather—which was turning cloudy, after such a fine beginning—Arlene broke the deadlock. She put down her brush and looked directly at Celia. "She's my mother, isn't she?" Her eyes were at once defiant and imploring. "My mother, not my aunt. Did you know it?"

Celia shook her head. There must have been gossip; but then Celia, being herself such a favorite target, missed out on a lot of gossip. "You mustn't—"

"I'm not ashamed of it!" flashed Arlene. "I'm not ashamed of anything about her! I don't care what anybody says, she's been the most— I love her the most of anybody in the whole world!"

"Of course you do," said Celia.

"Only why did she have to— Why did it have to be that way?"

Vulnerable, and yet somehow unapproachable, Arlene bent her head and beat her fists softly against the table. And the question—the unanswerable question that Celia, too, had asked so often and so fruitlessly—throbbed between them, seeming to wipe out the gulf of age and leave them face to face, two human creatures with a common grief, struggling to understand the why of life itself. To Celia it seemed like that. But to Arlene?

"Why, Miss Colby, why?"

To Arlene she must seem simply inadequate; the trusted guide failing, in this crisis, to provide the answer, or even a crumb of comfort. There was no answer, there was no comfort either, but Arlene still believed there was. She still half-believed that this mythical character, this Miss Know-it-all Colby of hers, was going to explain what couldn't be explained.

"You're expecting too much of me," cried Celia, bitterly and honestly. "Don't you see that I don't know any more than you do? I'm a human being too! It had to be that way just because. Just because Sophie's Sophie, and Lew's Lew, and you're you, and I'm me ..."

There, she was shocking the child; her great, innocent eyes were blank with astonishment. And no wonder. Celia herself was shocked at her own vehemence. She had not felt, until now, the full impact of last night. Lew and Sophie, she thought. A younger, uncoarsened Sophie. And a younger Lew, too discontented to have a conscience, frankly on the prowl—as he had been when Celia first met him. (Oh, Celia hadn't been too naive to know a wolf when she saw one. Not that it made any difference. She had been engaged, she remembered, really quite seriously engaged, and that made no difference either. By Christmas time of her first year in Turk Ridge she had been fathoms deep in love, and no longer engaged.) Lew and Sophie. And Arlene. Was that at the root of her outburst? A subterranean resentment against Arlene for being Sophie's daughter instead of her own?

"I don't know what's the matter with me, Arlene. I'm only making it worse for you, and I don't want to. Honestly, I don't want to. I just meant that you mustn't blame any of us. Sophie, or me, or Lew—"

"Blame Mr. Morgan?" gasped Arlene. "Oh, Miss Colby, I'd never blame Mr. Morgan!" In a coltish little rush, Arlene was kneeling beside her, her face alight with hero worship.

"Neither would I," said Celia. A little sadly: she was remembering how subdued and gentle Lew had been on the way home last night. "I wish I knew what to say, darling," he kept saying. "I wish I knew some way to make it up to you." She could have told him how—only she was such a lady, such a dyed-in-the-wool Penelope. Too proud to say what she wanted to say: "Spend tomorrow with me. Go fishing with Grover some other time." Too proud—and anyway, it wouldn't have worked unless Lew thought of it himself.

Well, he hadn't thought of it. He would give her a present instead, another extravagant peace offering. She had quite a collection, each one a memento of some slight, some unavoidable bit of bitterness. Like her platinum-and-diamond bracelet, commemorating the snub from the Penelopes. (For though Lew pretended to make fun of them, they represented—to him more than to Celia, actually; he had grown up on the wrong side of the tracks—the pinnacle of the social scale.) Or her sables, in memory of the dreadful solitary New Year's Eve she had spent in a Chicago hotel; Lew hadn't been able to get away, after all ...

And yet he always had "made it up to her" somehow or other—not by giving her presents, as he believed, but when he least intended to, by some humble word or gesture. For there was another Lew, beneath the veneer of self-assurance, a shy, unguarded Lew who melted her heart. That meltable heart of hers! There was no help for it. One Lew was as irresistible to her as the other. An incurable case of love.

"You think I don't understand anything," Arlene was saying, with fierce dignity. "You think I'm just a kid, I don't know what the score is. And maybe I don't get it, all of it. But some of it I do." Her face flooded with hot color, but she went on resolutely. "I've known about Aunt Sophie for quite a while. I mean I've sort of known that she wasn't just my aunt. I know about you and Mr. Morgan, too. He talked about you last night, Miss Colby, he said the most wonderful things about you ..."

"He did?" And there it was again, the little fountain of happiness inside her: she was the luckiest woman in the world, the one Lew loved, and she wouldn't change places with anybody anywhere.

"I think he's just super, Miss Colby. Just absolutely super. And Aunt Sophie does too, no matter what she said last night. She didn't mean all that stuff, she feels terrible about it, and she's scared he'll hold it against me and won't let me have the job— Oh, Miss Colby, he won't change his mind, will he? You don't think it will make any difference, do you?"

"I'm sure it won't. If you still want the job—"

"Want it?" Arlene clasped her hands dramatically. "I yearn for it! I don't care what Victoria—Miss Morgan—says, I yearn for it."

"Victoria?" A tingle, like a minute alarm, ran along Celia's nerves. She put her hand under Arlene's chin and looked down into the charming, eager face. "What about Victoria?"

"Nothing much. Just something kind of funny she said to me the other day, when I applied for the job. Mr. Morgan talked to me first, and then he called Victoria in and said I was hired, and when did she want me to start and so on. Well, then he had to go down to the lumber yard, so there we were alone, and it was so funny the way she said it. She'd been—well, not exactly snippy to me, but not friendly the way Mr. Morgan was either."

"Victoria's a reserved sort of person," said Celia carefully.

"Real reserved. It sounds snippy, what she said, and in a way it was, but in another way— I was all ready to leave, and I couldn't help it, I was so thrilled about the job that I told her so, and how I knew Mr.

Morgan was going to be a wonderful boss. 'Yes,' she said, 'he's taken quite a notion to you, hasn't he?' Okay, I thought, if you want to be that way about it, I can turn on the deep-freeze too." Arlene smiled icily, by way of demonstration. "'I'm sure I hope so, Miss Morgan,' I said, but she didn't pay any attention, she looked at me so funny, and she said, 'You're not so lucky. You poor kid. Just because he likes you. You're not so lucky.'"

It was eerie, the way Arlene caught the quality of Victoria's voice, and her mannerism of barely moving her lips when she spoke. For a moment it seemed to Celia that Victoria was there in the room, a pale, tense ghost haunting them with those few bitter words; her face seemed to slide over Arlene's like a mask. Two such different faces, and yet Celia found herself remembering what Victoria had been like as a young girl ...

Jealous, she told herself. It was only natural that Victoria should resent an upstart like Arlene, blithely trespassing on what she must consider her own domain. That was all it was. Just jealousy.

"She didn't sound so snippy anymore," Arlene said thoughtfully. "It almost seemed as if she might kind of like me."

But that was the strange, disturbing overtone that Celia wanted to ignore. It made of Victoria something much more than just the jealously devoted daughter, unwilling to share Lew's affections with anyone else. She became, besides, a victim—beloved, but a victim all the same—aware of her own fate, and sending out a pitying cry of warning to one in the same danger. (Fantastic, Celia told herself. Victoria and Arlene were nothing alike, and never would be. Hero worship or no hero worship, Arlene would never turn into the warped, ingrown creature that Victoria was.) And it made of Lew—why, it made him a menace, and his love a misfortune and a blight!

Celia gave her head a little shake, to clear it of such nightmarish vaporings. Her world came back into focus—here they were, she and Arlene (who was not in the least like Victoria), having a heart-to-heart in the big, shabby, familiar Home Ec room. No tragic ghosts flitted in the corners. There were the sewing machines against the wall, and outside the windows the gray spring sky and rain beginning to fall.

"Look, honey," she said, "you can't expect Victoria to welcome you with open arms. Not after all these years of being the one and only apple of her father's eye. It's going to take her a while to—"

Footsteps thudded in the corridor outside, the door burst open, and Bud, from Underwood's Store, peered in. He looked excited. "Miss Colby," he stammered. "They told me you'd be here, and Mom said we must let you know, being a special friend of Mr. Underwood's ..."

"Yes, Bud. What is it?" He stopped just inside the door, a gangling figure in his frayed sweater and grocer's apron, with the same beseeching expression in his eyes that used to be there when she called on him to recite in Freshman English.

"He—he got drowned some way, while him and Mr. Morgan were fishing. We just heard it. They're hauling him back to town now, and Mom said we must let you know."

"Grover's dead?" Her incredulous whisper bounced back at her from the sewing machines. Arlene, still kneeling beside her, gasped. Bud took a couple more steps toward her and thrust out his hand awkwardly. "Oh no, it can't be! Grover can't be dead."

Bud's eyes filled with tears. In a high thread of a voice that kept threatening to get completely away from him, he told her the few details that he and Agnes had been told. And when he had finished it was a fact: Grover was dead. (Grover. Not Lew. At the heart of her grief was that flicker of shamed relief. Not Lew. Grover.)

"Where is Agnes? At the store?" she asked. "Maybe there's something I can do—"

"Go right ahead, Miss Colby," whispered Arlene. "Don't worry about the place cards. I'll finish them up."

Celia stared blankly at the litter of brushes and paints on the table. "Yes. Thanks," she murmured before she followed Bud out the door.

There was not much that anyone could do for Agnes. Bereft, drenched in tears, she roamed the dim recesses of the store, reminded at every turn of Mr. Underwood's kindness, his wisdom, his impossible, impossible death. The window display—he had complimented Agnes, only yesterday, always so nice that way, appreciated every little thing. The new line of hats—he and Agnes had deliberated over the order, he claimed he'd be lost without Agnes, all ladies' hats were unbelievable to him. Just his little joke, of course, everybody knew what good taste he had. The candy counter—he had given away more than he ever sold, knew every child in town by name, yes, and by choice in lollipop flavors, too. Betty Licorice Peterson, he used to say. Susan Orange Fletcher. Bobby Raspberry Hall ...

The homely, loving details set Celia to weeping too. She could not shake off a recurrent feeling that this was a dream, at any moment Grover would trot in, dear, familiar, fussy Grover in his alpaca jacket. "Now, now, what's going on here? What's all this weeping and wailing and gnashing of teeth about?" The purest wishful thinking. Already Grover's voice, the patient but dignified tilt of his head, his eyes with their gentle twinkle, were fading, ever so slightly, into the past. But the picture of him as she had last seen him was still sharp-edged—teetering in the store doorway yesterday, enjoying his morning cigar, waiting for his few minutes' chat with her. And clearest of all, for some reason, was the clasp of Grover's hand—his warm, dry, steadfast hand folding itself over hers, seeming to say here I am whenever you want me, here I always will be …

"I knew something was wrong." Agnes was off again on still another mournful ramble. She wiped her poor tomato-red nose and drew a quavering breath. "The minute I laid eyes on him, after he came back from the bank, I could see it. He didn't look right, somehow. But I didn't let on. I says, 'Well, Mr. Underwood, you got it all settled, I hope?' I didn't want him to think I was snooping, but still at the same time— 'Oh yes,' he says, 'it's all settled,' and there was the funniest look on his face. 'We're going fishing tomorrow,' he says, 'Lew and me—that is, provided you'll let me have the day off.' And that was all he said about it. Not another word. It wasn't like him, Celia, I'm not trying to make out he told me every last thing about the store, because he didn't. But last year, when he got the loan from Mr. Morgan, didn't he come back all excited, just busting with the news, yes, and didn't he haul out a bottle of his Pa's brandy, and nothing would do but we must all have a nip, him and Bud and me, to celebrate. There was something went wrong, I know it just as sure as I'm standing here, it's my opinion that Lew Morgan turned him down—"

"Oh, he wouldn't!" cried Celia. "Lew wouldn't do a thing like that to Grover!"

"—drove him to his death," Agnes swept on, unmindful of where the chips fell. "Mr. Underwood wouldn't want to live, if he didn't have the store anymore. It meant the world and all to him."

"Agnes, stop it!" Genuinely angry for a minute, Celia took hold of the old woman's bony shoulders and gave her a little shake. "You're talking nonsense, and you've got to stop it right now. I won't have you spreading talk like that around town! There's not a word of truth in it. Do you think for a minute they'd be off fishing together if Lew had turned him down?"

It brought Agnes up short. "Well," she admitted slowly, "no. I guess they wouldn't, at that."

"Of course they wouldn't!" To her annoyance, Celia found that she was assuring herself as much as Agnes. She knew what Lew thought of Grover's business methods. Too well for complete comfort. Last year she had done a good deal of arguing in Grover's behalf—telling herself all the time that Lew was just letting off steam, he never really intended to refuse the loan. But this year she had not had a chance to argue; she had not even known that Grover was asking for another loan. A shadow of uneasiness crept over her.

But of course, if Lew had refused (and of course he hadn't) they wouldn't have gone off fishing together. Anybody could see that.

The need to see Lew—and to get away from Agnes—began to take on the proportions of an obsession with her. But according to Agnes' rather confused report, Lew and Doc Fletcher had gone back out to the river. Something official about the coroner's report. She might try to call him at home. But if he wasn't there, it meant coping with Victoria, and it was uncanny, the way that girl could make Celia feel. Like a streetwalker who had somehow got her hooks into Lew and from whom he must be protected, discreetly but firmly.

All the same, she decided, she would try calling him, as soon as she finished the coffee Bud had brought in from the Dew Drop Inn. Because if she didn't get out of here pretty soon, her own image of Grover would be reduced, like Agnes', to a sodden mass of recollections ...

Lew himself came to the rescue. Agnes hadn't gotten it quite straight: he and Doc Fletcher were only now setting out on their return trip to the scene of the accident. He looked deathly tired, but his arms around her were solid, she could feel the steady stroke of his heart against her cheek.

"Oh Lew! I can't believe it— Poor Grover—" She disgraced herself by threatening to pull an Agnes act of her own.

"There there. I know. There there. I tried to call you from home ... Look, this isn't going to take long. I'll pick you up when I get back. Where you going to be?"

"Do I have to stay here?" she whispered. "I mean—"

He knew what she meant. He knew Agnes. "We'll drop you off at home. Victoria's coming down. That's the reason we stopped, to tell Agnes she'll be here to help with the arrangements, whatever has to be done. No reason for you to stay at all."

Ten minutes later she was alone in her room—which was where she wanted to be if she wasn't with Lew—stretched out on her studio couch, watching the gentle rain outside her window, and shedding her own gentle tears for Grover. It would have touched him, perhaps pleased him a little, to see her crying like this for him. He had seen her cry so often, but always for Lew, wild storms of tears that no one but Grover knew about. And that no one but Grover—her old, true friend, the best she had ever had—knew how to deal with. How selfish she had been with him! Absorbed as she was in herself and Lew, she could not help knowing that in his own unspectacular way Grover had once been in love with her too; and yet she had spared him nothing. She had used him shamefully, and his own willingness to be used did not excuse her. "Don't mind me," he used to say, "I'm just an innocent bystander."

And it was that quality in him that she (yes, and Lew too) had imposed upon—that capacity for playing second fiddle, with quiet, endless devotion. He had never paraded his own emotions; and so it had been easy to fall into the habit of forgetting that he had any.

Ah Grover, she thought (now that it was too late), forgive me, forgive Lew, we never bothered to notice your feelings ...

She realized that she may have convinced Agnes, but not herself. In her own mind she was quite certain that Lew had refused to give Grover another loan.

So she was prepared for Lew's answer when she asked him about it, later in the afternoon. She waited until they were settled at last in the back room. She had driven out to his house in her coupe, after all; it seemed simpler, because Lew's car was loaded with fishing tackle and the blankets and provisions he had brought back from the shack. They were alone in the house: Evvie had the rest of the day off, and Victoria was still downtown, helping Agnes with the arrangements. Dort and Whitt and Johnny would come out later for a drink ("I feel we all ought to rally round," Dort had explained piously over the phone to Celia. "I can imagine how upset Lew must be.") but in the meantime they had this quiet, cozy hour together beside the fire.

"Yes, I turned him down," Lew told her. His head came up defensively; he made a point of looking her in the eye. "What about it?"

"I don't see how you could do that to Grover, Lew. You knew what the store meant to him."

"Oh, for God's sake!" He flung himself up from the couch, paced to the window and back, and stopped in front of her, hunching his shoulders irritably. "If you'll listen for a minute, I'll explain how I could do it. It was the only way to save the store. What good was it going to do Grover or anybody else for me to keep on, year after year, throwing good money after bad? He was already in up to his neck. What kind of a friend would I be if I didn't try to stop him from sinking in deeper? The way he was running the store, it was bound to fail, and the only way to save it was to force him into running it different. It would still be Underwood's Store, he'd still be the manager, even though the chain owned it. The only difference is he'd be making money instead of losing it. If Grover saw it, I don't see why in the hell you can't!"

"Did he?" said Celia.

"Of course he did! Do you think he'd have gone fishing with me if he thought I was doing him dirt?"

Her own argument, come back to haunt her. She stared up into his tired, flushed face, wanting so much to believe him, longing for him to make this up to her too, as he had all the other things. He had not quite done it yet. But he would. She waited helplessly.

"He was just the same as always this morning, the same old Grover, fussing around because I hadn't packed my stuff to suit him. Why, I've known Grover all my life, I could have told if he was sore at me."

"Maybe not. I mean— He was the kind that kept his feelings to himself. Maybe we took him too much for granted, Lew."

"But we talked about the store, out there at the shack! I told him pretty much what I've told you, and it was all right with him. I remember exactly what he said. He said, 'I'm not worrying about it. Why worry? It's all settled, and that's that.' Does that sound like he was holding it against me? And then we started off with our stuff, and there wasn't a thing out of the way, until—"

He stopped abruptly. His forehead puckered up, like a puzzled child's, and he sat down beside her—all his bluster gone—and fumbled for her hand. "I don't know how to tell you exactly. It's just this funny feeling I've got—"

Rain whispered outside the window, where darkness had already fallen. One of the logs in the fireplace shifted, loosing a little shower of sparks. Celia could hear her own quick breathing.

"All he had to do was grab ahold," said Lew. He sat with his shoulders bowed wearily, not looking at her now, but staring down at his hands. He kept clenching them, stretching them, clenching them again. "We'd stopped there on the path. He kind of stumbled and shoved against me—I damn near went over the bluff myself—only I got my balance, but not in time to catch him. But there still wasn't any reason why I couldn't have hauled him up. I don't understand it. I just don't understand why he didn't grab on to the line and let me pull him up."

"He must have gotten panicky. He must have lost his head completely," said Celia. Her voice was a little breathless; she was mentally running away from Agnes' words. Drove him to his death. Mr. Underwood wouldn't want to live, if he didn't have the store.

"It could be. But then the way he looked at me, just before he let go." He paused and swallowed. "I don't know how to describe it. Not exactly a grin ... I don't know what you'd call it. I think he was saying something, but I couldn't hear what it was, and the look in his eyes— Godamighty, Celia, he didn't look like himself. He didn't look like anybody I ever knew, or anybody that knew me. And then he just let go." His own big, square hands opened out helplessly, in mid-air, and the eyes he turned toward her were full of loss and bewilderment. She felt the familiar flood of tenderness.

"Lew. It was just an accident, Lew. You did all you could. You mustn't brood about it like this." Did she believe her own assurances? No matter. Just so Lew believed them. He must be comforted, at any cost. "You know that Grover wouldn't—"

She glanced up and saw Victoria in the doorway. All stark black-and-white; not a trace of color in her pinched, bitter face, nothing to soften the glitter of her eyes. Celia shivered. That girl, she thought; she hates me, and she hates Lew too. Whether either of them knows it or not.

Lew did not know. He was not able to put a name to the look he had seen on Grover's face; he could not even see it on his daughter's face. In his terrible innocence he had sprung up and was fussing over Victoria, drawing her in toward the fire. He did not see at all. But such an uncanny conviction of danger—not from Victoria alone; other dangers too—possessed Celia that it was all she could do to keep from crying out a warning. Look out! Lew! Look out!

At that moment he seemed to her a willful, heedless child with no inkling of the consequences of his own egotism, and with no defense against hate (perhaps he had earned it? Celia did not care) because it never crossed his mind that hate was there. Only Celia—who, knowing him, still loved him—could see and save him from the dangers closing in on him.

10

They had been fantastically lucky. "Only because we deserve it," Johnny assured her when she said she was superstitious about such things; it couldn't possibly last. "What's luck, anyway? When you get right down to it, it's simply seeing your chance and grabbing it. These boys that scream about their tough luck just don't have the nerve to make the most of what comes their way. That's all. We've made our own luck."

And of course they had. Dort just as much as Johnny. Even more so, if you wanted to go back to last night. It was she who had seen in Sophie the opportunity they needed. Seen it and leapt at it. And it was she who had diared, at last, to crystallize into words the unspoken idea that had possessed them both for so long.

But once the enormous first step was taken, Johnny's boldness matched hers. Today proved that. He was as quick as she to see how Grover Underwood's accident, cutting short the fishing trip, changed the pattern—or not so much the pattern as the time. Tonight, instead of tomorrow night. They made the shift without a moment's hesitation. After all, as Johnny pointed out, tonight was better. They were surer of Sophie, this way. They might have had to do some finagling to keep her from starting back to Chicago too early tomorrow night; now they didn't have to worry on that score.

The first stroke of luck came up at Lew's, when Victoria—and why she did it was anybody's guess; certainly Dort didn't know what made that one tick—walked out and left them alone in the back room. Luck? Or seeing your chance and grabbing it?

It was a chance that Dort might very well have muffed. Because she couldn't help it, she couldn't quite forget what Johnny had said last night about playing the Victoria angle. She knew with her mind that his sympathetic, "poor Victoria" routine was just an act. But there was another, primitive part of her that remained unconvinced and that now and then took over—mind and all. Like a fever. So if it had been left to her ...

But it wasn't. Johnny was on the ball, if she wasn't. "Now," he whispered, the minute they were alone. "Where is it? The gun. Where is it?"

It jerked her back to reality. "Wait," she said. "She hasn't left the house yet. She's in the hall, talking to Evvie. Wait till we're sure."

The sound of Evvie clumping upstairs came first, then the front door closing behind Victoria, then the whine of the vacuum cleaner.

"Here," said Dort. She opened the desk drawer. There it was, way in the back. Loaded? Yes; Johnny checked it before he slipped it into his jacket pocket. With that gesture—a throb of excitement shot through Dort—he committed himself. Both of them. It was a step as enormous as the one bridging the gap between wordless idea and spoken plan. From thinking to talking. And now from talking to doing. There was a vast difference.

Johnny didn't give her time to brood. After one quick, cool glance at her, he said briskly, "I'll keep an eye out for Lew while you type the letter. We've got plenty of time, and with that vacuum cleaner going Evvie's not going to hear the typewriter. Get going, sweetie."

They had already drafted the letter, last night, so as to be ready when the chance came. And here it was: Lew's portable right here on the desk, his stationery in the drawer. For it was a letter from Lew to Sophie. They had toyed with, and rejected, the notion of a telephone message to Sophie out at her brother's farm. Too risky. Telephone calls could be traced; and Sophie, dumb as she was, must know Lew's voice pretty well. Very possibly too well to be fooled by Johnny masquerading as Lew. So they had settled on a typewritten message, even though getting it to Sophie was going to be a problem ...

That was where they had their really phenomenal stroke of luck. Beyond anything they could have imagined. The letter was typed (it was a cinch to fake Lew's slapdash signature) sealed, and ready; they were tackling the problem of how to deliver it without themselves appearing to have anything to do with it—when bing, the doorbell rang, and who should be standing there but Sophie herself!

At first Dort, who had answered the door, could only goggle at her. Sophie had a scarf tied over her head (oddly becoming); and her bright green shortie coat was spotted with rain. Her face looked drawn. But determined, too, as if she had charted a course for herself and was going to stay on it, no matter what. The sight of Dort seemed to throw her off balance; for a moment she goggled too.

Then she said, "Oh, hello. I didn't expect— I mean, I wanted to see Lew. Mr. Morgan. Tell you the truth—" She made a hungry little snatch at the comradeship of last night— "I guess I owe him an apology. The way I acted last night. After he gave Arlene a job, and all. I don't know what got into me. So I just decided, the least I can do is tell him I'm sorry, and if he slams the door in my face, well, anyway, it don't hurt to try."

"He isn't here just now, but won't you come in anyway?" Dort's mind was working furiously. They couldn't, of course, just hand Sophie the letter; they couldn't afford that obvious a connection. But there must be some way. It was unthinkable, to have to waste an opportunity like this. To gain time, she kept talking, pouring out the story of Grover Underwood's death—anything to keep Sophie here until they could figure out a way.

Sophie had not heard about the accident. The easy tears sprang to her eyes: poor Mr. Underwood, the nicest man, why, one of the very first things she could remember was coming in to Underwood's when Pop did the Saturday trading, playing with the iron rabbit doorstops, and Mr. Underwood always gave her a stick of candy ...

She let herself be drawn into the hall. Automatically, Dort produced sympathetic murmurs; her ears were strained for some sound from the back room, some signal from Johnny. He must have recognized Sophie. Was he, too, mentally wringing his hands over the opportunity that must not be wasted, the chance that must be seen and grabbed?

When he opened the back room door and looked out, with an air of polite interest, Dort knew right away that he had figured out a way. His eyes had that glow. Her heart soared.

"Oh, Johnny," she said. "You remember Sophie, don't you? (You don't mind if I call you Sophie, do you?) We met her last night, at the hotel—"

"Of course I remember her." He came out into the hall, smiling; at once Sophie's hands got busy, fumbling with her scarf, smoothing her hair. "How are you, Sophie? Won't you come in and sit down?"

Dort raised her eyebrows at him as she followed Sophie into the back room, but all she got for an answer was a slight narrowing of his eyes. All right, so she didn't need to be cued yet. She would take it slow and easy until he gave her some kind of a tip-off. He could trust her not to foul things up for him.

"I'm sorry we can't offer you a drink," he was saying to Sophie. (The brandy bottle was no longer anywhere to be seen. Well, of course that made sense. Give Sophie so much as a whiff, and she'd be here till the bottle was empty. And whatever Johnny's plan was, it could hardly involve Lew's coming home and finding Sophie here.) "But the fact is, we're not sure where Lew keeps his liquor—"

"Oh no, thanks. Oh no, I wouldn't think of it," said Sophie. She licked her lips. "Not at this hour of the day. I never take a drink before five. You know, like they say, till the sun's over the yardarm. I can't stay, anyway. I just wanted to see Lew for a minute. Such a terrible thing about Mr. Underwood, Mrs. Morgan here was just telling me ..." She chattered on, and while she chattered Dort noticed—for what it was worth—that Johnny was unobtrusively steering her over to the easy chair beside the desk.

"Oh well, you can sit down for a minute, can't you?" he said. "Here. This chair's the most comfortable. Cigarette?" He bent over her attentively, offering his case and a light. There was no doubt about it; if anybody could make a woman feel cherished, it was Johnny.

With a grateful, flustered little sigh, Sophie sat down and crossed her ankles. There was something wistful in the way she looked around the room. As if she had often wondered what Lew's home was like and at last was finding out. "My, isn't it nice and cozy," she said. Her glance took it all in, fireplace, bookcases, couch, desk— All at once her eyes got bigger than ever. Her mouth fell open a little, and she leaned forward.

"Well, what do you know about that," she said softly.

Dort felt her own eyes drawn irresistibly to the focus of Sophie's attention. And it was all she could do to keep from laughing out loud. Because what Johnny had figured out was so simple, so easy and natural. Propped up on the uncovered typewriter was the square white envelope, with the name Sophie Barta printed on it in heavy black letters.

"What?" said Johnny, all innocent interest. "What's the matter?"

Sophie put out her hand, then, with a self-conscious glance at Dort and Johnny, drew it back. She laughed nervously. "Why, it's just— It's so funny. It's got my name on it!"

"What? Oh, I see," said Dort. She picked up the letter, peered at it as if she had never seen it before. "Why, it is addressed to you, isn't it? It's Lew's stationery. Looks like his printing."

Johnny stood beside her, peering too. "Well, well. Small world, isn't it? Or something. Looks like he was planning to deliver it to you by hand."

Dort put it down, delicately, on the arm of Sophie's chair. Still Sophie didn't touch it, except with her eyes. She couldn't keep them off of it. "Oh, do you think I should?" she said.

"Well, it's got your name on it," Dort pointed out. "I don't know. It's up to you."

"I know, but— I mean, why would Lew be writing to me?"

"You've got me," said Johnny. He lit a cigarette for himself. It was obvious that his interest in the letter was for politeness' sake only, because Sophie found it so remarkable. "But it seems that he did."

"Maybe something about Arlene?" offered Dort.

"Why, sure." Sophie let out a breath of relief. "I never thought of that. But that must be it, of course. Oh Lord, you don't suppose he's decided not to give her the job, on account of last night—" She looked up at them pleadingly, then back at the letter. She picked it up. At last. "Oh no. I can't feature him being that mean ... Well, what the hell, it was laying right there in plain sight with my name on it. So why shouldn't I open it?"

For another nerve-wracking moment she hesitated, while Johnny sauntered over to the window and looked out at the rain. While Dort clenched her teeth to keep from saying it out loud: Open it, for God's sake open it. Get it over with. She didn't trust herself to move until Sophie ran her chipped red fingernail under the flap of the envelope, pulled out the sheet of paper and unfolded it. She was a slow reader, and her lips moved as she read. Dort stole a glance at Johnny; he had stopped watching the rain, and though his attitude was still passably casual, his eyes weren't. They gleamed like opals in his dark face.

In a way, it was a masterpiece of a letter. Brusk, like Lew, not overly concerned with fine phrases or anything except the point. Which was that he wanted to see Sophie. Privately. About Arlene. Something strictly between him and Sophie; his family and Celia were to be kept out of it. That was why they would have to meet secretly. Could Sophie arrange to be in the summer house tonight, say between seven thirty and eight? In true Lew style, he assumed that she could, and launched at once into explicit instructions. She was to leave her car a couple of blocks away from his house, slip into the summer house, and wait for him there. He'd be there too, the minute the coast was clear and he could get away. Meantime, no telephone calls, please, on account of the family. He knew she'd make it if she possibly could. And he was hers, as ever, Lew.

It made a new woman out of Sophie. The drawn look around her eyes vanished, her cheeks flushed up, her lips parted in a tremulous smile of hope and excitement ... Who knew what golden visions she saw ahead for Arlene? Or what she might be reading into the letter's few careless endearments? Anything was possible, with a foolish romantic like Sophie. When she looked up her eyes were blank with happiness.

She's in the bag, thought Dort. She'll be there tonight, all right. Now if we can just get her out of here before Lew turns up—

But of course Sophie too was anxious to follow instructions and avoid Lew until the witching hour. She stuffed letter and envelope into her purse and sprang to her feet.

"Everything okay?" asked Johnny casually. "No dire news, I trust."

"Oh, no. Everything's swell." She turned eagerly to Dort; for a minute the simple-minded creature seemed on the brink of spilling it all, quoting Dort's own letter to her, word for word. But she caught herself in time. "It was for me, all right," she said. "Nothing very important. Just—just something he forgot to mention last night. Look, it's been real nice seeing you, but I've got to run along now. If you're still here when Lew gets back, tell him I found the letter and took it. He won't mind. In fact, he'll be— Well, anyway, thanks again for everything. I mean last night. And everything."

They saw her to the door, watched as she dashed out through the rain to her car and sputtered off. She almost missed the curve in the driveway, she was so busy scanning the grounds, spotting—for future reference—the summer house where she would wait for Lew tonight.

Johnny's hand closed over Dort's, exultantly. They did not speak until they were in the back room again; even then it was only a few incoherent, triumphant words, and a kiss that left Dort breathless.

"Johnny," she whispered, "we mustn't. Evvie might—"

"The hell with her. Let's get out of here. We'll tell her we can't wait any longer, but we'll be back later ... Now all we've got to do is make sure Lew's here too, on the spot at the right time. What worries me is Celia. How do we know she won't get him to take her out somewhere and gum everything up?"

"I don't think so. On account of Grover Underwood. She and Grover were pals from way back. I could even call her. Yes. Why not? Tell her we're all planning to gather up here for a quiet drink or two, we know Lew will want her too—"

"That'll do it. Ah, Baby, my beautiful baby with brains ... Come on, let's scram." He looked the room over, ducked back of the couch to retrieve the brandy bottle, and replaced it on the table.

"There's one other thing," said Dort. She went over to the window and performed a brief but major operation on the cord that pulled the green velvet drapes open and shut. "This gadget gets out of whack every so often. Nobody's going to be surprised if it doesn't work tonight." She tugged experimentally, and nodded in satisfaction when nothing happened. Nothing would happen, until they got a new cord. Tonight, with the lights on and the drapes undrawn, Lew—in his favorite chair, with his profile toward the window—would be spot-lighted, like an actor on a stage. An extraordinary feeling of power spread through Dort: she and Johnny had not only set the stage, they had written the play, they were running the whole show. It remained only for the cast to act out the roles assigned to them—and they had no choice, they could no more change the course of action than characters in a play could step out of their roles.

"All set?" asked Johnny from the doorway.

"All set," she answered, and a gust of ecstatic laughter shook her …

She never quite recaptured that feeling of limitless power. Doubts crept in, a superstitious mistrust of their own good luck. Fate might be only playing a cat-and-mouse game with them, teasing them with these preliminary bits of success. The main event still lay ahead. Plenty of time for disaster. Dort's throat went dry at the thought. And once, while she was brushing her hair, getting ready to go back to Lew's, she looked in the mirror and saw what seemed the face of a stranger, no one she had ever seen before. *Who are you? What are you doing here? What are you planning?*

But that was only momentary. The sight of Johnny, so coolly impervious to panic, brought her back to her senses. Johnny held the key to her whole life; who she was, what she was doing and planning, had no meaning without him. It had always been that way with her, and now—she saw it for the first time—it would be that way with Johnny, too. Whatever happened from here on in happened to them both; tonight's project welded them together, world without end, amen.

Perhaps he saw it too. For all his air of nonchalance, his hands, cupping her face for one last kiss, were not quite steady. "Come on," he said. "Let's go make ourselves some more good luck."

The others were all there when they arrived. They met Whitt in the hall; he was coming out of the kitchen with the ice bucket in one hand and a bottle of Scotch in the other. Errand boy, thought Dort as she submitted to his kiss; an errand boy, pure and simple.

The atmosphere in the back room struck her at once as peculiar, though it was a little while before she figured out why. Lew looked tired and rather preoccupied, but that was natural enough. And Celia's face showed traces of tears; that too was natural enough. She was sitting on the couch, with her head tilted up toward Lew in frank devotion, and the firelight dancing on her rich, untidy hair. Dort had always had a certain wary respect for her. Not that they spoke the same language, really; Celia's candor was incomprehensible, even a little shocking, to Dort. But she knew female electricity when she saw it. No, she had never underestimated Celia.

And at the moment there was nothing in either Celia's or Lew's manner to account for the peculiarly overwrought atmosphere in the room. Dort was halfway through her paces (sweet sympathy, as befitted a dutiful daughter-in-law), when she spotted its source. Victoria.

It was always easy to overlook Victoria, and she was standing outside the circle of fire- and lamp-light, with her back to the wall. She must have just come in. She was still wearing her raincoat; above its gleaming blackness her face was pinched and white. Her hands were in her pockets. Dort knew at once that they were clenched—as everything else about her was clenched, into a hard, tortured knot. Her eyes were fixed on her father in a stare that seemed almost obsessed; she saw nothing but him, she heard nothing, all her strength was concentrated in that strange, tense stare.

"Hi, Victoria," said Dort, and at the sound of her name Victoria's head jerked slightly, as if she were coming out of a trance. She closed her eyes.

"Hello," she said. Barely audible.

Silence descended, like a blight.

Then Lew said, "Victoria needs a drink. She's caught herself a cold or something." There was a faint edge of impatience to his voice. "We could all use a drink, when it comes to that."

"At your service," said Johnny, flashing his smile. "I'll tend bar. What'll it be?" (They had decided ahead of time on this maneuver, for safety's sake. Lew had a notably loose wrist with the Scotch bottle, and it behooved Johnny and Dort to stay sober tonight.)

There was quite a bit of bustle, with Johnny making drinks and Whitt helping Dort and Victoria off with their coats. Dort followed him out to the coat closet in the hall to ask, "What's eating on Victoria?"

But of course he didn't know. He mumbled something about a cold and aspirins. A cold! Aspirins!

"She didn't have a fight with Lew, did she?" Dort persisted. She didn't seriously believe that Victoria's odd behavior had any vital significance. How could it? But it was out of the ordinary, and tonight Dort felt a compulsion to investigate the slightest deviation. There should be no unexplained tag ends to trip over.

"A fight?" echoed Whitt. "With Dad? Good Lord, no! Why, Victoria's never had a row with Dad in her life!"

She'd be better off if she had, thought Dort. There had been something smouldering, like a subterranean fire, about that fixed stare of Victoria's.

But when they returned to the back room, Victoria looked as usual, colorless and trim in her expensive black suit, which might just as well have been a bargain-basement model, for all the good it did her. All Victoria's clothes were like that. In impeccably good taste, with absolutely nothing about them to catch anybody's eye. She sat, stiff and self-conscious, with her drink in her hand. A social nonentity, in the bosom of her family, as elsewhere.

"Did Johnny tell you, Lew?" asked Dort in her sprightly, daughter-in-law manner. "You had a caller this afternoon, when we were here before, waiting for you. Sophie whatever-her-last-name-is. She dropped in to apologize for last night, she said. She doesn't know what got in to her, to talk to you like that."

Lew shot a quick glance at Celia and then said easily, "Poor Sophie. She just had one too many. She doesn't mean any harm."

"That wasn't the way she sounded last night." Johnny gave a reminiscent chuckle. "For a woman who didn't mean any harm, she was talking a real good fight."

They were getting no rise out of Celia. (Not that that had been their purpose, anyway.) Her expression remained one of pleasant detachment, and this seemed to fluster Lew. He said, "Oh, well. Just a lot of talk—"

"May I have another drink, please?" Victoria was holding her empty glass out to Johnny. She must have finished it off at one fell swoop. "Pardon me, Dad, I guess I interrupted you. What were you saying?"

Her politeness was strictly mechanical; she had her mind on another drink, judging from the thirsty way she was waiting for her refill. Dort suspected that she hadn't heard a word that had been said. And it wasn't like Victoria to drink with such enthusiasm. Again she felt the twinge of uneasiness. There shouldn't be any unexplained tag ends, and Victoria was being one. Or maybe it was only Dort's own edgy nerves, conjuring up dangers out of nothing.

Except that she was not edgy. She felt a miraculous calm, and with it a heightening of her senses, as if she were seeing and hearing extra-clearly. Insignificant details—the pattern in the rug, the snap of the fire, the rain pattering on the leaves outside—seemed to spring out at her, fresh and distinct. Yet not distracting. Only Victoria, with her ill-timed vapors, remained a stubborn, puzzling nuisance.

After the tensions of the day, Lew was whole-heartedly relaxing. He sat (what a good boy he was!) in his favorite chair, with his feet stretched out to the fire. His face looked sad, rather dreamy, mellow with fatigue. "Who cares about food?" he said when, after a while, the subject was mentioned. "Evvie's not here. There's nobody we have to impress. Let's drink dinner tonight." Time was nothing to him; he let it slide by as if he had an endless supply. Once he got up and tried to pull the drapes shut; when the cord didn't work he grumbled mildly about "that damn contraption," peered out at the rain for a minute, and then sank back into his chair. And once—when for the third time Victoria broke into the conversation with an abrupt request for another drink—he turned to look at her in surprise. "Hey, what is this? You keep this up and you're going to get drunk, Baby."

"Yes," said Victoria, and held out her hand for the refill.

It was not quite seven thirty when Johnny made a trip to the kitchen for more ice. Dort went along to help. ("Oh no, Whitt, you've been doing all the work around here. It's time somebody else lifted a hand.") She waited—remembering to rattle the ice trays—while Johnny whipped out the back door. He was gone only a moment.

"She's there already," he said quietly. "Waiting in the summer house. I figured she'd be there ahead of time."

"We're all set, then," said Dort, and she saw his face with such clarity— the texture of his swarthy skin, a minute white scar on his chin, and below the shallow ridge of his brow his light-colored eyes ...

"That's right. All set. You're okay, aren't you?"

She nodded. "The only thing is, Victoria—"

"Forget her. She doesn't know what the score is. Forget her."

Which was ordinarily very easy to do. But tonight Victoria had worked herself up into some kind of a snit, no doubt of it. "What time is it?" she asked suddenly, and when Dort told her seven thirty, her eyes went wild, like a scared horse's. "Oh no, it can't be!" she stammered. "It mustn't be!" She got to her feet, clumsily, and stood there, swaying, with her hands pressed up against her temples.

"Victoria," said Lew sharply. "What's the matter with you?" He started to get up, but she shrank back toward the door, as if she thought he was going to hit her.

"Nothing. I'm all right. I just— I'll be back." She whirled. They heard her feet thudding along the hall and up the stairs. A door slammed. Then silence.

"I'll be damned," said Lew, "if I know what's—"

"I think I know," said Celia. She looked around at all of them candidly, then straight at Lew. "I think she's upset about—well, about me. About you and me. You can't blame her, in a way, for resenting me—"

"Resenting you! But she likes you! She's always liked you!"

Celia half-smiled. "You're not really very bright about women, darling. Ask Dort if she doesn't agree with me."

"Now you're putting me on the spot." Dort cocked her head judiciously. Though there was nothing to decide: Celia's theory hit the nail on the head. It explained everything. Except maybe the business about seven thirty, it can't be seven thirty. But then nobody could cover all the angles that went on in that screwed-up head of Victoria's. "But just between us girls, I think you've got something there ..."

"Women!" cried Johnny, throwing up his hands in mock despair. "They've got a logic all their own, bless their little hearts. Only don't let's try to grasp it, Lew. Let's stick to our rules and let them stick to theirs, and never the twain shall meet."

"I believe you," said Lew grimly. But he grinned a little. "For God's sake. Why Victoria should resent—"

"Never mind. We can straighten it all out later. I probably shouldn't have mentioned it. I wouldn't have, if I hadn't had too many of these." Celia tapped her glass ruefully.

"That's the thing about drink. It loosens the tongue, addles the brain, undermines the memory—" As at a sudden, dreadful thought, Johnny smacked his forehead and cast his eyes heavenward. "Oh Lord, *doesn't* it, though! The car windows. Now that I think of it, I could swear I left the back ones open. In all this rain. I can see it now, the flood waters rising, all the little flotsam and jetsam in the back seat ... Carry on at the bar, Whitt. I'll be back in a flash." He tore out the door. Not even a glance at Dort.

But she knew that it was now. It was going to be now.

"Whitt, darling," she said—just in case, errand boy that he was, he had any ideas about helping his old pal Johnny close the car windows— "Whitt darling, put a little sweetening in my drink?"

11

Once in her own room, Victoria stopped short, as if the drive of her terrible urgency had propelled her into nothing. Into a vacuum. Here she was at her goal—but why was it a goal? What had she meant to do when she pelted out of the back room and upstairs? The terrible urgency remained, pounding away like a useless machine, but she could not focus her will enough even to turn on the light. She could only stand here in the darkness, at the mercy of her plunging heart and brain. It whirled with images of faces—Dort's, Celia's, Johnny's, Dad's— and remembered voices saying half-remembered things. The past hour had been, for her, so full of sound and fury, and she must be drunk, all those drinks, yes, her head was splitting, that was why she could not remember ...

"It's almost seven thirty," said Dort's voice, and another, strangled-sounding voice cried out, "Oh no, it can't be! It mustn't be!"

Her head cleared. Seven thirty. One hour left. At this moment Fred must be driving through the dark, rainy night toward her and Dad and annihilation. "What's the matter with you?" he had rapped out, and she had been shrewd, she had not told him. He thought she was drunk. He did not know that she wished him dead. She herself had not known until tonight, but the pressure of the wish had been building up for too long, all her life; it had burst out into the open at last, and it was too much for her to bear. Only one thing could set her free. Death. Her own; or Dad's ...

Why not her own? She knew where the pills were. ("You haven't caught a cold, have you? Better take a couple of aspirins.") In Mother's bedroom; that was why she had come upstairs. Doc Fletcher had prescribed them for Mother's insomnia. Remember: no more than three at a time. Tiny packages of sleep, of escape. How easy it would be! No pain, no violence, only sleep blooming in her brain like a lovely, deadly flower. Why not?

She switched on the light beside the bed; in the mirror across the room a white, distraught face seemed to leap out at her in the moment before she turned and went noiselessly down the hall. Through the airless dark of Mother's bedroom—the smell of illness and defeat still hung here—she moved, to the bedside table. This was a secret mission; she did not turn on the light. She did not need to. The little bottle was there, in the drawer.

Why not her own death?

Fred was why not. Or perhaps not Fred, after all; but Dad himself, the streak of Dad in her that rose, a stubborn, fierce egotist, to fight for its life. To die now would be to miss everything forever, and she had already missed too much. Dad had kept her sealed off from life—while he himself relished it to the full. He had had his Celia and all the others; he had taken everything he saw that he wanted. Even now he held half of Victoria's heart in a crippling grip, and would, until he died. So crippling that she might never recover; she might always be the half-person she was now. But she had a right to find out. She would not be cheated out of her chance.

Death. Her own or Dad's. And because she was his daughter, fashioned in his ruthless image, it had to be Dad's.

Again the plunging, the whirling, the scraps of faces and voices. She was smothering. Air, she thought, and she stumbled over to the window and opened it wide. Like her own room, this one had a little balcony. She stepped out onto it; the vines that covered it rustled and stirred gently in the rain, and oh, it was cool, heavenly cool ... She took great gulps of the air. It smelled of night and wet lilacs and geraniums—for of course Mother had her everlasting potted plants here, too. A dog barked somewhere, and on the road beyond the maples and the summer house the lights of a car swept by on the way to town.

She steadied herself against the balcony rail. She was still holding the bottle of pills, the tiny packages of sleep that could as easily bloom in Dad's brain as in hers. Almost as easily. Yes. Why not? There was still time. If she were to go back downstairs—no longer beside herself, but the mousy Victoria that people seldom noticed—and make a nightcap for Dad ... Because she often did that; he liked her to fuss over him. And then if drowsiness were to overtake him—and why not? tired as he was—and she would still be there, fussing over him, shooing everybody out, getting him to bed ...

And Fred would come, and she would be free, and no one would know until tomorrow morning that there was anything extraordinary about Dad's sleep. Her mind stretched out, for a moment, beyond tomorrow morning. There would be questions. But who was going to believe that a model daughter like Victoria would wish her father dead? Her whole life stood behind her, an unimpeachable witness.

She closed her eyes and leaned forward, lifting her face to the cleansing rain. One last minute of innocence—but what was innocence without freedom?—and then she would do it. She would go downstairs and do it.

It was almost like a mirage. When she opened her eyes, there was only a screen of trembling springtime leaves between her and the lighted windows of the back room. She had forgotten how, from this side of the house, you could look down on the side yard and, back of it, the rear wing, jutting out at a right angle. With the drapes undrawn (that bothersome cord, always getting out of kilter) and the mellow lights inside, the back room might have been a scene on a stage, and the dark balcony where she stood a box. Yes, the effect was that fascinating, not-quite-real effect of a theater. She could see Dad quite clearly, in his chair by the window. Johnny—or maybe it was Whitt; she couldn't be sure—was fussing with the bottles on the table. She caught only a glimpse of Celia's gray dress against the couch. That was Dort's arm, winking with her wide rhinestone bracelet, holding out her glass toward whoever was making the drinks.

She gave a sudden sob. Dad, she thought, oh Dad, Dad, forgive me, I have to ...

Something outside the little stage of the back room window moved.

A darker, denser shadow among the lilac bushes close to the house. Almost directly beneath her. Wind? There was no wind; only the rain pattering straight down. A trick of her imagination? She waited. It moved again, something cautious and purposeful edging toward the back room window.

The feeling of unreality, that she was watching an exciting scene on a stage, held her in a spell. It did not occur to her to scream; she was only the audience; the danger—for that crouching figure was all danger, all sinister intent—was a theatrical one, and would be averted in the nick of time. She leaned forward tensely, peering through the gauzy curtain of rain. The figure melted completely into the shadows at the angle of the main house and rear wing. Then once more it emerged, flattened against the rear wing, sliding closer to the lighted window. Predatory as a tiger on the prowl. It stopped, just outside the yellow square of light. Now, thought Victoria from her place in the box, now they will see the danger and avert it in the nick of time, and I'll be able to breathe again.

But still the characters in the spotlight remained unconscious of any peril. She could see Dad's profile clearly. He was smiling. He sipped his drink. He tapped a cigarette against his thumb nail. In the background Whitt-or-Johnny crossed toward the couch, and more of Celia's gray dress shifted into view. Dort was no longer visible; she must have gone back to the hassock.

The figure outside the window moved again. Not all of it, only its hand. Victoria caught the glint of what the hand was holding, and in that instant the spell of unreality was broken. This was no stage scene. This was murder. They were going to kill Dad; she knew it with a flat certainty that needed no reason, that was its own unquestionable reason.

She did not think. What she did was pure reflex, as ancient and as much beyond her power to control as the beating of her heart. Her hand shot out blindly, closed on the geranium pot, and hurled it, all in one lightning flash of movement. And she cried out, a wild, warning scream.

There was a crash. A sound like a car back-firing. Dad leapt out of his chair. Someone shouted. In the second before she turned and fled downstairs, Victoria caught sight of someone else straggling across the yard toward the lighted window, from the direction of the summer house.

When she got downstairs she was still clutching the bottle of sleeping pills.

12

Dort got there first. The others were too bewildered—the crash, the shot, the scream—to do much of anything for a minute or two. But Dort was one up on them; she had been braced for the shot. Not for the crash or the scream. Wrong, it's gone wrong, babbled an idiot voice in her brain, as she streaked out the kitchen door. She couldn't make it shut up. Wrong, it's gone wrong …

At first she could see nothing through the chill haze of rain. Trees and bushes loomed up all around her, unfamiliar and menacing; her feet kept slipping on the muddy lawn. Panic took hold of her. "Johnny!" she screamed into the empty night, and all at once it was not empty, after all, and she was not going to lose her head. She heard him rather than saw him: a warning shush, low but fierce, that came from close to the house, beyond the rectangle of yellow light from the windows. Or perhaps it was the sight of Sophie stumbling across the yard from the summer house—just as they had planned—that got her back on the track. It had gone wrong, yes; all they could hope for now was the saving of their own faces. Could they salvage even that? The letter, thought Dort, and the gun, my God, the gun. They had wrapped it in Sophie's glove, but if Johnny hadn't gotten rid of it somehow ...

He came tearing toward her, making sounds of innocent excitement, and behind her she could hear the others. They had only a second. But it was enough.

"The gun?" she whispered.

"I threw it out into the yard. Carry on."

Here they all were—Whitt in the lead, then Lew, and behind him Celia and Victoria. Victoria, the unexplained tag end that had tripped them up; they had her to thank for that unearthly yell, Dort would bet on it. Whirling, she pointed at Sophie.

"There she is!" she cried out. "There she is! What's she doing, sneaking around here?"

It was not so much a question as a decree. The force of it made Sophie falter in her advance; she seemed—if not indeed to sneak—at least to shrink. "Now wait a minute," she stammered. "Now listen."

But she produced nothing for them to listen to, even if anybody had been so inclined.

"Who? What in the *hell* is going on here?" That was Lew.

And Whitt: "Dort! Darling, are you all right? You shouldn't have—"

"It's Sophie!" cried Celia, and darted across the yard. "Sophie, what in the world are you doing here? What happened?"

Victoria said nothing at all. Just stood there, with that sleepwalker look on her face. She had to be the one who had yelled. How much had she seen? Damn her. How much was she going to tell if she ever came out of her trance? They would simply have to out-talk her, she and Johnny …

Johnny started talking. "I don't know who I saw, but I saw somebody sneaking around out here. After I closed the car windows. I started back, but then I caught sight of this character, whoever it was. Close to the house, moving toward the back wing, the window … It looked suspicious, you know, somebody hanging around like that, at night. I thought I'd better find out what was going on. So I started following them, but then before I could see who it was, bam, something fell out of the sky, damned if I know what, and there was this yell, and—"

"It couldn't have been me!" Sophie burst out. "Because I was in the—" They all waited, but she didn't finish. She stopped short, guiltily.

One of them must find the gun, Dort was thinking. Should she …? No. Better if one of the others noticed it. Only not Sophie, please God; if it turned out to be Sophie, the show was over. Nobody could ever be persuaded that a guilty Sophie would call attention to the gun and her own glove. Dumb she was, but not that dumb. Just dumb enough; no one would ever believe, either, that she might be doing it out of craft, knowing that it would clinch her innocence. Not Sophie, please, not Sophie.

She might have known that it would be Lew. He wasn't like Celia and Whitt, diverted by the first side issue that came along. Nor like Victoria, locked away in an inaccessible world of her own. (If she would only stay there, where she belonged!) No. Trust Lew never to lose sight of the main point. Which was that a shot had been fired; so where was the gun? While the others gabbled, he was doing a little searching.

He found the flower pot first. "Here's what fell out of the sky," he said, and scuffed with his foot at the broken shards, the clots of soil, and the one broad leaf that still reared up straight, trembling in the rain. "Or rather, out of the balcony." Everybody gathered round to peer—Dort as curiously as the others. A potted geranium. Of all the ignominious agents of defeat! It must have missed Johnny by inches. It might even have grazed his arm before it crashed against the house. Certainly it— and the wild shriek that had hurtled through the air along with it—had spoiled his aim.

Lew wasted very little time over it. He left them to their questions and exclamations (Had it fallen of its own accord? A wonder it hadn't gone straight through the window!) and got on with his search. Out of the corner of her eye Dort watched as he circled off in the general direction of the summer house; she saw him when he stooped.

"Here it is," he called. "It's mine. My revolver." He did not sound surprised. "Come on," he added. "We might as well all get in out of the rain. Now, now, Sophie, it'll keep till we get inside. Pull yourself together."

Obediently, they all trooped inside. In the back room again, they fell into a nervous silence. Except for Sophie, who had dissolved into tears. The cat still had Victoria's tongue. Lew's too, for the moment; he was looking very thoughtful.

"I don't get it," Whitt said at last. As if he ever got anything. "Dad's gun, and somebody prowling around. I just don't get it."

"There wasn't anybody prowling around when I got there except her." Again Dort aimed an accusing finger at Sophie. "There she was, sneaking—"

"I was not!" Sophie's voice came out blurred but belligerent. She surged forward in her bedraggled finery (she had blossomed out in the sequin dress for her tryst with Lew), her eyes flashing. "Why do you keep saying that? I was not sneaking! I heard the racket and came running just like the rest of you!"

"Well, somebody was," said Johnny mildly. "Like I said before, I couldn't see who it was. And before I had a chance to find out, down came the flower pot, and all hell broke loose. The shot, and the yell, and whoever it was streaked off toward the summer house, and then you all came pounding out, and ..." He paused, smiling a little, ruefully. "And thus endeth my career as Sherlock Holmes, I guess. I'm sorry I turned out to be such a flop."

"It's not your fault, Johnny," Whitt hurried to assure him. "That's another thing, that flower pot. Did somebody heave it, or did it just blow down?"

For the first time Victoria spoke. Very low; a dry, whispery sound. "It was me. They were going to kill Dad, and I—" Victoria seemed to wait, along with everybody else. But no more words came. She swallowed a couple of times. Her eyes were stretched wide, but blind-looking. Lew went over and put his hand on hers gently, and she jumped as if she had been burned.

"Who was going to kill me, Baby? Don't look so scared. They didn't do it. Look. I'm right here. It's all right. Who was going to kill me?"

"I— I was— I—" Again the whispery sound died away.

"Yes?" prompted Lew patiently. "You threw the flower pot? Where were you?"

"The balcony. I—" She had something clenched in her hand; she was staring at it incredulously, as if it horrified her. All at once she sobbed.

Just once. She shed no tears, she did not turn her face away. Just the one desolate sob. What could anyone do about a sob like that? It was so far beyond comfort that there was nothing to do but pretend it had not happened.

Which was what Lew did. He talked quickly, like a man hurrying to put as much space as possible between himself and the scene of some irreparable disaster. "What's this in your hand? Oh, I see. Sleeping pills. So that's how it was. You went into Mother's room to get these— I don't know that it's such a hot idea for you to be taking this stuff, but anyway—and of course from her balcony you could see whatever was going on. Now we're getting somewhere." He smiled at her anxiously. "You thought they were going to—"

"They were going to kill you," Victoria repeated. "I know, because I— They were. I know they were."

There was an uncomfortable silence. Everybody looked at what was in Lew's hand. The gun and the glove. "Well," he said finally, "somebody was gunning for somebody, sure enough. What did you see? Could you tell who it was?"

In a way it was the most agonizing moment of the evening for Dort. Their only chance was to out-talk Victoria, and yet they did not dare say a word until this impossible creature made the opening move. It wasn't enough that she had ruined their plan with her benighted meddling; now they must wait in impotent silence while she decided what further damage she was going to do, if any.

Her eyes moved from the gun to Johnny. Back to the gun. She wet her lips. And then—it didn't make any sense, but then what did make sense about Victoria?—she looked down at the little bottle in her hand. She dropped it as if it had suddenly turned into a rattlesnake. Just opened her fingers wide and let it fall; it rolled under the couch, and there she stood, rubbing her hand against her skirt like Lady Macbeth and her out-damned-spot routine.

"I can't say," she said primly. "It was dark. I can't say who it was. Don't ask me anymore."

A long sigh escaped Dort. She sat down, carefully, on the edge of the couch.

Johnny gave everybody a sunny smile. "That makes it unanimous. We don't neither one of us know nothing."

A gust of uneasy laughter sprang up, and quickly died. Lew tossed the gun on to the desk. The glove he kept in his hand, turning it this way and that in an absent-minded way. Sophie couldn't take her eyes off it. He spoke as if to himself. "So where are we? Johnny saw somebody, he's not sure who, and Victoria saw somebody, she can't say who, and my gun turns up out in the yard with one shot fired. So somebody was aiming to kill me." He looked suddenly angry. "You all take it for granted I was the target. I wasn't the only person in the room, but apparently it goes without saying that I was the only one anybody would want to kill. The man of distinction. That's me."

"Lew." Celia put her hands over her eyes, as if to shut out a nightmare. "Lew, don't talk like that. I can't bear it."

"Well, they didn't get me," he went on grimly. "But they tried. I'm not sure what's the correct procedure in a case like this. Call the police? Just pretend it didn't happen? We could, I suppose. Apparently we haven't disturbed the neighbors or anybody else with our little commotion. We don't have to call the police."

"But Dad," said Whitt, "if there was somebody prowling around, I mean an outsider—"

"He's long gone by now. Nobody here but us chickens—and Sophie." He turned to her, not unkindly. "How in the hell did you get in on this act, Sophie?"

The question startled her out of her preoccupation with the glove, which he was still holding. She started to say three or four different things at once, gave up on all of them, and at last—after an imploring glance around the room—blurted it out. "I was waiting for you in the summer house. Like you said. In your letter—when I stopped in this afternoon there it was, right there in plain sight with my name on it, so why shouldn't I take it, they said so too, why shouldn't I take it, and I know you said you didn't want your folks to know, but Jesus, Lew, you see the spot I'm in. I don't want to make any trouble for you, but she said it was me sneaking around out there, and it wasn't. I wasn't sneaking. I came running out, just like everybody else, when I heard the racket."

She stopped to get her breath. Lew asked cautiously, "You said—my letter?"

"I've got it right here." She began burrowing in the ice bucket bag. "It was on top of the typewriter, where you left it. Right there with my name on it. They were here when I found it, they can tell you. Your daughter-in-law and that fellow, what's-his-name. Sure it's your letter."

This could get very ticklish, thought Dort. The letter was a great idea—with Lew out of the way, unable to deny having written it. But he was not in the least out of the way. He was right here, conducting the inquiry into what should have been his own death, knowing very well that he had not written the letter to Sophie, and perfectly capable of figuring out who had. Yes, very ticklish. There must be no fumbling.

Dort opened her eyes wide. "Letter?" she said blankly. "What letter? Do you know what she's talking about, Johnny?"

"Why, no. No, I don't remember anything about a letter. We were here when she stopped in—remember, Lew? I think we mentioned it to you this evening—and the three of us chatted a while, had a cigarette together. We left right after Sophie did. But I don't remember any letter." He turned to Sophie, all friendly interest. "Where did you say it was?"

"On the— Listen. Are you nuts, or am I? You sat right here, both of you, right here in this room, and watched while I ... Here it is. This'll prove who's nuts." Emerging victorious from the struggle with her handbag, she thrust the letter at Lew. "Here it is."

He read it through in silence. His eyebrows lifted a little; once or twice he chewed at his moustache. But all he said was, "Yes, indeed. Here it is."

All right, so he was going to play it noncommittal. Dort refused to be thrown off balance. "It's funny we don't remember," she said. "Are you sure, Sophie? Or— Wait. I bet I know what happened. It must have been when you were in here alone. While Johnny and I were in the kitchen."

"But you didn't—" The indignation in Sophie's eyes gave way to an expression of hurt bewilderment. "Why are you lying? I don't get it. You said I was sneaking around out there, and now you're making out like you never saw the letter ... I just— I don't get it."

"She thinks you did it, Sophie," said Celia in that uneven voice of hers. She went over and stood close to Sophie. "She thinks you tried to shoot Lew."

Celia the candid camera, thought Dort. Trust her to lay it out in black and white. "Now that you mention it," she said, "that's exactly what I think. I think she stole Lew's gun this afternoon, while Johnny and I were out of the room, and I think she made up all this letter business just so she'd have an excuse for being here in case she got caught. For heaven's sake, Celia, you were at the hotel last night, you heard what she said to Lew. If she didn't threaten him, she did everything but. And I know what I saw tonight. She was trying to sneak away from the window, only we got out there too quick for her, so she dropped the gun and made a big production out of running toward us instead of away from us. Who else could it have been that Johnny saw prowling around out there? Who else had a motive, and a chance to get hold of Lew's gun, and—"

"Now, Dort," said Whitt nervously. "Now, darling."

"I can't help it!" she cried, and she buried her face in his shoulder. "I'm not like the rest of you, I can't stand around cool and collected, as if nothing had happened! Something *has* happened! Lew wouldn't be alive, if it weren't for Johnny—"

"And Victoria," said Lew abstractedly. He was looking at the glove again, so he did not see Victoria cringe.

"All right, so it's my glove!" Sophie burst out. "Ask me and get it over with! That's all you need, isn't it? My glove, and the pack of lies she's told—go ahead, call the police, arrest me. I don't *give* a damn! I didn't do it, I tell you, I didn't do it!" She flung out her hands in desperation, as if appalled not only at the situation, but at herself—a disheveled, unbridled figure screaming out denials that no one believed. "I didn't do it," she whispered. Then her voice rose again. "Lew! Lew, you know me! You know I wouldn't try to kill you!"

Lew sat down heavily. For a moment his face looked bleak with confusion. "Somebody did," he said helplessly. Then he got a grip on himself. "Hell, Sophie, you might. If you'd had a gun last night— You were sore enough, then." His eyes, keen and steady as searchlights, measured her. He made up his mind. "But not like this. No. I won't buy it. You'd never *plan* to kill me. You've never planned any of the things you've done. You do them, and think about them afterwards. And that's how it would be, if you killed me. No. I think Dort's—mistaken."

Dort stood motionless in the circle of Whitt's arm. She did not want to look at Lew, but it was as if his eyes were pulling her head up remorselessly, making her face him. He was not quite smiling. But almost.

She knew right then that they were lost.

13

"Of course Dort's mistaken," Celia echoed, and she had a moment's illusion that all was happily settled: not that she had really believed Lew would swallow the notion of Sophie's lying in wait for him, creeping up on him, cold-bloodedly primed for murder ... It was too preposterous, and—she needn't have worried—Lew saw it. He wasn't the man to lose his head in a crisis, even when it was a crisis that threatened his own life. Once more Celia shut the memory of that crisis out of her mind.

It was *all right*. The danger was past. Lew was safe, and she must forget the hairbreadth margin of safety. He was here, as vital as ever, dominating the scene, smiling—rather oddly—at Dort. Dort, who was of course mistaken. And who stood, white-faced and tense, with Whitt's arm around her and those extraordinary eyes of hers watching Lew as if—as if her life depended on it.

Celia's illusion of happy security vanished abruptly, with no more fuss than a soap bubble bursting.

Whitt put into words her own unspoken thought. "But Dad," he said, "how else are you going to explain it? I mean—"

"Yes. How else?" Lew's eyes rested, with brutal contempt, on his son. "You tell me." He let the silence stretch out and out. "All right, then, I'll tell you. It's time somebody put you wise. I tried to, the other day, when you turned up with that cock-and-bull story about wanting your share of Mother's money so you could invest it in this red-hot restaurant deal. I knew they'd put you up to it. If you weren't such a fool you'd know it too. You want me to spell it out in words of one syllable for you? All right, I will. I'll—"

"Lew!" cried Celia, but he shook off her hand without even a glance at her. His eyes, merciless, pale with fury, did not swerve from Whitt. They impaled him; no matter how Whitt might shrink, he could not escape. He did shrink, he cringed; and Celia felt a wrench of pity. Lew must not do this. He must not do this to his son.

He did it. "Your charming, devoted little wife," he said. "And your devoted old pal Johnny— You bet they're devoted to you. They've been itching to get their hands on your money since the day they met you. For God's sake, how long are you going to go on being a sucker? You going to let them rub your nose in it the rest of your life? You're the laughingstock of the town, that's what you are! Everybody's sniggering over the way you're providing a love nest for your wife and her—"

"No, no, it isn't true, it's not so ..." Whitt put out his hands, like a schoolboy trying to ward off a rain of physical blows. And a terrible, burning flood of shame rose in his face.

Celia heard her own voice babbling out frantic protests, and Johnny's saying something indignant, and Dort's gasping in outrage.

But Lew drowned them all out, he thundered them into silence. "I don't give a damn about that part of it. It's nothing to me who sleeps with who. But nobody's going to try to kill me and get away with it." He smashed his fist down on the desk. "I don't care how much dirty linen gets washed in public, and I don't care whose delicate feelings get trampled in the process. They're not going to get away with it. Do I make myself clear?"

Johnny stepped forward coolly. "I can't believe you're serious, sir. Are you actually accusing Dort and me of—"

"You'd better believe I'm serious, sir. Maybe when you and Dort are on trial for attempted murder you'll believe it. Sir. Because that's where you're going to wind up, the both of you. Any further questions?"

"Just one or two minor points." It was not so much terror now, as a sense of ruin—both accomplished and impending—that closed in on Celia. Even so, she felt an incongruous flicker of something like admiration for this slick, light-eyed young man who refused to be jolted out of his nonchalance. This guilty young man. For there was no doubt in Celia's mind; guilt fit Johnny (and Dort) as flawlessly as innocence fit Sophie. He was going on smoothly. "Forgive me if I seem slow about catching on to all this. It's kind of a shock, you know, to be accused of attempted murder. Especially when the victim is somebody you've always considered a friend. I think I get the general outline now, though. I'm supposed to have tried to shoot you because I wanted your money? Is that it?"

"Whitt's money." Lew smiled wolfishly. "Don't leave Dort out of it. Never underestimate the power of a woman, you know."

"That's right. I forgot the love nest angle there for a minute. If I had the time, sir, I'd tell you that in my opinion you're a damn dirty-minded old man—" Ah, that was cruel, that old man thrust. Lew's face darkened, and Celia put out her hand automatically. But he didn't hit Johnny, after all; perhaps he suspected that was what Johnny wanted. "—and that you're fabricating this whole thing precisely because you *do* care how much dirty linen gets washed in public. You're mighty anxious, I notice, to keep Sophie out of the picture. Why, I wonder? She threatened you in public last night; the gun was wrapped in her glove; she was hanging around outside, waiting to meet you in the summer house ... But all this counts for nothing with you. You dismiss it with a snap of your fingers. It couldn't be you're shying away from airing something pretty smelly in your own backyard, could it? If all that Sophie hinted at last night is true, I don't blame you for wanting to keep her out of the picture. Even if it means throwing Whitt and Dort and me to the wolves—"

"Look, I'm not going to argue with you," said Lew shortly. "You can have your say in court. Save your eloquence for then. You're going to need it."

"You're going to need something harder to come by than eloquence, you're going to need proof, and frankly—not that it's any of my business, of course—but frankly, I can't see that you've got a ghost of a chance of proving one thing against either Dort or me."

He might very well be right, thought Celia. In the welter of her feelings she snatched at it; it was another argument against dragging the whole mess into court. And was that what she wanted, Lew's would-be murderers to be let off scot-free, with never a murmur against them? No. That wasn't right, either. But without proof, what would be accomplished? Nothing except the public, total destruction of Whitt, and somehow—it was a conviction with Celia—somehow the destruction of Lew too. For his own sake he must be prevented from completing the wreckage job he had started on Whitt tonight (tonight? Oh no, long ago, long before tonight). Call it saving him from himself, call it anything, only save him because she loved him.

She watched him helplessly. He was at ease now, leaning against the desk with his arms folded; it occurred to her that, in a way, he was enjoying himself. "Maybe I can't prove it," he told Johnny, "but I can damn well try. You never know what you're going to turn up in the way of proof till you start looking. That letter, for instance, the one to Sophie, telling her to meet me in the summer house. It's very interesting about that letter. Just when am I supposed to have written it?"

"I haven't the slightest idea," snapped Johnny.

"Neither have I. Last night? No, because last night I was planning to stay out at the shack. I had no idea I'd be back here tonight. Today, then. But just when? Not when I first got back from the river. Victoria was right here with me, she knows I didn't write any letter then. And yet when Sophie drops in a little while later, here the letter is, right out in plain sight, with her name on it. Waiting for her. I had left. So had Victoria. Only you and Dort were here. You and Dort and the letter."

"But there *wasn't* any letter!" Dort burst out shrilly. "We told you before. She made the whole thing up! Typed it herself, and brought it with her tonight in case she needed it. Neither of us ever laid eyes on it, or heard a word about it, until tonight. She's got to explain what she was doing sneaking around outside, so lo and behold, here's this letter that nobody else ever heard of before!"

"Uh huh." Lew turned, abruptly, to Sophie. "Sophie. Can you type?" She blinked at him. "Who, me?" she said.

"Of course she'd say that," Dort began, but Lew cut in irritably.

"Let's stop playing games, shall we? The fact is that I think you and your friend Johnny tried to kill me, and I'm going to do my damnedest to get you for it. Don't waste your breath on me. Save it for the sheriff when he gets here." He reached for the telephone.

"Wait, Lew!" cried Celia. "Please! You must listen to me. You mustn't—"

But he was beyond listening to anybody. Nothing short of physical force was going to stop him; and it was Whitt—the weakling, the jellyfish—who supplied the physical force. The paralysis of shame that had held him mute, all but stupefied, suddenly loosed its grip on him. He made a convulsive lunge forward, grabbing for the phone. It took Lew so completely by surprise that he staggered back, leaving Whitt sprawled halfway across the desk with the phone in his hands. He seemed to be trying to pull the thing out by its roots. He was half-sobbing.

"No, no. I won't let you. You can't do this to me ..." Another moment, and Lew had his balance again. But Whitt hung on with the strength of desperation. The brief, ludicrous struggle ended with the phone crashing to the floor and Lew gripping Whitt—collapsed and limp now—by his shirt front, shaking him as if he were a rag doll.

"I'll do anything I please to you or anybody else. You're not going to stop me. What's the matter with you? You mean to tell me you'd let that little bitch you're married to—"

"She isn't! I don't care if she is! I don't *care!*"

"You don't care. Why, you— What kind of a son are you? Don't you understand that she tried to kill me?"

"I wish she had!" It was a kind of whispered scream; it must have been pent up inside Whitt his whole life long, released at last by the pressure of hysteria. Not courage. His face was terror-stricken. But he could not stop now. "I wish I'd had the guts to do it myself! That's the kind of a son you've made out of me ..."

The room rocked into silence. For a moment Lew stood stock-still. Then, with a gesture of disgust, he flung Whitt away from him. "Get out of my way," he said. He turned, and Celia saw it in his face: nothing on God's earth could stop him now. Whitt's mutinous flare-up, as inconsequential as a tissue-paper fire, had already burnt itself out; he was cowering in the arm chair, his head in his hands.

Even though she knew it was no use, she made one more try. "Lew, wait. Stop and think before you call the sheriff. It's not going to help! It's going to make it worse!"

"Worse for Whitt, you mean. My heart is supposed to bleed for him?" His face seemed to have turned to stone; his eyes had the pale glare of ice. "You heard what he said. He made it clear enough what he'd do to me if he had the chance. And the guts. Well, he hasn't, and I have, and isn't it just too bad." He picked up the phone, reassembled it, and asked for Sheriff Lally.

Celia closed her eyes and waited. It was so still in the room that she could hear the whisper of rain against the windows. Out in the hall the clock chimed eight thirty.

"Is Joe there, Mrs. Lally?" The telephone crackled with Mrs. Lally's long-winded explanation; let that woman get started and you had your hands full stopping her. "Okay, okay. I'll try him again then ... No, no message. I want to talk to Joe. Okay, Mrs. Lally, okay." The phone was still crackling when he hung up. "The honorable sheriff is God knows where drinking beer. That's a free translation." He lit a cigarette. "So we wait. We make ourselves comfortable and wait. Won't you have a chair, Dort? Johnny?"

"No, I won't have a chair. And what makes you think I'll wait, either? There's nothing to—"

"Oh yes, there is." Lew picked up the gun and hefted it. "Just try not waiting, if you don't believe me."

At that moment the front doorbell rang, and Victoria bolted. There was no other way to describe it. She was out of the room and streaking down the hall before the first peal faded. A second, shorter peal followed. Then a man's voice, hearty-sounding to begin with, quickly sinking to a murmur that blurred with Victoria's.

"Now what?" said Lew. A man's voice meant, of course, someone to see him. He stepped out into the hall, and Celia followed him. By this time her nerves were strung to such a pitch of anxiety that even a casual caller seemed like a menace. She caught only a glimpse of the man, whoever he was; the hall light struck a gleam from his glasses. Victoria's back—and how rigid her attitude was, as if she were facing a firing squad!—blocked off most of him. She had not opened the screen door to him. Maybe he was a stranger to her, too ...

Celia could hear what the man was saying now: a bewildered protest. "But look here, Vicky—"

Vicky? Lew had caught it too; he moved forward, halfway down the hall. He still had the gun in his hand. Who was this, calling his daughter Vicky?

"I can't help it, Fred. It's no use, that's all. It's no use." Celia hardly recognized Victoria's voice, it was so strained and harsh. "Just go away. Will you please, please, just go away ..."

"Who is it, Baby? What's going on here?" asked Lew.

Victoria shuddered. She did not answer or turn around. But she shuddered, as if the invisible firing squad had done its work and in another instant she would be slumping to the ground.

"Vicky," said the man. She slammed the door in his face.

"Victoria," said Lew sharply. "Who was that?"

She waited—it seemed forever to Celia—until they heard the muffled closing of a car door, and a motor starting up. At last she spun around. Her hands were clenched at her sides. She looked like a wild animal at bay.

But there was no violence in her voice. "Nobody," she said dully.

Lew took a few uncertain steps toward her. "Nobody? But it must have been somebody you know, Baby. You called him by name. You called him Fred."

"Did I?"

"Why, yes. And he called you Vicky ..." He put out his hand, like a man groping for something in the dark, and Victoria made a queer, gulping sound. Then she rushed past him, up the first few steps of the stairway. She seemed to crouch there, her hands clamped on the banister, her face painfully twisted. A lock of hair had fallen down across her forehead; the disarrangement—so trivial, so uncharacteristic—shocked Celia.

"He's gone," she said passionately. "So what's the difference? He's gone. It was nobody. I told you before. It was nobody, nobody, nobody!"

Lew did not move. His head was tilted back in a defenseless attitude; a freakish shadow struck his face, scooping out hollows in his cheek and temple. He had shrugged off Whitt's open outburst of hate as no more than a passing annoyance. But whatever it was he saw in Victoria's face shook him to the core. Even after she had run the rest of the way up the stairs, he remained motionless, staring at the spot where she had been.

He turned blindly when Celia said his name. "I don't understand," he faltered; and pity swelled in her throat, because she saw that—for a moment at least—he did understand, and could not bear to believe.

14

Well, Sophie gave up. Maybe the rest of them knew what was going on, but she couldn't make head nor tail of it. She had gotten lost quite a ways back, when she finally caught on that Dort and Johnny were accusing her of trying to kill Lew. That had been the limit. After that Sophie gave up.

All she wanted now—all she had wanted for hours, it felt like—was to get out of here. Why she had ever come in the first place ... Well, for Arlene's sake, of course; because Lew's letter had seemed to her to promise so much. Only, from all Sophie could make out, it wasn't Lew's letter, after all. And anyway, she should have known better than to expect anything from him. For Arlene, or herself, or anybody else on God's green earth. Not Lew. He looked after Mr. Lew Morgan. Period.

But he never thought I done it, she reminded herself, and her heart suddenly swelled. Give the devil his due: for all his orneriness, Lew knew her, he hadn't let them make her out a murderer. Her glove, and Dort and Johnny lying their heads off about the letter, and still he had said I won't buy it.

Yes, but what about the sheriff when he got here? That Johnny had a smooth tongue in his head; and if Sophie knew Dort, she'd be making with the eyes for all she was worth, not to mention the rest of her equipment. And no matter which way the sheriff was going to jump, Sophie was stuck—just like everybody else—until he got here. Words, stately words like evidence, witness, testify, set up an awesome reverberation in her head. Just the thought made her throat go dry with apprehension.

They might as well face it, though: nobody was going to talk Lew out of getting the sheriff up here. Not even Miss Colby, nor his son, his poor nothing of a son— She stole another glance at Whitt, who still sat with his head in his hands, shivering now and then like a whipped dog. She didn't care, it wasn't right for Lew to do his son that way. It wasn't any way to do. A wife like Dort, and a father like Lew. Oh brother, thought Sophie, what a life Whitt must have led. When it came to that, Victoria ... You'd think Victoria Morgan would have the world on a string if anybody ever had. But Sophie would bet on it, that girl didn't know what it was to have a good time. Why, she looked as if—

The doorbell rang, and Victoria was out of there so fast it made Sophie blink. After a minute Lew stepped into the hall too, with Miss Colby tagging along, and—again Sophie blinked—Dort and Johnny didn't waste one split second, they made for the tall French windows like a bat out of hell.

Sophie hadn't opened her mouth, but Johnny gave her a shove as he went past. "One peep out of you, and you'll get it good," he whispered. Dort was already halfway through the window, without a backward glance at Whitt, who had lifted his head and was watching her groggily. It was Johnny who remembered. "What about you, Whitt? You going to—"

Whitt didn't take his eyes off Dort. His face twitched. "You don't need to worry about me. You're rid of me. That's what you wanted, isn't it? To be rid of me. Well, you are."

It was doubtful if Dort heard him at all. And Johnny didn't wait for him to finish. He slid out the window quick as a cat, and after that there was nothing but the fire hissing softly, and Whitt staring at the window, and Sophie standing there with her teeth in her mouth.

She eyed the French windows longingly. They had beat it; why shouldn't she? It would be easy enough ... except that it would be just her luck to get caught. And that would look great, wouldn't it, to be nabbed clambering out of a window behind everybody's back. No. She wasn't going to give anybody another chance to accuse her of sneaking around. (Dort's phrase. It still rankled.) She wasn't like Dort and Johnny; she hadn't anything to hide, and she wasn't going to act as if she had. Come to think about it—Sophie's breath quickened—they had like as not cooked themselves, once and for all. They were gambling on Lew's cooling off and dropping the whole business, now that they had scrammed. And he might; if Miss Colby had her way he would. It was a long shot, though. They had a head start, and it was anybody's guess what hideout they might be heading for, but it was still a long shot.

Compared to them, Sophie was going to look pure as the driven snow to the sheriff. There was just one thing: people were going to ask why she hadn't hollered her head off instead of standing here tongue-tied while they got away. The reason why was too complicated for Sophie to explain, even to herself. But people, such as Lew, were going to ask.

Unless she could make it look as if she too had been out in the hall. Why not? It was a free country, and she didn't need to worry about Whitt. He'd had his mind on other things than Sophie Barta's whereabouts. It wouldn't surprise her if he'd forgotten there was any such person. She started edging toward the door. He didn't bat an eyelash in her direction. A few more steps and she was out, and one glance told her that nobody in the hall was going to notice her comings and goings, either.

Victoria was part way up the stairs, leaning over the banister, and down below were Lew and Miss Colby—all three of them lost to everything except Victoria's words. She flung them at Lew, like a handful of pebbles. "He's gone. It was nobody. I told you before. It was nobody, nobody, nobody!"

Sophie got it, just like that. Brains she might not have, but she had always been able to smell romance a mile away. She felt an automatic, pleasurable quiver of excitement. Not to mention surprise: who would have thought that a Miss Priss like Victoria would come up with a love interest? A secret love interest; somebody Lew wouldn't approve of. And of course that figured. No matter who the guy was, he wouldn't be good enough for Lew's daughter, the apple of his eye ...

The quiver, the cozy glow, faded. There was something in Victoria's face that didn't fit either the role of star-crossed lover or apple-of-the-eye daughter. Something that reminded Sophie of—well, of Whitt when he had lashed out at Lew a little while back. But that was crazy; everybody knew that Victoria was her father's favorite, as devoted to him as he was to her. It was just crazy. Sophie shifted uneasily from one foot to the other. If this was what happened to you, when you had Lew for a father

It wasn't the same thing with Arlene, of course. Not the same at all. Arlene was just going to work for him. He wasn't going to adopt her or anything like that. He was just giving her a break because he had taken a notion to her (who wouldn't) and it wasn't the same thing at all.

Maybe Sophie had queered it for her, anyway. Blowing her top like that last night. Suddenly she hoped—she almost hoped—that she had.

Victoria had run on upstairs by this time, but it was another minute or two before Lew moved. And when Sophie saw his face, she couldn't help it, she felt so sorry for him, so damn sorry ... She actually took a step toward him before she remembered Miss Colby, who of course was there, putting her hands up to his face as if to shield him, just the way Sophie wanted to do.

But wasn't that something? For her to be feeling sorry for Lew Morgan, of all people, and damn it, damn it, wasn't she ever going to be cured? And as if that wasn't enough, she felt sorry for Miss Colby, too; poor, lucky Miss Colby who was going to marry Lew, and who was trying so desperately to keep things under control. Including herself. Just the sight of her tense shoulders made Sophie's back ache in sympathy. Maybe ladies—and Miss Colby was a lady, to the marrow of her bones— never blew their tops. Sophie wouldn't know. But if they ever did, it was on nights like this, over guys like Lew.

Again she shifted from one foot to the other. Embarrassment spread through her. She couldn't retreat to the back room now, she had to hang around and wait to be noticed, and once noticed, what was she going to say?

She sighed, more audibly than she intended, and at once Miss Colby turned around. "Why, it's Sophie! I didn't know you were here."

"I know it. I mean— Excuse me." Where *that* brilliant remark had sprung from she would never know. She remembered the purpose of her being here and tried again. "I came out when you did. I guess you didn't notice."

Lew still wasn't noticing much of anything, as far as she could tell. He looked as if he didn't know what had hit him, and he kept rubbing his forehead in a tired, uncertain way. But as he started slowly for the back room, he gave Sophie a sort of grin. "Poor Sophie. You've had a rough time tonight, too. Somebody owes you an apology."

"Not you. I'm the one that ought to apologize. For last night. Honest and true, Lew, that's why I stopped in this afternoon. After you offered Arlene a job and all—" She paused, not knowing whether she dreaded or hoped to hear what he was going to say.

"Don't worry about that part of it. Arlene's going to have her chance. I'll see to that. I guess I had it coming to me, whatever you said last night." He looked at Miss Colby, cautiously.

"In vino veritas," said Miss Colby. "Let's forget it, shall we?" Her voice sounded funny, but then she smiled. That million-dollar smile of hers that for some reason made Sophie feel even more like crying.

She hung back on purpose; it would be better all around for Lew and Miss Colby to walk into the back room ahead of her. Let them make the discovery. Lew stopped on the threshold. His back stiffened. Beyond him Sophie could see Whitt struggling to his feet out of the arm chair. He faced his father, glassy-eyed.

"So they've gone," said Lew pleasantly. He took a step toward Whitt.

"I might have known it. And you sat here and watched them, I suppose. Probably kissed them a fond farewell. Didn't you? Wished them better luck next time—"

It got Sophie, the way Whitt just stood there, swaying on his feet, and not fighting back with one single word, not even mustering up the spunk to run away from his tormentor.

Apparently it got Miss Colby, too. "I can't stand any more of this," she said suddenly, and whisked out into the hall. Sophie followed her and watched as she paced up and down, hugging her elbows as if she didn't know how else to hold herself together. Lew hadn't paid any attention to them; they could still hear him, lighting into Whitt for all he was worth. Talk about beating a dead horse, thought Sophie. And yet in a way she saw how it was with Lew: he had to work himself up into a rage out of self-defense, to keep from thinking about Victoria.

"It's just because he's upset," Sophie offered timidly.

But Miss Colby had paused at the front door, and was peering out, intent as a bird dog. Above the thunder of Lew's voice Sophie caught the sound of a car in the driveway. The sheriff? It couldn't be; Lew hadn't even left his name with Mrs. Lally. By the time Sophie got to the door, Miss Colby was out on the porch.

"Aunt Chat!" she gasped. "What in the world are you doing out, a night like this? Here, let me help you—"

But the raw-boned old woman toiling up the steps brushed her aside curtly. "No, leave me be. Like I told Bud, more hindrance than help." At last she hoisted herself up the last step and straightened painfully to her full height. She wore a voluminous coat that flapped around her knees, and a crocheted fascinator over her head. For a moment she seemed to Sophie like some great, strange, wheezing bird (for the effort of climbing the few steps had winded her), bearing fateful tidings; a creature from another world. Then the moment passed. It was, after all, only Lew's old Aunt Chat, as human as anybody else, standing here on the porch, with the rain whispering in the trees beyond and lending fuzzy haloes to the street light down at the corner and to the departing tail light of the car that had brought her.

"Come in," said Miss Colby. "Lew's inside—"

"You're the one I came to see. I've already told him, and you think he'd pay me any mind? Not him. All right then, I says to myself, I'll just get ahold of Celia, if he hasn't got the sense to listen to me maybe she will, I'll just get Bud to drive me out. Because one thing about it, I won't get a wink of sleep tonight anyway. I never do, when it catches me like this—"

"What is it, Aunt Chat? What's wrong?"

"It's like something had me by the throat." The old woman stopped her shuffling, jerky progress across the porch and unwound the tail of the fascinator from her stringy neck; Miss Colby was staring at it as if she actually expected to see a hand clutching it. (Well, so was Sophie, when it came to that.) "There's something terrible going to happen. I can always tell. I get this feeling."

"Something terrible?" echoed Miss Colby. "It's happening right now. It's already happened."

"I don't mean Grover," said Aunt Chat. "Bad enough, him getting drowned like that, but that ain't it. I'd know if it was. I mean Lew. It's come to me in a dream, and his picture falling off the wall—not once, mind you, but twice, twice in the same week—and this feeling I get … But try and tell him anything. Me and my signs, he says, the other day when I warned him. Scoffed, you know, treated it like a big joke, just the way he always does. Well, I says to myself, if he don't care what happens to him, I know who does, and I couldn't stand it another minute, Celia, seemed like I just had to find you and tell you, I don't care whether you believe me or not—"

"Oh yes," said Miss Colby. "I believe you." She was holding the door open for Aunt Chat, and in the dim light her eyes looked deep, deep, and darker than they really were. "Yes, I believe you."

The old woman was inside now; slowly, like a clumsy, rigid machine, she got out of her coat, lowered herself on to the hall piece, took off the fascinator, and folded it into a neat square. Her hands were trembling. Then her glance fell, apparently for the first time, on Sophie. "Who's this?"

"Sophie Barta. I mean Hoffman," said Miss Colby. "You remember her, I expect."

You bet she did remember. Sophie set her jaw and faced the familiar, Turk-Ridge-Ladies-Aid inspection. What saved her from the full treatment was the crackle of Lew's voice from the back room. He was no longer roaring, but no one could miss the edge of furious contempt in his voice. Aunt Chat cocked her head.

"What's he jawing Whitt about now? Where's Victoria? There's something going on here, don't try to tell me different."

Miss Colby closed her eyes. For a minute Sophie thought she was going to spill the whole thing. But then for some reason—maybe because she had noticed Aunt Chat's trembling hands, the quaver in her voice; maybe because Miss Colby herself was just too tired—she changed her mind.

"It's all right now. Lew got a little—upset about Dort and Johnny, and you know how he is, he always takes everything out on Whitt, but it's all right now. It's going to be all right. They're gone, and Victoria's upstairs, and it's all over now." She wasn't fooling Aunt Chat. Or herself, either; she let her voice trail away, and Sophie saw her tighten up, listening. Lew was trying to get Sheriff Lally on the phone again, but again with no luck.

"Joe. Joe who?" said Aunt Chat, who had been listening along with everybody else. ("Joe" was all she had to go on; Lew hadn't mentioned "Sheriff" or "Lally" in the course of his call.) She looked hard at Miss Colby. "All right, Celia, I ain't one to nag. There's no law says you've got to tell me what's going on. Only don't try to make out to me that everything's fine as silk. I wouldn't be here if I didn't know better. There's trouble hanging over Lew, I can see it as plain as I see you this minute, I can feel it like fog closing in on me, choking me ..."

Again she put her hand up to her neck, and Sophie caught herself swallowing anxiously, half-persuaded of a mysterious pressure in her own throat. She had always been a sucker for fortune telling, mediums, psychic messages; not, she said, that she really believed in them, it was just for the fun of it. But it was one thing, sitting in a candle-lit tea shop, shivering a little, giggling a little, while a fake gipsy read your palm for the familiar (and secretly cherished) signs—the tall, dark suitor, the journey, the unexpected windfall. It was something else again, listening to this matter-of-fact old woman foretell doom. No murky atmosphere here, no crystal ball or hoop earrings or heavy ring worn on the forefinger. The hall light fell flatly on Aunt Chat's withered face, topped with the scanty little bun of hair, on her decent percale dress, on her big feet in their elastic-sided men's shoes planted side by side. There she sat, peering through her bifocals at the future, and—it just showed you, once a sucker always a sucker—all but convincing Sophie that every word she said was the God's truth.

Except that Miss Colby, who was no sucker, was all the way convinced. "Oh yes, I believe you," she had said to Aunt Chat, and you could see that she did: her face was drawn, and her eyes looked haunted. She stood facing Aunt Chat, with her hands clenched in the pockets of her soft gray jersey dress. Sophie could hear her quick, nervous breathing.

"Mule-headed," said Aunt Chat. "'Lew,' I told him, 'you take care of yourself, boy, there's terrible bad trouble ahead,' but no, he's too mule-headed to listen to me, and—"

"But what shall I do, Aunt Chat?" Miss Colby burst out desperately. "You keep saying it, and I already know it, but what's the use when I don't know what to do? I don't! I don't know what to do!"

"Maybe he'll listen to you. He don't always act like it, but he does, Celia, Lew thinks the world of you, and if anybody can save him it's you. Like it says in the books, love conquers all. Maybe he'll listen, if the warning comes from you." Aunt Chat tossed her head stiffly. "Nobody's seen fit to tell me what's going on up here. I don't even know what to warn him about. I presume you're at least that much ahead of me."

But the dig was wasted on Miss Colby. She was staring off into space, intent on Lew, no one but Lew. "Yes, I can warn him." (Only, thought Sophie, what's she going to warn him of? She doesn't really know, any more than Aunt Chat. She's just snatching at the only straw in sight.) "I can try," said Miss Colby, in that warm, uneven voice of hers.

"For God's sake!" They all turned, and there was Lew in the doorway of the back room, staring at Aunt Chat as if he couldn't believe his eyes. A red streak of temper still showed in his forehead, but mostly he just looked flabbergasted. "How did you get here, Aunt Chat?"

"Run every step of the way," said Aunt Chat pertly. "Same as I always go everywhere. You were back there hollering at Whitt, the reason you didn't hear me." Her face mellowed into a smile; she even let Lew help her to her feet and down the hall—for he said at once the hall was no place for her to sit, she must come on back and make herself comfortable.

Whitt was more or less on his feet, propped against the mantel piece and looking as punch-drunk as anybody Sophie ever saw. But he went through some limp motions of greeting Aunt Chat, and for a few minutes there was a stir of false gaiety in the room. Maybe they would all get back to normal now, Sophie thought wistfully. Maybe Lew, having worked out his temper on Whitt, would change his mind about getting the sheriff up here, in which case—why not?—Sophie could beat it, just quietly get the hell out of here ...

Lew nipped that nice little hope before it even got to be a bud. "Sit down, Sophie," he said, and it might sound like a cordial invitation to some people, but Sophie knew a command when she heard one. "You can't leave yet. Why, the evening hasn't even begun." He sat down himself, and grinned at Aunt Chat. "So you just dropped in to pass the time of day? Don't give me that, Aunt Chat. If there's something on your mind—and of course there is—let's have it and get it over with."

"Taking considerable for granted, ain't you? You're not the only frog in the puddle. Maybe I didn't come to see you at all. There's other people up here too. Victoria, Whitt, Celia ..."

"Celia," said Lew. "Oh."

His eyes—amused and shrewd—switched to Miss Colby, and her face flushed up like a peony. She had counted on more time, probably a less public setting for her warning, that was clear enough. But, flustered as she was, she saw her chance and snatched at it.

"Yes. Me," she said, and in a little rush she crossed the room and sank down on the hassock at Lew's feet. "I'm the one she came to see, Lew. That is, it's about you, of course. Only she thought maybe if I told you, and I don't know how to say it, but you must listen to me—"

"I'm listening. But I don't need to. I've heard it before. 'There's something terrible going to happen.'" He touched her bright hair tenderly. But he had a mean, reckless look in his eye that Sophie didn't like. "You mean Celia didn't tell you, Aunt Chat? For once your signs and portents were right. Something terrible damn near did happen tonight. That is, if you call murder something terrible, and maybe I'm prejudiced, but I do."

"Murder!" Aunt Chat's face turned blotchy with the shock.

"That's right. Murder." Almost as if he was boasting, Sophie thought. "Oh, it was a sweet little scheme that Dort and her pal Johnny cooked up. It didn't jell, but if it had I wouldn't be telling the tale. You might as well know about it, as long as you're here. It's no secret—or at least it won't be for very long. They've skipped out, but they're going to wish they hadn't when I get my hands on them. I don't give a damn who knows what kind of a tramp my son married." He was on his feet now, pausing to cast another challenging glance at Whitt. But there was nothing to challenge: Whitt had obviously not heard one syllable. He had poured himself a drink, and he sat with it tipped in his hand, staring at nothing. Lew turned away from him in disgust.

"They tried to kill you," whispered Aunt Chat.

"But they didn't do it!" He went over and took her hands in his. An impetuous, boyish gesture. "Don't you see, Aunt Chat? The something terrible almost happened. But not quite. Because I'm here, I'm safe and sound. Your spooks got their wires crossed—come on, now, admit it— and we can all stop worrying till the next time. Everything's okay again!"

Well, it made sense to Sophie. And Miss Colby's face was tremulous, ready to break into a smile as soon as she saw that Aunt Chat was convinced. The old woman wanted to be convinced, too; her mouth worked in and out anxiously while she studied Lew's face.

But in the end she shook her head. "If it was okay I wouldn't feel this way. It would let up on me if there wasn't anything to worry about any more. And it ain't let up. Not a particle. There's more to come, Lew, you watch what you do because there's more to come."

Poor Miss Colby, thought Sophie. She couldn't laugh it off the way Lew did; she took it deadly serious. But she found in Aunt Chat's words a new angle for her warning, one that matched her own feelings. You could practically see the wheels going round in her head. What was Lew doing that ought to be watched, that might be dangerous?

"Lew," she cried, "don't call the sheriff. Please. Let it go. Supposing you can't prove it was Dort and Johnny? You'll be putting Whitt through the wringer for nothing. Sophie, too. Everybody. Even if you can prove it— Please don't, Lew. It won't help. It's only asking for more trouble." She didn't let herself holler. But her voice shook with the effort. Even Lew couldn't miss that. Not that it made him pause for more than a tick or two. His glance fell on the gun, there on the table where he must have put it. He picked it up, turning it absently in his hand.

"Listen to me, Celia. You don't seem to see my side of this. It's a damn funny feeling, in case you're interested, to know somebody wants you dead. Gives you quite a turn, as they say. Some way you can't quite believe anybody could hate you enough to—"

"Stop it!" This time Miss Colby did holler. All of a sudden she snapped. She put both fists up to her temples, as if to keep her head from flying off. "Stop it, stop it, stop it! Do you think I don't know they all want you dead! Yes, all of them. Dort and Johnny. Whitt. He said so. Grover ..."

"Celia!"

"Oh yes he did. You told me yourself, the way he looked at you, at the end. As if he was nobody you'd ever known, or that ever knew you. It was hate, he was hating you ... Even Sophie. She'd have killed you last night, if she'd had a gun. Even—"

She gave a terrified gulp, and stopped just in time. But it seemed to Sophie that the room throbbed with that not-quite-said name.

"Even who?" said Lew softly.

"Everybody!" She flung out her arms and plunged on. "All of them, they all want you dead. You have to know, because you mustn't die. I can't bear it if you die! Lew, Lew, you mustn't let them ... I haven't ever asked much of you. I've waited, I've stood it all this time, everything else. Only don't die. Don't let them kill you ..." She kept trying to say more, but it was swallowed up in sobs; at last she just stood there clinging to Lew, with the tears streaming down her face.

Well, so now Sophie knew: ladies blew their tops too. On nights like this, over guys like Lew.

He was patting Miss Colby's shoulder, but automatically, and when he got her over to the sofa, he didn't sit down beside her. His jaw was clenched, and that hard look was back in his eye.

"I vow, I wish you'd put that gun down," said Aunt Chat. "Makes me nervous, just the sight of it. You hear me, Lew?"

"I hear you," he said, without putting it down. "All right, so they all want me dead, do they? All of them, you said, Celia. And you're right, you know, now that I think of it, you never spoke a truer word. Even Grover. Even ... It would fix things great for all of them, if I were out of the way. Well, it's too late for Grover. But look at the rest of them. Sophie'd be even with me at last. Dort and Johnny could go their own sweet way, and don't think Whitt wouldn't be waiting to welcome them back with open arms and nobody to make rude remarks about what a damn fool sucker he is. And Victoria—"

Miss Colby, whose face was buried in her hands, made a strangled sound. He went on bitterly. "No, you didn't say it. But I'm saying it, I saw the look in her eyes, and my God I don't even know— What have I ever denied her? All she ever had to do was ask, her whole life long I've given her every damn thing she ever wanted, but she's no different from the rest of them. They hate me, every last one of them." He gave a sudden, ugly laugh and lifted the gun toward his head, as if every last one of them were there watching, and he were mocking at them. "Wouldn't they love it, though. Wouldn't it be nice and obliging of me, to do what they'd like to do and pull the trigger. Well—"

Whatever else he was going to say was cut off by Aunt Chat's frazzled screech of alarm: "No, Lew, no! Stop him, somebody!" It shot along Sophie's backbone like an electric shock. It cracked even Whitt's stupor; he lurched to his feet. Startled, Lew turned slightly, and in that instant Miss Colby sprang up, wild with terror, mindless with it, blind to everything but the gun in Lew's hand ...

"Don't do that!" yelled Sophie, but Miss Colby had already grabbed, the sound of the shot was already bouncing back from the walls, and Lew was slumping in her arms like a half-empty sack of flour.

For a minute the world and everybody in it seemed to stand still— Aunt Chat with her gnarled hands on the arms of her chair, frozen in the act of hauling herself up; Whitt with his mouth open a little; the gun still sagging in Lew's hand; Miss Colby's face blank and white as a sheet of paper.

Victoria broke the spell. The sound of the shot brought her tearing down the stairs; she stopped short in the doorway, haggard and glittering-eyed. Not a word, not a question out of her; she just stood there watching while Whitt called Doc Fletcher and they got Lew laid out on the couch. The inert weight of him shook Sophie. She stared down at his face, so remote now, so drained of all its fierce energy and arrogance, and at the dark, thick wetness creeping out from under his temple.

"Miss Colby," she whispered, but there was nothing to say, after all, and anyway, Miss Colby had not heard her. She was shaking all over, violently. She knows, thought Sophie; she knows, the same way I know.

"He's dead!" Suddenly Victoria was shrieking, jabbing her finger at Miss Colby and shrieking. "You did it! It was you! You did it!" Over and over again, the same words, splintering the quiet of the room. And Miss

Colby with her head tilted, as if she were listening politely. Only she was still shaking all over, and her face was empty, without radiance or charm, nothing now but a collection of imperfect features—over-square jaw, over-large mouth, slightly crooked nose.

Sophie couldn't stand it. She turned on Victoria. "Shut up. Don't you think she knows it? You wanted him dead, too. Everybody did, except her and Aunt Chat. They were the only ones ... You shut up. You leave her alone."

She put her arm around Miss Colby.

15

"I told him, you know," said Aunt Chat. "'Lew,' I told him, 'I wish you'd put that gun down.' I've always been that way, gives me the fidgets to see anybody fooling with a gun. And then I had this feeling ... Hadn't been for that, it wouldn't have hit me the way it did, him aiming that dratted gun at his head and talking so wild. I'd been in my right mind, I never in the world would have thought Lew was going to—"

"No," said Celia. "Of course he wasn't going to." But she hadn't been in her right mind, either. Like Aunt Chat, she had seen danger where there was none, and, intent on saving Lew, had brought about the very thing she dreaded.

This was her first call on Aunt Chat since Lew's funeral. A goodbye call, really, for she was leaving town the end of the week. She was not sure yet where she was going. Just away. Not that she had any hope of escaping from herself or the cruel machinery of her memory. But at least she could escape from other people's memories. Though, now that she was here, she was finding Aunt Chat's endless, mournful reminiscences less harrowing than she had expected. The place itself was so peaceful— this old-fashioned, pretty backyard where they sat, with the dappled sunshine like a blessing on their shoulders, and the contented clucking of the hens and the creaking of the lawn swing like an artless accompaniment to Aunt Chat's voice. And what she said had a rather ballad-like quality, as if it had all happened long ago and far away ...

"I keep telling myself, what's meant to be will be." Aunt Chat shook her head over the quilt blocks in her lap. Then she brightened. "One thing about it, it's made a man out of Whitt. I never thought I'd see the day when that boy would stand up to anybody on this earth. Not that I saw it with my own eyes, but from what I hear tell, that's just exactly what he did, not only stood up to his wife, but threw her out. Yes sir, her and that dark-complected feller that came back with her, all set to move in again. Threw the both of them out." She cackled in triumph. "I couldn't believe my ears."

Neither could anybody else, thought Celia, who had been there when Dort and Johnny came back. She remembered Whitt's air of astonishment at his own voice, thin but inflexible, answering Dort when she tried her blandishments, Johnny when he tried his old-pals approach.

"The gall of them," said Aunt Chat. "Of course Dort always wound Whitt around her little finger before, no reason to think she couldn't do it again. Especially with Lew out of the way. Oh, she was after the money, from the very first, and Whitt's well rid of her. I only wish Lew could have lived to see her get her come-uppance. Why, bless me if I don't think he'd have been proud of his son, for once in his life!"

"I wouldn't be too sure," said Celia. "Whitt sent her and Johnny packing, yes. But he let them off a lot easier than Lew would have, if he'd had his way. He was going to have them arrested for trying to kill him, you know." Instead, there was to be no public scandal; the rest of them had agreed, with one accord, to let the Dort-Johnny episode rest in decent secrecy. No, Lew still wouldn't have been satisfied with his son. He would have found a way to belittle Whitt's newfound strength— which, with Lew there to belittle, would most likely never have emerged at all. It was only because of Lew's death that Whitt had found himself capable of anything but cringing and grovelling.

"That's so," said Aunt Chat. "Well, then, *I'm* proud of Whitt! Whether anybody else is or not. Yes sir, and it's my opinion he'll make out all right now that he's got a chance to farm, the way he's wanted to do all along. He never wanted any part of the lumber yard. Or the bank either, he's glad to leave that to Victoria ..." But her voice faltered over Victoria's name and the image of strangeness and incurable bitterness that went with it.

"She said I killed him!" The words seemed to burst out of Celia; she heard them with a mingling of horror and relief. "And it's true, I grabbed the gun. If I hadn't grabbed the gun—"

"You wouldn't have, if I hadn't hollered. But I did, and you did, and somehow it just happened ... Victoria ain't herself, poor girl. It's a funny thing, Lew and his childern." Aunt Chat's faded eyes met Celia's, sadly. "He was a hard man. Hard on them that he loved, the same as on them he didn't. You musn't hold it against Victoria. She hasn't got anything left, with Lew gone."

"I haven't got anything left, either!" cried Celia. "At least she's younger, she hasn't spent her whole life waiting the way I have!"

"So?" Aunt Chat had her head reared back, getting the right angle with her bifocals to thread her needle. "First I heard about you and Lew doing any waiting. Mind you, I'm not saying I wouldn't have done the same. No, Celia, you've got a sight more than Victoria ever had, or ever will have. You just remember that when you get to carrying on."

"I'll tell you what I've got. You know it anyway. Everybody else in town does. Years of sneaking around, and those awful hotel rooms, and pretending I didn't care about all the gossip and the snubs ..."

"If it wasn't worth it," said Aunt Chat, "why did you do it?"

In the silence that followed, a wren in the grape arbor teetered her tail and exploded, loosing a flood of chattering, stuttering excitement.

"All right," said Celia wearily, "you win. It was worth it. I did it, and I'm not sorry, and now I'll move to some other town and teach in some other school, and— But do you think I'm different from any other woman? Don't you think I wanted a wedding ring, and a home, and children, like everybody else?"

"You're not so old." Aunt Chat appraised her candidly. "And like I used to tell Lew, he picked a good-looker when he took up with you. Let's see, what are you, about thirty-eight? Why, land, Celia, I had a miscarriage when I was past forty-seven!"

"If you're trying to tell me I'm ever going to forget Lew, ever going to get over this—"

"No such a thing," said Aunt Chat. "I was just remarking you ain't too old to have a family. So you've made up your mind to leave Turk Ridge. Well, I don't blame you. Where you planning to go for the summer?"

"What's the difference? Anywhere, just so it's away."

"All by yourself?"

"Who would you suggest I take with me? Victoria?"

The idea tickled Aunt Chat; her high-pitched laugh rang out. "Now that's one I hadn't thought of. There," she added, smoothing out her quilt block on the seat beside her, "now I think that's nice, if I do say so as shouldn't. I've always liked the star pattren. I was thinking to myself this morning, I just think I'll give this one to Arlene Barta when I get it done. She's a nice, obliging young one. Used to stop in every day, all through the bad weather, to feed the hens for me, and such as that."

"She's a darling." Celia felt the tears spring to her eyes; how long was it since she had given a thought to Arlene? How bewildered the child must be feeling, lost in the shuffle of unaccountable adult reactions, pulled this way and that by her loyalties, and with all her high hopes for the summer dashed to nothing. "Poor Arlene, she was so thrilled over the job Lew promised her."

"Oh well, there's always other jobs. Chili Joe's, places like that."

"Chili Joe's! Why, that's no place for a kid like Arlene! It's a joint, it's where Sophie— She musn't take that kind of a job!"

"Well, it don't seem like there's anybody much to stop her. I guess she feels like you do, kind of at loose ends. What was it you said? What's the difference where you go this summer or what you do. Only difference is, you can just get in your car and go, and Arlene can't."

"I could—" began Celia, and then there was a long pause, while Aunt Chat bent her head industriously over her sewing and Celia turned over in her mind what she had not said out loud. I could take Arlene with me. Why not? Why not? It was the first idea to strike a spark in her heart since Lew's death. A timid, wavering spark, a poor shadow of her old inner glow; she hardly dared believe it. But it was there: Arlene was the one person whose company she could find bearable this summer. Because she was young, with her eyes fixed on the future instead of the past; because the world was new and full of marvels to her; because— most of all—because she had nobody much but Celia left. Sophie? Yes; but what Sophie had to give was not all Arlene needed. The something lacking was what only Celia could give ...

"I must drive out to the farm and see Arlene," she said. "I can do it tonight."

"Be nice if you would. She ain't had it too easy. Though I'll say this about her Aunt Sophie, or whatever she is, I don't think she's as bad as she's painted. No sir, I've been misjudging Sophie Barta all these years. Couldn't anybody have been kinder than her, up there at Lew's the night it happened." Aunt Chat's voice threatened to quaver; she steadied it with a shot of indignation. "And that's another thing. I'll be switched if I know what she was doing up there in the first place. I said to Whitt, I said, 'Give me one reason, give me one good reason.' But of course nobody tells me anything."

"They don't need to," said Celia. She stood up. "You've already got it all figured out. I must say goodbye now, Aunt Chat. I've got to run along. No, no. No need for you to get up."

"Well, maybe I won't, then. Kind of hard for me to get around anymore. Pick yourself a pansy on your way out. There's some nice big ones in bloom right to the left of the gate." Her gnarled old hands, both of them, closed over Celia's. "Goodbye, Celia. You're a good girl. That's what I've told Lew, many's the time, 'Lew,' I says, 'that's a good girl, and if you had a lick of sense you'd leave Olive and her money and all the rest of it and get yourself a wife that is a wife.' But you know how he was. Couldn't anybody tell him anything. Mule-headed. And yet, I don't know what it was about Lew, but all the same—"

"Yes," said Celia, "all the same."

She walked quickly away, but when she reached the front gate she had a sudden impulse to go back, to thank Aunt Chat—she wasn't sure, just yet, for what—maybe even to kiss that tough, wrinkled old cheek. Because who knew whether they would ever see each other again, these two who had known Lew and loved him anyway?

She turned back, but she got no farther than the corner of the house. Because Aunt Chat was sitting in the lawn swing bolt upright, with the quilt block wadded up in her hand, and the tears that she had been too proud—or too brave—to shed in front of Celia squeezing their way down her withered-apple face.

So Celia never told her thank you, after all.

THE END

My Brother's Killer

By Jean Potts

1

Garth Sullivan decided to kill his brother on an evening that started out like dozens of other evenings. First the whack on his apartment door, then the ebullient Irish-tenor voice. "Hey, Garth, you in there? Come on down and have a drink with us."

"Us" being Mr. and Mrs. Howard Sullivan—Garth's brother and Pam, who had once upon a time been his girl. They were generous with their invitations because they felt sorry for him. (Poor Garth, glooming up there all by himself, it won't hurt us to ask him for a couple of drinks.) He knew it. Yet he seldom declined. Maybe because it was too much effort to concoct an excuse. Maybe because he was a masochist.

"I just got out of the shower," he called back. He always made for the shower as soon as he got home from the office. A form of ritual cleansing: he loathed his job. "Be with you in ten minutes. Okay?"

"Sure. Fine." And Howdy pounded back down the stairs, passing up the elevator, as usual. It was a decrepit little contraption, subject to paralytic seizures. Walking was quicker, even on its best days. But of course old Mr. Bauman, who occupied the other top floor apartment across from Garth's, couldn't have managed without it.

Pam had inherited the house, a shabby but solid old four-story brownstone; she and Howdy occupied the second floor and rented out the rest. Well, Howdy had always been lucky. Their apartment had considerable charm, in spite of the way it was furnished. The brand-new living room suite—Howdy's pride and joy—was the color of spoiled raspberries and fuzzy on top of that. A hideosity. Not to mention the plastic zebra-striped sling chairs and the frenetically figured drapes. But there were a few good old pieces, like the piecrust table handed down from Pam's grandmother. And nothing could blight the proportions of the great high-ceilinged room itself, or the simple grace of the fireplace.

There was a cheerful little fire going in it on this chilly May evening. Garth, in fresh shirt and slacks, with his lank tan hair sleeked down, stood in front of it for a moment, stretching his left hand out to the pleasant warmth. As was his habit, he kept his right hand in his pocket.

"What'll it be? The usual?" Howdy beamed at him from the bar, an elaborate job of chromium and padded imitation leather. He was a big fellow, beginning to run to fat, but still good-looking enough, with his high color and dark wavy hair. And then the ever-ready tongue, the heart-warming smile. His nickname suited him. Howdy the personality kid. Everybody's friend. "Right. The usual. And a whiskey sour for you, doll," he added, as Pam emerged from the bedroom.

After a year and a half, she was still not quite easy in her role of sister-in-law and inclined to overplay it. Tonight, as usual, there was the business of deepening dimples, outstretched arms, extra-cordial greeting—all of which Garth observed, as usual, with wry amusement, but with a pang of sorrow too. In the old days, before he introduced her to Howdy (yes, his own doing!) he had never rated this much of a glow from her.

"How does the new hairdo grab you?" Howdy asked as he handed around the drinks. "Pretty classy for a washerwoman, isn't it?"

"Oh, you," said Pam, and patted her topknot. She was always doing something different with her hair, which was thick, dark, and hard to manage. Not her best point. Tonight's arrangement struck Garth as more successful than most. It showed off her neat little ears, and the pretty slope of her neck.

He did not say so. Made no comment at all. For they were exchanging one of their husband-and-wife looks—Howdy fondly teasing, Pam trembling her lip in a fake pout. Far be it from him to intrude on these moments of togetherness. He sat down on one of the sling chairs (at least it got the damn thing out of sight) and waited for them to remember his existence.

The doorbell pinged tentatively. Howdy leapt off to answer it. His voice rang out from the little foyer. "That you, Eunie? Come on in, baby, join the party."

"We asked Eunice to come down too," Pam explained unnecessarily, and a little nervously. "Okay with you?"

"Sure. Why not?"

"Well. Sometimes you're not very nice to her."

"Me? Not nice to Eunice? Why, how you talk!"

Her face tightened up. After a moment she said, "Yes, don't I. And about things that are none of my business any more. Such as you."

A hit. A very palpable hit. He would have to wait till later to pay her back: she had already turned away from him to greet Eunice.

"Here she is," Howdy announced. "Our little Carrot-top."

It was an inaccurate description on both counts. Eunice was a pretty solid chunk of a girl, and her long straight hair was more pinkish than carroty. She had a lot of freckles.

"Hi, Garth," she said without looking at him. "Your hair looks great, Pam. Terrific. A whiskey sour? I'd love one. In fact, I need one. Utter chaos at the office, and when I got home guess who popped out and nabbed me before I could get my door open. If you hadn't phoned when you did, I'd have been stuck there yet."

"Oh dear," said Pam. "Sober? No, I suppose not."

"At the lady-of-refinement stage. You know. What was I doing about the servant problem? So difficult these days. Too, too distressing. And then the riff-raff you see on the street. Why, she can't step outside the house but what some low coarse fellow starts following her. I give her another couple of days. Then she'll be calling the police with another of her midnight horror stories."

Everybody sighed. The phases of Miss Crosby's drinking cycle were familiar to them all—especially to Eunice, since she had the other third-floor apartment. The pattern was predictable, but not the degree of intensity. Usually Mrs. Faye, the long-suffering and inventive superintendent, could be counted on to deal with the situation. If she gave up, then there was nothing to do but call Miss Crosby's brother and let him arrange to have her carted off to the sanitarium. He had washed his hands of her long ago, and never saw her except on these occasions.

"I can't help feeling sorry for her," said Pam. "She's got nobody, you know. All alone in the world."

Like everybody else, thought Garth; even the happy couple themselves, not that they would ever admit it.

"Yes, poor soul." Eunice gave another sigh. She had chosen the other sling chair, opposite Garth. But she was still not looking at him.

"Oh, I don't know," he said. "Mrs. Faye keeps an eye on her. And she's got you right next door. Just about the neighborliest neighbor anybody could ask for."

That did it. She blushed, violently—and unbecomingly, because of the freckles. And out of the corner of his eye he could see Pam tightening up again. It didn't necessarily mean that Eunice had confided in her: the kid's flaming face was enough of a tip-off. But his guess would be that Pam already knew. Yes. One of those cozy girly heart-to-hearts. Probably they had compared notes.

It was nothing to him, one way or the other. His discovery of just how neighborly Eunice could be was certainly not the result of any planning on his part, and he had no intention of pursuing the matter. He had checked her off as strictly ho-hum stuff when she moved into the house last winter. All that bubbling about her first job, her first very-own apartment; all that eager friendliness. Left to himself, he would have made no move to socialize with her. But Howdy and Pam often rang her in on their cocktail hours with Garth—presumably because they found him easier to take diluted than straight. Surely even Howdy, compulsive matchmaker though he was, couldn't have any ideas about pairing him off with Eunice.

She was still busy blushing. Howdy rattled his ice cubes and looked baffled. It was Pam who broke the deadlock.

"You haven't seen the new bedroom curtains, Eunice!" She bounced up off the sofa. "Now that they're up, I'm not sure about the color. Come on, tell me what you think."

Eunice lumbered off gratefully. She was wearing clumpy shoes and a long dress with a skimpy sort of flounce around the bottom. Oh pioneers.

Howdy waited until the bedroom door had closed behind them. "What was that supposed to mean? That crack about being neighborly?"

"It has to mean something? As far as I'm concerned, it was just a simple statement of fact."

"Oh, come on now. A simple statement of fact. It embarrassed the hell out of Eunie, and you know it."

Silences were apt to rattle Howdy, and this one did. He took a nervous gulp of his drink and eyed Garth—who preserved a face of bland innocence—with the familiar mixture of puzzlement, wariness and exasperation. "Damn it, Garth, what's the matter with you? She's a good kid, maybe not your type, but anybody can see she's got a yen for you—"

"Don't be silly. Of course she hasn't."

But of course she had. Like quite a number of girls before her; it was an odd fact that, lacking Howdy's personality and good looks, he had never had any grounds for envy on that score. Except when it came to Pam. Who was the only one that mattered.

Eunice couldn't have mattered less. He had acted out of idle curiosity on that evening last week when she asked for his help in getting her door open. "I don't know what's wrong. The key only turns halfway, I've been trying for half an hour and I can't make it work. Would you mind terribly? I hate to bother you, but there's nobody else around. Howdy and Pam are out to dinner, and Mrs. Faye isn't home either."

It had been an unseasonably warm, humid evening—which no doubt accounted for her troubles—and she had worked herself up into quite a sweat. She had also managed to jam the key, so that it took him a good ten minutes to persuade it back into business. He could hardly leave her to haul in her double armload of groceries by herself, and naturally once they were inside she offered him a drink. One thing led to another, the final destination being her studio couch, a rickety second-hand job that squeaked during the entire performance and at moments threatened to collapse. Idle curiosity on his part. And on Eunice's? If memory served, she had mumbled something about "love"; let her call the dreary little episode by any name she chose. There was nothing for him to feel guilty about: she had been as eager as she was clumsy.

And whether or not Pam had been treated to a replay of the details, nobody had passed them on to Howdy. He was back at the bar now, frowning as he poured himself a dividend, obviously unsure of his ground. Finally he said, "Okay. It's none of my business. But I've seen the way you treated other girls. You can be a mean bastard when you feel like it. I just don't want it to happen to Eunie, that's all."

"If I'm such a social menace, why ask me down here?" Smiling pleasantly, he stood up. "Thanks for the drink. I'll be shoving off."

It was a tried and true gambit. Howdy shot out from behind the bar to grab his arm. "Now wait a minute. I didn't mean it like that. You know how I am, me and my big mouth, always sounding off, if anybody's a social menace it's me ..."

Garth did know how he was: all his life he had been playing on Howdy's need to like and be liked. It was no part of his own make-up, thank God. Neither was Howdy's penchant for letting his tongue run away with him, or his bursts of temper that burned themselves out as quickly as they blazed up. He could no more hold a grudge than Garth could let go of one.

In due time he allowed himself to be mollified, accepted the refill Howdy pressed upon him, and sat down again in the sling chair. He even assumed an air of interest while Howdy—relieved at having, as he no doubt thought, talked his way out of another awkward spot—launched into a colorful account of his recent trip to Mexico. He worked for a construction materials outfit. Their top trouble shooter. Naturally. Like all Howdy's expeditions, this one had been terrific, fantastic. Garth let him run on, not bothering to point out that he himself had spent the better part of a year down there, as against Howdy's few days, and might just possibly have learned something about the place on his own.

The better part of a year, and the best part of his life, the crest of the wave for him. His one-man show of wood sculpture, at a small but prestigious gallery, had been a modest triumph; he even made some money from it, enough to finance the Mexican jaunt. It had been a dream come true, to explore, in footloose solitude, the country that had fascinated him since childhood. (For unfathomable reasons, as far as Howdy and Mother were concerned. But then they never understood why he wanted to mess around with all that wood, either. Not that they weren't proud and pleased at the success of his show. But flabbergasted, too: who would ever have thought it, people paying good money for those things Garth whittled!) Eventually his wanderings had brought him to the Don's estate, those high, bare hills beyond, and he had known at once that it was for him, the place where he could settle down and work. For of course the first show was nothing compared with what would come later; he was seething with confidence, ideas, energy.

"But I don't need to tell you," Howdy was saying, belatedly remembering. "After all, you've been there too. Might still be there, if Mom hadn't passed away when she did."

And if you hadn't wired me about it, thought Garth. And if I hadn't felt obligated to come back for the funeral. He still didn't know why: it had always been perfectly clear who was Mother's fair-haired boy. Howdy, not Garth. Not that he cared. Anyway, he had come back—for a few days, as he thought, a week at the most. Only then he had met Pam, and somehow time got away from him, and then there had been the accident that blasted all his hopes and plans.

Howdy cleared his throat. "Ever think about going back?"

"No. Why should I?"

"Well, you sure seemed to like it down there before."

"That was before. This is after." He took his hand out of his pocket and watched Howdy's eyes flick away, as always.

"All I meant was—"

He broke off, and no loss, as the girls emerged from the bedroom. Eunice had recovered from her blushing fit. Pam's hair was beginning to work out of its washerwoman's knot. Everybody was back to normal.

Including Howdy, who relaxed visibly. "Garth and I were just comparing notes on Mehico. He's the guy that knows, of course. I only had four days down there. Long enough to pick up a slight case of Montezuma's revenge, I grant you, but that's about it."

"Did you show him the present you brought me? Oh, but he's got to see it! Unbelievable. Wait a minute, it's right here, I'll get it." Pam charged across the room to the what-not cabinet where she kept her collection of miniature animals. Most likely Howdy's present was an addition to it—one of those crude, dime-a-dozen pigeons, or maybe a turtle or lizard.

No, it was something bigger, about the length and width of a largish book, but disproportionately thin, more like a tray or a plaque. Mildly curious, Garth leaned forward, and caught the glint of the stones that studded it.

After a moment of silent staring, Eunice said, "What on earth is it? I mean, it's great, but—"

Howdy exploded into guffaws. "Don't look at me! I was half smashed when I bought the thing, so your guess is as good as mine. It just seemed like a good idea at the time. There we were, some dump God knows how many miles out of Saltillo, and not a hope of getting back to civilization till morning. So naturally we hoisted a few. And take my word for it, that tequila is one powerful brew. Man, oh man!"

"Where did you get this?" Garth had it in his own hands by now, and he was on his feet, standing close to the floor lamp so he could really see.

"That's what I'm telling you. We kind of made a tour of the cantinas, see, and every place we hit, begad, here was the same scruffy little customer tagging along after us. His privilege, of course, but it began to spook Ed. He was sure the guy was fixing to get us in a dark alley and knife us, or anyway roll us. *Muy* rich *Norteamericanos*, you know. Me, I figured he was just hanging around hoping to scrounge a drink, and I stood him one or two, he was drinking cerveza, couldn't speak a word of English ..."

He chuckled, relishing his own story. "Actually all he was trying to do was turn a fast buck. And damned if he didn't do it, too. I'll give him this, he knew a sucker when he saw one. He waited to make his pitch till we were headed back, more or less straight, for the hotel. We thought we'd shaken him at the last place, but no, we hadn't gone more than a couple of blocks when we heard this hiss, you know the way they do down there, pssst, and out he popped from a doorway. By this time Ed was spooked for sure—not another living soul in sight, and dark as a pocket—but the guy had a bulldog grip on me with one hand, he'd pulled his merchandise out from under his shirt with the other, and he was gabbling away like crazy. Not a word of English, as I say, and what Spanish I know you could put in your eye, but that didn't keep him from getting his message across. A bargain, *muy precioso, muy bello*, he was doing me a favor to end all favors. And maybe he was. All I know is, whatever it is, I bought it. How about it, Garth? Did I get taken, or didn't I?"

"Who knows?" said Garth, who knew not only what it was and what it was worth, but whose it was: the scruffy little customer might be any one of the workmen around the Don's estate, acting out of greed or spite. Like Garth himself, in withholding what he knew from Howdy? For that was what he seemed to be doing—without making any conscious decision in the matter; he had spoken automatically. Now he added, "Depends on what you paid for it, I suppose."

"Yeah." Howdy made a wry face and hesitated briefly. "Well ... well, he wanted seventy-five for it, but I got him down to fifty bucks."

"Fifty bucks," Garth echoed in a hollow voice. He put the panel down carefully on the coffee table. The workman could have been motivated by simple dire necessity. The Don was not famous for paying high wages.

"I know. One tequila too many. But hell, it's only money, and the stones must be worth something. Maybe I could have them made into a necklace, Pam likes necklaces, or at least a bracelet."

"Break it up, you mean?"

"Why not? That's what I'll do, I'll take it to Lenny, he's due back from Europe next month, he's just the guy to do a bang-up job on it, and he'd give me a break on the price, too. Hey, Pam? It's no use to you this way."

"Oh, I don't know. I could always hang it on the wall. You're right, though, it would make a stunning necklace." They beamed at each other.

"Absolutely stunning," Eunice agreed.

"It's already stunning enough." As Garth reached to touch it again—beautiful, beautiful—he saw how violently his hand was trembling and drew back. "So why not leave it as it is?"

"Well, but it's no use this way," Howdy repeated.

No use. And therefore, of course, no excuse for being. Doomed to be dismembered: its stones reset into a trumpery necklace by that idiot Lenny, its exquisitely carved wood thrown away or split up for fireplace kindling. Why not? It was no use this way.

And still Garth did not speak out. By now he could not; words were literally, physically, beyond him. Through a white dazzle of hate he saw his brother's face with its smile that was supposed to be so engaging, his solid shoulders and chest with the big warm heart beating inside, oh sure, good old all's-right-with-the-world Howdy who lucked into everything, understood nothing ...

Nothing, but nothing. His proposal to destroy the panel—his gizmo, as he called it—was typical, one more in the chain of his offenses, and committed with the same blithe unawareness. Such a small offense, after all, compared with some of the others. The accident, for instance, or Pam. But it was the one too many for Garth; it propelled him into a surge of rage that transcended all the other rages of his life.

And they had been there, they had been there as far back as he could remember. Because Howdy had been there, Howdy the displacer, the charmer who could make their mother's eyes melt as they never melted for Garth. Howdy the destroyer ... She had always rushed to his rescue. "Stop it, Garth, stop it this minute! The idea, hitting your little brother, you ought to be ashamed! Just because he broke your mug, it was an accident, he didn't do it a purpose."

He could see the mug now, standing here in his dazzle of hate, with the chit-chat swirling around him. His beautiful, cherished mug with its border of vine leaves and the design of dusky grapes against the glaze, smashed to bits on the splintery floor where Howdy had knocked it. The lesser treasures, too—the scooter he had salvaged and patched up himself, his shinny stick, his airplane book that Howdy left out on the fire escape to be ruined in the rain. It was always an accident. None of it was ever done "a purpose." As if that made up for the damage.

It didn't. Neither did Howdy's tearful apologies, or the replacements he had now and then produced. "Look. I saved up to buy you a new mug. It's nice, isn't it? As nice as the old one?" An ugly, thick thing, lumps of birds, even on the handle.

All right. The mug. But not the panel. He was not going to vandalize the panel. Garth would see to that. And when the time was ripe for damage, it would by God be his kind, not accidental like Howdy's.

He sat down again, reached for his drink, sipped. His hand was no longer trembling. He had a feeling of remoteness, as if he were enclosed in glass, with the others out there going through their meaningless motions.

If they noticed how little he talked, they would think, well, at least he wasn't needling Eunice any more, and anyway, that was Garth for you, never the life of the party. It didn't matter, either, whether or not he followed the ins and outs of the conversation, as long as he took his cues, laughing when the others did, copying their expressions of surprise, concern, what-have-you.

The bit about Memorial Day came at the end, when he had refused another drink and was on his feet, heading for the door. Still insulated, shut off in his enclosure. He missed the first part of what Howdy was saying.

"—plenty of room, if you'd like to come too."

What? Where? Jolted out of his glassy retreat, he caught the expression on Pam's face. No welcome there. Stiff resistance. But Howdy rushed on, oblivious to the storm signals. "Hey, that's a great idea. Why don't you? Eunie's coming, the more the merrier. You can help us open up the cottage, the both of you. We'll be driving up Friday, if you can get away early. How about it?"

The cottage at Arrow Lake. Their mountain hideaway, as Howdy called it; he had bought it last summer from some guy in the office, in a jam for money or he would never—so he said—have let it go. Howdy and his bargains. There must be something that marked him to would-be salesmen as their man. The "scruffy little customer" in Mexico, for instance, heading straight for him with the Don's panel.

Garth's first impulse was to ease out of the invitation with some excuse. As he usually did: the Arrow Lake cottage was not his kind of place. But this time he hesitated, he wasn't sure why. Unless it was Pam, so obviously uptight, so plainly willing him to say No. Why not let her stew for a while? "I can't get off early, so that's out," he said. "Okay if I think it over and let you know in a day or two?"

Of course, Howdy assured him expansively: loads of time; a week and a half.

They clustered in the foyer to bid him good night. Eunice was smiling shyly, hopefully. A glutton for punishment. Howdy had his arm around Pam's waist. She stood stiff and straight, in no mood for togetherness.

Garth gave her a special parting grin before he took off up the stairs.

2

It was raining next morning, and Howdy's departure for the office was even more of a scramble than usual, because they had both overslept. When he was gone Pam made herself another pot of coffee and settled down by the window for an interlude of peace and quiet. Presently Mittens, having made sure the coast was clear—she was a cat who preferred human beings to stay put and keep their voices down—emerged from seclusion under the couch to join her.

Last night's quarrel with Howdy, fierce enough while it lasted, already seemed far away and long ago. They had made up in bed, the way they always did—anger, harsh words, reproaches, all consumed in a fine, purifying blaze.

She had lit into him the minute Eunice left. What in the name of common sense did he think he was doing, asking Garth up to Arrow Lake for Memorial Day week end? It was nerve-wracking enough, just to spend an hour with Eunice and him, knowing that sooner or later he would start needling the poor kid. And now here they were, faced with a whole week end of it, all because Howdy didn't know when to shut up. Why did he always have to drag Garth into everything ...

He fired up at that, of course. The more so, she suspected, because he was already having second thoughts himself, had probably realized before the invitation was out of his mouth that it was a mistake. He wasn't stupid. It was just that he got carried away on the tide of his natural conviviality.

Plus the other thing, the sense of guilt. That was at the root of his dogged attempts to draw Garth into their charmed circle, his and Pam's: he hoped at one stroke to ease Garth's unhappiness and his own conscience. It was an exercise in futility, and Pam used to try to tell him so. Not anymore. She knew when she was licked. Howdy didn't. He could not, would not, face the fact that he was never going to be able to make amends for his share in Garth's misfortunes. No amount of brotherly love and kindness could repair the damage that had been done that night two years ago.

All she knew about the accident was what Howdy had told her. Not one word out of Garth, either then or any time since. Stony, desolating

4

The telephone at the Arrow Lake cottage was in the living room, and Eunice was sleeping on the living room couch, so it was she who took the call that came in the middle of Sunday night. Groggy with sleep, she stumbled to the bedroom door and banged on it. "Howdy! Telephone!"

He came out, rumpled and croaking. "Who is it?"

"I think he said—the police?" It was only when she had said it aloud that the implications began to permeate. "I'm pretty sure. The police."

"Oh God." Pam appeared in the bedroom doorway, grappling with her robe, one sleeve of which was inside out. "Miss Crosby's gone berserk and set fire to the house. Or flooded it. Or something."

Howdy cleared his throat and said hello. It was a very one-sided conversation: the phone quacking away unintelligibly, Howdy listening. And Eunice and Pam watching him listen. At the end he said, "Yes. We'll be out. As soon as we can make it." When he hung up his face was gray. He felt his way to the nearest chair and sat down carefully. He kept rubbing his hands against the knees of his pajamas while he told them.

Garth. The rented car, abandoned near the beach. The suicide note stuck in the windshield, naming Howdy as the person to be notified, at the Arrow Lake number.

Pam sagged in the doorway. Howdy buried his face in his hands. Eunice heard herself whimper, and made a blind rush for the privacy of the screened-in porch.

They drove straight out to the Island, stopping in New York only long enough to drop Eunice off at the house. It was still too early for Mrs. Faye to be up and about, and just as well. A session with her would have held them up—an extra hour, probably more—and time seemed of the essence.

Not that it could possibly matter anymore to Garth. There was no doubt in their minds as to the nature of his "disappearance," as the police called it. He had come out here seeking death, and he had found it. The note made his intentions unmistakably clear. And he was not the sort to change his mind after writing that note.

"It was the kids tipped us off," the police explained. "They saw him Saturday night—well, more like Sunday morning—anyway, saw this guy down at the beach. Kind of mooning along, all by himself. He was still there when they left. They noticed the car again when they came silence. It was a couple of months after their mother's death; Garth—called home for her funeral—kept postponing his return to Mexico, drawing out the love-struck days with Pam. His pretext was that his help was needed in clearing out the old family apartment uptown, which Howdy planned to give up as soon as he could find a smaller one for himself. A plausible pretext: some of Garth's woodworking tools were still there, in the room he had rigged up as a studio. That was where he was the night it happened, absorbed in squaring up a piece of walnut on his table-saw, when Howdy ...

"He didn't hear me come in," Howdy had told her in a stricken monotone. "It never crossed my mind that he didn't know I was there. It should have, of course—that damn machine makes an ungodly racket, whining away—but I'd had one or two, I never stopped to think; God help me, I went over and slapped him on the back."

Garth was taken completely by surprise. His hand skidded into the path of the circular blade, which neatly severed his thumb and half his forefinger.

So much for his career as a wood sculptor. And so much, as it turned out, for his romance with Pam.

But why? she thought, and once again she felt the pang of grief and bewilderment. Why couldn't he believe that the accident made no difference to her? She had hung on and hung on, so sure that she could convince him. But he had seemed bent on losing her along with the rest; it was as if he found a bitter satisfaction in driving her out of his life. And into Howdy's. Yes. Into Howdy's. That was the final twist, all that was needed to make the vicious circle perfect.

Now, two years later, she could look back and see how inevitable it was that she and Howdy should turn to each other. Misery had been the bond in those first dark days; Howdy and his guilt, Pam and the failure of her love. Two separate miseries, but both rooted in Garth. There was no need for explanations between them, no obligation to make the kind of social effort an outsider would have expected. They were the insiders, the only two in the world who could make any claim to being close to Garth.

And for Pam at least there had been no one else to turn to. She had dropped out of college, and out of the old circle of friends, in the spring when she first met Garth. She had no brothers or sisters. No father that she could really remember; she had been too young at the time of the divorce. There was still a dutiful exchange of Christmas cards, his with a check tucked inside. He seemed to move around a lot. The last one had a Canadian postmark.

Her mother ... well, that was the summer when Mother finally, after who-knew-how-many alarms and excursions, married again and moved out to California. She had been too busy with her own affairs to bother about anyone else's. As she would have been in any case. You had to accept Mother for what she was, a charming, flighty, self-absorbed creature who skimmed through life only vaguely aware of what was happening to other people. She had not come back since; all the flurry of plans and promises to be on hand for Pam's wedding had somehow failed to materialize. Sketchy as she was about details, it was entirely possible that she did not realize Pam had wound up marrying not Garth, whom she had met, but his brother, whom she had not.

They were so different, so different. And of course that was the other thing that drew her to Howdy. After Garth's prickliness and catlike reserve, Howdy's easy-going warmth and open heart. There was no holding back on his part, no secret inner labyrinth inaccessible to her. (She had no real understanding of Garth's wood carvings. They were wonderful to her, all of them, simply and solely because he had done them.) Howdy was all hers, never mind the quarrels, in a way that Garth would never have been ...

She shifted the warm, purring weight of Mittens in her lap and stared through the rain-beaded window at the passersby across the street, hunched under their umbrellas, on their way to work. There was Garth, cutting across the pavement from the house, headed for the subway. No umbrella for him. No hat, either. Already his hair was plastered to his bony skull, his shabby old raincoat was streaked with the wet. She still felt protective about him. There was still, after all this time, the familiar little tremor of her nerves—like a reflex action—at sight of his wiry figure moving in that special, quick way.

A few minutes later Eunice appeared, at the gallop, with her see-through plastic umbrella held square over her head, like the cover on a cake plate. Though she herself was not so much a piece of cake—except to Garth—as an open-faced sandwich, thought Pam wryly. Everything right out in plain sight, poor kid; it was painfully obvious from the start that she had set her heart on Garth.

"I don't know why," she had said the other night when, once again, she was unbosoming herself to Pam. "I just—even before I ever saw him, I had this feeling, just from what Mrs. Faye told me about him ..."

So in the beginning there was Garth's tragic history—the stuff of fantasy for many and many a girl besides Eunice—with Garth himself as the finishing touch. It didn't matter that he wasn't the traditional tall-dark-and-handsome. He had plenty else to keep the fantasy going: the haggard look, the withdrawn brooding air, the impression he gave of pent-up intensity.

"I didn't think he'd ever be, you know, really interested in me," Eunice had confided tremulously. "But then yesterday when I got home from work, I don't know what it was with my key, I couldn't make it work, and ..."

Rapture, rapture. Eunice's Night of Nights, a real earth-shaker. Clearly a good deal less than that to Garth. Since then, a week and a half ago, he had not only made no effort to follow up, but last night he had gone out of his way to turn the knife in the wound.

And Howdy wanted him in on the week end at Arrow Lake! Well, he didn't know the whole story; and Pam hadn't told him, not even in the heat of battle. There wasn't much she could do for Eunice, but at least she could keep her promise not to tell anybody, anybody at all.

The doorbell chimed: Mrs. Faye, broom in hand, was taking time out from her daily chores to bring up the morning paper. Which meant she had something on her mind, something more than what she started out with. "That delivery boy. A day like this, and he can't be bothered slipping the paper inside the foyer, leaves it stuck in the outside door, if you please. It's half turned to mush. So help me, I've a good mind to report him." She paused for breath, smoothing down the apron which, with a shrunken old sweater, slacks, and a hairnet, constituted her working uniform. "No, thank you, dearie. I won't stop for a cup of coffee, I'm far enough behind as it is. The stairs and all the usual to do. And Miss Crosby's gone and spilled another bottle of beer in the elevator. Eunice was just telling me."

Ah ha, the key word at last. What Mrs. Faye had on her mind was neither the paper boy nor Miss Crosby—old hat, both of them—but Eunice, who didn't know enough to lock her fire escape window, bless her heart, and was therefore a special pet.

Mrs. Faye's eyes, round and green as gooseberries, lit up with indignation. "That's not all she told me, poor child, she was full of it, how you've asked Garth up to the cottage for Memorial Day week end too. Of course it's none of my business—" She always threw this in; actually she considered everything that went on in the house her business. With good reason: she and her husband had moved into the first-floor apartment twenty-odd years ago, and for fifteen of those years, ever since his death, she had been handling the job of superintendent by herself. She had also been giving Pam and the tenants as much mothering as the traffic would bear, to make up for not having any children of her own. "—but mark my words, it's asking for trouble, throwing the two of them together."

"Now don't get ahead of yourself. He didn't say he'd come. I doubt very much if he does. If it had been left to me, I wouldn't have invited him, but—"

"Well, I should hope not. After what he put you through. Thanks be to God you came to your senses at last. It's beyond me what you ever saw in him. Or Eunice either, come to that. It's plain as the nose on your face he doesn't give a snap of his fingers for her. He's just out for all he can get. Then he'll toss her aside like an old shoe, wait and see if he doesn't."

There was no need for Pam to wait and see. But she wasn't going to betray Eunice's confidences to Mrs. Faye any more than she had to Howdy.

"Honestly, Mrs. Faye, I don't think—"

"You remember I warned you when you first took up with him, and that was before he lost the use of his hand, poor fellow, it was bad luck on him, I'm not denying he's had his troubles, I'm just saying he was cross-grained to begin with. Born with a mean streak in him that was bound to come out, good luck or bad. I warned you. But would you listen to me? And now it's the same with Eunice. The same story all over again."

Not quite the same, thought Pam. Whatever his feelings about her now, time was when Garth had given a great deal more than a snap of his fingers for her. And she for him. She for him, until he crushed it out of her. But that lost "time was" made the difference between her own first love and Eunice's.

Mrs. Faye was pressing on, full tilt. "Oh, I knew it wasn't going to work, having him here in the house. Remember when that apartment came up vacant, I was dead set against offering it to him, I said at the time it was a mistake."

"I remember," said Pam. "I wasn't sold on the idea, either." But Howdy had shamed her into it. Where was her heart? She hadn't seen that furnished room of Garth's, or she wouldn't hesitate for a second. Why, it was enough to drive anybody up the wall, especially a guy who had nothing else going for him, poor devil, the least they could do was give him a chance at a decent place to live.

Pam sighed. Sometimes she wondered if it might not be the favors that rankled most with Garth—the favors he had no choice but to accept and could therefore never forgive.

Howdy wouldn't hear of it, of course, but a sharp, clean break would have been better for all concerned. Healthier. Safer? Once the word popped into her mind, she couldn't seem to brush it aside. There had been something about Garth last night, something sharkish about his parting smile ...

All right, then. Safer.

A couple of evenings later she ran into him on his way home from work. "Hi. Have a good day?" she asked. A fool question: she knew how much he hated his job. It was with an investment firm, a very small cog in a very big machine. Howdy had wangled it for him, through a buddy of his who owed him a favor and had known which strings to pull.

"Rhapsodic," he said. "Here, let me help you." He took over her shopping bag full of groceries, and when the elevator had shuddered to a stop on the second floor he waited while she unlocked the apartment door.

"Thanks. Just put them down anywhere." Howdy wasn't home yet. When she switched on the light Mittens peered out from the bedroom door, uttered a mew of welcome, and politely but firmly retreated. "Come in for a minute?"

"No, I can see you're in a hurry."

She wasn't, really. They weren't due at the Walls' for dinner until seven. But being alone with Garth was apt to send her into a mild fluster.

He didn't look in the least sharkish tonight. Rather wistful, in fact, hanging around there in the little foyer. "About the week end," he said.

She stiffened slightly. "Yes. About the week end."

"You're driving up Friday, right? I'm afraid that's out for me. They're pretty stuffy in my department about extra time off, especially when it's a holiday week end. I suppose I could get a bus up Saturday. But they don't go all the way to the lake, do they?"

"Stroudsburg would be the closest. I don't know exactly how far it is. Twenty, twenty-five miles."

"That far? Then I'd better just skip it. I mean, the hassle of meeting me, and all."

After a moment of twanging silence Pam said politely, "I'm sure Howdy wouldn't mind."

"I'd mind, though. Putting him to the bother. I impose on you too much as it is."

"Impose on us?"

"You know, depend on you. For sociability." His eyes were hazel, the kind that change from gray to green to brownish. Very dark at the moment, deep and brooding. "It's not as if I was all that good company, either."

"But you are, Garth. Very good company, when you—"

"Yeah. When I'm not being a bastard. Ahhh. The hell with it. I'm stuck with myself. No reason why you should be."

"But you mustn't just hole up for the long week end. If you don't come up to Arrow Lake"—and for the life of her, she still could not urge him—

"then why not someplace else? You used to love it at the shore, and you haven't been there in I don't know how long." She did know, exactly how long, and hurried on. "Anywhere. Just so it's a change of scene."

"Yes. It was great out there in East Hampton, wasn't it? Remember Babe and Waldo at The Nautilus? Still going strong, I suppose." He gave his shoulders a forlorn little shake. "Well. Well … don't worry about me, I'll make out. One way or another. You're right, of course. Time I pulled up my socks and got out on my own. Maybe one of these days I'll do it. So long, Pam. Be seeing you."

"You don't have to go yet. There's time for a drink if you'd like one."

"No. No, thanks." His voice sounded abstracted, remote. She couldn't see his face: he had turned and was fumbling with the door knob.

"Here. It goes this way."

She watched as he started up the stairs to his apartment, where nothing, nobody was waiting. He went fast, as always, but somehow heavier, no spring in his step.

"Garth," she said, and if at that moment he had looked back, she would have given in and pressed him to accept the Arrow Lake invitation.

But he did not look back. Maybe he heard her, but he did not look back.

She closed the door without calling his name again.

3

The little skirmish with Pam couldn't have been more satisfactory as far as Garth was concerned. After due consideration, he had decided against Arrow Lake as the ideal setting for Phase One of his plan. Otherwise he might have taken Howdy up on the invitation—if only because Pam so obviously didn't want him to.

Didn't want him, and yet had come within a hair's breadth of urging him to accept. The poor-pitiful-Garth ploy had worked like a charm; it was a pleasure to find he could still get to her. (Up to a point, of course. He knew better than to push his luck too far.) And it was she—not he— who had first mentioned the shore. With no prompting from him. How about that for a nice little bonus?

She would remember it later. And she would never forgive herself.

Beautiful, beautiful. Inside his own apartment, he stretched out on the couch and once more checked over the details of his plan. For that was what it was by now. The formless, furious resolve of four nights ago had crystallized into a plan, clearly charted from beginning through middle to end.

And in the process he had come alive again; it was a long time since he had felt so good, so—yes, so carefree. Liberated from boredom. This problem, unlike his meaningless drag of a job, absorbed him, body and soul. Each complication only added to the fascination of the whole. A new challenge; another puzzle to sharpen his wits on. And each time another little click of triumph when he hit upon the solution. It was always there, somewhere. Just a matter of finding it. Patience. But sometimes, too, a sudden thrilling leap of imagination ...

The plan, as it finally took shape in his mind, was devious. But then it had to be. He hadn't a chance in the world of getting away with the forthright approach. Even a purported accident, fatal to Howdy, with himself as the survivor, was far too risky. Somebody would be sure to dredge up all the reasons he had for hating Howdy and cast suspicion on him and his story, no matter how plausible. Somebody like Mrs. Faye, for instance. She had taken against him on sight, and had never made any bones about it. And she was devoted to Howdy.

So was Pam. Devoted to him. Married to him, and happily. Not Garth's girl any more. He had thought of her as his for a while, had let her get closer to him than anybody ever had or ever would again, but ... All right. The point was that she knew him too well for safety. Too well to imagine, as Howdy did, that he could be won over with a barrage of favors (galling) or the all-pals-together bit (tiresome). And much too well to be out-maneuvered on a matter of such crucial importance as Howdy's death. Give her the chance and she would be on him like a tiger.

So don't give her the chance. That was the name of the game, exactly what his plan was designed to accomplish.

He saw no reason why it shouldn't work, and God knows he had gone over it often enough, searching for flaws, some tiny oversight that could blow the whole scheme. Now he ran through it again, just to be sure. It was tight, as nearly fool-proof as he could make it. The unforeseeable flukes were beyond his control; he wasted no time worrying about them.

Some of the groundwork was already laid for Phase One. The rest he could manage handily during the week ahead. By next Friday, when the Howard Sullivans—oh yes, and Eunice, mustn't forget Eunice— departed for their mountain hideaway, he would have made whatever advance arrangements were possible and would be ready for action.

Ah, he thought, ah. Hurry Friday.

He was twelve minutes late getting into the office on Friday. His cell mate, always a dependable man with a cliché, raised his eyebrows and said, "Bankers' hours, hmmm?"

He mumbled something about a subway tie-up. Actually, it was saying goodbye to Pam and Eunice that had put him behind schedule. Howdy was already gone when he tapped on the apartment door. Some deal that required his presence at the office for a couple of hours before they took off.

"Oh. Garth." Pam greeted him rather breathlessly. "Do come in, I mean, if you can get in. You know how it is. Going up for the first time. Such a hassle."

There was a clutter of cartons in the little foyer. More of the same in the living room, and a couple of open, half-packed suitcases. Also Eunice, in jeans and a—well, not exactly a sweater, not exactly a poncho, either—fringe. She was trying to fit too many kitchen utensils into a too small shopping bag. At sight of Garth she dropped a clattering handful and turned the regulation patchy red.

"I just stopped by to wish you a happy week end." He held out his hand, and Pam took it. There was a smudge of dust beside that charming, curly mouth of hers. Her eyes didn't quite meet his. "Looks like you're going to have good weather," he added.

"I know. Marvelous. How about you? I hope you're not going to let it go to waste."

"Oh, I'll probably think of something. See how I feel tomorrow."

"You could still come up to Arrow Lake." Eunice gulped it out bravely. She was out of the living room by now, hovering just behind Pam. "It's not too late to change your mind. There's several buses tomorrow, that is, if you'd ..."

"Yes, why don't you?" That was Pam, nothing if not dutiful. "Honestly. It's no bother meeting you."

"Maybe another time. When I feel more sociable." He straightened his shoulders forlornly. "Tell Howdy I'm sorry I missed him. Have a great week end. I'm sure you will. Can I take any of this stuff down for you?"

"No, no. It can wait till Howdy gets back with the car. Thanks, anyway. And Garth—" Her eyes did meet his at last, concerned and sorry. "—you have a good week end, too."

"Sure. Don't worry." Without planning to do so, he kissed her. It was something he hardly ever did anymore, so she was probably caught off guard as much as he. By way of stabilizing things, he kissed Eunice too. She showed a tendency to cling, and he got tangled, but not seriously, in the fringe.

A last wistful wave, and he was off. A day of drudgery for him; of holiday excitement for them.

He sat down at his desk, cheek by jowl with his cell mate, who had by now passed on to the weather. He dealt with it in detail, analyzing the outlook for the entire week end, and not neglecting a comparison with conditions for the same period in previous years. The weather was one of his favorite topics of conversation. Another was the television programs he had watched the evening before. His job was on the same paperclip-counting level as Garth's; he was contented with it, and would remain so—and with whatever trifling promotions were meted out to him through the years ahead—until he reached retirement age.

His name was Arthur Morris and he lived in Queens. Height 5' 9 ½". Weight 175. Eyes hazel.

These items of information, and other pertinent data, were set forth on his driver's license, which he had lost last week—he would never understand how—and which now reposed in Garth's apartment, safely under lock and key.

"You wouldn't get me out on the roads this week end," Arthur Morris stated, "not for love nor money. With the wife in her condition?" A second little Morris was imminent, after what seemed to Garth the longest pregnancy in recorded history. "And the traffic like it's going to be, this kind of weather? No way. Thank you very much, I'll settle for a nice quiet week end at home. We're having the neighbors over for a cookout. Maybe we'll take in a movie. And that's it for yours truly."

After a pause Garth said, "It's different when you're all on your own. I'm kind of sorry now I decided not to go up to my brother's place. A long holiday week end, just hanging around town—it can get pretty damn long. I know. God, how well I know!"

"You do hole up quite a bit, and that's a fact." Arthur glanced at him nervously. Pep talk coming up. "But there's no reason why you should, if it gets you down. I mean, a guy like you, no family responsibilities, nobody to worry about but yourself. Why, you ought to be having the time of your life. You could at least go to the beach this week end, even if you can't afford anything else, and I gather from what you told me last week you're not too flush at the moment—"

"What? Oh. You mean that horse I bet on. The one that was sure to win, only he didn't." He had told Howdy the same story, against the day when the closing out of his modest bank account would require an explanation. And had stoically rejected Howdy's offer of a loan to tide him over. "I wasn't thinking about that part of it. We get paid today, don't we? And anyway, if I had all the money in the world I'd still be stuck with myself. Sometimes I think I'd be better off if I just ..."

"Now, now," began Arthur, and would no doubt have floundered on indefinitely except that the phone rang, summoning him to a conference with his immediate superior.

"I'll get back to you later," he promised Garth as he bustled off.

He didn't, though. It wasn't just the conference. It was the report due that afternoon, an absolute must, to hear Arthur tell it, the entire organization hung in the balance. At five o'clock he said a hurried good night, and that was it. Would he remember afterwards, with a pang of self-reproach, how he had let the day slip by without finding time for the added encouraging words that might have made all the difference?

Garth rather thought so. He lingered a moment after Arthur's departure, tidying his desk for what—if Phase One worked out as planned—would be the last time. One final poignant touch: he put the paperweight Pam had given him for Christmas in his pocket. Then he shut the door behind him and stepped forth into liberation.

Saturday morning when he came back from picking up the paper he found Miss Crosby seated on the floor of the elevator, sipping with regal air from a pint bottle of gin. What was left of a pint, that is, less than an inch.

"I'm afraid it may be stalled," she informed him chattily. "Though of course it's just possible I neglected to push the buttons in the right sequence. These mechanical operations. So confusing. Lovely morning, isn't it?"

He stepped over her feet in their high-heeled mules and pushed the buttons. Nothing happened. "It's conked out again," he said. "Can I help you up the stairs?"

"How very kind of you to offer. I'm quite comfortable here, thank you."

"But Miss Crosby, you'll ruin your coat—"

"Oh, this old thing!" She was wearing the purple velveteen job today. Her multi-colored turban hid all of her hair, except for the bangs, dry from decades of bleaching, which in turn hid her forehead. Below them, as always, were out-size dark glasses. That left out in the open only a small area of puffy white face, adorned with a cupids bow mouth, blurry at the edges. "This tacky old thing!" she cried, and took another sip of gin. "I really must get uptown and do some shopping one of these days. Except it's so tiring, not like it used to be, all those women, so common, pushing and shoving, why, even in the better shops ..."

Garth left her still talking and went down the hall to ring Mrs. Faye's bell.

Neither of his two news bulletins came as any particular surprise to Mrs. Faye. "I'll call about the elevator, but you know good and well what they'll say—if there's anybody there to say anything, that is. It's hard enough to get a repairman down here on a regular working day, let alone a holiday week end. That machine!" she added, with a touch of pride. "I declare if it doesn't seem to *know*—well, at least old Mr. Bauman's away, off visiting his son, otherwise he'd be marooned up there in number four

A for the duration."

She tackled Miss Crosby with the skill of long practice. "All right, now, dear, come along upstairs where you belong. How am I going to get my cleaning done, with you sitting here underfoot? Up you go. Here, take my arm." And, when Miss Crosby showed signs of digging in, the clincher: "You don't want me calling your brother, do you? Well, then."

The procession up to the third floor had a kind of shaky stateliness. Garth brought up the rear, carrying Miss Crosby's bottle of gin. Which apparently made him the court favorite. When she was settled in the decaying grandeur of her living room, she thanked him effusively. Mrs. Faye she chose to ignore.

"It's not that I mind her calling my brother," she explained to Garth. "It's just that I prefer to handle the details of my own personal relationships as I fee—as I see fit. As far as my brother is concerned, I make every effort to reserve judgment, though I must confess there are times when I ... but I don't have to tell you, Mr. Sullivan. I'm sure you understand exactly what I mean." Her bony hand tightened on his; the cupids bow mouth arched into an insidious smile of complicity. "After all, you hate your brother too."

It jolted the bejesus out of him, and no mistake. His ears clanged. His eyes dazzled. His hand went into an independent spasm, clenching instead of letting go as he ordered it to do.

Into the silence charged Mrs. Faye. "Now is that any way to talk! Why, I never heard of such a thing." Oh, hadn't she! He knew how much this flash of allegiance from her was worth—she was one of the danger points he had spotted from the beginning, she and Pam, and now muzzy, maundering Miss Crosby—but he was grateful for it all the same. "And after Garth's gone out of his way to be nice to you, too."

"Nice?" Miss Crosby gave him a look of cold distaste and severed her hand from his. "I was quite comfortable there in the elevator. I told him, I said, 'It's very kind of you, I'm sure, thank you very much, but I'm quite comfortable where I am.' Any gentleman would have tipped his hat and gone politely on his way. But not Mr. Garth Nice Sullivan. He's no gentleman." She went on to spell out in explicit terms what he was instead; her vocabulary was quite impressive, considering the delicate-flower image she was so fond of projecting.

Mrs. Faye cut her off sharply. "Now that's enough. I'm warning you, any more such talk and out you go." She marched to the door—Garth was already halfway through it—where she gave some sign of relenting. "You going to behave yourself? All right, then. Finish your drink and have a little lie-down. Do you a world of good. I'll pop in later and fix you a bite of lunch."

Behind her back Miss Crosby made a gesture at Garth, and again her mouth curved in that private, unnerving smile.

"No need to look so upset." Mrs. Faye sounded almost as exasperated with him as with Miss Crosby. "Of course it's none of my business if you want to start brooding over what a poor groggy creature says when she's too far gone to know up from down. Personally, I wouldn't give it a second thought. Just because she calls you a few names." It wasn't the names, and she knew it: there was no mistaking the speculative glint in her eye. She was hoping to draw him out. Well, let her hope.

"Who's brooding?"

"I'm just going by what I see. You've got a face on you as long as my arm." Her own face had tightened into its customary anti-Garth expression. "It beats me, anyway, what you're doing moping around here on a day like this. No wonder you get low in your mind, you're alone too much, that's the trouble, you ought to—"

"I know what I ought to do, all right, nobody has to tell me."

"Well! I'm sure I didn't mean to pry."

"Now don't get huffy. And don't take too much for granted, either. What would you say if I told you I'll be out of here as soon as I throw a few things in a bag and pick up the car I've rented?"

"I'd say good for you. And about time, too," she added tartly. "I hope, wherever you're going, you've got a reservation."

"Wherever I'm going." He gave a little laugh of forced gaiety as he started up the stairs. "The beach. The ocean. I haven't thought any further than that. I'll just play it by ear and see what happens. What the hell, I can always sleep in the car."

"Yes, I suppose so," said Mrs. Faye doubtfully. "Well, anyway. Have a good week end."

When he looked back from the top of the stairs she was still there on the landing, watching him.

"Well, blow me down!" Having done a double-take, Waldo reached across the bar at The Nautilus to shake hands. He was a big, moon-faced guy, unchanged from two years ago except that now he had sideburns. "Hey, Babe, look who's here!"

She let out a shriek of welcome and called Garth by name. That was her specialty, remembering people's names. Waldo's was remembering what people drank. Neither of them ever forgot a face.

"Scotch. Right?" Waldo poured him one on the house, plus a little something for himself and a splash of gin for Babe. "This calls for a celebration. Sit down, boy. Good to see you again. How long's it been, anyway?"

"Two years," said Babe. She hadn't changed, either; as skinny and sharp as ever. And as full of chit-chat—about nothing in particular. Especially not about Pam.

He asked about a room, knowing in advance what the answer would be. A holiday Saturday, after all, and late, getting on toward midnight. (He had timed it that way, had stretched out the drive with stops and detours so as not to get here too early.) Yes. They were full up, annex and all. If he had only given them a little notice ...

"It doesn't matter. I didn't get the idea until today." He stared absently into his drink for a moment, then glanced toward the corner table that used to be their favorite, his and Pam's. Another couple sat there tonight. The girl was blonde, nothing like Pam. "Maybe it wasn't such a good idea, at that. Coming back without Pam."

"I didn't like to ask," said Babe—quite gently, for her. "Naturally I wondered."

"It all blew up, not long after we were out here the last time. She married—somebody else."

Waldo cleared his throat in a commiserating way. Babe said, "I was afraid it must be something like that. You turning up by yourself, I mean. I'm sorry to hear it, Garth."

But not exactly surprised, he thought. Babe would have seen the handwriting on the wall, that last time. It was after the accident; he was at the morbid-fascination stage where he used to sit for minutes at a time gazing at his mutilated hand. They had come out here at Pam's suggestion. Her insistence, really: a kind of last-ditch gesture, he supposed, intended to prove that she was doing her utmost. Maybe she had actually believed that the place itself might work some magic. No use, of course. At least it had put a stop to her gestures.

"I'm sorry to hear it," Babe repeated. "Yes. You had a good girl there. A good thing going."

"Too good to be true, I guess." No guess about it. Even at the start he had been cagey enough not to let go entirely, tempting though it was to believe that Pam was his for keeps. And after the accident he had known damn well she wasn't going to stick. He had been right, too. Married to Howdy. *Happily* married to Howdy. Blooming for him as she had never bloomed for Garth.

"Tough," said Waldo.

"Well. That's life for you," said Babe. "Nothing to do but pick up the pieces and start over again. You're young, you'll find somebody else ..."

She dashed off then, to greet a crowd of newcomers. And Waldo was already busy with a flurry of orders from the other end of the bar. They kept an eye on him, squeezed in a few snatches of conversation in passing. No more of the sustained stuff. But those first few moments had been enough; Garth was satisfied.

He stayed on for an hour or so, another couple of drinks. Alone in the midst of all the chatter and laughter. He was conscious of his pathos. They shook hands with him when he left, and wished him luck. Babe agitated a bit about his not having a room for what was left of the night.

"It doesn't matter," he said, as before. "Don't worry about me. I'll make out, one way or another." He paused at the door for one last look at the corner table. The other couple were still there, absorbed in themselves. Then he walked out fast, got in his rented car, and drove to the beach.

There were no other cars parked on the rise, but from the dunes came the thrum of a guitar, voices singing. A beach party. He spotted them when he got out of the car, a bunch of kids off to the right, and chose the other direction for his own solitary walk.

The night was windless, starry, splendid. Under his bare feet—he had left his loafers in the car—the sand at the water's edge was chill and firm. For a while he could still hear the kids, then nothing but the endless surge and sigh of the sea. Hypnotic. And seductive. On and on he walked, farther than he intended, in a kind of mindless trance.

He came to himself with a start and headed back. His plan. Howdy. The Mexican panel. No, he was not ready to let the sea swallow him yet. Though, as he had once said to Pam, it would be so easy, so simple, a good way to die ...

The beach party was breaking up; he had timed things right. A couple of the kids saw him and waved before they straggled up to the road, trailing their blankets and guitars. He waited until they were gone. Then he went back to his car. It took him only a few minutes to change into the clothes he had bought last week. They were clothes—purplish slacks, striped pull-over, droop-brimmed hat—that Garth Sullivan would not have been caught wearing. Dead or alive. The discarded jeans and sweater, to be disposed of later, went into the little canvas zip bag which was also new, and which he had packed inside his larger case this morning. The note was already written; he stuck it in the windshield where, sooner or later, someone would be sure to notice it. That left only the finishing touches: dark glasses, the fake cast for his right hand (his money next to his wrist, inside it) and the kerchief for a sling.

He emerged from the car secure in his new identity. So much for Garth Sullivan, and good riddance. He was beyond the reach of suspicion. Now nobody, not even Pam, not even Mrs. Faye or Miss Crosby, could ever connect him with what was going to happen to Howdy.

back Sunday night. No sign of the guy, not even when it started to rain. And boy did it rain there for a while. Cats and dogs."

The kids stuck it out, huddled under their blankets; finally, when they were leaving, one of them spotted the note Garth had left up against the windshield. They could make out enough of it to shake them up and send them running for the nearest phone booth.

The note was characteristically terse: "I've had enough of life. No point in going on. Everything I own goes to Howdy and Pam. I blew what little money there was. Sorry about that. This isn't a sudden decision. And nobody's to blame, not even me. It's a good way to die, Pam knows what I mean. Many brave hearts et cetera." There followed his signature, Howdy's name, with the Arrow Lake address and telephone number, and as an afterthought: "They know me at The Nautilus."

The handwriting in the note was definitely Garth's? Definitely. Both Howdy and Pam could vouch for that. And they both confirmed that he had been moody, withdrawn, given to fits of depression.

"The Nautilus," whispered Pam.

Yes, Babe and Waldo at The Nautilus knew him, he had stopped in Saturday night, and their report on his state of mind—in a word, low—fit in with the suicide theory. Even so, there would have to be an investigation. If and when the body was recovered, then of course ...

"Is there any chance it will be?" Howdy asked huskily.

It depended on where he had gone in, and what time. You got one hell of an undertow, some places along this stretch of beach. On the other hand, it had been known to happen. There was always a chance.

But surely not a good one, Pam thought hopefully. A sea burial was what Garth wanted. Let him have it.

Meanwhile, the police got on with their questions. They had already heard, from Babe and Waldo, about the accident to Garth's hand and the short-lived romance with Pam; and apparently what they had heard satisfied them. Now they turned their attention to such matters as Garth's job, his living arrangements, his financial status, current girl friends, if any. (Eunice was not mentioned—why should she be?—poor kid, only another of Garth's one-night stands.)

Howdy's answers were as full as he could make them. There was so little to tell. An empty life. No point in going on. The phrase Garth had used in his note seemed more than ever apt.

When it was over, the police thanked them for their cooperation. Shook hands. Expressed sympathy. Assured them that they would be kept informed of any further developments.

Back in the car, Howdy said, "They have to go through the motions. That's their job. They have to investigate, just in case, even when it's perfectly obvious." His voice was still subdued, his normally ruddy face still gray with shock. "Maybe it was bound to happen sooner or later, no matter what. So it might not have made any difference—I mean, in the long run—if he had come to Arrow Lake with us. All the same—"

"Yes. All the same," said Pam. She fixed her eyes on her hands, clenched together in her lap. "I could have talked him into coming with us. A little urging, that's all it would have taken. But you know how I felt about him and Eunice together. I didn't want him, and I let him know it. I'll never forgive myself. Never."

There was a silence. Then: "*You'll* never forgive yourself!" Howdy burst out, and slammed his fists down savagely on the steering wheel.

They were not the only ones to suffer pangs of conscience. "I can't help thinking," Arthur Morris told one and all, "if I'd taken the time to talk to him a little more that last morning, I can't help thinking, it might have given him a different slant on things. He wasn't always easy to get through to, and God knows I'm no psychiatrist. Still and all, you share an office with a guy, five days a week, nine to five, you kind of tune in on his wave length, right? Even when it's a guy like Garth, strictly a loner, and prickly as all hell. Take it from one who knows."

A doleful pause, while Arthur pushed his horn rims back into position. "If only I'd taken the time. It never hurts, you know, a friendly word or two. We can all use a helping hand now and then. Looking back on it now, I think he was in a mood where the least little thing could push him either way. Over the edge or back on the beam. I might have been able to turn the trick for him. But it was one of those days. The bi-monthly report, just for openers, plus a stack of paperwork this high, you wouldn't believe the pressure. Somehow I never got back to him. I meant to. I told him I would. But somehow I never did."

Another pause. A windy sigh. "Well, there it is. I'll always feel I let him down. Maybe he was already beyond help and it wouldn't have mattered. That's not the point. It's one thing to try and fail. I didn't try."

And then the finale, in all its sombre profundity. "We pass this way but once," intoned Arthur Morris. "We pass this way but once."

Of all the distressing angles, Mrs. Faye bemoaned most the fact that without a body there could be no proper burial. "To think of it," she would say, her gooseberry eyes flooding with the tears that were always on tap, "the poor lad at the bottom of the sea, not even a grave to call his own. Oh, it's cruel, it's cruel ..."

She had made her about-face without the slightest difficulty, and in all sincerity: now that Garth and his mean streak were no longer on the premises, he was automatically transformed into that poor lad, a lost soul if she ever saw one, she would never forget the look on his face that Saturday morning when he told her he was going to the beach. "I know what I ought to do," he had said, and little did she think at the time of what he might mean, what he must have already set his mind to do, God help him.

She said a prayer for him, and lit a candle.

It was a busy time for Mrs. Faye. There was Eunice, who continued to cry a lot, and must be consoled with cups of tea and motherly advice. Howdy and Pam, too, though of course they had each other, and didn't give her much chance.

Old Mr. Bauman had come back from visiting his son with "a cold on his bronchials" and required extra attention: the vaporizer, the nice hot broth, the Vitamin C tablets. He was hard of hearing, and couldn't seem to take it in about Garth. Kept asking, though, and time after time Mrs. Faye would explain into his good ear: "He did away with himself. Drownded. They haven't recovered the remains. Looks like they never will. I told you before. Remember?" Mr. Bauman would nod and wheeze, Yes, he remembered—and then like as not ask all over again next morning.

As for Miss Crosby, she was tuning up for one of the more dramatic phases in her cycle. Perils lurked on every hand. Sinister male figures followed her on the street; she heard an intruder's footsteps creeping up the stairs in the dead of night, stealthy fumblings at her door; she caught glimpses of shadows fleeing on the fire escape. Give her a week or so, Mrs. Faye predicted, and no wheedling or bullying her out of it, she would be off on another spate of calling the police. The boys at the local precinct were well acquainted with Miss Crosby; like Mrs. Faye, they took her in their stride.

Finally, of course, there was Garth's apartment to be cleared out. The task fell to Pam and Mrs. Faye; Howdy couldn't bring himself to set foot inside the place. It took them only a day. Garth hadn't been one to accumulate possessions. The barest minimum of furniture, ditto with the clothes, a couple of his wood carvings (Pam broke down over those), a few books. And that was about it. Mrs. Faye, knowing everybody in the neighborhood as she did, had already found takers for all of it. She had also—though she held off mentioning it quite yet, better let it come from Pam herself, and anyway they'd have to get the painters in first—bent her mind to the matter of a new tenant. Personally, she was hoping for some young fellow with a steady job but no steady girl friend. Might be just the ticket to take Eunice's mind off her troubles.

After all, no use dwelling on the past, no use, either, letting a nice little apartment sit empty. Sooner or later they'd decide to put it up for rent again, and the sooner the better, in Mrs. Faye's opinion. For all concerned.

Her own memory of that last fateful Saturday didn't exactly blur as time went by, but it shifted in focus. What had struck her as the most vivid part at first—Miss Crosby's remark about brotherly hate, and its effect on Garth; froze him in his tracks, and no mistake—now seemed pale and insignificant in comparison with all that had happened since. It faded further and further into the background of her mind. She hardly ever thought of it anymore. Finally not at all.

5

His name, now that he was through with Garth Sullivan, was George Mettler. The furnished room he had rented before Memorial Day week end was in the West 20s. A dreary, gritty block of semi-slum apartments and rooming houses "For Men Only." In case anybody asked, his hand had been injured in an accident "at the plant" and he was on workman's compensation. The landlady did not ask; her sole interest was the weekly rent, payable in advance.

He had enough to live on, frugally, for several months, over and above the price of the plane fare to Mexico. Or, to be accurate, Arthur Morris' fare, for it was good old Arthur Morris' driver's license that would serve as his identification for the tourist card needed to get him into Mexico. Once there, with the Don's panel in his possession—and by then it would be in his possession—he had it made.

The panel, the panel. It was both beginning and end; not only had it triggered him into his plan, it guaranteed his success. Stingy as the Don was with his workmen, he would not haggle over an art piece like the panel. Oh, a little, of course: that was his nature. But in the end his joy at restoring it to its rightful place was sure to prevail. They understood each other, the Don and Garth. And they understood the value of the panel, both monetary and otherwise.

Unlike Howdy, who had chanced upon it, in his usual slap-happy way ...The enormity of it, the sheer, idiot luck! He hadn't the foggiest notion of what he had bought with his fifty bucks, the panel was still tucked away in the what-not cabinet, waiting for what's-his-name to get back from Europe and break it up so that the stones could be made into a necklace for Pam.

It was never going to happen. Never. Never. The panel was going to wind up intact, and back where it belonged. And Howdy—here, at last, was where his luck ran out on him. His fate, and that of the panel, had been settled the moment Garth laid eyes on it.

So he lay low in George Mettler's seedy room, waiting it out. Patience was as important as frugality: the interest of the police in his own death must be allowed to run its course before Howdy became a subject for investigation. He supposed there must have been a routine check of his suicide, though it hadn't made the papers. Howdy would rate a paragraph or two, under some such caption as "Construction Executive Victim of Mugging," with possibly a passing reference to the earlier tragedy in the same family. "It was only last Memorial week end that Mr. Sullivan's only brother" blah blah blah. Even so, Howdy's death would soon pass into oblivion, along with many another crime of violence, never to be solved.

The police angle was not the only reason for waiting. His next move was geared to fit in with the usual pattern of Howdy's and Pam's lives. And presumably his demise would cause some temporary disruption. Not that he envisioned either of them prostrated by inconsolable grief. Hardly. Still, some temporary disruption of their regular schedule, which for all its sketchiness had one or two fixed points. Like Wednesday evenings, when Pam worked as a volunteer night school teacher from six to nine and Howdy made a big production of cooking dinner for the two of them. It was one of their rituals of togetherness; on Wednesday evenings they neither accepted nor issued invitations.

Pam might or might not consider the suicide of her brother-in-law a valid reason for skipping her night school classes—she was very conscientious—but there was no sense taking unnecessary risks. He was counting on those three hours, with Pam out of the apartment doing her good deeds and Howdy messing around by himself in the kitchen. He had nothing to lose, and plenty to gain, by giving them time to get back on schedule.

Meanwhile, the days slid by. He spent them, for the most part, stretched out on the sway-backed bed, hands clasped behind his head, eyes fixed on the ceiling with its peeling paint and coating of grime. There was one crack above the window that reminded him of Mexico, the line of high hills that served as a backdrop to the Don's estate. That grandly austere line had taken his breath away the first time he saw it. Even now, the mere sight of a crack in the ceiling—but it really did have a little of the same sweep, especially if he half-closed his eyes— was enough to set up a faint vibration in his nerves or wherever it was that the remembered jolt still lingered.

The hills, like everything else in sight, belonged to the Don. Always had. Always would. He was a rickety jumping-jack of a man, with long yellow teeth and eyes as hard and glittering as jet. Camping, he announced, was not permitted on his property. The implication was that Garth should have known better than to ask, particularly not in the halting Spanish he had seen fit to produce for the occasion. The Don's statement was delivered with contemptuous finality, and in impeccable English. It had a curiously exhilarating effect on Garth. He met those jet eyes with a flat stare of his own. "Okay," he said. "Then how about giving me a job?" Because one way or another he was going to stay in this place; it was up to the Don to choose on what basis. His was more than an implication, it was practically an ultimatum.

Maybe that was what intrigued the Don, the sheer novelty of being on the receiving end of an ultimatum. Or maybe—his instinct in such matters was uncanny—he divined, correctly, that Garth would have worked for nothing. It was damn near nothing, the figure he came up with. For in the end, after an exhaustive inquisition, he agreed to take Garth on in place of the carpenter who had walked off the job two weeks ago. Good riddance, according to the Don. Still, it left him with a half-built set of bookcases on his hands ...

He named his damn-near-nothing figure. Garth snapped it right up. The bargain was struck. They both grinned a little, in mutual satisfaction.

As well they might. In the months ahead the Don would get his money's worth many times over. And would acknowledge it. Not in words, and of course not by raising the ante. But after the bookcases came other jobs, of a very different caliber; the fact that he entrusted them to Garth spoke for itself.

As for Garth, he was to discover that the bargain offered rewards far beyond the line of hills that had magnetized him in the first place. (It cropped up, that line, a recurrent motif in every one of his carvings from then on. In one, the one he left with the Don, he had almost got it right.) He had hoped for nothing more. The realization that he had stumbled on to a treasure house—it was the only word for the Don's collection, a treasure house—came as a second breath-stopper to him. He had never known such wood existed, such faultless grace and intricacy, as he saw in those ancient chests and cabinets, benches and tables. Oh yes, he had recognized Howdy's gizmo. He ought to, after the days and weeks he had spent painstakingly restoring the legs of the piece it belonged to. It had been a labor of love, an unexpected bonus tied in with the bargain.

Well, the Don was a bonus too, in his off-beat way. What sprang up between them couldn't be called affection or camaraderie or even liking. More a sort of wary rapport that bound them together willy-nilly. A feeling of kinship? Garth wouldn't know. But he had sensed it in the

Don's manner and tone, sometimes even in his eyes. It was what had prompted him to give the Don his best carving. He was glad he had done that. He was very glad to have known the Don.

Their bargain lasted four months. Then Howdy's wire arrived, calling him back to Mother's funeral. And to the disaster that was also Howdy's doing. All right. He had destroyed everything, everything Garth had ever valued. Now he would pay for it.

This was the point in his days of waiting when Garth stopped squinting at the crack in the ceiling and turned away from the lost past to the future. There was where his salvation and his sustenance lay, in his plan, already in progress, but by no means finished. Over and over again he checked it through in his mind, looking for flaws, trying to foresee the unforeseeable. It had endless fascination for him. Occasionally, too, he hit on extra little twists.

Like the day he called Howdy's office—poised to hang up if Howdy happened to be in—and had a rewarding conversation with his secretary. (No danger there, either; she had never heard his voice before.) She turned out to be quite a chatty type, dear girl, once she had reeled off the standard bit—sorry, Mr. Sullivan was not in, might she ask who was calling—and listened to his explanation. He had it ready, of course.

"Actually, it's Garth Sullivan I'm trying to locate. I'm based in Chicago now, just back here on a quick business trip, thought I'd give Garth a ring for old time's sake. Must be three four years since we've been in touch. I don't know his brother, never had the pleasure, but I remembered the name of the firm he was with—my wife's maiden name, one of those coincidences—and since I can't find Garth in the phone book I decided to give it a try."

She swallowed it whole and, in a hushed voice, gave him the tragic news. It was a real treat. He enjoyed especially his own final speech, requesting little Miss Chatty to convey to her boss his deepest sympathy. And it disposed of any lingering uncertainty about the success of his suicide charade. Unqualified. An unqualified success. He had thought so before. Now he knew.

He took long nocturnal walks that sometimes included the familiar block, downtown and east from where he lived now. The house seemed to draw him. At first he had to make himself keep to a steady pace as he passed it; his legs prickled with excitement, a sense of danger. But no one was going to recognize him in his impossible clothes, with his kerchief-sling and his hair growing longer by the day. Probably he could meet Howdy himself, in the dark like this, meet him face to face and pass as a stranger.

Once he saw, from across the street, Miss Crosby lurching out of the doorway; and once Eunice came clumping out in her clubfoot shoes with a couple of bags for the garbage can. Usually there were lights on in the second floor windows of Howdy's and Pam's living room, sometimes the flicker of shadowy figures moving behind the blinds.

He observed the leafing out of the spindly trees on the block, and the progress, against all odds, of Mrs. Faye's petunias in the sooty little scrap of front garden.

He kept tabs, too, on the windows of the fourth floor apartment he had occupied and noted, with a queer pang—as if it were not to be expected!—when they were stripped of their curtains and shades, exposing the emptiness of the room beyond. The gaunt outline of a painter's ladder. Nothing else. Of course they would rent the apartment to someone else. They would be out of their skulls not to. All the same, a pang ...

He took his walks. He observed. And he bided his time.

6

The new tenant was young, Mrs. Faye gave him that, though she didn't care much for his moustache. But nowadays they all had too much hair to suit her. He seemed friendly enough. And cheerful, which was more than could be said for the rest of the household. Like a tomb, it was; they could use somebody around here who hadn't forgotten how to laugh.

His name was David Jackson, and he was recently home from Vietnam, planning to go back to college, graduate school, next term. His father was a business friend of Howdy's, apparently enough of a big shot so that Howdy couldn't very well turn him down. Otherwise, no telling when he would have agreed to let anybody move into Garth's apartment. As if leaving it empty was going to bring the poor lad back to life. Actually all it did was serve as a constant reminder of the whole sorry business, and who needed that?

Practical as her own view of the situation was, Mrs. Faye felt that David's was a little too much of a good thing. "I know it's only because Dad leaned on him that I got the apartment," he said, when she undertook to fill him in on the details. "So his brother copped out. His privilege. I'll let you know if he comes back to haunt me."

No, it didn't seem quite proper, him standing there grinning at her, pleased as Punch with what other people's ill wind had blown his way.

"I wouldn't laugh if I were you," she said darkly. She moved toward the door, clutching the curtain rods which he claimed he had no use for, whoever heard of such a thing, no curtains, and as for some of the posters he had plastered all over the walls—well, she didn't know where to look, that was the honest truth, she simply didn't know where to look. There was precious little else in the line of furniture, aside from a couple of coal-scuttle chairs, a couch, a zigzag-patterned rug that was enough to keep you awake nights, and a lot of hi-fi equipment. Poor old Mr. Bauman, he could be thankful he was hard of hearing.

"Don't go off mad." He bounced over and gave her a little pat on top of her hairnet. Fresh as paint. "You were going to show me how to do the cupboard shelves. Look at it this way, baby. You can't expect me to break down and cry over some joe I never even saw. For all I know, he's well out of it. He must have thought so. I'd be a hypocrite if I—"

"All right. But a little respect wouldn't hurt." Actually, her mind was on the cupboard shelves. He needed showing how, right enough. A more helpless creature when it came to such things she had never seen.

"All the respect in the world," he assured her. "He had the courage of his convictions. I mean it. Seriously. And Howdy's a great guy, and Pam's a stunner, and you, of course, you're the girl of my dreams."

"Go along with you." She couldn't help it, he did make her laugh. She put down the curtain rods and added, "And how about Eunice?"

"Who? Oh yeah, Eunice. She's okay too."

Mrs. Faye sighed. "Did you get the shelf paper like I said?"

He had, indeed, enough for all the kitchens in the house and then some. She put in a pleasurable half hour lining the cupboard shelves for him—he was about as handy as a bear with four left feet—and arranging his dishes, what few there were. But then he didn't need many. As far as she could tell, he lived on hamburgers and cokes—not that he couldn't afford better: plenty of money in his background, that was plain enough. Look at the sports car he drove. His clothes, too, when he bothered to wear anything but those beat-up old jeans; and the silver and bedding he had hauled down from his folks' place in Connecticut. No, he just didn't know any better.

She had brought him a bit of ham for his supper. "Unless you're taking your girl friend out," she said. "Or there's enough for two, if you want to ask her here."

"What girl friend? You have to be on the scene to have a girl friend. Otherwise, forget it." He stared down at the ham; after a moment he pulled off a sliver and tucked it in under his pirate's moustache. "Hey. Not bad."

"Well, I should hope not! No lack of girls, now that you're back on the scene. Just a matter of looking around. Eunice, for instance. She could stand a little cheering up right now."

"Yeah?" he said through another mouthful of ham.

"You keep on, and there won't be enough left for your own supper, let alone anybody else." She picked up the plate and slammed it inside the refrigerator. All right, if he wasn't any more interested than that, far be it from her to thrust Eunice or anybody else down his throat. "Don't forget to return my plate. I'll be off now. I've wasted too much time as it is."

"Okay, I'm all ears. What's with our freckled friend downstairs? You mean she and Garth—"

"If you want to know so bad, ask her." She snapped it out with finality.

But there was no squelching him. "Right on," he called after her as she marched off. "Thanks for the ham. You'll make somebody a wonderful wife. Play your cards right and you might even hook me."

He didn't particularly want to know, and he didn't ask. Eunice told him anyway. Because, after polishing off the rest of the ham and making a few unproductive phone calls, he did wind up inviting her for a drink. If she needed cheering up, okay, he was pretty much at loose ends himself, what with one thing and another—vacation time, nobody answering their phone, classes not due to start for another couple of weeks.

So anyway, he asked her, and she said great, she'd be right up. She was, too. He hardly had time to break out the ice before his door bell chimed.

"I've been dying to see your place," she said candidly. "Mrs. Faye says it's a caution, what you've done with it." And after a moment of forthright gawking: "I don't know. It doesn't seem all that wild to me."

Which left him not knowing exactly what to say. On the one hand, there was "Sorry to disappoint you"; on the other, "Gee, thanks." She didn't give him time for either.

"Here, I brought you a house warming present." She thrust a box of fireplace matches at him. "They're supposed to bring good luck. I didn't buy them special. Somebody gave them to me for Christmas. I've only used a few."

A house warming present. It caught him off guard: the kind of homey gesture that nobody else he knew would make. He looked from the bright-colored box to her face—round, freckled, and at the moment pink with pleasure. Everything out in the open with Eunice. No tricks. No insulation, either.

It was the first time he had given her more than a passing glance. He remembered her hair, of course, the color of salmon, and tied back tonight with a hank of yarn that didn't match the shade of blue in her dress. It had a sailor collar and a pleated miniskirt. She was built like a sturdy child; no seductive curve of waist or ankle; a solid, country look about her.

"You're a good kid." He said it from the heart. "Let's have a house warming drink. Gin and tonic okay? Or there's—"

"Great." She plunked herself down on the couch. "Cheers," she said when he brought the drinks, and took a healthy gulp. Then she told him all about her job, secretary second grade with a real estate firm; about her home town in upstate New York; about her folks, two brothers and a kid sister; plus the highlights of her skiing trips last winter, terrific; and the course she was taking in art appreciation at the New School, also terrific.

He had figured on a fairly droopy session—after all, she was supposed to be feeling low over something or other—with heavy going in the conversation department. Now he began to wonder if she was ever going to run out of steam.

The break came in the middle of the second drink. He lolled in one of the bucket chairs, listening or anyway half-listening, and watching the light beyond the windows thin out from day to early evening. The sudden silence startled him. She was sitting bolt upright, hands to cheeks. "Oh," she said. "Oh. I'm talking too much, right? Excuse me. I always talk too much when I'm nervous."

"Why should you be nervous?"

"Well, because. Well, just for openers, I know why you invited me. You wouldn't have, only Mrs. Faye bugged you into it. Didn't she?"

"Not exactly. She kind of suggested. But I still wouldn't have asked you if I—"

"Like I'm a charity case or something. I don't want people feeling sorry for me, trying to cheer me up. I just want them to leave me alone!"

"Okay." He hesitated. But what the hell, if she could lay it on the line, so could he. "Okay, then why did you take me up on the invitation? You're so anti-social, why say Yes instead of No?"

"That's the other thing," she said, and she took a long, slow, careful look all around the room. Memorizing it. Absorbing the vibes. Or—if he had guessed right about her and Garth—remembering it; sure, that must be what she meant by the other thing, remembering the way it used to be and agonizing over the changes. Probably seemed like sacrilege to her. But then, just when he thought he had it all figured out, she whispered, "I wanted to see where he lived. Just once. I wanted to see his place."

"You mean you were never up here before? But I thought you and Garth—"

"Me, yes. Garth, no. He never even asked me for a date. That's the kind of nut I am." She held out for another moment or so, her face all screwed up and red in patches. Then she sort of doubled over and let loose with the tears.

Trying to comfort her was maybe a mistake. But he couldn't just sit there in the eye of the storm, so to speak, and pretend it wasn't happening. Because brother, was it happening. And never mind the bit about her wanting to be left alone, she hung on to him for dear life, pouring out her tale of woe along with the gulps and sobs. There was little enough to tell: the cocktail hours down at Pam and Howdy's, and the Oh Night of Nights night when she couldn't unlock her door. That about wrapped it up. You couldn't call it an affair. It was too meager, too one-sided. Okay. It was still a big deal to Eunice.

Eventually the strangled sounds she was making into David's shirt front eased off. She blew her nose and croaked, "I'm sorry, I didn't mean to unload everything on you like this, you must wish you'd never—"

"Don't worry about me. You all right now?"

She looked like hell, of course, all blotchy and swollen and bedraggled. His arm was still around her; he gave her a final pat and kissed her in what he meant to be a brotherly way.

But Eunice didn't take it that way. "Go ahead if you want to. It's okay," she said, and so help him if she didn't start undoing her sailor collar.

"Now wait a minute. What do you think you're doing? I mean, Chrissake, Eunice!"

"The realistic approach," she explained, with brisk authority. "It was in this book I read. The realistic approach versus the romantic. After all, sex is just something people do. Like taking a drink of water when you're thirsty."

After a moment of dazed silence he said, "That's how it was with you and Garth? Like taking a drink of water?"

"I didn't read the book until afterward."

She was too much. She was honest to God too much. He gave up. "The bathroom's to the right. Go mop yourself up and I'll take you out to dinner."

"Listen, if you're just asking me because you feel sorry for me—"

"Please." He cast his eyes heavenward, and off she clattered.

Sorry for himself was more like it, he thought glumly. But somebody had to look out for her, you couldn't let a babe in the woods like that run around loose.

He finished off her drink in a silent toast: Okay, Mrs. Faye. You win.

"I called the police again last night," said Miss Crosby. "But of course by the time they got here he was gone. Not that I'm blaming them, I'm sure they do their best, and as one of them said—such a nice young man, really quite handsome—said, 'Miss Crosby, we not only have to catch these jokers, there's got to be a violation of the law before we can make an arrest. As long as he didn't mug you or molest you in any way, it would just be your word against his that he was following you.' All well and good. But what I say is, things have come to a pretty pass when a lady's not safe stepping outside for a breath of air. He was right on my heels when I came in the downstairs door, a great hulking brute, I could hear him breathing ..."

Miss Crosby's followers came in two sizes—great and hulking or lean and tigerish. They were all hard breathers, and they never let her catch more than a glimpse of their faces. Sometimes, like tonight, she only Sensed a Presence. Half an hour ago, having stepped outside for a breath of fresh air at the corner bar, she had tapped on Eunice's door and announced in an ominous whisper that she didn't dare set foot inside her apartment, someone was lying in wait for her there. Was the lock jimmied? No. Had she heard sounds from inside? No. How did she know? She felt it in her bones.

Miss Crosby and her bones. The truth was not in them—as Eunice had once again demonstrated by unlocking the door herself and going in first. Nobody lying in wait, of course, unless you wanted to count the cockroaches who scurried for cover behind the stove when she turned on the lights. (She made a mental note to tell Mrs. Faye.)

She had been trying to make her escape ever since. But this time, as usual, she found herself trapped, with Miss Crosby blocking the way to the door, and no sign of a let-up in her monologue. Poor soul, she just wanted somebody to talk to. All the same, enough was enough.

"You'll have to excuse me, Miss Crosby, but it's getting late, and I really have to—"

"I know, dear, I mustn't keep you, you've been more than kind. You're sure you won't join me in a little nightcap? No? I think I'll have another, just a drop. I wouldn't dream of it ordinarily, but I'm in such a state tonight, my nerves, simply shattered ..." Glass in hand, she lurched to the table beside the window, poured herself quite a sizable drop, and then—before Eunice could make it to the door—let out an arresting, hissing sound.

"What is it? What's the matter?"

"That man," whispered Miss Crosby dramatically. She was pointing out the window. "There he is again. I've seen him before. There. Look. Across the street."

With a sigh of resignation, Eunice joined her at the window. All right, so there was a man across the street. Big deal. A shadowy figure in a wide-brimmed hat, walking along under the trees at a pretty good clip, apparently minding his own business. "What about him?" she asked, and she made as if to turn away.

But Miss Crosby grabbed her arm. "Wait! Wait till he gets to the street light. You haven't had a good look at him yet. Then you'll see what I mean. Because it's not just my imagination, I thought it might be at first, but—There! Doesn't it strike you too? The resemblance? Isn't it uncanny?"

"Of course not," said Eunice, much too quickly. "If you're talking about Garth—"

"I didn't say it. You did." Miss Crosby's cupids bow mouth curved into a smug smile. "Oh, I know. When did Garth ever wear such an outfit as that? But forget about the clothes. The way he walks, and the tilt to his head, and one shoulder pushed forward. Garth to the life. I knew you'd see it too. Uncanny. That's the only word. Uncanny. And notice how he keeps looking across at this house? He always does. As if he's watching. I can't help feeling there's something strange about him, something strange going on, ever since Memorial Day I've sensed it ..." Her voice went hushed and portentous. "There's no absolute proof that he's dead, you know. They never recovered his body."

"Don't be silly," said Eunice sharply. She pulled her arm free and headed for the door. This time she reached it without interference. Her good night was curt. Miss Crosby's was gentle, and even without looking back, Eunice knew that the smug little smile was still there on her face.

It couldn't have been Garth, of course. Only Miss Crosby—half smashed as she was most of the time, and scatty all of the time—could dream up such a possibility. Trust her to make a muchness out of nothing. Or practically nothing: Eunice couldn't deny that first wild leap of her heart, before her mind told her it couldn't be. After all, the world was full of look-alikes, talk-alikes, walk-alikes. It wasn't the only time she had seen someone who put her in mind of Garth. How often, especially during the first week after his death, had she been caught by a gesture, a slant of the head, a voice? And it always turned out to be a perfect stranger. She might as well get used to these fleeting resemblances; they would be with her as long as she remembered Garth, and she would remember him for the rest of her life. There would never be anyone else for her, never. She did not rule out sex episodes, why should she? As the book said, something people did. But real love, even when it was unrequited, like hers for Garth, was once and for always.

She knew what she knew, no matter how much David pooh-poohed the idea. He pooh-poohed it plenty. (For since that first evening, when she came apart at the seams, they had settled into a casual kind of comradeship. Potluck dinners at her place. Listening to records at his. He was inclined to lecture her, but usually she didn't mind.)

David didn't believe in real love. Or so he claimed. He looked pretty starry-eyed, Eunice noticed, the night he managed to get through to what's-her-name, the girl he kept trying to call, only she was always out of town or busy or something.

Could it be he was lecturing himself as much as Eunice? Could be, though she wasn't about to say so to him. No. There were some things she kept to herself. Not many—she admitted it; but that was one. The man she had seen from Miss Crosby's window was another. She knew in advance what David's reaction would be: How ridiculous can you get! And for once, she had to agree. Ridiculous. A typical bit of Miss-Crosbyism. Not to be taken seriously, any more than the perilous adventures she fabricated for herself, the followers she reported to the police, the premonitions and feelings in her bones. "Garth to the life," she had said. But the point was that Garth was dead, so it couldn't be, it couldn't possibly be.

Then, the next night, Eunice saw the man again. Not from the window this time, but from David's convertible. They had been to a rock concert uptown, and were cruising the block, on the lookout for a parking place; David was sounding off, something about the state of the world, she wasn't paying much attention ...

She must have let out a gasp, because he broke off in the middle of a word and asked what had hit her.

"That man." She heard her own voice echoing Miss Crosby's dramatic whisper. Felt again the inner lurch. Realized that her hand was clamped on the door of the open car, and that David was beady-eyed with curiosity. "Nothing, really," she stammered. "He looks like somebody I know. I mean, sort of like. Only I don't think it can be. No, no, don't honk at him or anything. Because it's probably just—"

The man was at the corner, turning up the avenue. That quick, purposeful stride, so like Garth that it gave her the shivers. He was wearing the same wide-brimmed hat that hid his face, the same striped sweater and sleazy-looking slacks. His right arm was in a sling. She hadn't noticed that the other time.

"We could follow him," said David in an off-hand way, and when the light changed he turned up the avenue too. "Why not? Give you a chance to make up your mind. Wherever he's going, he's not taking the subway. Or the bus, either. Does he live in the neighborhood, this pal of yours?"

"I don't know." She swallowed. "He's not exactly a pal, just somebody

I used to know. Back home. That's where I knew him, back home, we went to high school together. He was kind of a kook, but still, you know, one of the gang. Well, actually, we had a thing for each other for a while, only Mom didn't like him. He came to New York before me, but I never got in touch with him, so I'm not even sure he's still here. And even if he is, it would be pretty wild, wouldn't it, running into him like this ..."

Apparently she had hit on the right explanation as far as David was concerned. "Oh, I don't know. Maybe it's kismet," he said, and gave her one of his grins.

There wasn't much traffic, this late at night, not many pedestrians, either, so it was easy enough to keep the man in sight. But as impossible as ever for Eunice to get more than a passing glimpse of his face. She was left swinging like a crazy pendulum between Yes and No, No and Yes. She had lost count of how many blocks when at last he turned west from the avenue, and they were stuck with the light behind a cab, so she still couldn't be sure.

"Lucky it's a west bound street," said David as he negotiated the turn. "Otherwise we might have lost him."

It was a dreary street of warehouses, wholesalers, bodegas, and run-down apartment houses flanked by battered, overflowing garbage cans. Music blared from one of the crummy bars they passed, raucous laughter, the sound of quarreling voices. The man pressed on for two more blocks, single-minded and self-contained, before he reached his destination.

Not even an apartment house. Furnished rooms, with a Men Only sign. Key in hand, he went up the steps; then he took off his hat, and for a moment—before he opened the door and disappeared inside— Eunice saw his face, clear and unmistakable, in the street light.

Had she known from the start? It was not so much shock that she felt, more like a thump of confirmation.

"Okay," said David. "End of the line, and whether or not he's Mr. Right from the old home town, he can't be making it too big or he wouldn't be living here. Be that as it may—"

She did not wait for more. Did not stop to think, either. The car was barely moving; she was out of it in a flash, stumbling a little, but only for a step or two. She did take time to toss a few words David's way: something about wait for her, she'd be back in a minute, as long as they were here she'd like to make sure. She owed David that much. And besides, she didn't want him following her.

There was only the one doorbell, and when she rang it nothing happened for long, long minutes. The woman who finally answered it— after peering out at Eunice through the dingy glass—was large, sagging, and hard-eyed. She had the voice of a bluejay. "Can't you read? Sign says Men Only."

"But I'm not—I'm looking for a friend of mine. Garth Sullivan. Could I speak to him, please? It's important."

"Who? Sullivan? Nobody here by that name."

"But there must be! I just saw him come in!"

"Nobody here by that name," repeated the woman, and slammed the door shut.

Belatedly, Eunice remembered the sling. Maybe if she called the woman back, described Garth ...

And then? Garth had chosen to disappear—for reasons she could only guess at. He may have simply decided to put an end to the unhappiness of being Garth Sullivan and start again as someone else. Or he may have been faced with some private, acute problem that could be solved in no other way. Nothing of the sort had come to light; still, it was a possibility. In either case, he was not going to thank her for barging in on him, much less for spreading the news that his death was a hoax and that he was living here under an assumed name. If she wanted to help him—and she did, she did!—her best bet was to keep her mouth shut and leave him alone until she had had time to figure out the right approach.

All right. Before, she had lied to David instinctively (and a good thing, too) without thinking through her reasons except that it seemed the quickest way to shut him up.

Now she did so with conscious deliberation. "Well, that settles that," she said as she got back into the car. "It wasn't him, of course. I never really thought so. But it would have bugged me till I found out for sure."

"Yeah," said David. "You okay? You look kind of—"

"I'm fine," she said, and put an end to the conversation by turning on the radio.

7

The time of waiting was over. If Pam and Howdy had not settled back into their usual routine by now, they were never going to. And Garth himself was ready, had been ready for the past week. This was the Wednesday that would tell the tale.

Getting into the house posed no problem; he still had his keys. What gave him pause was the possibility of a chance encounter with one of the occupants. Mrs. Faye, for instance. She was always popping in and out herself, and she kept a sharp eye on everybody else's comings and goings. He wouldn't dare go through with his plan tonight if he ran into her—or any of the others, either. Even if they didn't recognize him, they would notice him as an outsider, wonder about him, remember him. After all, he had lived here, he knew how it was in a house this small.

At least the weather was on his side: overcast, threatening rain, not the kind of evening when Mrs. Faye would be outside pottering around with her petunias or gossiping with the neighbors. Not only that. When he circled the block in advance, he saw the Bingo Tonight sign in front of the church and knew that Mrs. Faye was safely out of his way for hours to come. Old Mr. Bauman never went out after sundown. Miss Crosby's windows were dark; she was probably either sleeping off the afternoon's drinks or tanking up at the corner bar. Lights glowed on the second floor, but with the shades and drapes drawn he had no way of knowing whether or not Howdy was there alone. There were also lights and drawn shades on the top floor, in what was no longer his apartment, but the new tenant's—whoever he or she might be—and the hi-fi was going strong. Eunice? He could not even check on her windows; her apartment, like Mr. Bauman's, was on the back. Nothing to do but trust in God.

All right. The coast was as clear as he could hope for, no one in sight except for a cluster of dog-walkers at the far end of the block. He crossed the street fast and pushed open the iron-grilled outer door. Once inside the stuffy little foyer he paused, listening for footsteps from within, the creak of the elevator. There was not a sound. His key turned smoothly in the lock. Noiseless in his rubber soles, he slid through the doorway into the hall with its twin lights on either side of the old-fashioned hall piece, its dark green tiles and striped wallpaper. The elevator arrow stood at two. Not that the indicator was any more reliable than the contraption itself. He took the stairway.

A couple of steps before the second floor he paused again to listen. If there was anybody there for Howdy to talk to, he would be talking. If he was alone, cooking up one of his creations, he would have the radio going to keep him company. Or so Garth had figured. But at first he heard nothing at all. Was the apartment empty, then? Quite possibly. They usually left a light burning when they went out of an evening. In that case he would either have to postpone his plan entirely or settle for the half-measure of taking the panel tonight and leaving the Howdy business till later.

He crept up the last step. There stood the elevator—as billed, for once, and empty. Among the keys on his ring was one to Howdy's and Pam's apartment, left over from the days when he used to look after Mittens during their week ends at Arrow Lake. He had planned to use it tonight, had looked forward with relish to walking in on Howdy, seeing the expression on his face change, as it was sure to, from blank incredulity to amazement to the final, futile alarm. Howdy or no Howdy, he could still use the key, pick up the panel (plus a few other odds and ends) and, again as planned, force the lock on his way out, to make it look like a run-of-the-mill sneak thief job. They might not even notice that the panel was missing, at least not for a while

At that moment he caught the murmur of a voice on the other side of the door. A masculine voice, but not Howdy's, and too soft and quick to be intelligible. Surely no radio or TV voice would come out so blurred, particularly since the set was at this end of the living room. And surely no real live person would be talking to himself. Okay. Whoever he was, whatever he was saying, whoever was with him—Garth could forget his plan for tonight. There would be another time, of course. It was just that he was primed for action now, now, and all for nothing, not even the half-measure as a consolation prize. He might as well get the hell out of here while the getting was good, before somebody saw him and blew his chances for another time.

What stopped him was Howdy's laugh, and after the laugh his voice—good old Howdy, always obliging—cluing him in, not all the way, but enough to keep him rooted there, straining to hear more. "Lenny." That was the one word he caught for sure. Because even Howdy's clarion tenor was subdued; he and his visitor must be at least half the length of the living room away from the door.

"Lenny." It had to be, it almost had to be, Lenny of Yesteryear Antiques, that half-baked dealer in junk, that artsy, brainless, self-styled creator of distinctive jewelry who was to be entrusted with the panel ... had the abomination already been accomplished? The thought turned Garth hollow, his forehead went clammy with sweat. He edged past the elevator, closer to the door, drawn by the terrible necessity to know.

Again Howdy obliged, and this time, though there were still gaps, the gist of what he said was clear. "... for her birthday, the end of next month. A surprise, that's why I asked you to come tonight, because it's her teaching night ... Not much time, I know, but I'll make it worth your while ... Something different, Lenny, something super-special, poor Pam, it's been a rough time for us both ..."

Garth leaned against the wall, weak-kneed with relief. There was still time, but not much, and that little only by the grace of God. If he had not hesitated the extra moment and heard the name Lenny

"Now don't worry, I'll extend myself." Lenny's voice was no longer a blur. Obviously he was moving toward the door too, on his way out. "After all, old friends like you and Pam, only too glad. I've already got an inkle about how it ought to be, no no, I'm not going to verbalize, that takes the edge off. Something super-special, take my word for it, and ready in time."

"One for the road?"

"I mustn't. I've got to run. Really. Group therapy tonight, I'll drop this off at the shop on my way, just make it, not a minute to spare."

There was more palaver, but Garth stopped listening. It was time for him to make himself scarce. From the sound of it they were in the foyer by now, practically at the door; in any case, he had heard all he needed to know, and what he knew went through him like a flash of lightning. His plan could be salvaged, after all! His whole plan, not just half of it. He need only nip part way up the next flight of stairs and wait there, safely out of sight, until Lenny was gone and Howdy was alone in the apartment. With Pam not due back for an hour, he had plenty of time. Then downtown to Yesteryear, snatch the panel, why, with luck he could be clean out of it by this time tomorrow night, if not actually in Mexico then on his way.

But before he could get past the elevator he heard somebody coming down the stairs. Two sets of footsteps clattering along fast, laughter, a girl's voice nattering on about whether or not it was raining yet. Eunice's voice; he recognized it with an inward thud. Eunice, of course. Who else? Trust her to show up at the wrong moment. He dare not risk running into her face to face on his way up the stairs, and the clicking of the lock on Howdy's door warned him that he could not make it down the stairs without being seen, either.

There was only one way out of the trap. He ducked inside the elevator and pushed the button for the fourth floor. If it stalled—

It did not. But as it gathered its whirring, clanking self together and tottered upward in a series of stately jerks he looked down and saw, through a haze of total shock, Miss Crosby sitting on the floor.

She was wearing high-heeled sandals and a flowered, garden party sort of dress. Her head was draped in a long chiffon scarf, its bedraggled ends flung dashingly over her shoulder. Setting down her can of beer, she extended her hand in a gracious lady-come-to-see gesture.

"Good evening. How nice to see you again. Though I must say it was very naughty of you, leading everyone to think ... Personally, I was never quite convinced, no, I felt it in my bones, but who was going to listen to little old me? Too fantastic. I doubted it myself, at first. Once I had seen you, of course—before now, I mean, oh yes, I spied you, more than once, across the street. I bet that's something you didn't know. Did you?"

He shook his head numbly.

"Oh yes, more than once, walking along—that's how I recognized you, by your walk—no more dead than I am. They wouldn't listen to me even then."

She had told them, of course. As she would tell them about this encounter; and though they might discount her story now, while his plan was still only a plan, the chances were all against their doing so afterwards. They. Their. Them. Pam, who knew him too well for safety. Mrs. Faye, who was his avowed, natural-born enemy. From the first he had seen them as the potential agents of his downfall. Miss Crosby had emerged as a threat only at the end, the last morning of his life as Garth Sullivan. Then, too, he had come upon her in the elevator. Then, too, she had smiled her little, knowing smile. "After all, you hate your brother too."

He stared down, fascinated, at her thin bird legs, genteelly crossed, her draggletail finery, her puffy face with its dark glasses and dry-straw bangs and cupids bow mouth.

"Naughty," she said, and she shook her finger at him archly. "You and your tricks. But you didn't fool me. I knew all the time you were up to something. I'm not going to ask what, mind you, far be it from me to pry. You have your reasons ..."

"Yes," he whispered. "I have my reasons."

He knelt on the floor beside her.

"Hey there." Howdy greeted them as they came down the stairs. He was wearing an apron, and he had stepped out into the hall to see a visitor on his way—a reedy, anxious-looking fellow with a flat package under his arm. "This is Lenny, kids. Eunie. And Dave Jackson, Dave's our newest addition. No use waiting for the elevator, Lenny. You just missed it, God knows when or if it will ever get back down."

"I'll walk," said Lenny. "In fact, I'll run. I'm late enough as it is. Nice to meet you, Miss Uh, and, uh, Dave—"

"Give you a lift somewhere?" offered David. "We're going out for pizza, and my car's right out in front. Be glad to drop you off. Any place short of Brooklyn."

"Perish the thought. Brooklyn. No, it's the Village, West Fourth, but I have to stop at my shop first, Yesteryear, it's on Greenwich, so maybe it's too complicated, too much trouble—"

"No trouble at all. Come on. Eunice can wait for her pizza. She's too fat anyway."

Eunice blushed, Howdy and David laughed, Lenny said, well, if they were sure they didn't mind. "Don't worry, Howdy," he added, tapping his package. "Super-special. And in plenty of time for Pam's birthday."

"Right. Remember, Eunie? That gizmo I brought back from Mexico?

We showed it to you one night when you were down here. You and Garth." As always, his voice sank on the name. He paused, looking into space, fumbling with his apron.

"Sure I remember. What is it, Lenny? Do you know?"

"Haven't the foggiest. Mexico's off my beat. There simply isn't time for everything, you know, and right now I'm into Oriental, not that I pretend to be an expert, but—Anyway, whatever it is, it's going to make a beautiful necklace. I'll be in touch, Howdy. Bye now."

"I told you it was raining," Eunice said when they reached the street. "I should have stopped to pick up my raincoat. Oh well. I'm not going back for it now."

They made a dash for the car, Lenny shielding the package under his jacket. "This is a godsend," he told David as he slid into the back seat. "Really. I'd never have gotten a cab. They all vanish, the minute there's a drop of rain. If I didn't have to leave this at the shop first, of course, but I wouldn't dream of taking anything of any value with me to therapy, not after the director's wallet turned up missing and he warned us he couldn't be responsible. And it's always a disaster for everybody if one member of the group is late." He leaned forward tensely to give directions. Up Sixth first, then across and down. He would say when to turn. After a moment of silence—apparently a rarity with Lenny—he fell back with a groan of such despair that even David, unflappable as he was, gave a little start.

Eunice turned all the way around. "Hey. What happened? What's the matter?"

"Oh no! I can't bear it," wailed Lenny, above the swishing of the windshield wipers. "Not again! I can't have come off without the keys to the shop ... But they're not here. I have. I've done it again. I remember now, I decided at the last minute to change jackets. I must have left them in the corduroy. They're not here. They're at home!"

David slowed down and asked, "Where's home?"

"Eighty-sixth," said Lenny in a hollow voice. "East."

"Oh. Well, we haven't got time then. To drive you home, I mean, all the way up town and back again to the therapy place. West Fourth, you said? Yeah. I don't think we can make it."

"Of course not. It's the story of my life, the same old self-defeating pattern. Why can't I break out of it? I try. God knows, I try. And then, just when I think I'm making progress—"

"Now let's not panic," said David. "Why not leave Howdy's gizmo with us? That way I can still get you to therapy in time and no sweat. I'll be home in the morning. You can pick it up then. Or if you'd rather, you could leave it in a subway locker overnight."

"I'd probably lose the key. It would be just like me. Would you keep it for me? Really? That would be marvelous. I can't thank you enough—"

He could try, though, and did, all the way to West Fourth Street.

"Yak yak yak," said David when they had left him behind. He gestured toward the package on Eunice's lap. "What is this thing, anyway?"

"Nobody knows. Kind of a plaque. Or a panel. With like carving, and stones set in it. I doubt if they're real." She gave him a brief run-down on Howdy's Mexican adventure. "The guy probably sold him a bill of goods. Garth seemed to think so. He spent quite a while down there a couple of years ago, before he hurt his hand. He didn't seem to know what it was, either." She had a sudden mental image, very vivid, of Garth that night, stroking the wood of the panel. He had set it down at last, so carefully, almost reverently.

Alive. He was still alive. For two days now she had lived with the knowledge locked up inside her, where it must stay—that was the one certainty—until she hit on some way of reaching him. Surely the fact that she had kept his secret would convince him that he could rely on her. For further silence, if he wanted it; for help, if he needed it. Once he realized that he had nothing to fear from her, he would ...

"Snap out of it," said David. "You act like you're in a trance or something. What's eating you tonight, anyway?"

"Nothing. Not a thing." She spoke quickly; otherwise she might weaken. It would be so easy, such a relief. Even a glance at him was risky: his homely face with the grandiose moustache, the nose that was not only too big but had a hump in it, the deep brown eyes. They didn't miss much, those eyes of David's. They had a way of drawing things out of her.

"I'm concentrating on a pizza place, is all," she said. "There's one up ahead. There. On the left."

Mrs. Faye's doorbell rang next morning at eight o'clock. She looked through the peep hole first—she always did these days; you couldn't be too careful—and saw old Mr. Bauman in his button-front sweater and visored cap, off for his morning constitutional.

"Excuse me, Mrs. Faye." It was his usual preface when he had a problem.

"Don't tell me the elevator's stalled again." No, of course not; he would have called her on the phone. Getting down the stairs was hard enough for him, and as for getting back up again, it was out of the question, a physical impossibility. Something with the plumbing, then? The electricity? A stuck window? The alternatives ran through her mind, familiar as a daily train.

"What? I'm sorry, I didn't quite catch—" His hand jerked upward to cup his good ear. Pretty shaky this morning, she noticed.

"Never mind. Not worth repeating. I say, it's not worth repeating!"

"I'm fine, thank you. Can't complain." He blinked at her. Settled his dentures. Came out with it at last. "It's Miss Crosby. In the elevator. I think maybe there's something wrong."

"Passed out, I suppose. At this hour of the day. I declare, if she isn't the limit." She bustled past him, clicking her tongue. "Well, I can't say I'm surprised. Now don't upset yourself, Mr. Bauman, I'll take care of it. I know how to handle her, God knows I've done it often enough in the past."

But this time was different. She opened the elevator door, took one look, and let out a banshee shriek that brought Howdy out on to the second-floor landing wanting to know what the hell was going on.

"Murder!" screamed Mrs. Faye. Time after time, the one word.

Within minutes she had roused everybody else in the house, too. David came pounding downstairs clutching a towel around his middle. Eunice was more or less dressed, hairbrush in hand. Pam was in robe and slippers. Wild-eyed, gasping out questions, they gathered in front of the elevator where Miss Crosby lay crumpled in her flowery dress, terrible-faced above the scarf that was wound around her neck.

David was the first to pull himself together. Into the stricken silence—for by this time Mrs. Faye had run out of steam and the others could only stare, dumb with shock—he said, "I'll call the police. Don't touch her, anybody. Don't touch anything."

As if any of them was likely to. They huddled together for comfort. Pam and Eunice had begun to whimper; Howdy stood between them, with an arm around each. Mrs. Faye still had her hands clapped over her eyes, and was praying. Presently Mr. Bauman shuffled to the staircase and lowered himself tremulously to the second step from the bottom.

"They'll be right here," David said when he came back from Mrs. Faye's apartment. He glanced toward the elevator door, closed now on its macabre occupant, and added in a subdued voice, "Do you suppose she was there all night? She could have been. Eunice and I didn't use the elevator when we came in. It was up on the top floor. Quicker to walk. Unless you used it, Pam, when you got back from school—"

She shook her head. "It was on the fourth floor then, too. I usually walk, anyway, unless I've got the shopping cart."

"Yeah, but no telling when Miss Crosby came home," said Howdy. "Except that—Hey, remember, kids, you were there when Lenny was leaving? And I said to him no use waiting for the elevator, he'd just missed it? I figured it was Miss Crosby going up then. She was always getting mixed up and pushing the button for four instead of her own floor. So even if I had noticed how far up it went, not that I did, it wouldn't have meant anything. I just assumed naturally—"

"Murdered!" burst out Mrs. Faye. "I thought she was drunk, God forgive me, I was ready to give her the rough side of my tongue. The poor harmless befuddled creature laying there murdered all night long, and not a soul to help her. He followed her in, the villain, many's the time she's told how somebody was following her, and nobody believed it was anything but a tale, ah, it's too cruel ..." She broke off and flew to open the door to the police.

From then on it was a constant procession. Detectives, medical authorities, photographers, more police swarming through the house in search of clues, coming and going in their cars. Eventually the sorry little bundle that had been Miss Crosby was removed, along with her handbag, stripped of cash, and what was left of her last six-pack—five cans untouched, one empty. Her brother was located and notified, after numerous phone calls; he was vacationing in Canada. Her apartment was checked: nothing missing or disturbed. The lobby door downstairs had not been forced. It looked indeed as if someone had followed her in and killed her for whatever money was to be found in her handbag. Probably not much. Her brother kept her on a short leash.

As to whether or not she had lain there "murdered all night long," in Mrs. Faye's phrase, that must wait for the medical report on the approximate time of her death.

Meanwhile, they all contributed their bits and pieces of information. About how they had spent the evening before. About the elevator, which only Miss Crosby and Mr. Bauman were in the habit of using regularly, and which had risen to the fourth floor about eight o'clock last night and as far as was known had stayed there until this morning. And about Miss Crosby's way of life, because these were not the regular precinct cops, who were well acquainted with her and wouldn't have had to ask.

"Check with Joe's Bar," said Mrs. Faye. "That's where she was headed when I saw her about six, poor creature, dolled up like she was going to a party. And they'll like as not know at the delicatessen what time she stopped in for the beer. She always went there, they let her run up a bill, more's the pity."

They had gathered in Howdy's and Pam's apartment for the questioning, and before it was over Lenny arrived, complete with police escort, and in such a state of agitation that he seemed about to fly apart. "What is this? I mean, what—The place crawling with cops, nobody allowed in, except I told them I was here last night, and—As if I hadn't been through enough this morning without—"

He listened, bug-eyed. "Miss Crosby? The lady lush? I remember seeing her once or twice, tottering along the street—" Tottering himself, he reached the couch and collapsed, shuddering. The detectives waited politely for him to regain his composure before querying him about his visit here last night. He could add nothing to what they had already heard from Howdy, David and Eunice. After therapy he had taken the subway home and gone straight to bed.

And what had he found when he reached his shop this morning?

"Broken into," he announced accusingly. "Again. That makes three times in the last six months. Yes, of course I reported it. For all the good it does me. I got off lucky this time. All that's missing is the petty cash. So it could have been worse. At least they didn't take my tools, the way they did the first time. This isn't a city anymore, it's a jungle! Unfit for human habitation! Wild beasts roaming the streets, murdering, stealing ..."

After a while, when the police cleared out, they all had a drink in memory of Miss Crosby. It seemed a fitting tribute. Old Mr. Bauman dropped off to sleep over his. Everybody else had a second. They dispersed one by one—Howdy and Eunice to their offices, Mrs. Faye to her chores, which today would include many a lengthy confab with the neighbors. Pam had a dental appointment, David a date uptown. Life, after all, must go on.

Lenny was the last to leave. What with the morning's disruptions, too shattering, disaster piled on disaster, it was no wonder that he forgot what he had come here for in the first place, or that no one thought to remind him.

The panel remained where it was, in David's apartment.

8

The waitress in the coffee shop across the street was a middle-aged, plain-faced woman who took a kindly interest in her regulars. "Oh, wow," she said when at last Garth dragged himself down there. "If you don't look like the morning after the night before!"

"Coffee. Black."

"Maybe a glass of tomato juice?"

He shook his head and watched dully as she padded off to the coffee urn. A hangover. Okay. It was as good a diagnosis as any. The symptoms were all there: the pounding in his head, the parched interior, the jangling of the wires that connected him with reality. Then, too, there were the freakish lapses in his memory of last night. Black-outs, they were called; drunks took them as a matter of course.

He had been stone cold sober, sharply aware of what he was doing and why. And at the beginning his mind had worked with lightning precision. It was only after his futile ransacking of Yesteryear Antiques that he lost his cool. Well, yes, there was that strange little hiatus in the elevator. He remembered kneeling beside Miss Crosby, reaching for her scarf while she prattled on, befuddled to the end; and then he remembered fleeing up the stairs to the roof and down again by way of the fire escape. The moments between were like a row of asterisks, weighted with significance, completely lacking in specific details.

He knew what the asterisks stood for, all right. Miss Crosby had given him no choice. He had had no choice afterwards, either. He didn't dare go back to Howdy's apartment. If someone rang the elevator bell and found Miss Crosby—as someone might at any second—the roof would cave in on him and his plan, and no picking up the pieces. But he could still go through with the other part of his plan. Or so he had reasoned at the time, confident as he was of finding the panel at Yesteryear ...

"There you are, Mr. Mettler," said the waitress as she set the steaming cup down in front of him. She knew all her regulars by name, first name in most cases, and for those who felt the need, she was always ready to lend a sympathetic ear. "Hand coming along okay? No sling today, I see."

He had forgotten it. Another one of those mental lapses. Minor, of course; the fake cast was still there, and his money safe inside. All the same, it shook him up a bit. He mumbled something noncommittal, without looking up from his *Daily News*. He had already leafed through it; there was nothing about Miss Crosby. But as he took his first sip of coffee her name sprang out of the air behind him. He turned warily: some guy back there with a transistor radio tuned to the eleven o'clock news. "... the body of the forty-seven-year-old woman, apparently the victim of a mugger who followed her home last night, was discovered this morning, strangled and robbed, in the elevator of the four-story house ..."

She had given him no choice. And by now he had lived with the thought of murder—but not this one, not this one—too long for it to pack much of a wallop. The row of asterisks remained. So did Miss Crosby herself, as a complication, an added, unforeseen hazard. Because now, for a while at least, the police would be buzzing around the house. That was all he needed. One more hazard. One more frustration.

He felt again a surge of last night's rage. It had come on him gradually, during his search of the jumble of junk known as Yesteryear Antiques. He had walked down there from the house, stopping at an all-night cafeteria on the way to get out of the rain and to kill some time. There was no point in arriving before Lenny accomplished his mission, and as for his own mission, the later the better. Getting in was simple: the block was dark, deserted, and there was a back door, accessible from the alley. The lock was new, but the old wood of the door itself was easily forced with his clasp knife; two minutes' work and he was inside the back room, where Lenny evidently produced his creations, and where on the work table—very thoughtful of him—he had left a flashlight.

But from there on it was all fiasco. For a while he could not believe it. The panel *must* be here. No reason to panic, just because it was not out in plain sight, as he had expected. In spite of being rushed for time, Lenny had paused long enough to tuck it away somewhere. That was all. Garth had gone on searching, methodically at first, then, as the rage built up inside him, with less and less regard for caution. He had torn the place apart—not in panic, but in rage.

To be cheated out of both his prizes, just when he was so close to grasping them! The best opportunity he would ever have, and what had it come to? An added complication. The two dollars and thirty-three cents from Miss Crosby's handbag; five dollars and a handful of change from Yesteryear's petty cash box. Plus a rage hangover, indistinguishable from the ordinary kind except that it could not be cured with a glass of tomato juice or a hair of the dog or any of the other standard remedies.

He had given up at last and left Yesteryear. The interlude that followed was pretty much a black-out except for a few fractured memories of prowling the Village streets in the rain. He had wound up—by what means he had no idea—back in his room, stretched out on the lumpy bed, as incapable as a drunk of purposeful thought or action.

The panel, the panel. Hunched over the lunch counter, he tried to focus his twitching mind on finding it. As he must—and soon, before Lenny began his brainless, blasphemous work on it. Howdy could wait. The panel could not. It was probably safe for today: Lenny would be too upset by the break-in at Yesteryear, and too busy putting it to rights, to settle down to his "creative" depredations. But that was as far as the time margin could be stretched.

He had met Lenny a couple of times. A fool. Howdy of course was taken in by his artistic pretensions, his nervous, fake-chic patter. Pam liked him for other reasons. He was so kind and gentle, she said, so anxious about everything, and yet so sweet. All right. A gentle, anxious, sweet fool who nevertheless had it in his power to destroy not only the panel but Garth's whole plan.

"'Bye now. Have a nice day," said the waitress as he slid off his stool. The coffee had not helped. He felt light-headed, shaky, mistrustful of his own mental workings. But he had nothing else to rely on. And no time to waste.

The first phone booth he passed was occupied. In the next two the instruments had been pulled out by the roots. He entered the fourth. There was even a directory. Sealed off, sweating, he found the number and dialed.

David's date uptown was at the Guggenheim with Marian, and he had hoped to prolong it into a luxurious, leisurely lunch, possibly beyond, into one of those golden times he remembered from past summers, afternoon melting into evening, evening into night, and the two of them too bemused to notice. Not that he had expected it to be exactly the same, but still ... He had seen her only once since he got back, at a big brawl of a picnic where everybody knew everybody except him. And today wasn't what it should have been either. His fault, maybe: he knew he wasn't at his best, Miss Crosby's death had thrown him out of kilter.

Anyway, there was just the museum; after that—much as she would adore lunch—Marian was due back at her aunt's apartment, they were all leaving tomorrow at the crack of dawn for the Cape, she simply had to do some last-minute shopping, not to mention packing.

He listened in a kind of sad embarrassment, and left her at her aunt's apartment with an empty, all-gone feeling.

Okay, okay. He got the message. About time, God knows. She had done everything but spell it out. Before he came home, with her letters, which had dwindled to a skimpy little trickle; now that he was home, with her spate of excuses. Yes, it was about time.

He had a luxurious, leisurely, and very lonely lunch. It was mid-afternoon by the time he got back to the house. Mrs. Faye was across the street, too busy gabbing with the super of the brownstone facing hers to give David more than a wave of the hand. Inside, all was profound, graveyard silence. If there were any cops still around, they were lying low. In the elevator, perhaps; he did not investigate. He wondered if anybody except Mr. Bauman, poor old boy, would ever again set foot inside the thing.

The silence in his own apartment was even more brooding. But somehow it didn't seem proper to turn on the hi-fi. For a while he fidgeted around. For another while he just sat, staring out the window and remembering something Miss Crosby had said to him, in one of her less lucid moments. "Forgive me for mentioning it, I wouldn't for the world want to put such an idea in your head, but haven't you ever sensed something strange in your apartment? Like a presence? As if it might be haunted? No? But of course you didn't know Garth. Such a strange man. Nothing like Howdy. Different as night from day. It would be like him to haunt the place ... But we don't really know he's dead, do we? No actual proof."

"Right," David had said cheerfully. "So that rules out the ghostly presence bit. I mean, you gotta be dead before you can haunt."

Miss Crosby and her boozy notions. He was in a mood, that was all; otherwise he wouldn't even have thought of it. In a mood, and the place was so damn silent, and—

Nobody had believed Miss Crosby's tales about guys following her either. Yet the fact remained that she was dead, murdered, presumably by one of those alleged figments of her imagination.

Well, but that didn't prove anything about her other notions. There was a big difference between muggers and ghosts.

When his eye fell on the package from last night, Lenny's package, he felt an instant lifting of spirit. It had slipped everybody's mind this morning, including Lenny's, though he had undoubtedly come for the express purpose of picking it up. Why not save him another trip and return it to him now? Anything beat sitting here arguing with himself about ghosts.

He remembered the address from last night. A fifteen-minute walk. Just what the doctor ordered. He set off briskly, already restored to his usual buoyant state of mind.

After the telephone call Lenny rather lost track of things. Yet shaken as he was he had gone on working—in fits and starts, to be sure, and mindlessly, like a wind-up toy—still, he had managed to restore Yesteryear to some sort of order. Somehow he never got around to carrying out his first impulse, which was to lock the door and put up the Closed sign. Just one of the things he kept losing track of. So there had been the usual quota of browsers, among them a woman who actually bought the pitcher-and-bowl set he had been trying to unload for months. Quite a coup, really; ordinarily it would have set him up no end.

Now the wind-up toy had whirred to a stop, and he sat hunched on the piano stool near the door to the back room, his hands between his knees, his mind fumbling uselessly and ceaselessly with the telephone call. He might have imagined it? No. The anonymous whispering voice could not be wished out of existence. Neither could his own voice blurting out the answers. He hadn't had the self-possession, let alone the courage, to lie or stall. All right. He was no hero. No great brain, either. But bright enough to know where lying or stalling would get him. Especially since the whisperer had spelled it out for him in considerable detail. And Lenny couldn't help it, he had this thing about violence, he simply couldn't ...

Once more the bell above the door jangled; once more he stiffened in panic over the unlocked door, the Closed sign left unhung. And only the one dim light burning in the shop, so that all he could make out was a dark, faceless figure pausing in the doorway, fuzzily silhouetted against the dazzle of sun.

"Hey, Lenny! You around? I can't—Oh, there you are."

He recognized the voice, David's, and croaked out a greeting. It was all he could manage. Perched on his stool, clenched in on this new anxiety, he watched as David picked his way toward him. He was carrying something. A package under his arm. Again he paused, no doubt waiting for his eyes to adjust to the change in light.

"You okay, Lenny? I mean, you seem kind of—"

Quiet. That was the word he was groping for, of course. Lenny the non-stop talker was not living up to his reputation. Instead of giving out with his customary chatter, he was sitting here practically in the dark, and in unnatural silence—unnatural even to a casual acquaintance like David. The only way to restore the semblance of normality, and it must be restored, was to start talking.

Say something, anything, no, not anything. Not, God forbid, the telephone call. But something, because David still stood there watching and waiting.

"I'm exhausted, is all. Absolutely exhausted." And he launched into an account of his day's work, he hadn't stopped for a minute, literally, not for a minute, how could he, with the place in such utter chaos, though he had been tempted more than once just to lock up—what was he saying, why bother?—just walk out and leave it for the next thief to paw through ...

It was quite a good imitation of himself, he thought. Maybe a little feverish, but that was understandable under the circumstances. On a wave of confidence, he sprang from his stool and switched on the overhead light. Yes. He had come through with the expected: a rattle of words, lots of them in italics, that didn't need to be followed too closely. David had relaxed into comfortable, slightly absent-minded listening; now that there was enough light to see by, his glance kept straying off to the assortment of objects around him.

"Yeah," he said when he got the chance. "Must have been some job, getting everything squared away. Quite a place you've got here. Great. Not that I know much about such things. This, for instance. What the hell is it?"

"A candle mold. A rather unusual one," Lenny told him, and went on from there, snatching at the diversion, spinning it out as far as it would go and beyond, almost persuading himself that he could stave off the evil moment forever.

He couldn't, of course. Now there was nothing, but nothing, more to be said about candle molds. Now, with his tongue withered in his mouth, he stared at the package David was holding out to him. "Here. Howdy's gizmo. You forgot it this morning, I didn't think of it either until after I got back from lunch. I didn't have anything else to do, so I brought it down to save you the bother of an extra trip—"

"No, no! I don't want it!" He shrank back, knocking against the piano stool, his arms flailing—a reflex action, completely beyond his control. It was the same with his voice; he heard, was appalled by, and could not curb its lunatic police-siren swell.

David stood rooted, like a kid in a game of statues, still holding out the package, floundering for words. "Don't want it? But how about Pam's birthday present? I mean, you were all enthused last night, and now..."

"I can't, I simply can't do anything creative, the state of mind I'm in. It's too much. The break-in here. Poor Miss Crosby. Everything. I know better than to try. I'd only make a hash of it. No. I wouldn't dream of touching it now."

"Well, sure, naturally you're too uptight right now. But later on, after you've had time to—"

"Maybe. But these ghastly connotations it has for me. I'm not sure I'll ever be able to shake them off. I can't help it, that's how my mind works, one look at the thing, and I'd like as not go to pieces all over again. The way I did a minute ago. Too ridiculous. You must have thought I was around the bend for sure."

"You did sort of blow up," said David mildly. "Okay. What do I do? Take it back to Howdy?"

Another surge of panic. Lenny felt his forehead go clammy. "No no, I mean, that is, not quite yet. You could be right, you know, what you said about later on, maybe I'll feel up to it later on. If I don't, of course, I'll have to tell Howdy, no question about that, but for the time being—"

"I get it. For the time being you want me to keep it for you. Right? Well, no reason why I shouldn't, I guess." He hefted the package, rubbed his moustache, eyed Lenny thoughtfully.

"If you wouldn't mind," gulped Lenny, in shamed relief.

So it was settled. Except that at the end he almost ruined everything— one of the self-defeating impulses he was famous for—by calling out urgently, "David!"

It brought David, who had been on his way out, wheeling around to ask, "What? What's the matter?"

And for a terrifying moment he teetered on the brink, the very brink, of plunging into a headlong, suicidal account of the telephone call. The holding-back effort left him weak and trembling. "Nothing," he stammered. "I just—Thanks, David. Thanks for everything."

"Don't mention it. Be seeing you."

The door opened and shut. Alone with his conscience, Lenny buried his face in his hands.

David was halfway home before he figured out what was eating Lenny. (As something obviously was: hardly a word out of him at first—Lenny, who hadn't shut up for a minute except to catch his breath during their previous encounters—then the fit of compulsive gabbling that didn't in retrospect ring quite true; then that queer final moment when David could have sworn he was on the point of letting go, only to pull back just barely in time.)

The guy was scared out of his wits. Uptight was one thing. Scared was another.

Since this morning something had happened to put the fear of the Lord into Lenny. And it had to be something connected with the package: one look at it and he had practically gone up the wall, anybody would have thought David was trying to hand him a coiled rattlesnake.

Supposing David hadn't made it so easy for him by offering to keep the package a while longer? Or what if, at the end there, he had pushed Lenny into telling him what was really the matter? It might not be too late, even now.

He hesitated briefly, then turned around and went back. But a second chance was too much to hope for. Yesteryear was closed up, unlit, deserted.

He shifted the package to his other arm and once more set off for home. Thinking hard, and getting no place in particular. By the time he reached his own apartment he had come to only one conclusion. As long as he was stuck with the job of caretaker for another couple of days, he might as well have a look at what he was caretaking. After all, he was entitled. Everybody else had seen it. Howdy's gizmo. Kind of a plaque, according to Eunice, or a panel, with carving, and set with stones that were probably not real.

But before he got the brown paper wrapping off, his door bell pinged twice, Eunice's signal, and there she was, all set for a rap session on Miss Crosby. She had run into Mrs. Faye when she came home from work, so she was full up and spilling over with the latest news bulletins.

"She was there all night, in the elevator, sure enough, they've fixed the time more or less, between seven thirty—that's about when she left the bar, and she stopped in at the delicatessen for beer—and nine thirty or so. Just think, if we'd taken the elevator down, we might have caught him. Or at least seen him. This way the police haven't got one single solitary clue. Oh, of course they say they're 'investigating.' They've got to say something. But one of them as good as admitted to Mrs. Faye, there's nothing to investigate, unless they catch these muggers in the act they might as well forget it."

"He didn't have to kill her," said David. "She was such a skinny little thing, and probably half looped."

"All the way looped. Too looped to notice there was somebody behind her when she came in the front door. Because the lock wasn't forced, he must have followed her in. The bartender said he sort of hinted that maybe she didn't need another drink, and she flounced out in a huff. No, he didn't have to kill her. But sometimes they do it out of spite, you know, if they're desperate for a fix and don't get but a few dollars. Or he could have heard us and panicked."

It was an unnerving thought. They mulled it over in silence. Then, as Eunice's eye fell on the package David had started to unwrap, she perked up a bit. "Oh, I'd forgotten all about that. Lenny must have, too. I guess we all did, what with one thing and another. Don't tell me you haven't taken a look! How could you resist?"

"I was just about to when you rang the bell," he admitted.

"Well, go ahead. Howdy wouldn't care. He showed it to everybody else."

"I know. You told me." He picked up the package and loosened the last bits of tape that held the wrappings in place. "Hey," he whispered. He ran his fingers reverently over the dark, richly carved wood. It was as mellow to the touch as to the eye. Genuine or not, the gems that studded it flashed with deep fire colors as he turned the panel this way and that.

Eunice was staring at it, too, with the big-eyed look that meant she was remembering Garth. Who hadn't seemed to know what it was, either, or what its value might be. But he couldn't have failed to recognize its beauty, thought David. He stroked the wood again. Who cared about the dollars and cents angle, or the practical utility of such an object? The fact of beauty was enough.

"Seems a shame to break it up. Whatever it is," he said. Whereupon Eunice's eyes got bigger than ever, and brimmed with tears.

He slipped Howdy's gizmo back inside the brown paper and changed the subject.

Later that night, without Eunice or anyone else to distract him, he took it out again. It looked the same as before. Great. Rare. Precious. Not that he was any judge, of course. He didn't even know how to go about checking on the value of this sort of thing. Museums? Art experts?

Jewelry appraisers?

But he did know that the mere sight of the package was enough to scare the hell out of Lenny. Who wasn't exactly the strong, silent type. It shouldn't take much pressure to get him to open up.

David dug the phone book out from under the stack of last week's newspapers in the corner and ran through the Websters—a nice, unambiguous name, only one way to spell it—several times. No luck. Information was sorry, but they had no listing for Webster, L. or otherwise, on East 86th Street.

It was like Lenny to have an unlisted phone number. Or maybe his apartment was a sublet. However. He could always be reached at Yesteryear.

It would provide a project for tomorrow, thought David, something to help stave off the memory of Marian chattering so compulsively, protesting so much too much, and then the long overdue thud of loss …

He couldn't seem to get to sleep at first. But then he hit on the device of reciting to himself all the advice-to-the-lovelorn jazz he kept handing out to Eunice. That did it. Two and a half paragraphs, and he was out like a light.

9

Eunice sat propped against the couch cushions, ball point pen in hand, yellow ruled pad in lap, diet-cola and pretzels within reach, and eyes screwed up in concentration. She was composing a letter to Garth.

True, she had no clear idea of what she was going to do with it if and when she ever got it written. No point worrying about that part of it yet. The immediate problem was to find the right words.

"You can trust me," she wrote. "I haven't told anyone, not anyone at all, and I never will if you don't want me to. You don't have to explain to me, either, if you don't want to. But I can't help it, I think about you all the time …"

Not today. The shock and disruption of Miss Crosby's death had overshadowed everything else, even Garth. It was David who had brought him back to center stage in her mind, David and the panel or whatever it was.

The look in his eyes when he saw it; the way he touched it; the tone of his voice saying, "Seems a shame to break it up"—all so like Garth that the memory of that other evening last spring rose up and swamped her. One memory led to another, of course; once more she ran through her meager hoard, right up to and including the image of Garth in his cheap clothes, unlocking the door of the rooming house where nobody by the name of Garth Sullivan lived. She had not dared go back to ask about him again. Even if she got past the landlady, Garth might not give her a chance to explain that his secret was safe with her. Instead of trusting her, as he could and should, he might go leaping off to some new hidey-hole, this time for good and all, out of her reach forever.

Wasn't a letter equally risky? Maybe yes, maybe no. One more question to be dealt with later. Meantime, there was something comforting about opening her heart to Garth, if only on a piece of paper he might never see.

"I never really believed you were dead," she wrote. And believed what she wrote. "Everybody else did, and still does. I mean, what else was there to think? What with your note and everything. But somehow I had this feeling, deep down inside, that you had to be alive and that someday I'd see you again. And sure enough ..."

He would sneer at that, she supposed. It did sound quite a bit like Miss Crosby and her prophetic bones. Poor creature, she hadn't been that far off, after all. Not about Garth. Not about somebody following her, either. Though of course these things happened every day. Muggers all over the place, on the lookout for an easy mark like Miss Crosby, and sometimes killing—needlessly, out of panic or spite or whatever.

Once more Eunice's glance flicked toward her door, securely locked and bolted, with the chain in place. Besides, the police were keeping an eye on the house. It wasn't exactly fear she felt, anyway, but the same chill that had crept over her earlier, in David's apartment, when they both realized that Miss Crosby's mugger might have panicked because of them.

She reached for another pretzel and got back to her letter. In the end she fell asleep over it, there on the couch—to wake, disoriented and cramped, at three in the morning and stagger off to bed, forgetting to set the alarm.

So it was only by the grace of God that she came to half an hour behind schedule, barely in time to make it to the office. You had to have what the supervisor considered a valid excuse for being late, and oversleeping wasn't one of them. The murder of your next-door neighbor was acceptable, but that had been yesterday. Today was today. At the last minute she snatched up the rough draft of her letter to Garth and stuffed it into her purse: maybe, while the supervisor was out to lunch, she could sneak enough time to type it out, see how it looked in broad daylight.

As things turned out, she never got the chance. Some kind of a crisis boiled up in the head office that kept everybody hopping—including the supervisor, who ordered lunch in and ate it one-handed, the other hand being busy firing re-types back at Eunice and the rest of the underlings. So much for personal matters. She counted herself lucky not to be stuck for more than ten minutes after five.

When she got home she found Mrs. Faye outside, fussing over her petunias, with David dishing out unsolicited advice from the sidelines. Since his one attempt at helping her with the weeding, some time back, she had forbidden him ever again to set foot inside the railing that enclosed her treasures. They broke off their amiable bickering to fill Eunice in on the day's events. There was nothing to report as far as Miss Crosby's murderer was concerned. And never would be, in Mrs. Faye's opinion. She wasn't blaming the cops—they were good lads, they did their best—but what chance did they have? It wasn't as though the villain had stolen anything identifiable or used a weapon that might lead to his undoing.

"Her own scarf," said Mrs. Faye with gloomy relish. "Choked to death with her own scarf. It doesn't bear thinking about. No, and neither does that brother of hers. Oh yes, he was here today, him and his hoity-toity airs. Blaming me, if you please, for not looking after her better. Me! If he had his way, of course, he'd have put her away years ago, locked her up with never a human soul to give her a kind word. The man's got a stone for a heart. No more feelings than a fish. His own flesh and blood murdered, and all he can think of is he had to cut his vacation short, and how much can he get for her furniture. It's no wonder she hated him. She did, you know, she ..."

It wasn't just that Mrs. Faye's voice dwindled, first to a whisper, then to nothing at all. Her face, too, changed from indignation to blank bemusement. She stood still, fumbling her apron and gazing into space.

"Well?" said David. "What are you looking so spooky about?"

"Spooky, is it," she said, but without her usual fire. "I was just remembering. Funny how things slip your mind. She was in the elevator that day too, sitting on the floor, polishing off a pint of gin. Memorial week end was when it was, just before Garth— He came and got me. Because the elevator had gone off, wouldn't you know, a holiday. It took the two of us to get her up the stairs and into her apartment. She could be stubborn, when she took the notion, and the only way to handle her, God forgive me, was to threaten to call her brother. That's what set her off, that's when she said to Garth— oh, I can hear her now, plain as day—'I don't have to tell you,' she said, 'you hate your brother too.'"

"She said that to Garth? That he hated Howdy? But it's not true!" cried Eunice.

"Exactly what I told her. And him too. He wasn't one to show his feelings, but I could see it gave him a turn. Whoever heard of such a thing, I told him, it was just the liquor talking, don't give it a second thought. That was the last I ever saw of him. He must have already had it in mind, what he was going to do." Mrs. Faye's eyes went rounder, greener, spookier than ever. "To think of it, dead now, the both of them. Her murdered. Him by his own hand."

There was a moment of silence while they thought of it. In their different ways. Then Eunice made tracks for the door. With her secret swelling inside her, and with a face like hers—an open book, David had told her more than once—it wasn't safe to stay.

"Hey, where you going?" he called and sprinted after her. "Pam asked us for a drink, if you're not doing anything else."

She wasn't, of course, and she hadn't the presence of mind or the strength to improvise. It probably wouldn't work with David, anyway. "Okay. Fine." She kept her head bent while she dug out her keys and checked her mail box. Big deal. The phone bill and a supermarket ad. She stuffed them into her bag, next to the draft of her letter to Garth. Which she resolutely refused to think about until she was alone.

The drink with Pam and Howdy stretched into several, and they all wound up eating dinner at the Italian place a block away. So that by the time she was alone she was beyond thinking of anything but shucking off her clothes and falling into bed.

After all, she had written the letter more for herself than for Garth. It would keep till tomorrow ... She sank like a stone into sleep.

Not so David, whose day had been free of head office crises and supervisors to keep him hopping. Pretty much a blank of a day, in fact, aside from the session down at college working out the conflicts in his schedule with his advisor. The project he had counted on—getting hold of Lenny—had come to nothing. He must have dialed Yesteryear's number a dozen times, for all the good it did him; and when after he was through at college and walked over for a look at the shop, he found it locked up, the Closed sign still hanging in the door. Now what? The therapy place on West Fourth? He tried it in desperation, only to be snapped off at the ankles by the director, a beaded, bearded type in a batik smock. It was not their policy to keep a file of such irrelevant data as home addresses on the group members. Even if it were, it would not be their policy to divulge any information of any kind to an outsider.

That seemed to be the end of the line—until, back home again, he had met Pam on his way upstairs. "Oh, hi," she had said. "I tried to call you earlier. How about coming down for a drink with Howdy and me, five thirty or so? Eunice too, if she's not doing anything else."

"Sure. Great. By the way, you don't know how I can get in touch with Lenny, do you? At home, I mean. He's not at Yesteryear."

"He isn't? Well. Well, I expect yesterday was too much for him. The robbery, and on top of that Miss Crosby. He's probably having one of his nervous crises. Why do you want to get in touch with—Oh, of course. Howdy's gizmo." Like everybody else, she knew the reason for Lenny's Wednesday evening visit and its aftermath; Howdy's original plan—to surprise her with the necklace for her birthday—had been lost in the shuffle when Miss Crosby's body was found. "Come on in a minute and I'll check."

Watching her while she pawed through a fat little notebook beside the telephone, David had thought what a mixture of gawkiness and grace she was, what a study in contrasts. Like her neck, so delicate, so vulnerable—all the more so for the decisive set of her jaw above it. Like her dimples and creamy skin—topped off by hair that wasn't a total disaster, but damn near it. Like her eyes, melting one moment, snapping the next. And in spite of her poise, there was something tremulous, a touch of pathos ... All those contradictions. Did they explain how, once having been in love with Garth, she had wound up marrying someone as different, according to all reports, as Howdy?

"Sorry," she said. "We haven't got anything but the Yesteryear number, either." She went on to explain how they had wandered in there one evening last fall, and had struck up a casual friendship because Lenny was so obliging about tracking down that nice old oil lamp for them. And so grateful when Howdy was able to steer a couple of good customers his way. They had included him in their big Christmas bash, had occasionally invited him for a drink. That was about as far as it went. He used to live in the Village, but she seemed to remember he had moved uptown not too long ago, a sublet she thought, or maybe with a friend.

"It doesn't matter," David said. "Thanks, anyway. See you later."

There had been no further mention of Lenny during the evening. Not much mention of Miss Crosby, either. It was as if they were conspiring, all four of them, to stave off the dark thoughts that would have possessed them if they had been alone. They had hung in there, working hard at the lively chit-chat; when now and then silence struck they had rushed with one accord to fill the void—Howdy with another drink all around, Pam with her snacks, Eunice and David with God knows what inanities. Though toward the end the extra drinks caught up with Eunice and she practically fell asleep over her spaghetti.

Well, David probably wasn't all that sharp himself. Now, back in his own apartment, he kept drifting off into aimless reveries about this, that and the other. Marian, of course. Lenny and the panel. In the middle of shucking off his clothes, he got it out again and had another look. As if, by staring at it hard enough and long enough, he might hope for a revelation. He thought about Garth, too, Garth, who had lived here, whose face had looked out of the bathroom mirror—this was while he was brushing his teeth—hundreds of times, who might or might not have hated his brother—you had to take Mrs. Faye's tales, especially the spooky ones, with a grain of salt. And Miss Crosby, snuffed out while, a few feet away, they socialized with Howdy and Lenny in the hall.

He was back to Marian when the phone rang.

The voice that answered his muzzy Hello was tense and guarded. "Are you alone?"

"Who is this?"

"Lenny. If you're not alone, say 'Wrong number' and I'll call back later."

"Oh. Hi. I didn't recognize your voice at first. Okay, I'm alone. Matter of fact, I've been trying to get you all day."

"You have? Oh God. What's happened? Are you all right?"

"Sure I'm all right. Any reason why I shouldn't be?"

"Yes. No. I don't know." Lenny made an audible effort to pull himself together. It took a while, and it wasn't an unqualified success. "David, listen to me. No one must know. I mean nobody. If you breathe a word of this to one living soul, I'm done for. I may be, anyway, but at least if I tell you—It's not fair not to, I'd be an utter rat, because now I've gotten you into it too, and—"

"Maybe if you started at the beginning," suggested David. "Like what it is you've gotten me into."

"Yes. I'm sorry. I'm doing this all wrong, the way I always do everything. What I've gotten you into ..." Lenny's voice dried up on him. He lapsed into silence.

"Okay. Something about Howdy's package. Right?"

From the other end of the line came a half-sob, possibly of relief. Then: "I told him you have it," said Lenny, as if this were the definitive statement, no further clarification necessary.

"Told who? The beginning, Lenny. Start at the beginning."

"Yes. Well. He called me at the shop yesterday morning, not long after I got back there from Howdy's. I don't know who, or why, or anything except that he's after Howdy's gizmo. 'The package you picked up last night.' That's how he put it. He talked in kind of a whisper. Too unnerving. 'Where is it?' he said, and when I said, 'It's not here,' he said, 'I know that, buster. I wouldn't be calling you if it were. What did you do with it?' So he's got to be the bastard that broke in and tore the place apart. He was looking for the package. David? You with me?"

"With you," said David. "Go on. What else did he say?"

"That if I didn't tell him where it was, or if I tried any funny business like calling the police or anybody else, he'd beat me to death. By inches. I'd rather not go into the details, if you don't mind. He was pretty graphic. And I can't help it, I'm a coward. So I told him. Not only that, I weaseled out of taking it back yesterday afternoon, knowing perfectly well what I was letting you in for. Yellow, all the way through."

"I wouldn't say that. You had guts enough to call me tonight."

"Only because I couldn't live with it on my conscience. And even then I'd have been too scared, except my home phone's unlisted, so I don't see how he could possibly—"

"Neither do I. He talked in kind of a whisper, you said. Are you sure it was a man?"

"What? Practically sure. I mean, the things he said. No, it didn't sound like a woman. And take my word for it, he wasn't kidding. He wants the gizmo, and he'll stop at nothing but nothing, nobody but nobody, to get it. That much I'm sure of. Absolutely, one hundred percent sure."

"In other words, I'm next on the list."

Lenny groaned, then burst out wildly, "And I'm to blame! It's all my fault. I didn't have to steer him on to you, I could have told him I'd lost it or something. But no, all I could think of was how to save my own skin, never mind what happens to you. I'll never forgive myself. Never. I don't deserve to live!"

"Calm down, Lenny. Nothing's happened to me so far. Or to the gizmo. It's still here, safe and sound. He hasn't tried any tricks with me yet."

"He will. And if he finds out I warned you, David, he'll—" After a moment of whirring silence, Lenny added with desperate, tremulous courage, "He said not to call the police, but I'll do it if you think I should. They'd have to give us protection. Wouldn't they?"

"You mean like round-the-clock bodyguards? For both of us? Just on account of a threatening phone call?" The cops must get scores of such reports every day; David couldn't help wondering how seriously they would take this particular one, coming as it would have to from Lenny, with his gift for chaos, melodramatics, hysterics.

"No, I guess not." Lenny breathed a deep sigh of relief. "But somebody's got to do something! I mean, here's this maniac running around loose, and—"

"It's his move," David pointed out. "So let him make it. Now that you've warned me I'll be ready for him."

"How do you mean, ready?"

"I don't know yet. I'll have to think."

The first thing he thought of—once he had managed to knock it off with Lenny and hang up—was the gun he had brought back with him from Vietnam. It was an Army automatic, confiscated from an enemy soldier. A souvenir that he didn't especially want (it was just one of the things you did because the other guys were doing it) and had certainly never expected to have any use for. Well, maybe he had expected wrong. He felt rather sheepish as he dug it out from under a tangle of socks in the chest of drawers, but he also felt reassured.

Because he wasn't about to hand over the panel without a struggle. On that point at least his mind was made up.

Wide awake now, and never more sober in his life, he got on with his thinking. His hunch had been right: the panel was some kind of a rarity, maybe not priceless, but valuable enough to spark the break-in at Yesteryear—which was pretty much a burglar's dream—and the threatening call to Lenny—who intimidated easily. Okay. The situation had changed since then. Not that this house was exactly a citadel, or David a hero. But thanks to Lenny he was forewarned, and thanks to the gun he was more than just theoretically forearmed.

His smartest move might be to sneak the panel out of his apartment to another, safer hiding place. Let this joker, whoever he was, a maniac according to Lenny, break in as he had done at Yesteryear; and with no better luck. And let him try intimidating David; he wouldn't have any luck there, either. Well, but what if he realized that Lenny had squealed and took it out on him? Lenny didn't have a gun. Wouldn't know what to do with one if he had. Was a self-confessed coward, yet had scraped up the courage to get on the phone tonight.

So? So the alternative was to keep the panel here and hole up himself, standing guard on it and waiting for the guy to make his play for it. Surely he would be forced into action before long. Like a couple of days? There was a limit to how much holing up David could take. But the guy must have his limits too, and he must be getting a little itchy by now. After all, it was more than a day and a half since he found out from Lenny where the panel was; two full days and nights since the break-in at Yesteryear. What was he waiting for? Why didn't he—

David sat bolt upright, suddenly struck by another, even more pointed question. How had he known about Lenny's visit here Wednesday night to pick up the package? How, unless he was here too, out of sight but not out of sound of their voices while they stood in the hallway talking? Wednesday night. The night of Miss Crosby's murder, which had quite possibly occurred during the course of that same four-way conversation.

It was too much to believe, the idea of two separate intruders bent on two separate crimes—murder and the Yesteryear burglary—lurking in the same small house at the same time. You couldn't rule out either of the crimes. They had both been committed. No question about that. If you ruled out one of the intruders, then you were left with only one possible conclusion: they were one and the same, the guy who had burgled Yesteryear in search of the panel was also the guy who had murdered Miss Crosby.

Wait a minute. Now wait a minute. It wasn't all that sure. He could have learned about Lenny's visit in some other way than listening in on their yak-yak Wednesday night. After all, Howdy wasn't what you'd call the close-mouthed type; he had undoubtedly told the saga of his Mexican gizmo to everybody handy. Might well have taken it into the office to show it around, and if he happened to stop for a drink on the way home, he would do the same with his bar acquaintances. Wouldn't think twice about answering any questions anybody might ask. David could hear him. What was he going to do with the thing? Why, have it made into a necklace for Pam's birthday, this pal of his, Lenny, ran the Yesteryear antique shop down on Greenwich, designed jewelry on the side ...

Lenny would have been equally obliging. A compulsive talker if there ever was one; only too grateful to find an attentive listener among the browsers who dropped in at his shop. Especially one who showed so much flattering interest in his jewelry creations. David could hear him too. Did he get many commissions? Well, not as many as he would like, these things took time of course, but the one he had now, or rather would have, he was to pick it up Wednesday night, too fascinating ...

No, the guy needn't have been here Wednesday night. He didn't have to be murderer as well as burglar. It wasn't all that sure.

But when at long last David crawled into bed the panel went with him, hugged against his chest; and the gun was planted close at hand, on the table beside him.

<h1 style="text-align:center">10</h1>

Saturday Noon

"Summer flu," pronounced Mrs. Faye. "It's going around. Wouldn't surprise me if you're running a temperature." She laid her hand against David's forehead. Diagnosis confirmed. "Poor boy. I thought yesterday you were looking kind of peaked. Now there's no need for you to stir out of the house this week end. I'll bring up some nice soup for your supper, lots of liquids, that's the best thing. Fruit juice. I'll get some for you, no trouble, I'll be going out anyway to do my own marketing."

"I don't feel much like eating," said David, who had just stowed away two hamburgers and a coke. But what Mrs. Faye didn't know wouldn't hurt her. And he had to give her some explanation for holing up in his apartment. What better excuse than a touch of invalidism? She had snapped it right up, only too pleased at the prospect of somebody to fuss over. Well, he would welcome the fussing, it would help pass the time. "Is Eunice around? Maybe she'll come up and keep me company for a while later on."

"She's gone to the beach. They picked her up half an hour ago. Quite a crowd of them, from the office. The one with the car was a real nice-looking boy. Why don't you call your girl friend?"

"She's out of town. Anyway, what girl friend?"

"I wouldn't know, I'm sure. Just an impression I got from Eunice. It's none of my business, of course." After a pause—in case he cared to argue the point—she went on briskly. "There now, dearie, you have yourself a little lie down while I finish the stairs. I'll look in on you again as soon as I get back from the store. Cheer up. Another couple of days, and we'll have you right as rain again."

It looked like a long couple of days to David. What with Eunice gone and all. She might at least have told him she wasn't going to be around today. That way he wouldn't have counted on her.

He stared disconsolately out the window. The summer Saturday emptiness of the street. The hazy, whitish sky. You could get one hell of a sunburn on a day like this. Especially if you had pink hair and a blotchy skin. He just hoped she had sense enough to stay under the beach umbrella.

Saturday Early Evening

It started out as one of their quiet evenings at home. Neither Pam nor Howdy was in a socializing mood. Miss Crosby was too much with them; though by now they had talked themselves out on the subject, her death pressed in on them, a numbing, immovable weight. Maybe we ought to get out of here, Pam thought again, just sell the house and make a fresh start. This time she kept the thought to herself. She had mentioned it once, and Howdy said she was out of her skull, bad things happened everywhere, she knew that, so what was the sense of moving, it wasn't as if the house was jinxed ...

No, of course leaving the house was no answer. The bad things that had happened here—first Garth, now Miss Crosby—would go right along with them, part and parcel of their lives.

Meanwhile, a quiet evening at home. Pam with her knitting, and

Mittens snuggled beside her on the couch. Howdy sprawling in the arm chair with his trade magazine. Background music purling out of the radio; the kind of music Garth used to refer to as cough syrup.

Was Howdy remembering too? Or was it one of his clairvoyant moments when he seemed to read her mind? She could feel him watching her, and out of the corner of her eye she caught his irritable gesture as he switched the radio off. She did look up then, and they exchanged rather wan smiles. But that was the first danger signal, as she recognized in retrospect.

"Where did you say Eunie went?" he asked. "Oh yes, the beach."

"And according to Mrs. Faye David's nose is out of joint. She also claims he's got summer flu, though he didn't sound very sick to me when I talked to him on the phone. You know how she is. Anyway, she says he didn't like it one little bit when she told him about Eunice. It set her up no end. She's been trying to promote a romance there ever since he moved in. Who knows, maybe she'll pull it off yet."

"What do you mean, maybe? As far as I can see, it's in full swing. With or without any outside promoting. They're always running back and forth, having dinner together, so on and so forth. Don't tell me that's Mrs. Faye's doing. She may have dropped a few hints at first, but they're on their own now."

"Okay, they pal around and all that. But David's got another girl in the offing. He told me about her once. Out of this world. And I'm not sure Eunice—I mean—" Watch it. Thin ice ahead. She put her knitting aside and jumped up. "Wait a minute while I check the casserole."

It didn't work, of course. When she came back from the kitchen Howdy was prowling back and forth in front of the window. He had his clenched look. "I trust you're not starving," she offered cheerily. "It's going to be a while yet. Shall I fix some crackers and cheese?"

"You were saying about Eunice."

"Was I? Yes, of course. Only now I can't remember what I was going to say. A mind like a sieve. Move over, Mittens. I'm entitled to some of the couch too, you know. And stay out of my knitting, it's loused up enough as it is."

No use. She knew from the way he planted himself in front of her that he was bent on picking a fight. "So you can't remember." His tone was ominously silky: Mittens effected a dignified descent from the couch and departed; Pam jabbed away at her knitting. "Then supposing I refresh your memory. It's the just-pals bit with Eunie and David, no romance, because he's got another girl and you're not sure Eunice—you mean— End of quote."

"I still don't remember. Stop making like a prosecuting attorney and sit down."

"Not till we get this squared away. Because, I've got news for you, we're going to. This time I'm not going to let you weasel out of it. Garth. That's what you meant. You think Eunie's still too hooked on him to make it with David. Once in love with Garth, always in love with Garth. That's it, isn't it? Well. You're the kid that knows."

Silence always enraged him on these occasions. All right. By now she was as bent on a row as he was. She remained silent.

"The kid that knows," he repeated. When she still did not speak, he snatched the knitting out of her hands and grabbed her by the shoulders. "Don't try to deny it. You were in love with him when I first met you, and you—"

"Take your hands off me! Of course I don't deny it. Of course I was in love with Garth. How many times do we have to go through this? You keep at me and at me ... What about you? You never so much as looked at another girl before me? Ha!"

"That's different."

"You bet it's different. For the main and simple reason that I don't nag you to death about them."

"Right. You don't care enough. And I got over the other girls when I met you. You never got over Garth. Even now when he's dead—"

"If I haven't gotten over him, it's because you won't let me! Like tonight. A nice quiet evening, and look what happens. I didn't start this. You did. How can I forget him when you keep dragging him in? Yes you do, you always have. Right from the start. Whose idea was it for him to live here in the house? Not mine, I can assure you. I knew we'd be better off making a clean break of it. But no. You had to drag him in ... All the favors you were forever doing him. Couldn't you see he hated you for them?"

He bent over her, his face darkening. Okay. He had asked for it. She stared back, scared, braced for violence. But it didn't come.

"He had more than that to hate me for," Howdy said bleakly, and turned away from her. "Aaahhh, what's the use? The hell with it!"

"Howdy," she began. But he was heading for the door, and did not see her hand stretched out in tentative conciliation. "Howdy, where are you going?"

"Out. Don't bother waiting up for me."

"Okay, if that's the way you feel about it! Go ahead. Get drunk. See if I—"
The door slammed behind him.

Late Saturday Night
Garth circled the block, reconnoitering. No sign of the police. If they

were still watching the house, they were doing so from inside. It was one more chance he would have to take. A small one: the cops weren't likely to overextend themselves on a case like Miss Crosby, a run of the mill mugging, and by now three days old.

Three days was all he could afford to waste. First, because he was running low on cash; he had his plane fare to Mexico, but precious little to live on in the meantime, and it was a longer meantime than he had allowed for. Second, because if he waited too long he risked losing track of the panel again. As long as it remained in the hands of this guy David, in the apartment Garth still thought of as his own, to which he still had the key—Fine. Great. Perfect. But could David be counted on to keep it indefinitely? Supposing he had already unloaded it on someone else? As Lenny had unloaded it on him.

Lenny had been only too eager to cooperate, once Garth got him on the phone. Sniveling little bastard, of course he wasn't going to squeal to the police or anyone else. Too scared. And too bird-brained to connect the break-in at his shop with what had happened to Miss Crosby.

But this guy David was an unknown quantity ... All right. Why borrow trouble? There was a better than even chance that he still had the panel. Time enough to worry if it turned out otherwise.

He was either out tonight or he had gone to bed. The windows of the top floor apartment were dark, Garth noted from across the street. So were those of the third floor, naturally, now that Miss Crosby was no longer in residence. As usual, there were lights on the second floor, which might or might not mean that Howdy and Pam were at home. The other houses in the block were no better lit, and as quiet; the street was deserted except for Garth. Almost like a ghost town. Not quite, though: he was on the point of crossing over to the house in the middle of the block, when a taxi came cruising around the corner. He stepped back just in time to avoid its headlights, and continued on his way—briskly, so as not to seem like a loiterer. At Fifth he turned downtown, then doubled back toward Sixth.

At first he could not believe it. A stroke of good luck, after so much of the other kind? It might be his imagination; since Wednesday there had been occasional moments when a sort of mental tremor rocked him and he felt—briefly, briefly—out of touch with reality.

But no. It was really and truly Howdy, headed uptown on the avenue. Not exactly weaving, but on the other hand—as he himself would have put it—not the soberest man in town. Garth had seen him like this often enough before. The crumpled look of his light summer suit; the tie, loosened no doubt during some "deep" impassioned discussion with his neighbor at the bar; the stride that was by turns purposeful and meandering.

Howdy was on his way home after a long, liquid evening. By himself. So Pam was either out of town for the week end, or more likely, in Garth's opinion, and again he knew the pattern, they had had one of their periodic fights.

Silent in his rubber soles, he followed at a discreet distance as Howdy made the homeward turn. For some reason known only to himself, he stuck to the side of the street opposite the house, as Garth had done earlier. He seemed unsteadier now, maybe dubious about the reception he would get from Pam. He needn't worry, thought Garth bitterly; her fits of anger lasted no longer than Howdy's. With both of them, it was easy come easy go. They didn't know the meaning of hard-core, abiding rage.

He needn't worry. Pam would be waiting with open arms, that curly mouth of hers warm and eager for kissing, her eyes deepening, deepening as they used to do for Garth.

He drew the knife from his pocket and crept forward, a cat stalking a pigeon. The street was deserted again, and under the trees the shadows were thick. But until he was within striking distance—and he was not; there was still a gap of twenty feet or more between them— he must be patient, super-patient, and careful, super-careful, so as not to betray his presence. The pigeon must be taken by surprise, with no advance warning, no chance to escape the sure, swift pounce.

Better safe than sorry, as their mother would have said. Had said, God knows how many times. She had a great stock of such platitudes. A sallow, gaunt woman, like Garth in looks. But Howdy was the one she loved, the one who was like their father. He had died young (as Howdy would), unremembered by either of them; only the photograph she kept on the chest of drawers: Howdy's open, good-humored face, his smiling Irish eyes and wavy hair. A house divided. Yet Garth, unloved and unloving, had felt it his duty to come back from Mexico when she died. He did not know why. Because Howdy had taken it for granted that he would? Or was it a gesture toward Mother herself? Not affection, but recognition of the hardness of her life and the granite streak in her that had kept her from buckling. She had raised the two of them single-handed; had cleaned other women's houses, hotel rooms, offices, to feed and clothe them, grimly determined to hold them together as a family. And though Garth's wood carving was a puzzlement to her, she had accepted it, making her own gesture of recognition toward him and his granite streak.

Anyway, for whatever reason, he had come back. It didn't matter why. All that mattered was the final consequence—this present moment, this here and now of inching closer to his prey, knife in hand, silently, by barely perceptible degrees, diminishing the gap. It was almost narrow enough. Not quite. A few more paces, before they reached the street light ...

Those few extra paces would have made all the difference. But he was cheated out of them. Of course. Hadn't Howdy always been the lucky one? So why should his luck desert him now? It didn't. Without warning, he flicked away his cigarette, squared his shoulders, and set off briskly across the street toward the house. And Garth sprang after him, propelled by the explosion of rage inside him, no longer capable of caution. Howdy reached the middle of the pavement; behind him, in the full glare of the street light, Garth raised his knife, ready to strike.

Somebody yelled: "Howdy! Look out! For God's sake, Howdy! Behind you—"

It was a man's voice, loud and urgent. It came from somewhere up above. As he turned and fled back into the shadows, Garth caught a fleeting glimpse of the figure at the window of his old apartment, arms flailing in wild warning. A glimpse, too, of Howdy standing there, befuddled, not looking behind him, but upward.

"Huh? What? That you, Dave? What the hell—"

"Some guy with a knife, behind you! Get in the house quick!"

"I don't see anybody ..."

Garth waited, well out of the range of the street light, for a few moments; then, sticking close to the shelter of trees and houses, he slipped off toward Sixth. The building just his side of the corner was being torn down. He had noticed this demolition project before. It was well under way: the walls were practically leveled, with only the gaping skeleton of the doorway still standing. He ducked through it, into the dank-smelling heaps of rubble beyond.

A safe hiding place? Or a trap? No; they would expect him to behave like an ordinary mugger and get out of the neighborhood, as fast and as far as possible.

And he could see the house from here. That outweighed everything else.

From his vantage point, crouched behind a pile of bricks, lumber, oddments, and a gas stove with its legs in the air, he watched the police car roll up and the two cops heave themselves out. They stayed inside half an hour or so. When they emerged, they paused for a cursory look up and down the block, then got back in the car and drove away.

So much for the official investigation. Well, no crime had been committed. Yet. Besides, Howdy had not seen him. Only David, the one person in the house who was not equipped to recognize him and who therefore did not count.

He felt a little light-headed, after his burst of rage, but otherwise calm, cool, confident, the way he used to feel last spring, in the first halcyon days of working out his plan. Never mind that tonight's try, like Wednesday night's, had misfired.

Next time, he thought. Next time.

11

"How many drinks have *you* had?" Howdy inquired jovially.

"Not as many as you," said David, who had had a couple, all right. Out of boredom, and in the vain hope that they would make him sleepy. "Listen, Howdy, this guy I saw, he meant to kill you. If I hadn't happened to look out the window just then—" Again out of boredom. Sitting there in the darkness, staring out at the deserted street, waiting for something that with every dragging moment seemed less and less likely to happen.

"You're sure you weren't, what do you call it, hallucinating? Or, hey, maybe you're delirious. Mrs. Faye said you were running a temperature."

"I am not delirious. I am not drunk. I was not hallucinating." In desperation he turned to Pam, who had come racing out into the hall when she heard the commotion. They were still in the hall, outside her and Howdy's apartment. "Don't you believe me, Pam? Didn't you see anything?"

"I was on the couch, nowhere near the window. Of course when I heard you yelling I looked out, but by that time Howdy was on his way up the stairs, and you were on your way down. There wasn't anybody in sight on the street then."

She and Howdy could hardly take their eyes off each other. You'd think they had been parted for at least a decade, the way they had fallen on each other's necks. All the more reason for them to take David seriously. He knew what he had seen, and they better believe it.

Left to himself, Howdy wouldn't even have called the police. What was there to report? Nothing had happened. Okay, an attempted mugging. But by now the guy, if he had been there at all, whoever he was and whatever he had in mind, was long gone. You couldn't expect the cops to comb the city for somebody who hadn't done anything.

"He meant to kill you," David repeated. "Pam ..." She snapped out of her trance long enough to say, "Yes. Of course we've got to report it."

The police showed up in record time, possibly because Miss Crosby's death had been reported from the same address less than a week ago.

It was one of the first things they asked. "Any connection with the lady got herself murdered here the other night?"

Howdy hooted at the idea. "You mean that old wives' tale, the murderer returning to the scene of the crime? A lot of bull." For the answers to all their other questions he referred them, with a wave of the hand, to David. "Here's your boy. Me, I don't know from nothing."

David did his best—which was none too good—to dredge up a description of the man. Tall? Short? Thin? Fat? Black? White? "I don't know. I didn't really see his face. He had on this hat, kind of a wide brim. Dark jacket and pants. It was all over so quick, and I saw him from above. Medium size, not as tall as Howdy. Not fat. Skinny. And fast on his feet." He paused, thought of something else, and produced it eagerly. "Oh, and he's left-handed. He had the knife in his left hand."

What kind of a knife? Was he sure it was a knife? Not something else, like maybe a broken bottle?

"I suppose it could have been. He held it like a knife, and it sort of flashed in the street light. I took it for a knife. Whatever it was, he meant to kill Howdy. That's for sure."

One of the cops cleared his throat. The other one sighed. Both preserved an expression of kindly patience.

Would he be able to identify the man if he saw him again?

"I—I didn't really see his face. It was all over so quick." He had said that before. It sounded just as lame the second time around. He might as well give up. "No. No, I couldn't identify him."

That was the first time he felt it—a faint twitch of memory, too brief and too deeply buried to get hold of. One instant there, the next instant gone.

He didn't linger after the police left. Howdy could have said, "I told you so," but settled for, "Well, that's that."

"All the same," said Pam, "I still think it was right to call them. Even if they can't do anything."

"A waste of time. Theirs and ours both." David paused with his hand on the door knob. "They figure I imagined the whole thing on account of I'm uptight about Miss Crosby. I could tell by the way they acted when they were leaving. The way they told me to take it easy, try to get a good night's sleep. They think it was just a case of nerves on my part."

They both took time off from star-gazing at each other to protest. Without much conviction, though; and Pam added, "We've all been on edge, of course. Only natural, after what happened to poor Miss Crosby."

Much more of this, he thought as he plodded up the stairs, and they'd have him doubting what he had seen with his own eyes. No, by God, he *had* seen it! The flash of the knife, the catlike figure, intent and full of menace—the mental image was still with him. Vivid. Undeniable. Real as the stairs under his feet. Everybody else could write it off as imagination. He knew better.

The third floor was silent, and there was no light under Eunice's door. She and her beach playmates might have decided to stay over for another helping of sunburn tomorrow. Or, here at the back of the house, she could have slept through the whole bit. Like Mrs. Faye, who was also on the back, and who was going to blow her top when she found out what she had missed. For his part, David was thankful; she would have put in her two cents' worth about his summer flu and the temperature he was supposed to be running. The credibility gap was plenty big enough without her.

Eunice. Again he felt the twitch of something not quite remembered. Something to do with Eunice? But again it slithered away before he could get hold of it.

He dozed off on the couch at last, still working at it. And when he woke up there it was, out in the open, staring him in the face. The guy he had seen prowling after Howdy tonight bore a striking resemblance to the guy he had followed that night with Eunice. The same wide brimmed hat and dark clothes, the same wiry build and speed of movement. All that was missing was the sling. On his right arm? On his right arm.

Nobody she knew, Eunice had said after they tailed him to that dump in the West 20's. A case of mistaken identity. He had wondered a little at the time—the look on her face when she got back in the car, and the way she clammed up on him—but he had ended by taking her word for it. Why not? What business of his was it, anyway?

So he had figured then. Now was different. Because if Eunice really did know the guy they had followed that night, and if he and Howdy's enemy were really one and the same ...

He sat up and looked at the clock. Seven thirty. He had slept longer than he realized. Of course Eunice, assuming she was back in her apartment where she belonged, would be fast, fast asleep. Poor girl. But life was like that. He had questions to ask her, questions that wouldn't wait and that only she could answer.

The phone rang as he reached for it. Snap, crackle, pop. Then Eunice's voice: "David? Sorry if I woke you. Wow, is this a lousy connection. Unbelievable."

"Where are you? Listen, Eunice, I was just going to call you. Because there's something—"

"I can't hear you. Can you hear me? We decided to stay over. Anne's folks have this place out here, you ought to see it, super, so we're staying over till this afternoon. Tell Mrs. Faye, will you? Otherwise she'll worry."

"Okay. I'll tell her. Listen, Eunice—"

"What? I'd call her myself, only I don't know her number. David? Are you there? This lousy connection."

Plus the hullaballoo her playmates were making in the background. Giggles. Squeals. A blare of radio soul music.

"I'm here!" he yelled. "I said I'll tell her!"

"You'll tell her? Is that what you said?" Her own voice faded as she turned toward the playmates. "Hey, pipe down out there. I'm trying to make a phone call ... Thanks a lot, David. We'll be back tonight. See you then."

"Wait! I have to talk to you. It's *important*. Give me your number out there and I'll call you back. Hold it, Eunice. Wait!"

But the snap, crackle, pop had ceased. He was speaking into a vacuum. He slammed down the phone and lapsed into obscenities.

After a while, when he had calmed down enough to think straight, it dawned on him that Eunice wasn't the only angle of approach open to him. Not necessarily the best one, either. Because if she had lied to him before, how could he be sure she wouldn't go on lying? He might get farther on his own. After all, he had been along that night, if only for the ride; he could find the rooming house again. And then ... He didn't know yet. He would think of something when the time came.

Who needed Eunice? There was more than one way to skin a cat.

It was only when he was showered, shaved, dressed and ready to leave that his eye fell on the panel, laid out on the bedside table. Jesus, it had gone clean out of his mind, lost in the shuffle of last night's doings. Now it all came back with a thump—Lenny, the panel, the threatening phone call, the scheme he had hatched to hole up for the week end and stand guard against whoever was after it. The thought of how close he had come to whooping off on the new trail, leaving his apartment wide open to theft, made him shiver. And don't forget, the character who was bent on stealing the panel might just possibly, not for sure, but possibly, also be Miss Crosby's murderer. That possibility gave him priority over Howdy's would-be attacker. Right?

Right. Glumly, David crossed to the window and looked out. Empty street. Overcast sky. Endless summer Sunday. The hell with it. The thief would most likely wait until after dark, anyway. If not ... He went back, slipped the gun in his jacket pocket, and hauled his raincoat out of the closet. It had patch pockets, roomy enough for the panel. Carrying the raincoat over his arm, he let himself out and locked the door behind him.

Mrs. Faye must have gone to early mass. At any rate, she was nowhere in sight on the first floor, and there were no bustling sounds or radio playing in her apartment. Good. For the moment he could do without her fussing over his health, her prying into where he was going and why. True to his promise to Eunice, he left a note on Mrs. Faye's door before proceeding quietly on his way.

Daylight didn't really do anything for the rooming house and its surroundings. There wasn't as much noise, now that the bars were closed, but you got a clearer view of the grime and decay. Half a dozen skinny kids were playing stickball in the middle of the street, and a left-over drunk lay sprawled beside an overturned garbage can. David parked in the next block and walked back, still carrying his raincoat complete with cargo. From across the street he eyed the rooming house. No signs of life behind its dingy windows and crumbling front. It seemed to him to have a sly, knowing look, like the face of some seedy character hauled in for questioning and determined to give nothing away.

And he didn't even know where to begin with the questioning. Like who to ask for.

Eunice had at least had a name. For all the good it did her. He remembered the finality of that door slammed in her face. The landlady had wasted no time in chitchat. It figured, of course. Rooms. For Men Only. Men who were on the skids, either temporarily or permanently; no doubt an endless procession of them, distinguishable to the landlady only on the basis of whether or not they came through with the rent.

Still, a name would have been an opening wedge.

The coffee shop didn't look like much. But it was open. More than could be said for any of the other hole-in-the-wall eateries in the block. He went in and picked a stool that gave him a view of the rooming house. No problem there: he had the place to himself except for an old fellow at the other end of the counter. And the waitress, who was johnny-on-the-spot, not only with the cutlery but with a nice, chirpy, "Good morning. What'll it be?"

Her face was nice too. A plain, kind, middle-aged face with no-nonsense rimless glasses and neatly scalloped graying hair. She reminded him of his fifth grade teacher. Miss Woodruff. The same dedication to her job. The same big seat. Under her cheering influence he decided he was hungry and ordered the works. The eggs turned out to be not too great, but that wasn't Miss Woodruff's fault. He ate them anyway, so as not to hurt her feelings, along with everything else, including the extra order of toast she slipped him.

Business picked up a bit while he was eating. Regulars, apparently. Miss Woodruff called them by name and knew without their telling her how they took their coffee. There was a good deal of kidding around and what seemed to be another installment of a confidential life story from one customer. The customer, as it happened, from the rooming house. David had seen him emerge, had felt a little spurt of hope as he watched the door opening. No such luck, of course. The emerging figure was much too big and beefy, nothing like what he was looking for.

All the same, it gave him an idea. Miss Woodruff and he had already done the routine socializing about the weather and so on. Now, as she paused to check up on him, he said, "Okay with you if I don't shove off quite yet? The guy I was supposed to meet ought to be along any minute now. I'd go across and ask for him only he said it's better not to bother the landlady. So if you don't mind—"

"Sure. Take your time. He's from the rooming house? I couldn't help but notice, the way you've been watching it. You don't have to tell me about that landlady. Nobody bothers her if they can help it."

"Yeah. So he said. Come to think of it, maybe you know him. Kind of a skinny guy, with his arm in a sling, at least it was in a sling a while back, I'm not sure about now."

It was all Miss Woodruff needed to know. She came through nobly. "Mr. Mettler! Sure. Well, I can't say I know him, not like I do some of the other boys. He's not all that regular a customer. Now that you mention it, he hasn't been in the last couple of days. And then he's not much of a talker. Keeps to himself. How about that! Mr. Mettler."

So now he had the name. They beamed at each other—David gratefully, Miss Woodruff with bright-eyed curiosity.

"I don't really know him, either," he admitted, and went on less truthfully. "It's one of those things, a friend of a friend. I've got some stuff I want to sell, tools and like that, and he claimed he was interested. But here he is, half an hour late. After all, I haven't got all morning."

"Now, now. What happened is, he's probably just overslept himself."

"Okay. Five more minutes, and landlady or no landlady, I'm going over and wake him up."

"Well. If you say so. Coming, Joe." She padded off in her rubber-soled oxfords to refill Joe's cup.

He took off five minutes later, on the dot, leaving her the tip she deserved but obviously hadn't expected. "Many thanks. 'Bye now," she said, and threw in a dubious "Good luck" as he went out the door.

The landlady lived up to advance billing, all right. Eyes like rocks. A voice like gravel.

"Not here anymore," she announced with satisfaction when he asked for Mr. Mettler. He had had the presence of mind to plant his foot in the door; otherwise she would have slammed it.

"You mean—"

"Not here. Moved out. Didn't leave no forwarding address. They never do."

"I see. That is—When did he leave?"

"Friday. He was paid up, I'll say that for him." She rattled the door knob. Looked down pointedly at his foot. Decided, no doubt with regret, against crushing it.

"There must be some way I can get in touch with him. It's important. How about the place where he works?"

"You're asking me?" She uttered a cawing, derisive sound—presumably her version of a laugh—that reduced what little was left of him to rubble.

He removed his foot. She slammed the door. So much for the Mettler caper.

It was beginning to drizzle, in a spiritless way. Not enough to make putting on his raincoat worthwhile. The weight of the panel in its pocket reminded him that he was stymied on that front, too. Him and his bright ideas. Where had they gotten him? Up the wall was where. Up the goddamn wall.

But then, as he was unlocking the car, Old Robby's name popped into his mind. Okay, so it was snatching at straws. Even assuming that Old Robby hadn't died, or moved to Timbuctoo, or lost all his marbles—even so, there was no guarantee that he could throw any light on the panel.

On the other hand, there was no guarantee that he couldn't.

Well, then, thought David. Well, then ...

12

Throughout Sunday Garth bided his time. He had left his hiding place in the rubble and slipped across to the house just before dawn. All was safe, spellbound silence as he let himself in—they might have changed the lock, but no, his old key still worked—and crept up the stairs. Past Howdy's and Pam's floor, past Eunice's, past old Mr. Bauman's and what used to be his; David Jackson's now, according to the mailbox lettering downstairs. On up the iron steps that led to the roof. The door gave a soft snick as he unlocked it; carefully he eased it open, to keep it from creaking. There was a chance, of course, that someone might notice it was no longer locked. But not much of a chance.

And the roof gave him the lookout post he needed. Or so it had seemed at the time. Later he was to find something better. Much later—after the hours of oblivion, sleep, whatever it was that had engulfed him up there under the pearly sky, huddled behind the low parapet. He surfaced from it at last, feeling disoriented, obscurely betrayed, oppressed by dreams he could not remember. The sense of disaster sharpened when he looked at his watch. Eleven o'clock. What had he missed? Who had come or gone while he should have been watching?

Rain was falling. Must have started quite a while ago: his clothes were damp through, and there were puddles in the depressions of the roof. He peered out at the street. A couple of people carrying home the Sunday paper. A couple more walking their dogs. No one from the house. Again, the sense of disaster.

But then, and just barely in time as it turned out, he had thought of the closet on the top floor. It was never locked. Mrs. Faye used it as a catch-all for her cleaning stuff, and since she didn't clean on Sundays there was no danger of her barging in on him. Yes, but if that bastard David Jackson or even old Mr. Bauman should happen to pop out into the hall and catch him on the iron stairway, as either of them might very well do

Well, he had made it. Had steeled himself to ease the roof door open again, not knowing what might lie beyond it, and when there was nothing, no one, had ducked into the closet with its smell of lemon oil, its pail and mop, its shelf for dust cloths and vacuum cleaner attachments. It was deeper than he remembered; room enough for him to sit on the floor if he hunched his knees.

Minutes after he had settled himself he realized by what a narrow margin he had made the switch from lookout post to listening post. The elevator was wheezing its way upward. There was the customary clank when it reached its destination, the pause while it gathered its strength, then the sigh, as of satisfaction at a job accomplished against all odds, of its door opening. Brisk footsteps. A tentative tapping sound.

After a moment of silence came the click of a lock being turned, and Mr. Bauman's thready voice: "Ah, good morning, Mrs. Faye. I didn't hear you—"

"Sh." She went on in a piercing whisper. "I just came up to check on David, make sure he's all right before I leave for Queens." Queens, thought Garth. She had cousins out there. Often spent Sundays with them. "He must have gone back to sleep. Best not to disturb him. Poor lad, he's getting over the summer flu."

"Fine, thank you," said Mr. Bauman. "I thought I'd wait downstairs for my son. He'll be along any minute to pick me up."

"Got your umbrella, have you? Yes, I see you have. Too bad the weather isn't nicer. Eunice out there at the beach, and all. They stayed over. I found a note from David when I came back from early mass. She'd called to let us know she was all right."

"No, I'm not planning to stay overnight," Mr. Bauman explained. "Should be back by nine thirty. Ten at the latest. Depending on the traffic."

"Now watch your step. I said, watch your step getting in. It's taken to stopping a little low, I notice." The elevator heaved another sigh and once more ground into action. Presently all was silent.

Including the apartment next door. Where the panel was, and where he presumed David was, too; conked out, asleep. He would have preferred it otherwise, of course—David out somewhere for the day, with the coast clear for him to let himself in with his key and get the panel. Because he couldn't risk leaving it till after he had dealt with Howdy; he must be all set to get the hell out, and not a minute to spare.

Meanwhile, patience. Sooner or later his chance would come. Sooner or later. He settled down on the closet floor and composed himself to wait.

"'Bye, everybody, see you tomorrow!"

Stiff with sunburn, euphoric with pizza and camaraderie, bemused from lack of sleep, Eunice clambered out of the car and waved as it drove off, trailing farewell messages and a throb of music from Chris' transistor. It was four thirty and raining, not hard but steadily. Coolish. Nice. As she turned toward the house, fumbling in her shoulder bag for her keys, she saw Howdy and Pam coming toward her, arms linked, cozy under their umbrella. They had had a late lunch down in Chinatown and somehow, without really planning to, had walked all the way home. They smiled dreamily at each other, at Eunice, at the world.

"Don't bother digging your key out. I've got mine right here," said Howdy. "How was your junket? Have a good time?"

"Terrific. Except today it rained. That's how come we came back so early. Anne's folks have this place, fantastic, right on the beach, plenty of room for us to stay over. We had a cook-out last night, oh, and Chris asked me to a party next week end—"

"Come on in. Tell us all about everything." Pam had untied her head scarf on the way up the stairs; her hair sprang out, wilder than usual. Funny, how little difference it made sometimes. Like tonight. When Pam felt good, she looked good, never mind her hair. Eunice, on the other hand ...

"Oh wow, look at the red nose!" It was David. He must have come in right after them, and had stopped halfway up the stairs to inspect and, naturally, to comment. "Just wait till it peels. Your legs, too. Talk about living color. How about a coke, or something to eat? I've got stuff up at my place. I want to—to hear about your week end."

"So do we," said Howdy. He unlocked the apartment door and swung it wide. "Right this way, folks. Glad to see you're up and around, Dave. From what Mrs. Faye said, you were holed up for the day, sleeping it off. Summer flu, or whatever the hell it was ailed you last night. I've got my own theory, but—"

"I'm okay," said David shortly. He came on up the stairs and followed them inside. With no great enthusiasm. He was carrying his raincoat over his arm, sort of nursing it.

"I didn't know you weren't feeling good or I wouldn't have called you this morning. And so early," Eunice began.

But he was pretty short with her, too. He was okay. Don't worry, he had passed along her message to Mrs. Faye. Had left her a note when he went out this morning.

"You've been out all day?" said Pam. "Then that's why Mrs. Faye didn't get any answer when she tapped on your door. Are you going to catch it when she gets back from Queens and finds out what you've been up to! She's all steamed up, anyway, over missing the excitement last night."

"What excitement? What happened last night?"

"Well." Pam glanced at David. He was perched, in a transient way, on the edge of the sofa, still hugging his raincoat. His face turned a slow, stubborn red.

"Go ahead and tell her, Dave," Howdy sang out from the kitchen where he was breaking out the cokes. "It's your story. Nobody else's."

"Then don't knock it."

"Hey now, don't get sore. I didn't mean it that way. All I meant was—"

"I know. You think it's just a joke. Well. It wouldn't have been so funny if I hadn't spotted the guy and hollered when I did."

"What guy?" Eunice burst out. "Will somebody please kindly tell me what this is all about?"

So then David gave her the story, with a take-it-or-leave-it air, practically daring her to believe it. She could see why, of course: Howdy's refusal to take him seriously, plus the brush-off from the cops. But he had no call to be like that with her. As good friends as they were to each other. Or so she had thought. He wasn't acting very friendly now. Kind of shut off, as if he had something more on his mind, something he wasn't telling. Like what, though? And why was he holding it back? Ordinarily she would have asked him, flat out. But she felt too uncertain of everything, including herself, too fuzzy and slow in the head ...

"Miss Crosby!" she gasped. "Did the police think there was any connection?"

"Sure they did. In their book that's how come I saw what nobody else saw. Hysterical reaction to the Miss Crosby deal."

"Now, David," Pam protested. "They didn't say anything of the kind."

"They thought it, though. Can't blame them, I suppose. They must get this kind of flak all the time. Somebody's murdered, and right away kooks like me start having delusions."

"But you're not that kind of a kook!" cried Eunice. "I mean—"

Howdy guffawed. David grinned a little, in spite of himself. Pam saw her chance, and changed the subject: she had some great stuff for sunburn, she had just remembered, she'd get it right now, for Eunice's legs. Which weren't all that bad, actually, but okay, who was Eunice to argue? Let Pam have it her way. She slathered the stuff on with a free hand, meanwhile steering the conversation back to Eunice's week end. "We want the full details. All about everything."

Eunice tried. But her heart wasn't in it anymore. She didn't think David was listening, and wondered why he bothered to stick around.

She found out soon enough. "I want to talk to you," he said, the minute they were outside in the hall. He hadn't wasted any time getting her out there; the merest hint that she was ready to leave, and he was on his feet, snatching up the zippered flight bag that held her essentials, and hustling her toward the door. Goodnight. Thanks for the coke. Be seeing you. Bang, bang, bang, and that was it. "Come *on*," he added. "Don't start rummaging for your key or we'll be here all night. It beats me, how you ever find anything in that damn saddle bag of yours."

"You don't have to be so snotty about it," she said. But she stopped rummaging and plodded along behind him, up the stairs to his place. He faced her, tight-lipped, unsmiling. In spite of the all-gone feeling in her stomach—not that she was scared. Of David? Too ridiculous—she managed to keep her head up while she waited for whatever it was that was coming. This was his show. Let him get it on the road.

"It's about the guy I saw last night," he said at last. "And I did see him, Eunice. I wasn't making it up."

"I believe you. No matter what Howdy and the cops think. If that's all that's bugging you—"

"That's not all. I didn't get a real good look at him, of course. He was off like a shot when I started yelling. Describe him to the cops? Identify him? Forget it. Especially when they were giving me the fish eye, anyway. But then I began to get this feeling like I had seen him before, somewhere, sometime. It didn't click until this morning. Just before you called me. If we hadn't had such a bad connection ..."

"Lousy."

"Yeah. Eunice. Remember the night a couple of weeks ago, you saw some guy you thought you knew and we followed him to that crumby rooming house?"

"What—What about him?" The all-gone feeling was worse. Much worse.

"I think it was him last night."

"You think it was—You're crazy! You've gone bananas!" she cried, above the roaring in her ears. "What are you trying to prove, anyway? I wasn't even here last night! And it was all a mistake, that other time. I told you what the landlady said. There wasn't anybody there by that name!"

"What name did you ask for? Mettler?"

"Mettler?" She stared at him blankly.

"That's the name he was using. One of the things I found out when I went back there this morning."

"You mean you saw him? You talked to him? One of the things, you said—one of the things you found out ..."

"Cool it, baby. No, I didn't see him or talk to him. He's gone. Moved out Friday. Without leaving a forwarding address. They never do. Quote, unquote."

"Gone," she whispered. Garth, oh Garth. Gone before she had found a way of getting through to him, and there would be no second chance. For a moment everything else faded away, and there was only Garth, her last sight of him, standing in the rooming house doorway, gaunt, lonely, locked in on himself and his secret.

It didn't last long. Not with David right there in front of her, his eyes trained on her like a couple of cameras, recording whatever showed in her face. And apparently plenty had showed: "Are you all right?" he asked. "You look kind of funny. As if you'd just seen a ghost."

She couldn't help it, she shivered. Let me out of here, she thought. But fast. Ridiculous to be scared of David? Ridiculous not to be, was more like it.

"Not me," she said. "If anyone's seeing things around here, it's you."

"Oh, is that so! Then why did you say you believed me about last night? Just humoring me, I suppose. Never argue with a maniac. Or did you— Yeah. You changed your mind when you found out I recognized the guy. That's it, isn't it? Because you recognized him, too. I thought so, the night we followed him. Now I'm sure of it. Listen, Eunice. Whatever it is you know about him—"

"I don't!" She made a panicky, scuttling move toward the door, but his hand closed on her arm. "I don't know anything! I told you!"

"Okay. You told me. All a mistake. Nobody you knew. Now how about telling it like it really is?"

"Let go of me! It's none of your business! Calling me a liar!" Out. Out. She had to get out of here. She wrenched free, and when he grabbed for her again she swatted him a good one with her shoulder bag. It was stuffed to the gills, and no mean weapon; but as it connected, with a soul-satisfying smack, its clasp gave way and everything—well, half of everything—flew out, to bounce every which way onto the floor. Keys, sunglasses, her paperback *Great Gatsby,* her chain belt, eye shadow, wallet, change purse, you name it—all the things she couldn't live without, plus the junk she had crammed in there and forgotten about. "Now look what you've done!" Sobbing, she dropped to her knees. With escape so near, to be reduced to this scrabbling anticlimax—it was too much.

"Oh, sure," said David bitterly. "I suppose I walloped myself, too."

There was a red welt on his cheek, running from moustache to ear. She saw it when he picked up a couple of curlers and tossed them into the bag. All right. He had asked for it. And he'd get more of the same if he started in on her again.

He didn't. "Think it over," he said as she opened the door. "When you come to your senses let me know."

"I'm never going to speak to you as long as I live!"

Tears choked her. She slammed out and pounded downstairs.

It had been a long vigil for Garth, huddled in the cramped quarters of his listening post. Long, and for the most part quiet. Once he thought he heard sounds from downstairs—Howdy and Pam? Coming or going?—but the top floor remained sunk in silence. Nothing to listen to but his own breathing, his own heart beating, the rustle he himself made when he shifted his position.

He may have dozed off for a while. He hadn't slept much lately, or eaten much, either; the last two nights, since Friday afternoon when he moved out of the rooming house, had been spent on park benches, when he wasn't walking the streets. But if he did doze off, it was lightly, nothing like the oblivion up on the roof, and when at last there was something to hear he was instantly alert.

Footsteps coming up the stairs. Voices. One of them was Eunice's; when he heard the key turning in the lock he knew the other one had to belong to David. The bastard hadn't been in there sleeping at all. Must have been already up and away when Mrs. Faye tapped on his door …

After the one lightning flash of fury he got himself back under control. So. He had missed an opportunity. He could not afford to waste his time or strength agonizing over it. Not unless he wanted to risk missing the next one too.

He hadn't been able to hear what they were saying while they were on the stairs, much less now that they were inside the apartment. There was no let up in the talk session, whatever it was about, maybe a prelude to Eunice's Good Neighbor act. As he recalled it, she hadn't shut up for more than a couple of minutes. Well, apparently she had met her match in David. There was more of his voice than hers.

Then all at once she gave a yelp—"Let go of me!" it sounded like—and there went the Good Neighbor theory. Unless, of course, she had changed her tactics: the silence that followed seemed to indicate something of the sort. But no. Or anyway, not yet. The door opened, with a wrenching sound; her voice came through, strangled but intelligible, "I'm never going to speak to you as long as I live!" Bang. Clump clump down the stairs, sobbing all the way.

The classic lovers' tiff exit line. David's cue to take off after her—if not right this minute, then soon. Only a little longer to wait for the coast to be clear. Inside the closet, Garth unkinked his knees and cautiously rose to his feet.

13

It took David a while to simmer down after the scene with Eunice. She had teed him off, no doubt about it. Lashing out at him like that, storming off ... Though what burned him, what really burned him, was that he hadn't been able to get the truth out of her.

Well, supposing he had been able to, what then? He wasn't at all sure it would give him a lead on this Mettler character, whoever he was.

The name clearly meant nothing to Eunice. She hadn't known, either, about his moving out of the rooming house until David told her. And surely her reaction—the stricken finality of her voice saying "Gone"— meant that she didn't have any more notion than David of where to find him again.

She knew who Mettler really was, though. Knew, and wouldn't admit it; for some crazy screwed-up reason she was still sticking to the story she had cooked up at the start.

Nobody she knew. All a mistake.

What David should have done, of course, was pin her down then and there, the night they followed Mettler to the rooming house. Because she was a lousy liar; he knew all along she wasn't leveling with him. But how could he have foreseen it was going to lead to this? And who was he to go prying into her business? There was no reason why she should tell him every last thing, good friends though they were.

Not anymore. He had blown that just now, along with his chances of ever finding out what she knew about Mettler.

The hell with it. He sat down on the couch and drew the panel, still in its brown paper wrapping, from his raincoat pocket. There at least he had something to go on. The one small plus in a day of otherwise total frustration.

Old Robby had neither died nor moved to Timbuctoo. There was his name in the phone book, at the familiar Riverside Drive address; and there, on the first ring, was his voice, also familiar—high-pitched and irascible, the voice of a man with no time to waste on social amenities. "Yes, yes, I remember you. I'm going to the movies. I always go to the movies on Sunday. I'll be back at three, if you want to stop by then." Slam went the receiver.

As for Old Robby's marbles, well, he seemed to have the same number he started out with; and there was a difference of opinion about whether that made him a brilliant scholar and teacher or a crackpot, self-styled authority on everything. David's mother, who was related to him in some complicated, five-times-removed way, sided with his admirers; Dad with his detractors.

Anthropology was supposed to be Robby's beat, but even during his academic career there had been no holding him to the one field, much less now that he was retired. He stayed put more than he used to—no more expeditions to remote corners of the world or lecture tours—but he continued to fire off a barrage of monographs, articles, treatises to scientific journals of practically every stripe. He lived by himself, with a rapid turn-over in housekeepers to cook and clean for him, and a long-suffering daughter who lived across town to quarrel with when things got a little dull.

"How's your mother?" he asked as he ushered David into his study. "A nice woman. It's beyond me what she saw in that fellow she married. You look like him," he added accusingly.

Robby himself was small and sprightly, with a flounce of fluffy white hair around his bald spot. His eyes were bold and piercing. He was wearing a plaid suit—rather subdued for him—and an out-size bow tie. When he failed to get a rise out of David with his opening gambit, he switched to himself and his latest appearance in print. "Here," he said, plucking a journal from the stack on his desk. "That's going to make them sit up and take notice."

David had hoped for something that might lead to the subject of the panel. No such luck. He made a polite show of interest, anyway: "So now you're into geology."

"Why not? If you're looking for an argument, young man—"

"I'm not," said David hastily. He drew the brown paper parcel from his pocket. "What I'm looking for is—well, I want to pick your brains."

That was obviously fine with Robby. He watched, bright-eyed, as the panel emerged from its wrappings, and when David handed it across to him he bent over it in absorbed silence for what seemed like a long time. Finally he asked, "Where did you get this?"

So David gave him the story as he had heard it from Howdy. The trip to Mexico, the purchase of the panel, the plan to break it up for the sake of the stones. (He thought Robby winced a little at that part.) He did not go into the later developments. They were for him to deal with. All Robby had to do—if he could—was identify the panel, and it wouldn't help him any to know about the robbery at Lenny's shop or the threatening phone call. On the contrary, it would only distract him. "Fifty dollars," he said thoughtfully. He put the panel down gently on the desk and leaned back in his swivel chair. "Of course it may be only a reproduction. Plenty of them around, I daresay, some really quite excellent."

"All right. A reproduction of what?"

Robby paused again, savoring his secret. Then he said briskly, "Part of a Spanish chest or desk. They liked things ornate, you know. Lots of compartments, and a fancy door for each. Jewels, carving, the works. Here, you can see where it fit on. You mean to tell me you never even saw a picture of one of those pieces?"

"I'm majoring in economics," said David apologetically.

"No excuse. These specialists with their blinders on. Oh, I know what they say about me. Spreading myself too thin. Dabbling in this that and the other instead of sticking in a rut the way they do. As if you could pigeonhole things like that, one science hermetically sealed off from all the others and never the twain shall meet! Of course they meet! They're all connected, even economics, all merging somewhere or other, like rivers flowing into the sea ..."

"Yes, sir. Part of an old Spanish piece. You think it's valuable, then?"

"What's that? Oh." It took Robby a moment to thump back to earth. "Valuable. Depends, first of all, on whether or not it's authentic. The experts can tell you. I can't. They have their methods. Second of all, assuming it's authentic, is it the only part left, or is the original piece sitting around somewhere intact except for one door? If the former, well, your market would be the collectors and dealers, and don't expect me to quote prices, because nobody on God's earth can predict how much any one of them might be willing to fork over for any given item at any given time. If the latter, and if it could be restored, then it belongs in a museum and the sky's the limit."

A hell of a lot of ifs.

But Robby had one more up his sleeve. "Even if it's only a reproduction, it looks like a good one to me, and good reproductions can be worth a nice piece of change, too. So I'd say your friend got a bargain for his fifty dollars, come what may."

"Yes. A bargain." In the light from the desk lamp the panel seemed almost alive, a creature from another world, rich and strange. Once again, David could not resist touching it. At the same moment Robby's hand reached out too; there were the two sets of fingers—one gnarled with age, the other square and strong—drawn together in brief rapport.

Then Robby switched off the lamp and stood up. End of brain-picking session. He had squeezed it in. Now he was clearly in a fidget to get on with whatever his schedule called for, after always going to the movies on Sunday.

"One last question," said David as he scrambled to his feet and began rewrapping the panel. "Those experts you mentioned. Could you give me the name of one? Because that's the first thing, to find out whether or not it's authentic."

Robby could and did. "You'll have to wait till tomorrow. He's never at the Museum on Sundays. About using my name ... Oh, he knows me, all right. You bet he does. We had a great old run-in some years back. A great old run-in. Well. Water under the bridge. And no question about it, he knows his stuff. Tell him I said so. That ought to bring him around."

He cut David's thanks short and propelled him toward the door, full steam ahead. Once there, he paused long enough to fix the parting guest with his glittering eye.

"Good day to you, young man, and good luck. Even though you didn't see fit to tell me the whole story."

"Sir?"

"You heard me," said Robby, and shut the door on David and his package.

So he hadn't been quite as much the master of the situation as he imagined. Still, he had done better with the old boy than with some other people he could mention. Howdy, for instance, refusing to believe that somebody was out to kill him. And Eunice, with her lies and her temper tantrums.

She had rushed off without her flight bag, he noticed. So? So he could take it down to her and ... No, damned if he would. Let her come after it.

And let her go on trying to protect Mettler, or whatever it was she was doing. Had she changed her mind and decided that Mettler, not Garth, was the Great Love of her Life? He wouldn't put it past her, with her weakness for lost causes. Okay. Let her.

He had other things to think about. Like the panel. Even without Robby's confirmation, he had known that it must be valuable. Somebody else knew, too. The somebody who had broken into Lenny's shop to steal it and, when he didn't find it there, had terrorized Lenny into telling him where it was. The somebody, don't forget, who might just possibly have murdered Miss Crosby. Maybe that was why he had made no further move to get the panel; a murderer would be pretty leery about coming back to the house until he had given the cops time to clear out and things to quiet down in general.

Mettler hadn't been too leery to come back; and anyway, his target had been not David and the panel, but Howdy. But if you ruled Mettler out of the panel business, then you were left with one whopper of a coincidence: two separate and distinct crimes in progress, both focused on the same small house. It seemed like too much to David. There must be a link somewhere. He felt it—shades of Miss Crosby—in his bones.

What to do about it was something else again. He had already made all the moves he could think of, only to be blocked on every front. The panel thief hadn't showed up. Eunice wouldn't tell whatever it was she knew about Mettler, and Howdy shrugged off last night's episode as a piece of hysterical hallucination, and Mettler himself had lit out for God knows where. Even Old Robby's expert wasn't all that much of a prize. Presumably he would be able to put some kind of a price tag on the panel. But as for throwing any light on the missing link—No way. Besides, he couldn't be reached until tomorrow.

David prowled across to the window. From there to the kitchen. From there to the couch, where he slumped down and stared blankly at the floor. It could stand a cleaning. A good cleaning, as Mrs. Faye would say. Not the lick and a promise job which was all it ever got from him. He'd have to get her up here again one of these days. Fluff from the zigzag rug in the corners, and the rug itself was crummy, matted down.

Not to mention the clutter of newspapers, books, junk mail that he kept meaning to throw out … He thought at first that was what it was, under the chair, and he wouldn't even have bothered to investigate except that something else had rolled under there too, something round and shiny that he didn't recognize as one of his own belongings. Then after a moment it registered: all that corruption that had spilled out of Eunice's saddle bag when she let fly at him. Of course. They must have missed picking up a couple of items, and no wonder.

The shiny round thing turned out to be stuff for her eyes. Purple. While he was at it, he might as well retrieve the piece of junk mail, too. Only that wasn't what it was. The realization hit him, wham, the instant he unfolded the sheet of yellow ruled paper. Eunice's headlong handwriting. A letter. A draft of a letter, judging by the number of lines crossed out, words changed or squeezed in every which way.

He rocked back on his heels, heart thumping, eyes racing. Phrases leapt out at him: "You can trust me ... I haven't told anyone, not anyone at all, and I never will if you don't want me to ... I never really believed you were dead ..."

After that first breakneck reading he went through it again, just to make sure. It still said the same thing. Crazy, crazy, and yet it made sense of all the puzzling bits and pieces that hadn't fit before ...

They clicked into place now, each one part of the chain that stretched back and back—only Garth knew how far. Garth the unhappy, unlucky loner, whose body had never been recovered, who had more than one reason to hate his brother, who could not have failed to recognize the value of the panel, and who by this time was in so deep that he had no choice but to go on.

David stumbled to his feet, clutching the letter. Eunice? Faced with the letter, she would have to admit ... Yes, but it was Howdy's brother. Howdy's life. He, not David, was the one who needed the gun. And right now. The back of David's neck prickled with urgency, a sense of time running out, danger closing in.

He wrestled the gun out of his raincoat pocket; that was the first thing, to get it and the letter to Howdy. Eunice, the panel, all the rest could wait.

The feeling of urgency swept over him, stronger than ever. Like something hot and wild breathing down his neck. He took the stairs down to Howdy's apartment three at a clip.

14

After the ritual ten rings Lenny hung up and sat, chewing his thumb nail and giving himself sound, sensible advice. Watch it. Don't do anything rash.

But rash or not, he knew he had to get out of here. Now, this minute. Here being his apartment where he had cowered like a mouse in its hole since Thursday night. Now being Sunday afternoon, four o'clock of the longest day in his whole entire life.

He couldn't take any more of his own miserable company, his own terrifying thoughts. They had been bad enough, God knows, on Friday; his warning call to David was an act of desperation, not courage, and for a while at least it had eased his conscience.

Besides, Friday he had still been benumbed by the trauma of it all, even less capable than usual—his poor old rattletrap brain!—of keeping on the track. So it wasn't until today that he had made the connection …

And he couldn't get through to David on the phone. The reason didn't have to be sinister, of course: David could have gone away for the week end, he could be spending the day with his girl friend, et cetera, et cetera. But supposing it wasn't anything like that? Supposing instead he was lying in his apartment, dead or dying, murdered for the sake of that damn package Lenny had unloaded on him? It was even possible that he had out-maneuvered the maniac, somehow managed to nail him single-handed. He had no way of letting Lenny know. Because of the unlisted telephone number, which (naturally) Lenny hadn't had the sense to give him.

"I have to get out of here," he said aloud. His voice creaked like a rusty gate.

It was drizzling, he discovered when he reached the street, but he did not go back for a raincoat. After all, he did have his beret, and the apartment, once such a haven of refuge, now seemed like a prison to him. Liberated, once more in touch with the human race, he stepped forth. Destination unknown. Or anyway unacknowledged. Maybe underneath he had already set his course. Meanwhile, what his conscious mind didn't know wouldn't hurt it. It was still busily turning out sound advice. Don't do anything rash. Watch it.

Be that as it may, after several blocks of walking he boarded a Fifth Avenue bus that happened to come along at the right moment, with a dawdler of a bus driver who must be running ahead of schedule and managed to hit the red light at every corner. Not, of course, that Lenny was in any hurry. He got off at 20th Street and continued downtown on foot. By now he was tensing up again, no longer able to pretend that he did not know where he was headed. But not able to turn back, either. It was like Friday night, when he had been goaded by desperation into calling David.

The drizzle was turning into rain, gentle but steady. He squelched along in his moccasins, shoulders hunched, beret pulled down over his ears. The sound of Howdy's voice sent him into a trembling, sweating skid.

"Hey, Lenny! What's the matter, you haven't got sense enough to come in out of the rain?" The warm hand clasping his, the big smile, the solid, comforting presence—for a moment Lenny was close to tears. "How about stopping in and having a drink with us? You look as if you could use one."

"Well—"

"Great. Come on. I just have to move the car and pick up some cigarettes, then we're in business."

The car was in the next block; Howdy found a spot for it across the street from the house. "Here we go." But he stayed where he was, behind the wheel. After a sharp, sidelong glance at Lenny he said, "Okay, fella, let's have it. What's wrong?"

"Nothing, really. Except that—" A nervous gulp. A sickly smile. "I guess it's just now getting to me, Miss Crosby, the shop break-in, everything. No new developments, I suppose?"

"None. Unless you want to count Dave's mugger last night."

"Oh God," whispered Lenny. It had happened, then. "He mugged David and stole the ..."

"What? Who?"

"Dave's mugger. Isn't that what you said?"

"Yeah. But I didn't mean it like that. Dave wasn't mugged. Nothing was stolen. Personally, I'm not sure *anything* happened, though Dave still insists he saw some guy sneaking up on me with a knife in his hand, all set to let me have it. There's only his word for it. I sure to God didn't see anybody. Or hear anybody, either, except Dave yelling bloody murder at me out the window. But okay, nothing would do but we must call in the cops."

"And the cops did their usual nothing." Lenny spoke automatically, preoccupied by the violent rattling in his mind. Some guy sneaking up on Howdy, not David. The maniac? No. Howdy, not David. Nothing had, thank God, happened to David. But if not the maniac, then...

"Well, what could they do? By then, of course, the guy was long gone. Assuming he was ever there at all. I'm not sure it wasn't just Dave's imagination working overtime. Anyway, that's the story. Such as it is. Now how about yours?"

"Mine?"

"Oh, come on, Lenny. You're not just in a sweat, you're in shock. Practically a basket case. It's got to be something more than delayed reaction. And that's not all. Who did you think mugged Dave? What did you think he stole?"

So. It had been pure wishful thinking, of course, to suppose that Howdy would let those tell-tale words pass unnoticed. He might be slapdash, but he was also shrewd. And kind. There was the danger. He had put his questions not in a bullying way, but with so much warm concern and sympathy that once again Lenny was tempted to let it all pour out, the maniac's threatening phone call, everything, as he had done with David. Yes, but with David there had been his conscience, spurring him on in spite of terror. With Howdy there would be only the relief, the enormous, treacherous relief of doing what came natural.

Watch it. Don't do anything rash. Yet he had to say something. Howdy was waiting.

"The panel. You know, your gizmo." He drew a shuddering breath and floundered on. "I can't get it out of my mind. Like it's a jinx or something. And David's still stuck with it, my fault, I've put off taking it back. Or wait. Maybe he hasn't still got it. Maybe he turned it over to you, and that's why—"

"That's why what?" demanded Howdy. He turned for another searching look at Lenny. Who sat like a lump, too paralyzed to utter. "That's why what? I don't get it. Or wait a minute. Maybe I do. You mean the mugger thought I had the panel and that's why he went for me instead of Dave? I don't have it. Haven't seen the thing since the other night when you picked it up. Haven't even given it a thought, to tell you the truth. What with all the other things that happened that night."

Again he paused, his eyes alight with wild surmise. "Look, Lenny, if you're right and somebody's out to steal the panel, then it hooks up with the robbery at your shop. Or rather, the non-robbery. Because nothing was stolen. Right? Just the petty cash, and the whole place torn apart. Like the guy couldn't find what he was looking for. And of course the panel wasn't there, you'd left it with Dave when you discovered you didn't have your keys."

"Oh wow." Lenny forced a laugh. "It doesn't take much to set you off and flying, does it? Just because the panel wasn't there."

"Well, a little more than that. You've got to admit it's possible ... We don't even know what the panel is, let alone how much it's worth. Hell, for all we know it's the long-lost treasure of the Incas."

"Now really, Howdy. Really ..."

"You're the one that started it. You and your jinx. Okay. So it's not all that valuable. It's got to be worth something. Otherwise why would anybody try to steal it?"

"But we don't know anybody is trying to steal it!"

"Don't we?" Howdy eyed him thoughtfully. "You were mighty damn quick about jumping to the conclusion that's what Dave's mugger was after. Supposing you're right, and this guy, whoever he is, either mistook me for Dave or got his wires crossed about who's got the panel by now ... I know, I know. Sheer speculation. But why not? What have we got to lose? Could be he's just the hired hand, and his boss is leaning on him to deliver, yeah, because the panel wasn't at the shop where it was supposed to be, and so he—Wait a minute. Hey, now, wait a minute."

Lenny shivered and closed his eyes. There was nothing he could do about his ears, where the change in Howdy's voice—from soaring ebullience to the hush of shock—echoed and reechoed. He knew what the change meant; had known from the start that, even without the maniac, Howdy might make the connection too. Well, now he was making it.

"Lenny. It just this minute struck me, God knows why it didn't before. Listen, Lenny. He must have been in the house that night. The night you picked it up. How else would he know it was supposed to be at the shop? We didn't know ourselves. Remember? It was only at the last minute that I got hold of you, and you weren't sure whether or not you could make it. He must have been there, waiting for a chance to nick it from me, must have heard us all yakking out there in the hall when Dave offered you a lift down to Yesteryear and—" With a gulp, Howdy took the final, inevitable leap. "Miss Crosby. Holy Mother of God. He has to be the one that killed Miss Crosby. That's it, isn't it? That's what's got you so scared."

Lenny let his breath hiss out. There was a moment of weirdly peaceful silence.

Then Howdy said, "Let's face it, the cops may not buy this. Or Dave, either. We can't leave him out of it. He's got the panel."

"He'll buy it," said Lenny. So would the cops, once they dug the whole story out of him. As they were sure to do. He had managed not to tell Howdy (just barely, and for all the good it did him) but he would tell the cops. He simply hadn't the strength not to.

Surely, having bought the story, they would be duty-bound to protect him against the maniac?

Clinging to this forlorn hope—but what else was there?—he stumbled out of the car into the rain and followed Howdy across the street to the house.

15

"You'd better tell me," Pam had said.

As well she might. After all, when she opened the door there was David, looking pretty wild-eyed, he supposed—even without the gun, which was out of sight in his pocket—pushing his way past her, demanding to see Howdy. Bad news personified.

Bad news that she would have heard in any case; furthermore, judging by last night's episode, she was less likely than Howdy to pooh-pooh the idea that his life was in danger. If she could be convinced, then maybe between the two of them they would be able to convince Howdy when he got back from moving the car or whatever the hell he was doing.

David had given it to her straight: "It's Garth. He's not dead, he's alive, he means to kill Howdy, it was him last night ... Here. Eunice knows he's alive, she recognized him the night we followed him ... Here. This proves it." And he had thrust the letter at her.

She was still clutching it; her other hand was clenched into a fist and pressed against the hollow in her throat. From the arm of the couch, where she had landed when her knees buckled, she stared up at David. Waiting for him to go on? But he had already told it all.

Except for the gun. He drew it from his pocket now. "Howdy's got to have some protection. I mean, we don't know how long it's going to take the police to track Garth down. Or when he'll try again." She continued to stare, speechless, blank-eyed. "Pam. Are you with me? Do you get what I'm saying?"

Her mouth trembled, fumbling for words. "Eunice couldn't have been mistaken? That night you followed him?"

"I don't see how. She got too good a look at him when he took off his hat. Not only that, but we tailed him all the way from here. It's not as though she just caught a passing glimpse of him."

"No. No, of course she wasn't mistaken." Those dark, dazed eyes, staring at him. No spark of hope left in them. "Neither were you, last night. Oh God, if only she had told me—"

"She didn't know any of this was going to happen. She still doesn't know about the panel business. I admit I blew it just now, calling her a liar right off the bat. That did it. She threw her tantrum and flounced out before I had a chance to tell her."

"About the panel. Or—" She swallowed violently. "Or Miss Crosby. She never did him any harm, it wasn't like Howdy and me, he has a right to hate us ..."

"She recognized him," said David. "There was no other way to shut her up."

"But Miss Crosby was always making up weird tales! Nobody took her seriously."

"You would have, after Howdy."

She made a distracted pass at her mop of hair, with the result that still more of it sprang free of the barrette that was supposed to keep it in check. Then she reached for the gun. "I don't know if I can make him believe—But he has to. He'll have to believe it if I tell him. He thinks I still—that I never got over Garth. You'll stay and help me, David? Please? There. That's him at the door now."

The door burst open, and Howdy charged in, with Lenny in tow. Or rather, what was left of Lenny, the shrunken, bedraggled remains. He hung in the background, while Howdy swept forward, in full spate. "Listen, doll, we just figured something out, Lenny and I, hey there, Dave, good, just the guy I wanted to see, it's about the gizmo—" He broke off to goggle at the gun in Pam's hand. "What in the name of God are you doing with that?"

But Pam had apparently once more been struck dumb. She could only thrust the gun toward him, urgently, wordlessly.

Was she leaving it all to David, then? She couldn't be; as she herself had pointed out, it was her word, no one else's, that would carry the real clout for Howdy. So what stopped her was Lenny's presence? Could be. Probably was.

Okay. If that was how she wanted it. "It's mine," said David. "For you. Take it, Howdy, we'll explain later. First let's hear about the gizmo."

As if he couldn't already guess. Poor Lenny, with his face of woe and his congenitally loose tongue. It wouldn't take much pressure from Howdy to break him down.

"Yours, Dave? Oh sure. From the Army." It was a relief to see that Howdy knew how to handle a gun; his examination of the Colt .45 was brief, interested, and expert. "Okay. I'm not going to give you an argument. Last night I thought you were out of your skull. Now I'm not so sure. Wait till you hear, and you'll see why. Because here's the thing, this is what I mean about the gizmo ..."

And he launched into his story, full steam ahead.

Eventually Eunice's fit of hot weeping eased off into nothing more than an occasional hiccoughing gulp. She sat up on the couch where she had flung herself when she first came in and blew her nose. It hurt. So did her sunburned legs. So did her throat, raw from all those wild sobs, and her chest, where something that felt like a chunk of cement still lodged, undissolved by the flood of tears.

A good cry was supposed to make you feel better.

Not this one.

And then—oh no, she couldn't bear it—she discovered that she had left her flight bag up at David's. Her tooth brush, her hair spray, her pantyhose, the only pair she had left that was fit to wear to the office tomorrow.

He must have noticed the bag by now. Wouldn't you think he'd have the decency to return it? No you wouldn't. Not smart-ass David. Prying into what was none of his business, bullying her, making up that crazy story about last night. Of course it was crazy. Of course it was made-up. Of course Garth wouldn't ... And he had the nerve to call *her* a liar! Her only regret was that she hadn't whopped him harder.

Now he was no doubt sitting up there, smirking to himself over the fact that she was going to have to eat those famous last words of hers. "I'm never going to speak to you as long as I live!" All right. Since she had to, she would speak to him again, two words and two words only. "My bag." She would then turn on her heel and depart. In dignified, irrevocable silence.

She avoided looking at herself in the mirror until she had splashed her face with cold water. Even so, it was pretty gruesome. Not that she cared. She gave her hair a couple of swipes with the brush, picked up her keys, and was off, not bothering to step back into her clogs.

Halfway up the stairs she paused, alerted by a snick of sound from above. Like a door opening. The elevator? Old Mr. Bauman? Could it be that David had decided to act like a gentleman for once in his life and return her property? Or maybe it was nobody, just the old house itself creaking, settling down for the night. She moved upward a couple of steps. Then she stopped transfixed, her heart plunging like a bronco.

She had thought never to see him again; and he was there, miracle of miracles, it was Garth. In that first dizzy moment nothing else mattered.

"Garth," she whispered.

It jolted him visibly. He half-turned, as if to duck back into David's apartment—that was the snick of sound she had heard—but instead pivoted again toward her, and eased the door shut behind him.

"Eunice?" More of a sigh than a whisper. "Ah ... Eunice." Still as a stone he stood, bone-thin in his sleazy clothes, his face shadowed by the broad-brimmed hat, under his arm a package wrapped in brown paper.

"Garth—"

"Shh. No point in raising the household, is there? Darling," he said. And he started toward her, quickly yet dreamily, a kind of sleep-walking glide. He seemed to be smiling.

She watched spellbound, riveted to the stairs, not even capable of unclamping her hand from the banister. The drum-thump of her heart, the rasp of her breath, and all at once a babbling whisper that was her own voice. "Nobody knows but me, I knew it was you, but the landlady said ... But I didn't tell anybody, not even David ... Honest and true, Garth ... I never told ..."

"That's good," he said gently. He put the package down on the step beside her. He was that close now, close enough so she could see his face, bone-thin like the rest of him, and set in a strange, sleep-walker's smile. His eyes were lighter than she remembered, with yellowish flecks, glittering and fanatic in his sallow face.

But all she could do was go on babbling: "You can count on me, Garth, you know how much I ... I won't tell anybody if you don't want me to ..."

"Of course you won't," he assured her, with deadly gentleness.

And at last the spell that had held her fast—too long, too long—was broken. She turned and fled for her life, down the stairs at a crazy, stumbling lunge. He was after her, swift and silent as lightning; once, twice she managed to wrench free of his wiry grip. She had reached the landing when she tripped and thudded down on her knees.

It was all over. No escape from those clutching hands. In the instant before they locked on her throat, screams ripped out of her—primeval, unearthly screams that ended in a gurgle, in silence, in nothing.

On the floor below Howdy, having laid out the main points of his theory, was now well into the wrap-up. "So there it is. It's got to be the same guy, the one that's after the gizmo, and the one that killed Miss Crosby. Or anyway that's how I see it. If I'm wrong, I don't see how but I could be, okay, it's still something for the cops to work on, more of a lead than—"

The yells, two and a half of them, tore through the room with the shattering speed and force of a cyclone. For a moment the air, the very walls seemed to shudder. A terrible stillness followed.

"Jesus," said Howdy. He grabbed the gun from the coffee table and made for the door. David was already there, grappling with the damn lock, which stuck at first, then suddenly gave way and sent the door flying open and him crashing back against the foyer wall. Howdy charged past him into the hall; by the time he got himself pulled together Pam was out there too, even Lenny had made it, only to lapse back into his catatonic state.

He had known what it would be, and it was: halfway up the stairs Eunice sprawled, a limp, disjointed bundle, with Garth crouching over her. The commotion below had alerted him; now, at Howdy's shout, he sprang up, quick and poised as a cat, and faced them, faceless in his wide-brimmed hat. His left hand whipped to his slacks pocket, out again, with the knife gleaming in it.

Howdy's shot slammed him against the banister; the hat spun from his head, the knife clattered out of his hand, and he slid in slow motion down to the landing, while the roar of the explosion ricocheted from wall to wall and at last racketed itself out.

"Garth?" said Howdy, because that was the word Pam had shrieked as he fired, was still shrieking, rocking back and forth, with her hands clenched against her eyes. He lurched across to the figure at the foot of the stairs and sank down, groaning, "No, oh no, oh no ..."

David, sprinting up the stairs, caught a glimpse of blood bubbling up from Garth's chest, eyes staring out of a bony face. Then he was beside Eunice. She sagged in his arms like a sack half-full of sawdust; she was a kind of mauve color and her neck was dented with dark bruises. But she was breathing, he thought she was breathing, yes, there, she gave a little whimper. After a moment her eyes flicked open and she croaked out something about "Garth" and "package."

"I know, I know." He could see the package up there on the stairs, and he could hear Howdy's anguished voice down below.

"The panel? But I would have given it to you, my God, Garth, you knew that. All you had to do was ask me." He was kneeling, with both his hands pressed against the bright bubbling, trying to hold his brother's life inside him. "Garth, Garth, I didn't know it was you, I didn't mean to—"

"I meant to." In a last spasm of will, Garth reared upward; the ceiling light fell directly on the stark planes of his face, gray under the sheen of sweat. But his eyes flared, still alive with the hate that consumed him. A lifetime of hate—Howdy would never again be able to pretend otherwise—and a lifetime of bitterness in the twist of his mouth. He spoke through a bloody froth. "I meant to. But you always were the lucky one ..." The froth turned to a gush. The flare in his eyes went out. He slumped.

Howdy got to his feet slowly, like a stricken old man. He looked down at his hands.

"Lucky," he said. "Lucky."

THE END

Jean Potts Bibliography
(1910-1999)

Mystery Novels:
Go, Lovely Rose (1954; winner Best First Novel Edgar Award)
Death of a Stray Cat (1955; reprinted in omnibus as *Dark Destination*, 1955)
The Diehard (1956)
The Man With the Cane (1957)
Lightning Strikes Twice (1958; reprinted in the UK as *Blood Will Tell*, 1959)
Home Is the Prisoner (1960)
The Evil Wish (1962; finalist Best Novel Edgar Award)
The Only Good Secretary (1965)
The Footsteps on the Stairs (1966)
The Trash Stealer (1968)
The Little Lie (1968)
An Affair of the Heart (1970)
The Troublemaker (1972)
My Brother's Killer (1975)

Mainstream Novel:
Someone to Remember (1943)

Short Stories:
The Lady Afraid (*Woman's Home Companion*, Feb 1942)
You're All I've Got (*Woman's Day*, March 1942)
The Other Woman (*Collier's*, Aug 24, 1946)
Restless Redhead (*Liberty*, Feb 1948)
The Box of Apples (*McCall's*, March 1949)
A Family Affair (*McCall's*, Nov 1949)
The Bracelet (*McCall's*, Dec 1951)
The Heart Must See (*McCall's*, Apr 1952)
The Engagement Ring (*Thrilling Love*, Oct 1952)
Let's Start All Over Again (*American Magazine*, Apr 1953)
The Girl He Didn't Marry (*Woman's Day*, Jan 1954)
A Long Day's Journey (*Cosmopolitan*, July 1954)
The Ideal Gift (*Family Circle*, Oct 1956)
The Withered Heart (*Ellery Queen's Mystery Magazine*, Feb 1957)
Murderer # 2 (*Alfred Hitchcock's Mystery Magazine*, Jan 1961)
Just Like Jessica (*Redbook*, Feb 1963)
The Only Good Secretary (*Cosmopolitan*, July 1965; condensed version of
   novel)
The Inner Voices (*Ellery Queen's Mystery Magazine*, Apr 1966)
In the Absence of Proof (*Ellery Queen's Mystery Magazine*, July 1985)

Two on the Isle (*Ellery Queen's Mystery Magazine*, Jan 1987)
The Lady Macbeth Case (*Ellery Queen's Mystery Magazine*, Nov 1990)

Family Circle "Family in Trouble" series (commentary by John L. Schimel, M.D.):
Families in Trouble (April 1969)
Families in Trouble - Alone Again! The Agonizing Problem of A Lonely Wife (June 1969)
Families in Trouble - "My Youngster Is Taking Drugs" (Oct 1969)
Families in Trouble - "My Job Made A New Woman Out Of Me!" (Feb 1970)
Families in Trouble - The Credit Card Nightmare (March 1970)

Unpublished Short Story:
Lady Bountiful

More suspense classics from...

JEAN POTTS

"Potts has a turn of phrase that cuts like a knife."—Paul Burke, *NB*

Go, Lovely Rose / The Evil Wish

A 1954 Edgar Award winner and a 1963 Edgar runner-up paired together for the first time. "If Hitchcock had written a novel, it would have been similar to *The Evil Wish*...two masterpieces."
—Don Crinklaw, *Booklist.* New introduction by J. F. Norris.

Home is the Prisoner / The Little Lie

"In Potts' fictional world there are no true good or bad characters, just many shades of gray, but she writes them in a way that makes you care about them, warts and all."
—*In Reference to Murder.* New introduction by J. F. Norris.

The Only Good Secretary/The Man With the Cane

"Miss Potts displays again her peculiar genius for portraying people who might live in the next block from you, in a genuinely fine and absorbing story."
—*San Francisco Chronicle.* New introduction by Bill Kelly.

Footsteps on the Stairs/The Troublemaker

"... propulsive enough to keep the pages flipping fairly quickly... If you enjoy the classic, traditional murder mystery, then surely you will be pleased with Jean Potts."
—*Paperback Warrior.* New introduction by Curtis Evans.

"A mistress in the art of dispensing psychological suspense."
—*Liverpool Post*